An Improper Situation

DEFIANT HEARTS BOOK 1

Sydney Jane Baily

cat whisker press
Massachusetts

This book is a work of fiction. Names, characters, places, and incidents either are products of the author's imagination or are used fictitiously. Any resemblance to actual events or locales or persons, living or dead, is entirely coincidental.

Published by cat whisker press

Cover: Philip Ré
Book Design: cat whisker studio
Editor: Chloe Bearuski

ISBN: 0615701191
ISBN-13: 978-0615701196

DEDICATION

To my exceptional dad
James George Baily
whom I miss every single day

Many times I call you.

OTHER WORKS

The RAKES ON THE RUN Series

Last Dance in London
Pursued in Paris
Banished to Brighton
Gretna Green by Sunset

The RARE CONFECTIONERY Series

The Duchess of Chocolate
The Toffee Heiress
My Lady Marzipan

The DEFIANT HEARTS Series

An Improper Situation
An Irresistible Temptation
An Inescapable Attraction
An Inconceivable Deception
An Intriguing Proposition
An Impassioned Redemption

The BEASTLY LORDS Series

Lord Despair
Lord Anguish
Lord Vile
Lord Darkness
Lord Misery
Lord Wrath
Eleanor

PRESENTING LADY GUS

A Georgian-Era Novella

ACKNOWLEDGMENTS

A big thanks to the following: My three beta readers — Toni Young, Holly Meyerhoff, and Pamela Schwotzer; Gregory Smart, librarian at the Boston Public Library, who found the necessary information about and images of Boston in the 1880s; copy editor Victoria Piercey, who found seriously egregious errors; Marliss Melton, who not only is my dear friend but also paved the way as a bestselling author of romantic suspense; my children for putting up with me sitting at my desk typing, staring, typing, typing, staring, typing.

And, of course, thanks to my mom, Beryl Baily.

CHAPTER ONE

✦

1884, Spring City, Colorado

Charlotte heard the wagon wheels and the horse's hooves from where she sat at her desk, and a frown crossed her otherwise clear features.

"Blazes!" she exclaimed. She was not expecting anyone. Moreover, except for Sarah Cuthins, the doctor's wife, Charlotte and her other neighbors weren't, well, neighborly enough with each other for uninvited visits. And she could tell just by listening that it wasn't Sarah's buggy coming down the dirt road.

Anyway, she couldn't see who it was even if she tried to look out the window, as books were piled high in front of it. Books were, in fact, the dominant feature in the study—on history, modern and ancient languages, classical architecture, mathematics, even oceanology, entomology, and geology.

In the middle of them all, Charlotte sat at her large desk, which had once been her father's. Currently, and always in fact, newspapers and other papers were strewn across it. A faded globe perched precariously on one corner, a lamp on another.

She lifted her fingers from the keyboard of her typewriter. The invention itself was over a decade old. Her machine, however—the one extravagant purchase she'd made that year— still felt brand new. Anything that took her from it was of great annoyance.

Standing, she absentmindedly tucked one strand of hair behind her ear. Then she reconsidered and twisted the rest of her waist-length hair to form a loose knot at the base of her neck. It wasn't tidy, but it was better than going to the door all undone.

The wagon was obviously stopping outside her door, so she had no choice except to greet its passengers. Lord, she hoped no one wanted coffee. For that matter, she hoped no one wanted anything, as the kitchen was as bare of food as she was of hospitality and time for interruptions.

Crossing the worn yellow and blue rug, Charlotte automatically stepped over the small hole in the floorboard as she strode into the front hall. It was cluttered with her shoes, coat, umbrella, and various knickknacks. She took note of the comfortable mess with a slightly hopeless shrug.

When a sharp knock resounded from the other side of the door, startlingly loud in the silence, she froze. Then she took a deep breath.

"Coming." Charlotte hoped she didn't sound as irritated as she felt. No one respected other people's deadlines!

Yanking open the door, she nearly slammed it shut with surprise. Instead, she stepped back with a murmured, "Oh, my!"

Before her was a tall, dark-haired man with the most strikingly vivid blue eyes she'd ever seen. Astoundingly, he was dressed in a well-fitted suit of the neatest charcoal stripe. Out here, in the middle of nowhere!

However, what caused her extreme disconcertion was not his devilish good looks alone but rather the two young children standing on either side of him.

A young girl with two tidy blond braids was holding the man's hand and staring up at her intently. A little boy who had hair remarkably similar in color to Charlotte's own, shimmering with all the colors of autumn, and who barely came above the stranger's knee, clutched the man's tailored pant leg, causing a severe pucker.

"I understand this is the Sanborn homestead."

His voice, deep and pleasant, brought her attention back to him. She looked up dazedly, her own eyes blinking at the late spring sunlight behind him. Perhaps the whole apparition of handsome man and small children might simply disappear if she willed it.

"I am Charlotte Sanborn." Automatically, she stuck out her right hand to the stranger.

He looked at her hand, his face surprised.

"The writer?"

It was her turn for an expression of surprise, as a tremor of trepidation danced down her spine.

"How on earth . . . ?" she began. No one outside of Spring City knew that she was "Charles" Sanborn, the acclaimed writer, and she doubted even all of Spring knew or cared.

"Excuse me," he added, "I knew you were a woman, but I thought you would be older. That is, I'm delighted to meet you."

A genuine smile crossed his features for the first time, and taking her extended hand in his free one, he shook it with a firm grasp.

Charlotte felt a shock of warmth and strength, and realized it had been a long while since she'd touched someone else's skin.

"It is an honor and a pleasure," he continued. "I've read much of your work."

His voice was as warm as his hand, and she flushed.

Charlotte was used to praise, having been hailed as a voice of her time for the past few years by the editors with whom she had contact. She was successful in her own uncelebrated and quiet way, of course under the guise of her pseudonym.

However, knowing that this man had sat down with her work in his hands caused her to feel strangely exposed.

"Thank you," she said and stopped. She was waiting. He was waiting.

The children were waiting, too, but less patiently. The little boy tugged on the man's pant leg.

"Are we goin' in?" he asked, looking not at Charlotte but up at the tall man, who gave him a smile that stirred Charlotte's sentiment.

"Oh, I do apologize," she murmured, still thinking of the man's genuine smile. "Where are my manners?"

The little girl just stared at her as if she was wondering the very same thing, and Charlotte moved quickly aside to let them enter her home. She felt for all the world as if she had suddenly stepped out of her own life. A few moments ago, she could never have imagined a man and two children standing in her entryway.

"I am sorry to barge in on you, Miss Sanborn," he began, as his eyes took in the untidiness and the disrepair in one quick glance, "but after we arrived in Spring City, I discovered, of course, that there was no telephone system in place as yet."

They must be from the east, she concluded.

"I think it will be a while yet before those of us in Colorado have the benefits of Mr. Bell's invention." Having exhausted that topic, she waited again for him to explain himself.

"We hope you are not too inconvenienced, but we tried to be here as close to the appointed time as possible, barring a few mishaps along the way." This statement caused both the children to giggle, apparently having been the cause of some of the mishaps.

Charlotte frowned. "The appointed time, sir?"

"The trains were running late along the Topeka-Santa Fe line. A Pullman sleeper had overturned," he stated.

She nodded, finding nothing more to say, since the entire conversation so far was making no sense to her, and she usually prided herself on her quick understanding.

After a long moment, the man frowned. "Miss Sanborn, the children are tired. We stopped only briefly in Spring City to get directions, and I'm sure they would benefit from a short nap while we talk about their situation. Then, perhaps, some supper would be in order."

"Supper?" she repeated. The situation wasn't getting any better. Why would this family come to her house and demand a place to sleep and eat?

She pressed her hand to the side of her head. Having worked steadily for days to meet her editor's deadline, she was plum tuckered out. Charlotte was sure that was the reason none of this was coming clear to her.

"Miss Sanborn, is everything all right?" Even this tall, handsome stranger seemed a bit agitated now. His dark eyebrows formed the oddest pattern of straight and wavy lines as he frowned.

"Everything is just peart," she began, "except I must confess. I haven't the slightest idea who you are." She felt better for acknowledging the corn, as her neighbor called it.

It was the stranger's turn to flush. "How is that possible? I sent the letter myself."

"The letter?" At least this wasn't a random visit by lunatics wanting food. Perhaps soon she would get to the bottom of this, and she could return to her work.

"Yes," he affirmed. "Are you telling me that you never received correspondence from the offices of Malloy and Associates, posted about a month and a half past?"

"Malloy?" The name sounded familiar, but she couldn't place it.

"I've been awfully busy, Mr. . . . ah . . . ?"

"It's Malloy. Reed Malloy." He said it slowly as if speaking to a child, but his voice registered a tone of definite annoyance.

"You needn't get in a pucker, sir. I didn't realize you meant that you were—" but Charlotte broke off, deciding to ignore his tone.

"Let me take a look in my study. It's possible that something came and got overlooked. Editors forward a lot of mail from people who read my work. I don't always get a chance to look through it right away," she added apologetically.

Turning away, she entered her study, stepping delicately over the unsightly hole. The good Lord knew she often let papers and envelopes pile up. It was an unfortunate habit, and she would have to allow that it looked as if it had put her in some deep trouble now.

She heard them follow her, all three of them trailing behind, as she went to her desk and began to sift through the papers on the edge of it. When these finally slid to the floor, she bent to try another pile that already had collapsed off of a small oval Pembroke table, with its leaves always in the up position to accommodate more stray papers and books.

"It's amazing that your work, which seems to come from such an orderly mind, can be created here, in this chaos," observed the man behind her.

At his tone, she looked up. He seemed genuinely displeased, and she felt a little like a naughty school girl in front of the teacher. His sapphire eyes bore into hers for a second, and she felt the same jolt as when he had touched her hand.

She was the first to look away, continuing to rummage through the papers and then moving to a stack of Scientific American mixed with Yale Literary Magazine, ignoring his remark.

Charlotte wanted to tell him how she used to be organized, how she used to have food in the pantry and wood ready for the fires and not a speck of dust anywhere. She wanted to, but it would be a bald-faced lie. It had forever been this way—chaotic, at best. Her mind, however, was sharp and orderly and with it, she created works that were concise, easily understood, and a step ahead of her peers.

"Some of us have time to do housework," she commented lightly, "while others of us put our minds to more important things, such as . . . aha!"

"Did you salvage something, Miss Sanborn?"

She stood up and faced them, triumphantly waggling the cream-colored envelope with Malloy and Associates embossed in blue lettering on one side. "Here it is."

Charlotte recalled now having received it, even remarking over the blue ink and placing it on her desk to read after dinner, and then . . .

She stared guiltily at the dark-haired stranger with his flashing eyes. The seal had not even been broken.

"Perhaps you should open it and see why we're here," he continued evenly, crossing his arms over his broad chest, "although perhaps you could do that somewhere where we can all sit down. The children are growing tired."

"Of course." She had been caught out again without her best manners. Her mother would be appalled. While for the sake of Charlotte's father, her mother, Regina, had grown tolerant of the lack of societal niceties in the West, she had, nevertheless, tried to instill in her bookish daughter a sense of manners and the finer graces.

Charlotte was failing miserably on all counts, knowing in her heart this was why she welcomed her own isolation.

"Please, come this way." She passed between the boy and girl, who still stared at her as if she were a prize exhibit at the fair, and headed down the hallway to the parlor.

Tossing open the door, she froze. How long had it been since she'd used this room? It was dark and musty, and frankly, it smelled like a horse blanket.

"Excuse the state of the room. I don't entertain much. Let me just air it out a bit, but do come in and find a seat."

In the dark gloom, she could barely make out the furniture, all relics from her parents' day. She went directly over to the windows, pulling aside the heavy curtains, and opening the shutters, letting the fresh spring air flood the room, bringing with it the scent of the purple-flowered fireweed that grew all around the house.

Unfortunately, when she got to the third window, she opened the curtains and saw cracked panes of glass and a board nailed onto the sashes from the outside. Hastily drawing the curtain closed, she hoped the elegant man in her parlor had not noticed.

She turned to face her guests, who had spread themselves gingerly around the room. By the look on his face, it was undeniable that Mr. Malloy had seen the poor repair job. The little boy sat directly next to the man on the high-backed sofa in front of the rough stone fireplace with its faded, embroidered screen and an old rifle hanging above. The little girl had taken one of the moth-eaten, petit-point cushioned chairs that her mother had worked hard to create.

Charlotte was well aware of the dust still settling after they'd seated themselves. As she crossed the room, she noticed Reed Malloy's expression of disapproval. Inwardly mortified and feeling her stomach tense under the peculiarity of the situation, she sat in the only seat left, a small mauve-colored chair with bits of horsehair sticking out where it shouldn't be.

Taking the letter out of her skirt waistband, she opened it. Skimming the salutation and the niceties, suddenly she caught her breath.

"I take it you've reached the part where—" he began.

"Blazes!" Charlotte jumped out of her seat. "Ann gave the children to me? Is she mad? Does she understand—?"

"She is deceased, Miss Sanborn."

Charlotte sat down again slowly, her gaze darting to the children, who didn't seem to understand that the adults were speaking about their mother, Ann Connors. She turned her attention again to Reed Malloy, looking decidedly grave, his eyebrows once more in a fierce, straight line.

"Yes, I had heard, and I'm sorry. My aunt, Alicia, the children's grandmother, wrote to me about the tragedy."

Charlotte didn't bother to add that it was the sole time she'd heard from her aunt since her own parents had died nearly a decade earlier.

"You must understand, Mr. Malloy, I have never met my cousin, and we had only exchanged a few letters during the years. To say we were not close would be to put it mildly. My parents moved here from Boston before I was born." She paused, remembering what her aunt's letter described.

"It was a collision between my cousin's carriage and a horse car, as I recall. I know it is doubly hard with their father having died two years ago—"

"Three," Reed Malloy corrected, his glittering gaze never wavering.

"Three," she agreed, nodding. "In the light of this, I ask, why me as a guardian? Why not their grandmother?"

He stretched one arm out along the back of the sofa, glancing at each of the children, then his gaze fixed once more upon her.

"For one thing, their grandmother, your aunt, is nearly seventy years old. I don't believe your cousin thought that Alicia Randall would be an ideal mother."

Seventy! Charlotte hadn't known her mother's older sister was so much older.

"Secondly," he continued, "while you, Miss Sanborn, might not have given much thought to the eastern branch of your family, your cousin obviously gave a great deal of thought to you. Ann Connors had read all your work. In fact, it was she who first introduced me to your literary endeavors. She was one of your greatest admirers."

Charlotte felt as if she'd been socked in the stomach, and a lump rose into her throat at the thought of a cousin who knew so much about her when she, herself, hadn't even felt much grief at the announcement of her death . . . until now.

However, her life was set, and she liked it that way. She had no close friends, only acquaintances with whom she corresponded. Various editors checked in with her to assign an article or push her to keep a deadline. And she had one younger brother, Thaddeus, who popped up from time to time, making her miss him all the more when he went away again.

It was no life for children, and she was not the woman to raise them. How could she ever have imagined that her cousin would do such an absurd thing?

"It is simply out of the question, Mr. Malloy. I am profoundly sorry that you and the children wasted a trip. And I do apologize for not having opened your letter. I didn't recognize the seal and assumed it was a letter from a reader, which I would have looked at eventually."

She paused as she stood up, wondering if there was a way to seem less harsh but failing to think of one.

"However, and I do apologize again, but undoubtedly you can see that there is nothing I can do." As she finished, she spread her hands, giving a slight shrug.

Reed Malloy said nothing for a moment. His blue eyes merely narrowed at her. Then he stood up, dominating the room.

Charlotte held her breath a moment while he seemed to come to some decision. She waited for him to yell at her, grab the children, and burst from her house.

Instead, perfectly under control, he said, "It is I who am sorry, Miss Sanborn, but there is no choice here."

About to protest, she let out her breath in a rush, but he continued before she could speak a word.

"You have ample space, which was my main concern for a woman living alone, even if the house is in need of some repairs. As for your objections, you have made no valid ones, nor can make any as far as I can see."

"Really, Mr. Malloy—"

"Miss Sanborn, your young cousins will be no financial burden to you as their upbringing has been well-provided for. All you need offer them is shelter, basic human kindness, and a moral and intellectual example, which I believe you are capable of if I have read your works correctly. Can you not offer all of these?"

Of course she could! That was hardly the point. It was that no one had asked, and had someone done so, she would have said emphatically no. She had never had the desire to be a mother, nor had she any such desire now, not even when faced with the two sweet little urchins seated in her parlor. She refused to be bullied by his tactics.

"Mr. Malloy, neither my character nor my house is at issue."

He inclined his head slightly, acknowledging the way she had maneuvered out of that trap.

"Rather the question pertains to my inclination, which is strongly to the negative. I live a solitary life here." She gestured around her, taking in the house and the stretch of land outside her windows.

Her father had set up his homestead just a fifteen-minute walk outside of town, not too far from a mining camp in the foothills, yet far enough away from the bustle of Spring City that wagons weren't going by their window every minute, or even every day.

In recent years, the city bustled infrequently, only when miners came through discussing gold strikes or travelers mistook the area for one of the healing hot mineral springs. Spring City was down to one theater, for both opera and plays, and that was threatening to close any day now.

"There are no other children close by, though there is a school in town," she added thoughtfully, then bit her tongue before continuing. "Mr. Malloy, I am not a heartless individual. I wish the children no ill will."

She looked toward the two children now. Having comprehended that the adults were discussing where they were to live, they knew instinctively they weren't wanted, not by her. And they were no doubt relieved, Charlotte thought. They stood up, once more anchoring themselves to Reed Malloy, who absently stroked the top of the boy's head.

"Honestly," Charlotte rushed on, feeling like the hard-hearted cad she was professing not to be, "I simply want what's best for them, and that does not mean living here in a remote environment with a peace-and-quiet loving writer, who has absolutely no idea about raising children. Can you understand that?"

"At least we are in agreement that we both want what's best for the children," he said, as if he hadn't heard anything else she'd said. He glanced at each child, and Charlotte could see that he cared for them. Then his glance returned to her.

"And your suitability is a question in my mind. That's why I didn't blindly follow Ann Connors's last wishes, but accompanied them out here myself." He thought a moment. "Yes, if we're both worried about the same thing, then the answer seems obvious, wouldn't you agree?"

Charlotte began nodding even before she asked, "And what would that be?"

"Why, for me to stay here with you and the children, of course, to assess the situation. If I find that you are unacceptable after all, then I'll wire their grandmother, and we'll see if other arrangements can be made."

Seemingly satisfied with his pronouncement, he began to usher the children out of the room.

"Let's go, little ones, upstairs to your room. Auntie Charlotte will show you the way. Won't you?" He turned to her, the look on his face daring her to contradict his words in front of his tired wards.

Charlotte was still reeling from his highhanded manner, the way he seemed to treat her as if she were auditioning for a stage role. Unacceptable, indeed! Not to mention the unfamiliar address of "auntie," and the utterly improper suggestion that he should stay under the same roof with her.

Despite all that, after taking another look at the children's faces, she nodded again. Brushing past them, she headed for the stairs. She was sure she had said no, and very firmly, too. Yet somehow, all three of them seemed to be staying.

"Meanwhile," Reed Malloy continued, "I'll ride to town and wire my office that I shall be delayed indefinitely. Do you need me to pick up something for supper, Miss Sanborn?"

"Oh, yes," Charlotte said gratefully, forgetting for a moment that, if it weren't for him, she wouldn't need to be providing supper for anyone but herself. He was the source of all this confusion, yet she thought only of the empty cupboards and bare shelves in her pantry. Even her root cellar was rootless!

"Yes, whatever you and the children are accustomed to, Mr. Malloy."

Giving her a quick nod, he vacated her front hall. The infernal man seemed to be quite pleased with himself! To her sudden horror, Charlotte realized she was alone with the children and she didn't even know their names.

CHAPTER TWO

"Well, here we are," Charlotte said, smiling weakly. First things first. She turned to the boy, who looked a few years younger than his sister.

"What's *your* name?" she asked, realizing how terrible it was that she didn't even know her own kin's names.

The little boy seemingly felt the same way for he screwed up his face, which instantly became beet red, and then burst into tears as he reached suddenly for his sister's sleeve.

"He's Thomas, ma'am," the girl said at once. "He doesn't take to strangers. Are you really our aunt? Why are you alone? Are you a spinster?"

"Oh dear," Charlotte murmured. Maybe children were as difficult as she'd always suspected. She had given up with her brother, letting Thaddeus fairly run free after her parents' deaths. It had taken all of her time just to keep the house together and food on the table. Some said he'd turned out to be a bad egg, though not to her face.

Without answering any of the little girl's questions, Charlotte tried again.

"And what's your name?" She hoped for a better response than what she'd received from young Thomas.

"I'm Lillian Winifred Connors."

Was it Charlotte's imagination or had a tone of superiority crept into this little person's voice?

"Well, Miss Lillian, as to your questions, yes, you may consider me your aunt." She thought it best not to go into the technicality that they were actually second cousins. "I'm alone because I choose to be, although I believe you are correct in classifying me as a spinster."

Charlotte was leading the way up the stairs as she spoke. "Careful of the fifth step up," she added over her shoulder, and they all stepped over the stair with the splintered wood and missing baluster.

Charlotte opened the second door to the left of the landing.

"I'm afraid you'll both have to share this room if Mr. Malloy is going to stay as well. There's . . . nothing in the way of toys or—" She broke off as the children stood in the middle of the sunlit room and surveyed it.

It was fairly pleasant with its four-poster bed and a bureau that had belonged to Charlotte's grandmother, which her parents brought with them from the east. Her mother's rocking chair was in one corner of the room, and Charlotte noticed a cobweb across the other. She hustled over to sweep it away with her hand.

"I'll get you some clean towels and you can wash up. Perhaps simply a sponge bath for starters? The bathing room's next door, and the water closet is beside that when you need it. I'll bring some water up."

They hadn't said a single word. Probably it was extremely different from what they were used to, but she couldn't be expected to have a full-blown nursery at hand.

At least there was an indoor "outhouse," thanks to her mother's persistence and her father's ingenuity with one small windmill. She remembered the day that she and her brother, still a toddler, watched her father install the contraption that pumped water to a pipe in the attic where gravity sent it down to the water closet and the kitchen faucet. Unfortunately, the water stopped there, which meant she still had to haul it to the bathing room.

Charlotte went downstairs to the pump to draw one bucket of cool, clean water. In the bathroom, she deposited half in the chamber set's blue pitcher and the rest in the accompanying wash bowl on a low table with a porcelain top. From the bureau in her own room, she then took two towels.

By the time she returned, the children appeared a bit more relaxed, no longer standing together like huddling sheep. Thomas was peering out the window at his new surroundings, and Lillian was opening drawers, which she closed with a bang as Charlotte entered the room.

"That's all right, you can look around." They both just stared at her so she put the towels down on the bed. "Why don't you get cleaned up full chisel and then take a quick nap until Mr. Malloy returns. Then we'll have supper. Okay?"

She had no idea how to speak to children, but this was apparently a failure, she thought, heading down to her study. They had not responded, though Thomas looked as if he might explode into tears again at any moment. *Man alive!* How would she ever get her work done and meet her deadline in two days?

If Mr. Malloy intended to see whether she was fit to raise children, she would show him how utterly unfit she was. He would come to understand for himself that she didn't have the time for this, and he would take the children and get back in his wagon, and then onto the train heading east.

Yes, she thought, feeling better as she settled behind what used to be her father's desk in the cluttered study. Everything should wrap up rather swiftly, if not immediately.

Thirty minutes later, she heard horse's hooves again and realized that she had been lost in her work and hadn't heard the children making any sounds of movement overhead. She supposed they'd chosen to nap before washing.

Perhaps she should check before Reed Malloy entered, and she stood up with a nervous flutter in her stomach. Then Charlotte caught herself and sat down again. No, of course not.

She would let him go upstairs, after all she wasn't the motherly type and wasn't about to start proving otherwise.

There was a brief knock, then he entered the front hall without waiting as if he already lived there and was a family member, instead of an unwanted guest. Charlotte merely stared at him through her open study door, not moving from behind the desk.

"I hope you don't mind," he said, glancing at her before dumping what appeared to be coarse feed bags in her entryway. "They're not as dirty as they look." He ran a hand through his dark hair causing a lock to fall over his forehead in rather rakish abandon. "I have a few more in the wagon."

Charlotte stood up, wondering why the sight of a male in her hallway caused such a flurry of odd feelings—in her brain, in her stomach, even in her knees, which seemed less steady. Inspection of the bags revealed them to contain not grain but apples, freshly baked bread, eggs, a fully cured ham, and some assorted vegetables.

He'd gone whole hog! The house hadn't seen food such as this since she still had her younger brother to take care of. For Thaddeus, she would have prepared a feast every day if she'd had the money or the culinary know-how.

As for herself, she occasionally received cooked meals from her nearest neighbor, Sarah Cuthins. When Sarah's only daughter had married nearly a decade earlier and moved away, the wife of Spring City's doctor had turned her kindly eye on the eccentric, young writer. Often, though, Charlotte went into town for a mid-day meal.

Good lord, it occurred to her that Reed Malloy would expect her to drop everything and cook for them. Her brother could have told him not to expect too much in that regard. Plain to simple was Charlotte's limited range of cooking, and she'd stopped even that when Thaddeus left four years earlier.

Still, she decided to make an effort and began to tote the food down the hall, past the parlor, and into the kitchen where she found a few more cobwebs and not the thinnest layer of dust, mixed in with some tinned goods and a few sacks of cornmeal and potatoes. All she ever used the kitchen for was heating water for bathing, coffee or tea, and cooking the occasional egg.

She placed the bags of food carefully in the middle of the maple block table, where her mother's cook had made tasty creations before Charlotte had to dismiss the woman upon her parent's death. Locating a duster, she began to wipe down the surfaces. At that moment, Reed Malloy's dark head appeared in the doorway, followed by the rest of him and two more bags.

"You have a grist of food here. It would seem enough for your entire visit," she commented.

"Oh, probably not, Miss Sanborn, but it's a start."

Charlotte stared at him. There was that feeling again, the strangeness of not being alone and of there being a man, a distinctly attractive man, in her kitchen. She watched as his deep blue eyes quickly took in the state of its disuse.

"I have to tell you, Mr. Malloy, that I find this extremely . . . all-overish."

He raised his dark eyebrows, clearly puzzled. She set down the duster.

"Uncomfortable, I mean. Your staying here is unorthodox to say the least, and—"

"If you had welcomed the children with open arms," he interrupted her, "I would be on the next train out of here in the morning." His eyes had taken on their steely appearance again, as if he were thinking something unkind about her.

She swallowed. "I told you, that is out of the question."

"Well, then," he said, brushing his hands together, dismissing the topic. "If you can clean up here a bit and fill a kettle as well as another pot with water, I'll bring in some wood from . . . ?" His eyebrows raised again.

She was speechless for a moment, caught up by the manner in which he was taking over her kitchen, not to mention her life.

"The wood pile is on the left. I'll show you," she added, unable to help the overly sweet tone of her voice.

Charlotte was starting to wonder why she hadn't sold the small homestead and moved herself into rooms in town. There would have been no question of dumping two children on her if she'd lived above a restaurant or the general store. She made a mental note to check into that after Reed Malloy and his charges left.

"Over there." She gestured with the kettle to the stacked wood under a small lean-to, and then proceeded to prime the pump with a vigorous up-and-down motion. Luckily, Sarah's cousin didn't mind splitting wood for a small fee, and one of her father's old friends maintained the pump.

Once in the kitchen again, Reed began a fire in the stove, and Charlotte started washing down the table and counters for the first time in a long time. She emptied the bags onto the now clean table and gingerly began organizing piles of food. Suddenly, she glanced up to find Reed's blue eyes upon her.

"Eventually, it has to be prepared," he mentioned dryly.

She nodded at that. "Well, then, Mr. Malloy, help yourself." She crossed her arms. He blinked at her.

"Please," she continued, "since you already seem to consider my home yours and the children's, consider my kitchen your kitchen as well. Besides, about the only thing I can make is Indian pudding, and I doubt you bought molasses. Now, if you'll excuse me, I've got work to do."

Not waiting for an answer, she headed down the hall quickly, her face feeling flushed and her ears perked waiting for the sound of his steps behind her. They came after a moment, but his footfalls went right past her study door and up the stairs.

Briefly, there was silence followed by Reed Malloy's voice, bellowing to her, "Miss Sanborn, would you come up here a moment?"

She sighed. It was beyond the pale. What had happened now? She trudged up the stairs, dragging her feet.

"Yes," she began as she entered the room that used to be her parents' bedroom, but stopped short at the sight of the children, still in their clothes sitting quietly on the bed looking, if possible, even more miserable than before.

Just then, a yawn split open Thomas's mouth, and Lillian stifled one of her own with her small, white hand. There were circles under their eyes and a slight paleness to their skin.

Charlotte frowned. "I thought they were going to wash up and take a nap. They look positively peaked," she added.

Reed looked at her as if she were the stupidest person he'd ever met. "Did it not occur to you that they need assistance with their clothes, with the hot water, with turning down the bed? Miss Sanborn, even you must be able to see that they are small children in need of some kindness and consideration, if not motherly tender love and care."

He finished on a harsh tone, and Charlotte pursed her lips. "I will do my best to assist *you*, in taking care of them," she said pointedly, "for the time that you are all here. What do you want me to do?"

She avoided looking at the children, whom she was sure would be staring at her as if she were a monster from one of their fairy tales. Her brother had been like a marten or a gopher, always grubby but able to do for himself. It simply had not occurred to her they would want a hot bath rather than merely washing their hands and faces.

With her small offering of help, however, the tension eased, and Charlotte soon was working side-by-side with the children's lawyer. Thomas and Lillian seemed to have more intricate layers to their clothing than she and Thaddeus ever had, and she could see why they needed help to undress.

Meanwhile, Mr. Malloy heated water downstairs and, in a moment, transformed himself from a well-dressed Bostonian into a regular washerwoman, rolling up his sleeves and preparing to bathe the boy.

Not that he could ever be considered regular or ordinary, Charlotte admitted, not with his striking profile. And then there were his well-defined muscles, which were in evidence as he wrestled Thomas into submission with one strong arm while scrubbing him with the other. She sat on the bathroom rug with Lillian while Reed soaped Thomas all over.

There were many stray suds flying around the bathing room, a few slips in the claw-foot tub, and even some laughter. Charlotte noticed Reed's gentleness that shone through his strength, as he tried to keep the whole affair from dissolving into chaos.

After Thomas was out of the tub, Reed picked him up and vacated the room. Charlotte pushed her worry over her deadline into the back of her mind before gingerly helping the girl with her bath. When they were done, she put Lillian into the bed next to an already-sleeping Thomas and followed Reed out of the room, closing the door behind her.

"Nothing will do them better than that nap," Reed said without turning.

Charlotte looked at his broad, muscled back. Unfortunately, his tone was once more one of irritation. A sigh escaped her. Being with people was downright draining.

His face as it turned to her held none of the tenderness she'd witnessed for the children. Instead, the coldness had reentered his sharp glance despite her assistance with their baths.

"I'll let you get to your work, Miss Sanborn, and I'll see about the supper."

She hesitated. "Do you really know how to do that?"

He looked surprised, his expression softening. "What? Cook?"

"Well, yes. Most men . . . that is, I don't think I know of any around here who could do for themselves. Except maybe beans or boiled eggs. But then, my circle of male acquaintances isn't that large. Still . . . ," she shut her mouth to stop the babble.

He gave her a long look, one eyebrow raised. "I assure you, Miss Sanborn, I can cook. Not a great number of dishes, but a limited repertoire learned at the insistence of my mother, two aunts, and three sisters who were determined to enlighten me when I would have preferred to spend my whole day playing outside. Shall we go downstairs?" His tone seemed to have softened, too.

She nodded and swept past him feeling foolish for having questioned him. As for his "limited repertoire," she had no doubt that it was wider and better than her own. At the bottom of the stairs, she hesitated again, but he simply went past her into the kitchen without inviting or asking for her help.

She shrugged. Well, it *was* what she wanted. She returned to her study, closed the door, and forced herself to concentrate. Despite the distractions, the piece on the farmers' recent political gatherings was going well. She dove into it and forgot all else.

That is, until the grandfather clock in the hall chimed, letting her know that nearly two hours had passed. She heard Reed Malloy call up the stairs, "Supper, you sleepy heads. Last one at the table does the dishes." She heard his step outside her door, but he paused only a moment before continuing to the kitchen, followed moments later by what sounded like a herd of bison coming full chisel down her stairway.

So, she was not to be invited to this repast in her own home. And the smells coming from the kitchen made her stomach pang with hunger. Her last real meal had been noontime the day before at the Fuller Hotel dining room in town. This morning she'd had nothing more than a tinned biscuit. She looked hopefully into the tin perched on the edge of her desk.

Empty, as was she.

Charlotte could hide in her study and starve to death or go out and ask to join them. After all, it was her kitchen. The alternative was to drive into town, but that would look ridiculous to her visitors.

Pushing aside the strand of hair that was always falling out of the knot, she stood up. Land sakes, she hated being humble.

She didn't bother going to the kitchen. Charlotte could hear them in the dining room, *her* dining room. Not that she minded, not that she ever used it. In fact, it made her think of being very young and of adults and white lace tablecloths and fine china.

She remembered her mother making her and her brother be on their best behavior, even though their father sat with his nose in a book and, much to her mother's annoyance, didn't even notice when Thaddeus dropped his peas on the rug.

Charlotte pushed the door open quietly, trying to shake off those old thoughts. Her glance quickly took it all in: Reed Malloy at one end of the table, her mother's end, still in his shirt sleeves, and the children on either side now dressed more casually for having dressed themselves.

He was serving them mashed potatoes from her grandmother's pink-flowered china bowl. It looked absurdly feminine and fragile in his large hands. Thomas was talking animatedly about the animals he'd seen from the train window during the trip.

Reed looked up after a second and saw her. Thomas froze mid-word, and his sister turned around to see what could have caused the disruption. Charlotte felt as though she were an intruder and would have turned around and fled, but Reed stood up and smiled at her.

"Won't you join us, Miss Sanborn?" He gestured to the chair opposite him as if he were inviting her to *his* table.

"Yes, thank you, if you're sure there's enough."

She was painfully aware that she hadn't helped cook the food, nor had she paid for it.

"Certainly. I would have asked you earlier, but I didn't want to disturb your work." He sounded genuinely gracious to Charlotte's ears. "Please, sit down. Will you have some baked ham and succotash?"

She did, and helped herself also to a cool glass of ginger beer from the pitcher on the table. Reed's culinary abilities were unquestionably beyond her own.

"This is a huckleberry above a persimmon," Charlotte told him honestly.

He froze with his fork halfway to his mouth. "Thank you, I think."

When she smiled encouragingly, he shrugged and remarked, "It's plain New England fare," leaving Charlotte to wonder what fancy fare might mean to him.

"Well, thank the Lord it's not calf's head," she returned into the silence that followed. Reed broke out laughing, while

Charlotte blushed at her own outspokenness. Some folks might call it blasphemy, her denouncing a local favorite.

A loud "ugh" came from Thomas, who forgot to close his mouth as he chewed.

As for the company, Charlotte was pleasantly surprised. The children were well-behaved and interesting after they got over their initial shyness. Thomas even offered to tell her about his room in Boston.

"Oh, how boring for Aunt Charlotte," Lillian cut him off. The little girl had already taken to calling her that sometime between the dishing out of the mashed potatoes and the passing of the bread. Charlotte found it startling but not altogether unpleasant, and considered, as she chewed thoughtfully, that these children were actually her flesh and blood.

"Nonsense, Lily. May I call you Lily?" The girl nodded. "Let your brother tell me about his room. I'm sure you had a lovely home in Boston."

"Oh, yes, Aun' Charlie," Thomas said, trying out her name for himself, "much bigger and prettier than this."

Lily gasped, appalled as any eight-year-old little girl could be at her younger brother's manners, but Charlotte only laughed, having never had delusions of grandeur concerning her parents' homestead. Also, there was the odd warmth in her chest when Thomas inadvertently used the nickname her own brother always called her. *Charlie.*

Catching Reed Malloy's glance, she received a friendly wink from him. Charlotte felt a blush creep up her face and was pleased that Reed excused himself to fetch the dessert of fresh berries and cream.

In truth, she couldn't remember when she had enjoyed a meal more, but she didn't think it prudent to say this to her guests lest they decide that was enough to make them all stay permanently.

Supper over, Charlotte helped stack all the dirty plates in a pile and carry the leftovers to the kitchen. Then she started down the hall to her study.

"Excuse me, Miss Sanborn," Reed Malloy began, coming out of the kitchen after her, "there is the matter of the dishes."

She opened her mouth to protest, but then Thomas came out, too.

"Last at table," the little boy said, pointing at her.

Charlotte looked from Reed to Thomas. She could hardly refuse in front of the child, and she could tell by the slight smile on Reed's face that he knew it.

Reed shrugged. "It's only fair," but his look told her that he was enjoying her dismay. Soon, she was in the kitchen, up to her elbows in soap suds scrubbing the dishes and the pots. She'd forgotten how much preparation a meal could take by the look of all the dirtied pans. She turned at Reed Malloy's footsteps.

"Do you want me to finish?" he offered, but Charlotte thought it was without much enthusiasm. It was perfectly fair that she do something for benefiting from the delicious food, and she told him so. He gave her a genuine smile, and she though it quite effective at making the heat rise in her cheeks.

She shook her head and turned to the sudsy water, hearing him take a seat at the kitchen table. All her nerve endings seemed acutely aware of his presence behind her, making her all-overish again.

"Where are the children?" she asked into the silence, hearing him pour himself a cup of freshly brewed coffee.

"In your parlor, reading. I've started a fire."

"Reading?" Charlotte echoed, somewhat surprised. She went on scrubbing thoughtfully.

"Yes, Miss Sanborn, they *do* read. At least Lily reads and Thomas follows along. Though they're not yet ready for your articles."

"Speaking of which," she said, suddenly feeling hurried, "I'd better get to it or my editor's going to have something highly disagreeable to say to me at the end of the week." She rinsed off the last dish and stood it on the counter with the rest before reaching for a towel.

"Here, I'll dry," Reed offered, smoothly taking the towel from her grasp, their fingers touching for the briefest second.

She looked up into his face, startled by the energy in this one man, not only glittering in the depths of his blue eyes, but almost—she would swear it was true—sparking off his fingertips where they touched her. Charlotte moved away quickly.

"Pour yourself some coffee," Reed suggested, picking up the first dish, "and tell me about your work before you go."

He propped his lean hips against the counter and began to rub the plate with the small white tea towel. For the first time that Charlotte could remember, instead of feeling sure about her ability and proud to discuss her work, she felt awkward. All she knew was that she didn't want to appear foolish in front of this man, who was obviously interested and waiting.

She dropped her eyes from his, grabbed herself a mug, and poured a steaming cupful. "Hmm, chicory," she said as the coffee's aroma reached her nostrils. He nodded.

"Well, the story as I know it and as I'm telling it is that the farmers' small gatherings are becoming larger and more political. Are you aware of the Grange, Mr. Malloy?"

"I've heard of it, The Patrons of Husbandry, but they're not exactly active in the heart of Boston."

"No, I don't suppose they are, but they might start to make their impact felt as far as your fair city. They seem to be gaining power in regulating railroad rates, and it is my opinion that it's about time. After all, in the east, you need their crops, the farmers need to get them to you. And the railroad needs to survive but by fair rates, not by gouging and abusing the farmers."

Charlotte went on reeling off facts and figures until Reed had finished all the drying. He had the grace to look impressed, and Charlotte realized she was still standing by the door.

"I hope you won't think it rude if I close the study door again. I'll leave you to see to Lily and Thomas," she added.

"We won't disturb you anymore tonight."

It didn't sound to her as if there was any condemnation in his words.

"Well, then, Mr. Malloy, I'll bid you goodnight. Thank you for the fine meal, and for the coffee." She saluted him with her mug.

"Anytime, lady writer," she heard him murmur as she left the room. She should be annoyed, but in truth, she felt a little thrill run through her at his words. From someone else, she would think them patronizing, but Reed Malloy seemed to offer them as a genuine tribute.

As she settled in behind her desk, Charlotte mused on the fact that the warmth she felt was not only from the coffee. It came as well from the innate feeling of peace and security of having another living being, three of them, in the house with her.

She had missed this feeling when Thaddeus left and then she had forgotten it, but now that a sense of companionship had returned, she welcomed it. Perhaps she would try to make the most of this unexpected visit from Reed Malloy and his two charges.

That was what she thought until all hell broke loose around one o'clock in the morning.

CHAPTER THREE

Charlotte was out of bed and on her feet before she was completely awake. Her heart was pounding uncomfortably and her hand shook as she fumbled to light her bedside lamp, before covering it with its glass chimney. Then she heard the scream again, followed by Lily's voice, yelling.

Charlotte threw open her bedroom door and bounded down the hallway, colliding with Reed Malloy. She felt herself bounce off of his hard chest, and she nearly dropped the oil lamp.

"What in blazes is going on?" she asked, as they responded to the commotion coming from the children's room. "The children are waking snakes!"

"Thomas has nightmares," Reed explained, as he threw open the children's door.

Charlotte took the scene in instantly over Reed's shoulder, her lamp illuminating the room. Lily was kneeling on the bed, yelling at her little brother who was thrashing around in the bed clothes. He screamed again.

Reed was beside him in an instant. He took hold of both of Thomas's shoulders and raised the boy to a sitting position. He shook him gently. Before long, the little boy was awake, blinking with large, startled eyes. Then Lily hugged her brother.

"Was it the same?" Charlotte heard the little girl ask. Thomas nodded, and the two of them curled together, snuggling down under the blanket. It tugged at her heart. How much harder it must be for them to lose their parents than it had been for her. She had been six years older than Lily and had not been carted halfway across the United States to a stranger's house—only to find themselves unwanted. The guilt welled up at once.

They seemed all right on the surface, but of course, inside, they must be vulnerable and bewildered. And they looked so small in the middle of the four-poster bed.

"Is there anything I can get you?" she asked, still clutching the light in front of her as if it were a beacon. Thomas yelled ice cream, and Lily giggled. Charlotte was amazed at their resiliency.

"I was thinking more along the lines of warm milk," she offered.

"I think that would be a good idea," Reed agreed, turning to strike a match, which he held steadily to the wick of their bedside lamp. A soft, amber glow filled the room.

Reed followed Charlotte out into the hallway.

"You might catch cold going downstairs dressed like that," Reed said as she reached the top of the stairs.

She turned to him, saw where his gaze was falling and looked down.

"Oh," she gasped. She was in her shift of the softest white lawn. And with the light in front of her as she led the way, he'd been able to see clearly the shape of her figure from behind. Now, he was no doubt getting a good look at the front of her. She blushed scarlet, thrust the lamp into his hands, and disappeared into her room.

Of course, he had been perfectly respectable, wearing a set of black silk pajamas, even if they did emphasize the firm shape of his muscles when he moved.

Hearing him go down the stairs, Charlotte leaned against the back of her door, feeling a strange tingling in her stomach . . . and lower. She wondered if she should bother to join him. In a moment, she groped in the dark for her robe and threw it on before heading for the kitchen.

Reed was already stoking the fire in the wood stove when she entered. She went to the cold storage and took a bottle of milk from where it lay nestled in the ice and straw.

"Has Thomas been having nightmares long?" she asked, measuring out two cups of the frothy white liquid into a pot. When no answer came, Charlotte looked up at Reed.

He was taking in her new attire with a disconcerting glance from her head to her feet, which peeked out from beneath the hem. Charlotte wiggled her toes self-consciously until his gaze returned to her face.

"You're wearing a banyan," he remarked, which she thought quite rude.

"My father's," she muttered, smoothing her hands over the outrageous peacock blue silk of her Indian gown, as she called it. There was nothing subtle about the rich purple curlicues woven through the damask, but when her mother's robe wore out, Charlotte had naturally decided to make use of her father's morning gown. She had long forgotten such a thing might be considered improper.

Reed shook his head abruptly as if to break up his thoughts, and then he addressed her question.

"I found out about Thomas's nightmares for the first time on the train. We had a sleeper car from Baltimore," he continued, as he took the pot from her and set it on the stove. "Lily told me that he has been having them since they moved from their own home to their grandmother's. Thomas barely knew his father, so his death wasn't as traumatic."

He ran a hand through his hair, making it stand up on top. "Both feel the loss of their mother greatly. I think it'll take some time, and they need to feel secure, not as though they're being shuffled around."

His pointed look made her flush again, not with embarrassment this time but with shame. This man had expected her to be that security for them, and she had let them down. Mutely, she pointed to the pot where the milk was starting to bubble, and he turned away. She sighed.

"The sooner you take them home, Mr. Malloy, the better."

"Home!" he echoed, his voice harsh. "They don't appear to have one at the moment. You know, I didn't even hesitate when Ann asked me to put you down as their guardian should anything happen to her. In your writings, Miss Sanborn, you seem far more compassionate than you are in person. But perhaps you care more for the plight of unknown farmers than you do for your own family."

He poured the steaming milk into two cups and, with a scathing look at her that again took in her ridiculous outfit before resting on her scarlet face, he walked past her down the hallway.

Charlotte was mortified. She *was* compassionate! She was just unsuited to . . . *To what?* she asked herself, leaning her palms against the work table. To being motherly? What about wifely? *Couldn't she love anyone?* Couldn't she reach out and be like other people? Didn't she need anybody? She thought of her parents, of Thaddeus—her Teddy—and of the years she'd spent alone.

She straightened. No, she didn't *need* anyone. If she did, she would have been crushed years ago and would be a sad, lonely woman even now. And she was not. Not at all. Wearily, she climbed the stairs, pausing only to listen to the voices of Reed and the children. He was telling them a story. A lump rose in her throat. Teddy used to love it when she told him stories. It was something she'd always been good at.

She hesitated a moment before returning to her bedroom. She was not welcome in the room with her guests, not while the condemning words of Reed Malloy still reverberated in her mind, not while he blamed her for causing Thomas's nightmares to continue. It was an odd sensation, feeling estranged in her own home.

"Mr. Malloy, this is intolerable." Charlotte had waited until the children went out to explore their new surroundings after breakfast, but she could hold her tongue no longer. "It caps the climax! You cannot simply show up unannounced—"

"But we were announced," he interrupted, moving to the sideboard to fill his coffee cup before sitting down at the dining room table. The remains of eggs, bacon, and potatoes were starting to stick to the plates.

She sighed. "Granted, you sent me a letter informing me of the decision made by my cousin and *telling* me that you were coming. I still think it an odd and even unorthodox practice that I was not told of the guardianship when you drew up the will."

Reed shrugged. "Ann Connors had assured me that she'd asked you beforehand, which was why my letter may seem indelicate to you now. I suppose she was worried that you would turn her down. Be that as it may, these children are your relations. How can you think of putting them out?"

His deep cerulean eyes bore into hers as if he was personally affronted by her callousness.

Her fists clenched under the table in frustration. *Was the man such a thick-headed coot?* She knew she could tell him until she was blue in the face that she was not a suitable parent, and he would blindly carry on trying to enforce her cousin's wishes. Even his words, attempting to play on her conscience and her sympathies, were nothing short of aggravating.

"The Randalls thought nothing of putting my family out when my mother married my father," she told him, thinking of Regina Randall Sanborn's proud sorrow when she was cut off from her family after the wedding.

Indeed, her mother had referred to herself with bitter humor as an orphan on more than one occasion, all because she married "beneath her" according to some outdated class code. No one from the east had ever sent cards of congratulations on Charlotte's and Thaddeus's births, nor invited them to be a part of their world.

"And so you repay the insult by shunning little children?" His eyebrows were up in exaggerated disbelief before forming that infuriatingly straight line of disapproval.

"Don't be ridiculous," she countered. "I merely bring it up to show that . . . that I am not without understanding of their plight, although the circumstances are different. My mother was an adult, marrying a suitable man whom she loved and who loved her back."

That was perhaps a slight misrepresentation of the odd and somewhat tempestuous marriage of her parents. "But these are children coming to my care when I am neither skilled in parenting, nor willing to adjust my life for such a reason at this time."

"But you raised your brother," Reed Malloy said quietly.

Her eyes darted to his. How much did the man know about her anyway? His expression was closed now. No condemnation, no judgment.

"I was forced to," she said, her voice sounding dry. She smoothed her napkin between her fingers and swallowed. "We were poor as Job's turkey, but I did the best I could under the circumstances. I will not be forced again."

A wave of melancholy washed over her, and she felt as if, against all reason, she might cry. Resentment over her parents' death, the hardship she and her brother had endured for so long, the pressure on her at such a young age as she'd struggled to keep them both clothed and fed, and then Teddy leaving her all alone. It had been beyond difficult.

Finally, she was moderately successful at the one thing that she cared about and that demanded all her time and concentration, her writing—only to find another horrible death had caused the cycle to begin again. Why did she always get the little end of the horn? Why must the lot fall on her to pick up the pieces? But then there was the very real dilemma of Thomas and Lily.

She wanted to have a conniption fit right then and there! Instead, Charlotte stood up, not looking at Reed's face, which she was sure would hold contempt for what he thought was her outright selfishness. "I have errands I must attend to."

She should have returned to her assignment, but she couldn't. Forgetting her bonnet until it was too late to go back for it, she headed to Spring City on foot at a leisurely pace to clear her head. She walked barely noticing where she was, sorting out what adjustments would have to be made if the children stayed, thinking ahead to when they came of age and left her, probably to head east. She knew how that would feel.

Teddy had left at seventeen, and she had walked around the house for days wondering how she would cope with so much time on her hands, with no one to do for. She had already started writing by then, and she began to spend all her time at that endeavor, submitting to anyone and everyone who would read her work.

Eventually the hollow feeling had gone away. But the little ones would want her to open her heart again, without reserve. She knew that instinctively.

Without thinking about where she was going, Charlotte ended up at the cemetery, a short distance outside of town. There was a slight breeze blowing, and she could smell the carefully tended grass and the fresh scent of wildflowers that bordered the area.

Pushing open the white gate of the fence that encircled the grassy plots, she headed for her parents' graves, buried side by side, as they had lived and died.

John Sanborn, loving husband and father, and Regina Randall Sanborn, loving wife and mother. That was supposed to say it all, but it didn't. It didn't describe the happy times in their home with a fascinating father and a beautiful and elegant mother, a genteel lady from Boston's highest society.

Charlotte knew Regina had wanted more out of life than Spring City, for herself and her children, but had loved her husband so much she would make any sacrifice.

Occasionally, there had been tense moments, Charlotte remembered, especially when her father became increasingly frustrated at his inability to find anything resembling a gold strike or when he secluded himself in his study for what seemed like days on end, reading and writing, until Regina had almost physically hauled him out herself. And even then, he brought a book along.

But he *was* a loving husband and father, trying to share what captivated him in the only way he knew how, by reading to them and telling them stories. Every outing, when they could drag him along, was an adventure.

And Charlotte had grown up early, as her mother's confidant, playing out their own version of society in their little parlor, and as her father's helpmate, on the occasional times that he brought his young daughter into the study and explained his ideas to her. Those had been relatively carefree times.

Quietly, Charlotte touched each headstone then hugged her arms around herself before moving a little way off to sit in the shade of a large fir. All around her face, tickling her cheeks, she felt the strands of hair that had fallen out of the untidy knot.

She started to smooth them, then pulled loose the rest of her long chestnut hair, combing her fingers through the silken skeins to untangle them somewhat while she thought.

Those times had ended far too soon, when she was just fourteen and Thaddeus barely nine. There had barely been time to grieve at first, so great was the shock.

The sound of hoofbeats brought her out of her morbid thoughts. The sinking feeling in her heart matched the downward curve of her mouth as she looked up and saw Reed Malloy approaching. Perhaps he would pass by into town, she hoped, as she scrunched herself closer to the huge tree. But he looked over and saw her. Obviously, he had been searching.

Charlotte watched quietly as he tied up the horse that had pulled the wagon he'd rented only yesterday to bring the children. The next moment, he was striding into the cemetery.

"Miss Sanborn, are you all right?" He stood close, looking down at her.

His question surprised her, and she lowered her gaze. She'd expected him to rail against her for walking off, to yell at her that the children were hungry or upset, anything but to worry about her own well-being. It was almost her undoing, as emotions she couldn't even identify washed over her.

"I am feeling thoughtful this morning," she told him finally, swallowing a lump in her throat. How could she explain to him about her worries, about the ghosts from the past, or how she feared letting the children into her life? He had already mentioned his own aunts and sisters and a mother when he talked about his cooking. His childhood sounded rich in love and protection and caring.

She'd learned the previous evening over dinner that his father had also been a lawyer, and Reed had naturally followed in his respected footsteps. Oliver Malloy had passed away three years earlier. Reed was devoted to his mother, Evelyn, and his sisters. How could he understand that she had carefully created a world of safety in which she needed no one and no one needed her?

Reed again surprised her by sitting down not more than two feet away.

"You do look thoughtful," he told her, "and a trifle sad."

She flushed at the gentle tone in his voice, similar to the one he used with the children. Charlotte had not discussed her feelings with anyone since her parents died. This was foreign to her. She looked to their graves, and he followed her glance.

"Your parents?" he asked.

She nodded but said nothing.

"I'm sorry if our arrival has brought up memories of your own parents' deaths. I know you understand what Lily and Thomas are going through. Better than I ever could."

His eyes were so brilliant and blue as they looked at her, and she knew they could bestow the gentlest of looks as well as the most scathing. Such intelligent eyes, behind which she knew he would reason that because she understood how the children felt, she more than anyone should want to take them in, unless she were cold and heartless.

Yet his voice sounded anything but condemning. She took a deep breath and told him.

"My parents died of cholera when I was a young woman."

"Perhaps not quite a woman," he offered.

She shrugged, then added, "Fourteen years old. It is as clear to me now as if it had happened yesterday. A cholera epidemic swept through Spring City so quickly. My parents were in town when the quarantine was put in place. They had already been infected by water from the well that serviced the restaurant where they dined that night."

She took a deep breath so she could speak evenly. "It was their wedding anniversary. Doc Cuthins sent a message to me and to all the homesteads outside of town to stay away They still thought it came through the air at the time. He called it *miasma*, a poisonous vapor."

Shaking her head, she looked toward the town, feeling as if she could see through the years. "The next message that came, three days later, said both my parents were dead. They died within half an hour of each other." She stopped, wondering at her own outpouring of words on a subject that normally stayed buried deeply inside her.

"I'm truly sorry." He reached out and touched her, simply a momentary brush along her hand, but it brought her out of her reverie. She focused again on his face.

"It must have been terrible for you and your brother. I remember when the cholera epidemic swept through Boston. I was very young, but no one who lived through it could ever forget the summer of '54. I lost an aunt and uncle. I can remember all those treatments they tried: first the laudanum then the acetate, the morphine, even red peppers. Nothing helped."

"No, nothing," she agreed. It had been a nightmare, but it was behind her now. Except that the untimely death of Ann Connors was bringing it all up again

The thought of becoming a surrogate parent once more reminded her of the struggles and the hard times and then, the inevitable loneliness, which she had coped with by developing a self-sufficient attitude to match her opinionated manner. And she would not put her writing on hold again. It was the only thing that had kept her sane.

She looked him squarely in the eye. "I do understand Thomas's nightmares and Lily's quiet, solemn stares," she told him, her voice as soft as the slight breeze that lifted the strands of hair off her shoulders.

Reed raised his hand, perhaps to take hold of hers or to touch one of those errant locks. Charlotte didn't wait to find out. She flinched away in the same instant and then stood up abruptly. Turning her back on him, she took the few steps toward her parents' graves.

"I understand that what the children need is a secure home and a heart full of love and generosity to make their own hearts the same way." She clasped her hands, realizing that they were trembling yet unsure of the reason why.

"And can't they find that here?" So silently had he approached from behind that she jumped slightly at his deep voice inches from her ear.

She didn't trust herself to speak for there again was that urge to cry. A lump sat solidly in her throat. A part of her cried out silently that it was her turn to be given a home and love. *Didn't she deserve that, too?* In the end, she shook her head.

"I believe you are wrong, Miss Sanborn. I think you have a world of love to give." She felt his hands on her shoulders—capable, strong hands that turned her to face him. He looked into her overly bright eyes, shining like green emeralds, and smiled. "I know you are capable of that love, even if you haven't realized it yet."

The timbre of his voice was shaking her very soul, and the blue spark in his eyes seemed to have lit a fire deep within her in that instant of standing so close and of touching and speaking of love. For she felt a warmth start in the pit of her stomach, and it heated up as it spread through her.

She knew in that instant that all the years of feeling proud of her self-sufficient isolation were a sham. She was a coward, afraid to love because of the pain that it caused. Afraid, indeed, of this exact feeling that encompassed her now.

God help her—to love and be loved was what she wanted more than anything else in the world, if she could but conquer her fear. She held her breath as the swirl of knowledge and sensations coursed through her mind and her body at his nearness.

A frown crinkled the soft skin between his dark eyebrows. He was looking into her eyes and probably seeing her whole soul laid bare in their green depths. The frown deepened a moment and then he lifted his hand to cup her gently pointed chin.

It was a bold touch, but he looked as mesmerized as she felt, as if he wasn't even aware of what he did. The shock of his fingertips on her skin made her gasp, and the spell was broken. They both stepped back.

"We should return. I left the children to come look for you."

His voice sounded gruff to her ears, and he was already striding ahead of her. She had to move almost at a run to keep up with him.

"They should be all right," she called after him. "Nothing much ever happens in Spring City," she said more to herself. Nothing except for the thrilling arrival of Reed Malloy.

"Still," she added, "there are a few critters to worry about if they're playing outside."

They arrived at Reed's horse. One horse.

"I'll walk home," she offered immediately.

"Nonsense," he said, his voice firm again. "The horse is a good strong one. I'm sure it can take both our weights."

Charlotte started to protest, looking behind her in case someone from the town should see her there with a strange man, but the road was blessedly deserted.

Before she knew it, he was bending down to create a cradle with his hands.

"Go ahead, Miss Sanborn. Step up."

She looked uncertainly at him but did as he suggested and placed one booted foot on his hands. She had to rest her palm on his shoulders, just below the nape of his neck, as he hoisted her high. He felt rock solid under her touch. In a moment, she'd grabbed the pommel and swung her other leg over, landing gently on the large mare.

While his back was to her, untying the horse, she quickly arranged her skirts yanking them down as far as possible before he turned. As he did, she saw his eyes go to her slim calf above her leather high-lows, but he said nothing, merely handing her the reins. Then, to her astonishment, he grabbed her ankle, and she gasped.

He pulled her foot out of the stirrup and moved her leg as far forward as she would let him. Then he stepped into the vacated stirrup and swung himself up behind her.

She gulped. It was peculiar, the feeling of his thighs, muscled and firm, against her own. She sat up straight to keep from resting against his broad chest, but there was nothing she could do about her rear end pressing intimately against his inner thighs.

Her cheeks burned at the thought of his body so close to hers. Then unexpectedly, Reed's arms came around her, and she gasped again, feeling instantly foolish when all he did was take the reins from her hands and flick the horse into beginning their journey.

"I . . . I could walk without any trouble," she told him, turning slightly to see her hair whipping him about his face.

"Blazes, I'm sorry," she muttered, trying to grasp the flying strands as the horse set off at a good pace.

He only smiled. "I much prefer your hair worn down," he told her. "I don't know which is prettier, your hair or the horse's mane."

Charlotte recognized that he was laughing at her discomfort and quickly faced forward, keeping a firm hold of her hair with one hand. He must think her as skittish and silly as a schoolgirl.

That thought and the continuing feeling of his legs, warm against her own, did nothing to calm the heat in her cheeks. She scolded herself for her runaway emotions. After all, she was *not* a girl but a woman of twenty-four.

Old enough to have had a lover, she added to herself, or to be a married woman with babies. *Certainly old enough to ride on a horse with a man.* But this particular man was playing havoc with her senses.

"These 'critters' you mentioned?" came his voice, so close behind her.

Without turning, she said, "Coyotes occasionally. Rattlesnakes, but hardly any. I just take the shovel to them. And wolves, once in a blue moon. Even less, since the bounty increased on their pelts."

"Even so, that seems an inordinate number of threats," he commented.

She laughed, thinking how it must sound to someone who had lived in the city his whole life. "Thaddeus and I played outside our whole childhood. Nothing ever bothered us. If a wolf comes by, you stamp your feet hard and yell, and it runs off. Same with the coyotes."

Even though it was less than a handful of minutes by horse, Charlotte had never been happier to see her home than when they rounded the grove of pine trees that grew on the edge of the Sanborn homestead. She was ready to jump off the horse but waited patiently as Reed slowed it down for the last few yards. She had the notion again that he was enjoying this far too much and gaining his amusement at her expense.

She bore it out regally, even waiting for him to assist her from the saddle after he dismounted. This was accomplished with an economy of movement as Charlotte aimed to deny him another view of her woven cotton stockings.

However, there was no denying the scorching touch of his hands at her waist, a sensation that seared right through her blouse to her skin as she slid from the saddle. Too close! As he set her down, she stepped back quickly and bounced off the side of the sweating horse. She didn't miss the glimmer of a smile in Reed Malloy's blue eyes.

"I'll put the horse in the stable," he told her looking down at her flushed face. "Why don't you check on the children."

Pleased to escape, she didn't even argue with his command and hurried off to find Lily and Thomas. As it turned out, they were playing happily in the parlor, having built a sturdy castle out of chairs. It was only once inside and away from Reed's presence that Charlotte concluded the heady feeling of being so close to him was a fairly pleasant, if unfamiliarly disconcerting, one.

With a shameful wickedness that surprised her, she wondered what it would feel like to have his entire body up against her own. And on that note, she retired upstairs to take a cool sponge bath, not even giving a thought to the unfinished article that waited in her study.

CHAPTER FOUR

Charlotte was up early the next day, closeted in her study until nearly noon.

"Hallelujah," she exclaimed, jumping up from her desk after sealing the manuscript in a large brown envelope. She had never been more relieved to finish an article. With it out of the way, she could better deal with Reed Malloy.

She ran her fingers through her long hair and assured that there were no large snarls, she twisted it up quickly into her usual functional knot. Leaving her study, Charlotte headed outside the house where she could hear Reed and the children laughing over something.

Stopping at the back steps, she paused at the sight of Reed running for all he was worth to catch Thomas, who dodged with nimble ease until he finally ran between Reed's legs.

"You're still it, Uncle Reed," Lily called out.

Charlotte spotted the little girl in the lower branch of her only apple tree that grew near the small paddock. Alfred, Charlotte's ancient horse, standing next to Reed's rented mare, seemed to be watching with some interest over the fence.

Charlotte felt she and old Alfred had something in common, both watching but not participating. She hungered for the laughter and the delight in the children's faces. She sighed and took a seat on the steps, feeling as fenced in as her horse.

Reed turned and spotted her. To her amazement, after a momentary pause, he headed straight for her at full chisel. She shrank back on the steps, her eyes wide, as he came to a grinding halt, directly in front of her. His eyes seemed to match the clear Colorado sky, and his hair, usually neatly brushed, was curling up all over his head, with one irresistible lock hanging over his brow. Her hand itched to twist his soft, dark hair between her fingertips.

He grinned down at her, and Charlotte felt her breath catch in her throat. His hand snaked out and lightly slapped her own, leaving a slight stinging.

She looked at her hand then up at him, too amazed to speak.

"You, Miss Sanborn, are now it." With that, Reed darted off to stop behind the apple tree where Lily still perched.

"I'm it," Charlotte repeated. So, she was not going to be allowed to remain an observer after all. How wonderful! She recalled playing the game when she was a small girl, before . . . before it became impossible to play. Later, she'd watched Teddy with some of the children in the school yard, and there were some moves she still remembered.

"Then beware, all three of you," she called out, standing up and racing down the steps, heading first toward Lily.

The little girl scampered higher up in the tree, just out of Charlotte's reach. Reed had dashed away the moment Charlotte started running, so she turned to Thomas who hovered near by, clearly wanting to be chased.

He screamed with glee as she closed in on him and then darted around her. He was good at this—small, elusive, and quick—and Charlotte nearly tripped herself up. She paused and then, without a care for impropriety, bent down and pulled the back hem of her skirt forward between her legs before tucking it into her waistband.

She looked down at her new guise, resembling a Turk from one of her father's history books. At least she wouldn't break her neck.

Not caring a whit for her white stockings, she took off in pursuit of Thomas once more, hearing Reed cheer her on.

Out of the corner of her eye, she could see that he had relaxed, standing nearly close enough to reach. Lily dropped to the ground, and Charlotte pretended to head for her. At the last minute, she changed direction, charging directly at Reed.

His face registered his surprise, but he had no time to react before she threw herself at him. Literally. She hit him like a buffalo on a rampage, helpless now to stop her momentum.

Reed couldn't withstand the onslaught, falling over and taking her with him onto the soft grass. Her hair, having come out of its loose knot, flew all around them in a wild whirl of reddish brown.

Charlotte felt his warm, hard body beneath her, then on top of her as they rolled. She had closed her eyes at the last moment and heard the children's laughter.

When she opened her eyes, her vision was filled with Reed looking down at her, his dark-haired head framed by the clear and bright azure sky above.

The coolness of the grass beneath her seeped through her thin cotton dress, but the front of her was aflame where the weight of his muscles pinned her down. It was a delicious heat that burned through her. Her entire body was tingling with a pleasurable sizzle.

When she opened her mouth to catch the breath she'd knocked out of herself, saw his glance dart to her parted lips.

"You certainly play to win," he murmured.

Teddy had always said the same thing. It was he, in fact, who had taught her that maneuver, striking the opponent like a cannonball. She'd been on the receiving end once or twice. However, she never thought she'd use it on a fully grown male.

Without thinking, she said, "And you are it, Mr. Malloy."

He opened his mouth to respond, but the children's giggles stole his attention. He stiffened, his whole body tensing on top of her, as if caught by surprise.

In truth, the sensations swirling through her—and the smell of Reed's maleness mixed with the fragrance of fresh grass, the dazzling light of day, the soft breeze carrying hundreds of spring aromas, not to mention the feel of his thighs and his chest—had caused her to forget that she and this man were not completely alone in the world.

Reed glanced once more into her eyes, his expression unreadable, before rolling sideways, to lie on his back beside her as the children ran up.

"That was great, Aunt Charlotte," Lily said. "Who's it now?"

"He is," Charlotte replied, jerking a thumb toward Reed. She laughed, feeling breathless and sat up, freezing a moment later at the feel of his hand on her back. He brushed up and down, and she realized foolishly that he was only removing blades of grass.

It didn't matter, her heart felt as if it were beating at double its normal rate. He was sitting up beside her now, and she let the curtain of her hair fall between them to shield her blushing features.

He rose to his feet, and Charlotte looked up as he offered her his hand. She hesitated, then grabbed hold of it. It was as she remembered from their first handshake, warm and strong, and this time she felt the broadness of his palm as it closed around her own.

In a moment, she was pulled to her feet as if she weighed no more than a child. He didn't immediately release his hold as their gazes met again, and she saw behind the amusement a glint of some dark, mysterious emotion swirling interestingly in the depths. Finally, he released her.

With his touch removed, Charlotte felt released from the frozen moment.

"How about some lunch?" she offered. She could see by the sun that it was past noon. "You three must have worked up quite an appetite with such carryings-on." Frankly, she admitted to herself, she didn't think her constitution was up to any more physical contact with Reed Malloy.

As if he understood that, he agreed. "Lunch it is."

The children ran on ahead.

"Your writing must be coming along well," he ventured.

He referred, of course, to the fact that she'd come out of her study at all. She gave him a smile filled with all the joy she felt at being done with her writing for the day, at having shared a delightful moment with her cousin's children, and most of all, at how alive Reed made her feel.

"I'll take that beautiful smile as a yes."

That afternoon, Reed offered to take her completed assignment into town to the post office, which was just a desk in the corner of the general store. Her article would leave on the express train. Meanwhile, he could attend to his own business using Spring City's telegraph system. This meant, of course, that she stayed alone with Thomas and Lily.

To Charlotte's amazement, she enjoyed sitting with the children while they played. There were make-believe games, followed by hide-and-seek, first in the house and then outside among the wildflowers and pine trees that grew in abundance on her property.

Lily said it was as pretty as some of the Boston Public Gardens where her mother used to take her to play. Charlotte only wished that it looked as it had in her mother's day, with a cultivated flower garden on either side of the front door, a vegetable garden in the back, and red and yellow roses climbing about on trellises all around the house.

By late afternoon, when Charlotte heard an approaching horse, she looked up expecting to see Reed. Instead it was Sarah Cuthins, her round, smiling face abruptly changing to shock at the sight of two children playing in front of Charlotte's house.

"Whatever have we here?" her neighbor asked without any pretense of disinterest as she drew her horse to a halt. "Why, what sweet little ones."

Charlotte went over to meet the doctor's wife. Straightaway, Thomas ducked behind Lily who came to stand by Charlotte.

"These are my young cousins from Massachusetts. Lillian and Thomas Connors. Children, say hello to Mrs. Cuthins, my neighbor."

Lily murmured a polite hello. Thomas, of course, said nothing.

"Well, I can see now why you haven't been by for a meal, Charlotte. I was worried about you. But it seems you've had your hands busy." Suddenly her round forehead frowned deeply. "How did they get here? Are you feeding them?"

Charlotte didn't take offense at that one. Sarah knew her too well.

"They came by train, and yes, they're being fed. They're having three meals a day."

She didn't feel the need to add that she wasn't the one cooking the meals. After all, neighborly need-to-know only went so far. Then the expected figure of Reed Malloy upon a horse came into view around the pines.

Charlotte felt butterflies take flight in her stomach. She wasn't at all sure she wanted Sarah to know that a bachelor, and a handsome one at that, was staying in her house.

The doctor's wife turned toward the sound of the horse and then looked at Charlotte with raised eyebrows. "And this is?"

"The children's solicitor from Boston," Charlotte finished in a tone that she hoped sounded as if no more information would follow.

If anything, Sarah's eyebrows rose higher, her warm brown eyes opening wide. By that time, Reed had dismounted and was striding toward them.

He stood beside Charlotte and the children, and looked down at the bulky figure of Sarah Cuthins. Charlotte hastily made introductions.

"So happy to meet you," Sarah said, actually sounding coquettish when faced with a dashing stranger from the east.

"The pleasure is all mine, madam," Reed returned.

"Well," Charlotte began, "it's time we got the children washed up and started the . . . ," she faltered. It was too early for supper.

"Started the chores," Reed finished helpfully. "Children, you heard your aunt. Say good-bye to Mrs. Cuthins." This met with the same immediate success as all of Reed's orders, and the children murmured farewell before scampering inside the house.

Obviously, Sarah wanted to stay and chat. However, since no invitation was forthcoming, she could do nothing but allow Reed to help her onto her wagon seat.

"I guess I'll be off then, seeing as you're all right," she added. "Oh, the food! Since it's already cooked, you might as well have it. There's enough for *all* of you," she put in, looking questioningly at Reed. He only smiled.

"How kind of you," Charlotte said, taking down a basket and handing it to Reed before taking a second one from Sarah. "Your cooking is always a treat."

"Yes, well, I hope your ready-made family likes it, Charlotte. I'll be seeing you soon. Good day." Sarah clicked the reins, turned her horse and wagon around in a wide arc, and started down the drive. She had a bemused smile upon her face when she looked back at them at least twice.

Charlotte groaned as they walked toward the house.

"What?" Reed asked, stopping on the front porch and balancing the basket casually against one knee.

"It'll be all over the valley before sunset," she told him, sitting on the swing that she'd repaired so many times over the years she couldn't count.

He began pawing through the contents of Sarah's offering, finally pulling out a custard tart. Satisfied by his choice, he looked up at her.

"What?" he asked again before taking a big bite of the treat.

She sighed. *How could the man be so dim?*

"That the odd female writer has a man of no relation and two children staying with her."

"At least the children are relatives," he offered, but it was clearly not meant to ease her mind, and Charlotte grasped that he'd known all along what was worrying her. And he was amused!

"It's not funny, Mr. Malloy. *I* have to live here. What if my neighbors want to ride me out of town on a rail?"

Perhaps he was trying to look serious, but he was failing. He finished up the tart in two more bites.

"I didn't think you cared a fig for what people thought of you. They all think you're eccentric anyway, don't they?"

That hurt. What's more, she *did* care. She longed to fit in, if only she knew how. She had feared for years that it was too late, that any attempts by her to enter into the social life of Spring City would be rebuffed, and she would be laughed at.

But what did Reed Malloy think? That she was odd, that she didn't care about anyone else's opinion? Did he think she was made of stone?

The expression on her face must have been morose, indeed, for he came to crouch before the swing, his gaze locked on hers.

"I was speaking in jest. I'm sure that the good people of Spring City think that you're as upstanding and straitlaced as they are. Even more so, since you live the life of a hermit."

She winced. "I never meant to be a hermit."

She tried to laugh as if none of his words mattered. But failing dismally, she lowered her eyes and started to play with the red cloth covering the basket on her lap.

"What did you intend for your life? You don't like being thought of as eccentric or as a hermit or as a wanton woman." He was speaking so plainly, he deserved an honest answer.

"I guess, at this point, I'd settle for ordinary."

Without warning, his hand was on her chin, raising her face and forcing her to look at him. "That you'll never be, lady writer. Don't pretend to be any different from who you are." He paused, seeming to search her green gaze for the very essence of her being, and she was certain his head moved a little closer to her own. "But don't hide from what life has to offer either. There's more to the world, Miss Sanborn, than this homestead outside of a little town called Spring City."

He was going to kiss her. She knew it, absolutely, from the look on his face to the intensity in his sapphire-blue eyes. His hand was still on her chin. All he had to do was hold her there and then bring his mouth a little closer.

"We're hungry," came Lily's call from inside the screen door.

Charlotte gasped, and she watched Reed's eyes widen slightly with surprise. Then he smiled.

"As for the rumors, they will all blow over," he said, fixing her with that intense gaze once more, filled with mischievous laughter, "or maybe we'll give them a real reason to gossip."

With that threatening statement, he took the basket from her, retrieved his own, and left her alone on the porch, her pulse still racing.

Charlotte stared after him, trying to calm the flutter that seemed to have taken up permanent residence in her stomach.

CHAPTER FIVE

The peculiarity of having them in her home began to wear off by the following week. The awkwardness of running into Reed Malloy when she went to the water closet or came out of the bathing room in her father's banyan, of finding a man's razor by the porcelain wash bowl and men's stockings hanging on the line—all of these had happened and been passed over and were now being ignored as if such occurrences had always taken place.

Amazing, as far as Charlotte was concerned, was that items broken for years were fixed as if by magic, such as the hole in her study floor and the cracked stair tread. She would hear Reed whistling outside with a saw in one hand, the kids sitting nearby chatting with him, and then by the end of the day, the repairs were done. She always thanked him, which he would shrug off, giving her an enigmatic smile.

She thought that, perhaps, he was using her home as a welcome change from all that he knew in the city. He was dressing in denims bought at Webster's store in town, barely combing his hair, sitting on her porch swing at all hours with one of her father's books in his hand—one day *Uncle Tom's*

Cabin, another day *The Count of Monte Christo*—and happily wielding a hammer when necessary.

After nearly two weeks with her visitors, Charlotte was starting to wonder how long this could go on with her hiding in her study, Reed and the children discovering things to do during the day, and then everyone congregating for meals.

As far as Charlotte could see, this had nothing to do with her being an adequate guardian when, except for occasionally lending a hand at bathing time, she was doing little in the way of parental duties. Reed Malloy was not only doing it all. He seemed to be relishing the assignment immensely.

And, of course, she was relishing the sight of him in his well-fitting denims!

That evening was another delicious supper, and she added a little more butter to her boiled potatoes while shooting a quick glance toward the man at the other end of the table. Should she say something to him tonight?

The children were settling in comfortably, too comfortably perhaps. They'd rearranged their room and were talking about sending for their toys. Reed seemed unconcerned with his business in Boston, having mentioned the capability of his law partner.

The truth was, even now, when she knew something had to give, she was loath to say anything and disturb the peaceful arrangement they'd fallen into so quickly.

Her writing had not suffered. In fact, she'd taken some comfort in knowing there were other people in the house, and without having to forage for food in town or at the neighbor's, she'd had more time to complete her work.

Reed had sent off another article for her that afternoon on his trip to town. She had spent an agreeable afternoon playing with the children. More games and flower-picking and—

"A dance?" came a veritable squeal from Lily that brought Charlotte out of her reverie, as she mashed yet another boiled potato under her fork. She realized she'd been staring at Reed without hearing a word he was saying.

"That's what I said." He helped himself to seconds of the peppered and salted roasted beets. "A barn dance. And we're all invited."

Charlotte nearly choked on a piece of roast beef. As it was, she coughed loudly and, with eyes watering, asked, "What do you mean 'We're all invited'?"

Reed stared back at her. "Exactly what I said. Even you, Miss Sanborn."

"Even *me*," she repeated indignantly. "Of course, me! I live here. But how could *you* be invited? I mean, no one even knows you."

"Despite that, Miss Sanborn, it's a friendly town, and when I was at the post office today, or rather at Jackson's," he clarified, referring to the general store that handled the mail, "I saw the notice about the dance. While I was looking at it, one of your townspeople—Miss Prentice, I believe—told me to come along as they could always use another dance partner."

Charlotte thought of the petite Miss Prentice with her tightly wound blond curls and her big blue eyes and wondered just how long her conversation with Reed had lasted.

Of course, Eliza Prentice would latch onto a fresh bachelor the moment he wandered into town, thinking nothing of striking up a conversation with a stranger and immediately asking him to a dance. She was an incorrigible flirt, despite the fact that she was already betrothed. But how much had Reed told Eliza about his accommodations?

"Are you sure you're telling me everything, Mr. Malloy?"

His eyes widened visibly, but he said nothing. The children looked from one adult to another, visibly excited over the idea of a dance.

"Are we going?" It was Thomas this time, and he actually sounded eager to venture out in public.

"Yes." "No." Their adult voices were simultaneous.

Narrowing her eyes, Charlotte glared at the opposing counsel.

"Does the whole town know that you're staying here or not, Mr. Malloy?"

"I assure you, I always maintain the utmost discretion. Of course, we don't know what Mrs. Cuthins might have imparted." His grin was broad. "As far as the fair Miss Prentice is concerned, I'm here on business, which I am, am I not?" He didn't wait for a reply. "Of course," he added, "everyone will see we're together when we enter the dance."

The kids squealed again, assured that they were all going, but Charlotte was not budging.

"I'm definitely not going, and I'm not at all convinced it is a dance for children, *my* cousin's children, Mr. Malloy, but I am sure you will have an enjoyable time." She hoped that sounded firm and final because she could see that Reed Malloy had other ideas.

As expected, he fixed her with a challenging look, accompanied by the children's protests.

"Why can't we go, Aun' Charlie?" Thomas asked, stuffing a piece of meat in his mouth at the same time.

"Don't you like to dance?" Lily added as if she couldn't imagine such a thing. She eyed Charlotte with wonder.

"I'm extremely busy right now, children. And . . . I, well, I don't go to dances often." *Try never,* she added silently. "As for you—"

"Who would have thought it?" Reed said slowly, interrupting her words. "The highly opinionated, independent Charlotte Sanborn is a wallflower."

"A wallflower!" she said horrified. Thank God the children wouldn't know what that meant. She would never have phrased it thus.

"A shrinking violet, then?" he offered, his tone helpful although his eyes were glittering.

In truth, she was quite shy, and something about groups made her feel a bit lost. Anything that she could say so well on paper, never came out of her mouth with the same finesse and effect.

Charlotte sighed. This was getting too complicated by far. The sooner the children and their handsome lawyer were out of her house, the better. Suddenly, Lily exclaimed aloud as her knife slipped, and she cut her finger. Charlotte was out of her chair instantly, taking hold of Lily's hand and pressing the small wound tightly with a clean napkin to staunch the bleeding.

Lily looked very pale, and Reed stood up, putting his hand on her small shoulder.

"I suppose we're supposed to cut the meat for them," he said.

If Charlotte hadn't known better, she would have sworn he seemed a bit off-kilter, sounding doubtful for the first time since she'd known him. Maybe it was the sight of blood on the little girl's hand.

After a moment, Charlotte peeked under the napkin. "There, it's not bad at all. It's barely a graze. The bleeding has stopped." Teddy had done much worse many times. "Come on, Lily, let's go clean it up a bit."

Reed started to follow, but Charlotte shook her head, still holding onto the little girl's hand. He was fussing like an old biddy, and it would only make Lily more frightened.

"There's no need for you to come along, Mr. Malloy. It's a small cut. All it needs is a clean piece of gauze. You and Thomas finish your supper."

She hustled the little girl up the stairs to where she kept a few medicinal items. Charlotte was beginning to think it would be good for the children to experience the freedom of the West. It seemed they were coddled much more than she or her brother ever were. It was also relieving to know that Reed Malloy wasn't completely at ease playing a mother hen. She had started to think he was damned near perfect at everything.

"Aunt Charlotte?" Lily broke in to her musings, shifting in the chair as Charlotte applied witch hazel with a clean piece of cotton cloth.

"Hold still," she admonished gently.

"Aunt Charlotte?"

"Yes, Lily?" She was cutting a small piece of gauze.

"We can go to the barn dance, can't we? My finger won't ruin it?"

Charlotte looked up from what she was doing, holding the gauze firmly in place. But there was no manipulation in the little girl's face. She simply assumed they would be going and would blame herself if they didn't.

Charlotte felt her heart melt. Certainly, the children could use a little amusement and gaiety in their young lives that had already experienced such bereavement. She looked away from Lily's soft brown eyes and began to tie the end of the gauze.

"No, honey, your finger won't ruin it. By the time of the dance, you probably won't even have to wear the bandage. Now, how about some dessert?"

It was late by the time supper was over and the children were bathed and tucked in bed. It was story time, and Charlotte was now expected to do the honors since she had done so with great success each night since the game of tag had bonded them all together more closely.

While she was sure Reed Malloy was as well read as herself, he seemed content to sit in the rocking chair by the window, his face shadowed, and listen to her. Charlotte sat on Thomas's side of the bed, her back turned to Reed. Both children were commanded to keep their eyes closed or the story would stop.

Lily held her bandaged finger out straight on top of the bed clothes, and Thomas turned on his side. Both their faces held rapt expressions as Charlotte conjured a kingdom of princes and princesses, and fairies both good and slightly bad, and, of course, dragons and griffins.

By the time she finished telling the old tale she remembered her father reading to her out of a big book with illustrations, the children were fast asleep. Charlotte turned to Reed and he nodded, blowing out the lamp. Together, they tiptoed out of the room and down the stairs.

"You did well tonight," he offered as they stepped out onto the front porch for some air.

Charlotte was glad the dark, clear night hid her blush. "Thank you for saying so, Mr. Malloy. I could tell stories from now until Judgment Day, and I don't think I'd grow tired of the telling, although I hope most of my readers stay awake for the outcome."

He laughed, and Charlotte liked the sound, deep and genuine.

"You are a consummate story teller, Miss Sanborn, but I was actually referring to your handling of the situation with Lily's finger."

"Oh." She made a minor mental adjustment, withdrawing the first mistaken compliment and substituting the other in its place.

"I am finding that being with the children is easier than I envisioned, but then," she continued, moving toward the porch swing, "we're all only playing around, after all. School is not in session, and I haven't cooked a meal or shopped for provisions since you got here." She couldn't help smiling at him. "You have been here constantly lending a hand and keeping them out of my way while I work."

Reed followed her to the swing, and Charlotte moved aside quickly, startled when he sat down beside her, but she continued her thought.

"It is not real life, Mr. Malloy." *I wish that it were*, she thought to herself. She could certainly get used to this, all of it and all of them.

He remained silent a moment, looking straight ahead across her front yard to the long line of trees that went up as far as the road to town. She was aware of her heart beating faster, just because they were alone and he was far too close. She told herself she was a fool, to be moved simply because a man was near, but his muscled leg against the side of her skirts felt warm and powerful.

She had to concentrate when he started speaking, and stop herself from thinking of the strong, sensual lips that were forming the words.

"I don't know what to tell you, Miss Sanborn. I am not a man to give up, and you don't seem a quitter to me, either. What I'd like is for us both to be on the same side, then I'm sure we can work this out."

He looked down at her. "Your cousin wanted you to be their guardian. You don't want the responsibility because of your work. The children want a home and are excited by coming out west. Their grandmother wants them, but Ann didn't want her to raise them. I've got a law practice to which I must return, but I can't shirk my responsibility as executor of the will."

He brought one ankle to rest comfortably on the knee of his other leg, as he draped his arm along the back of the wooden swing. That was almost her undoing, the feel of his fingers resting ever so lightly behind her left shoulder. It was as if all her skin was superbly sensitive, honing in on whatever part of his body came close to her.

"You're a smart woman," he concluded. "You tell me how I should tie this all up in a neat package and make everyone happy."

She stared at him and was at a loss for words. They could not be on the same side since they were of opposite opinions as to where the children should live. If she let them stay, it wouldn't be the same as it was now. There would be all the little details to work out, and she wondered if the upkeep money he'd mentioned covered her need to hire a woman to help with the cooking and cleaning.

Could she concentrate on her writing with them in the house? She would be there with them alone, and Reed Malloy would be thousands of miles from Spring City. She sighed and turned away. *Why should that be the one thing uppermost in her mind now?*

"Thanks for the input," he said, wryly.

She laughed, and the sound was foreign to her own ears. It startled her, and she raised a hand to her throat. "Well, it has been fun."

"That was the last thing I expected you to say."

"Do I seem such a stick?" Charlotte was extremely interested to learn Reed's perception of her. He was a man who must know a lot of people, many of them women, and she wondered how she compared.

"No," he said firmly, with a shake of his head. "Your laughter is lovely, and not heard often enough. You have your priorities, and they don't seem to include any amusements. Instead of being a wallflower, Miss Sanborn, try being a wildflower."

She should have been affronted at his presumptiveness, but she smiled at that curious image he'd conjured. "I do have to support myself, all on my own hook, even though I need very little money for my lifestyle."

She stood up, moving away from him to lean against the railing, resting the side of her head against the porch post. She surveyed the stars of the sky so familiar to her, aware all the time that he was studying her profile.

"I honestly don't know how to resolve this situation," she confessed. "I only know how I live my life, for good or for ill. It seems to have suited me so far. If I had the children, then I'd need . . . a wife, I guess." She looked at him.

He appeared as startled at that as she felt, then they both laughed. He stood up, too, and suddenly the porch seemed to be much smaller. With him standing so close, she could feel the heat from his body, and absurdly, she wanted to be enveloped by that warmth. He made her feel as if something special was always happening.

It was probably the strangeness of having an adult male in the house who wasn't her father or her brother. But she couldn't take her eyes from his blue gaze, which seemed to be looking at her so earnestly. She didn't know enough about Reed Malloy to guess whether he was affected by her presence, too, but he did have a curious expression on his usually confident face.

"And do the pressures of your career mean you cannot go to a barn dance, Miss Sanborn?"

So that was what was on his mind. She smiled crookedly. "No, I believe I can manage one dance, much better, in fact, than I can manage two children." *Or one man,* she added silently, needing to escape before something foolish came out of her mouth.

But when she would have moved, he startled her by placing one steady hand on the porch post above her head. She craned her neck to glance at it, then looked at him to see his own gaze riveted to the throbbing pulse point she'd exposed on her slender neck.

"Mr. Malloy." Neither query nor statement, her whispery voice sounded strange to her ears. It was more a plea for mercy, she thought. It brought his eyes up to lock on hers.

He was silent a moment. She could almost see the struggle waging within him. She had the feeling then, as she'd had before, that he wanted to kiss her, but he was torn by something, something barely powerful enough to restrain him.

He raised his hand to her neck and, with a slightly callused thumb, stroked down the side of its white column before lightly caressing her unyielding jawline. Once, twice.

"Miss Sanborn," he said at last, his voice a deep timbrous sound that vibrated with the rhythm of her heartbeat. "I believe it's time we went to bed."

"Bed," she repeated, her eyes widening as the porch floor seemed to slip out from under her.

CHAPTER SIX

Charlotte lay awake far into the night. She burned over the blamed ninny she must have appeared to Reed, blurting out the word *bed*, just as he had dropped his hand from the post and moved to let her pass by. Clearly, he had meant nothing untoward by his statement.

She'd hurriedly bid him good night and gone inside, but she plainly heard him through the door, "We'll see, lady writer, we'll see."

About the children was all he meant, she'd assured herself. However, in her gut, she knew they were now dancing around another subject altogether and that he was as affected by her as she by him.

It was more difficult that night to accept being a twenty-four-year-old virgin than it ever had before. She felt hot and prickly, as she thought of Reed's face and his hands and those muscles in his rear end, perfectly displayed when he wore his jeans. It was a long night, indeed.

The next morning, Charlotte not only acknowledged that her visitors were all staying through another week, but that they were going to a dance together. And she was looking forward to it, until the questions started popping into her mind: Was Reed her escort or was he going to dance with every woman there, including Eliza Prentice? And what was she going to wear?

True, it was merely a barn dance, but all her clothes were hopelessly worn out. She couldn't remember the last time she'd gone to Miss Finney's in Denver or even to their own small "house of fashion" located in one corner of Jeremiah Webster's piece goods store.

Occasionally, Mr. Webster had some factory-made clothes that were, if a little plain and pragmatic, at least decently priced. She'd bought a few blouses there over the years. However, most of the women in Spring City relied on their Sears Roebuck or their Montgomery Ward catalogues, or they sewed their own creations.

From what Charlotte had seen, some of them were quite adept at dressmaking.

For her part, she could barely sew on a button, let alone create a dress appropriate for a dance even if there was time. Regina Sanborn knew solely the art of needlepoint and found that too tedious to teach her daughter. Her mother's dresses had always been made by seamstresses when she'd lived in Boston, and Charlotte remembered overnight outings to Denver when her mother needed something new.

Charlotte's own dresses had been bought at Miss Finney's until she was fourteen, and then . . . . She frowned.

She had probably bought two plain dresses in the past ten years. Everything else was recycled from her mother's wardrobe. She did not mind in the least wearing her mother's clothing, although she had worn out most of her skirts, not to mention finishing her growth at about three inches taller than Regina.

Her eyes refocused on the work at hand. The article in front of her was supposed to be on the problems between the farmers who were cordoning off more and more land with barbed wire and the cattlemen who were running out of places to drive their cattle. She had barely begun it as she couldn't keep her mind on the task at hand.

"Blazes!" She looked around guiltily, which made her madder. This was her home, and she could curse or daydream if she wanted, but by God, she would not be daydreaming if it weren't for that infernal lawyer who had somehow got the upper hand.

They should have been gone by now, Charlotte fumed, except she wasn't driving them out. Instead, she'd been polite and caring and almost . . . motherly. And worst of all, she was enjoying their company too much by half!

She still didn't know how to answer Reed's question from the night before. How could she help him work out the problem of what to do with young Thomas and Lily? She only knew that today she wasn't getting any work done. She might as well make a good showing at the one town dance she was ever likely to attend.

Gathering up her blue beaded purse and making sure she had enough money inside it, she hung it from her wrist, and placed a well-worn, favorite bonnet on top of her head. Reed was outside with the children, who were good about being quiet when she was writing, or supposedly writing. The three of them turned to her as soon as she stepped out the back door, and she felt a brief moment of panic.

How would she explain abandoning her work for a silly whim? Reed was already looking at her with that quizzical gaze. She didn't want him to know she didn't have anything proper to wear or that it mattered to her if she did. Then she had a stroke of brilliance.

"Come along, Lily. We need to get you a dress for the dance." She watched as three mouths seemed to drop open at once. "Well?"

"But I already have a dress, Aunt Charlotte."

"Oh. You brought it with you from Boston?"

The little girl nodded, and Charlotte saw a smile spread on Reed's face. But she wouldn't give up.

"Hm," she faltered. "What about you, Thomas?" She would prefer to have the little girl with her but any port in a storm, at that point.

He just shook his head. Then Lily's face brightened. "I need a new pair of stockings. White ones," she added for emphasis.

"Well, there you are," Charlotte said gratefully. "How could you get slicked up for a dance without white stockings? Come along, get in the wagon. Mr. Malloy, I trust you'll look after Thomas."

"As a matter of fact, I need a new tie, myself. We'll all go into Spring City together."

It was Charlotte's turn to be caught open-mouthed.

"Really, Mr. Malloy. You went to town yesterday. Why don't you let us choose one for you?"

She was determined not to have Reed there while she picked over the clothes at Webster's. She couldn't ask Lily to keep silent about it, but she could at least stop the man from seeing it for himself.

He looked as though he might argue, but then, to Charlotte's surprise, he acquiesced.

"All right. I'd like that." He stooped down to the little girl. "You mind your aunt, and pick me out a handsome tie." He reached into his pocket and pulled out his billfold. He handed the little girl some money and gave her a pat on the top of her silky blond head.

"A V-spot," Lily exclaimed, her eyes as big as saucers at being given the responsibility of minding five dollars.

Charlotte, feeling victorious, drove old Alfred harder than usual to town. Lily held on tightly beside her with one hand, the other still clutching the money. The only conversation between them was when Charlotte turned to ask if the little girl's finger was bothering her today.

When Lily glanced at her, she saw immediately that the girl was delighting in the fast ride. They smiled at one another.

"I'd almost forgotten my cut," was all she said. Then after a pause, she asked, "Can I drive the wagon one day, Aunt Charlotte?"

Charlotte considered at what age she had first held the reins. "Perhaps on the way home, you can try it for a bit, sitting here on my lap."

She wasn't sure if that was the motherly thing to do. Perhaps she should have told her she was far too young. But looking at Lily's widening smile, Charlotte didn't care a hang if it was the motherly thing or not. They said nothing more until they pulled into town.

"It's so much smaller than home," Lily observed.

"Yes, I'm certain it is."

Charlotte had, of course, seen artist's renderings in newspapers, even the occasional daguerreotype, of eastern cities, such as Boston and New York. She knew they had to be ten times more impressive in reality. What did it feel like to walk along the broad paved avenues and witness the sights and sounds?

She took the little girl's hand in her own and they headed straight for Mr. Webster's store. Charlotte nodded to some passersby and greeted others. Her visits to town were frequent, to the restaurant and to the general store to send off her articles and to get information wired to her from far and wide as she researched her stories, but this excursion was out of the ordinary.

When she approached the ready-made clothing section, Webster's teenaged granddaughter, Anna, appeared out of nowhere to help her, eyeing both her unlikely customer and her unknown companion.

"This is my cousin, Lillian, from Boston," Charlotte explained. "She needs some white stockings for the dance on Saturday."

"We can suit her up, over here." Anna led the way to a shelf of stockings and proceeded to pull out an assortment for Lily, some plain, some with a little flower pattern.

Charlotte had only a vague idea of what was appropriate for a little girl and had one eye on the rack of dresses in the corner. She started toward these, saying, "Whatever Lily wants is fine. I'm sure the two of you know more about this than I do."

They weren't even listening to her at that point, and she lifted her skirt and fairly scurried over to the dresses, hoping she could pick something out quickly and with minimal attention. But she had barely begun to look through them when Mr. Webster appeared.

"Ah, our famous writer," he said with a twinkle in his eyes.

Charlotte smiled at him. "That's kind of you, Mr. Webster." Charlotte remembered how she'd always adored coming to see him with her mother. He used to have sweets in his pockets for her and Thaddeus, and always a pleasant word. Lord, he must be as old as the hills, but he still looked the same.

"Is our biggest frog in the puddle looking for something special?" His voice was kind but Charlotte wondered a moment if he, too, thought her strange.

"Oh, not particularly, just a dancing frock, nothing too flashy." She tried to sound casual as she continued to paw through the meager assortment, but she could tell already that there was nothing here exactly as she'd hoped.

"There's nothing there," he echoed her thoughts, "that will suit, I reckon." He said this without artfulness, studying her detachedly and looking over the dresses himself. "But let me think a minute. I may've got something upstairs." He yelled over to his granddaughter, "Anna, go get that dress in my office."

"What dress, Pappy?"

"The one from Denver." He turned to Charlotte. "It was routed here by mistake, and I was fixin' to return it." He looked back at Anna who hadn't yet moved. "Bring it here, girl, quick-like."

Precisely what she'd hoped to avoid, thought Charlotte, as Anna hustled up the stairs—Mr. Webster making a big fuss over her. How embarrassing! Right then, Lily came running up, smiling broadly.

"I've found the perfect pair, Aunt Charlotte. Look." In her hands were a pair of the sheerest, palest white stockings that Charlotte had ever seen and up each side was a row of faux pearls.

"Oh, my. I hardly think . . . do you . . . I mean, is that what you normally wear?"

Lily dissolved in laughter, and Charlotte thought how good it was to see the little girl looking genuinely happy. She imagined it had been a sour time the past few months. She hated to have to tell her no, but those stockings!

"Not for me, Aunt Charlotte, for you, for the dance."

"Oh." What more could she say? How did Lily know she longed to have all the feminine finery necessary to make it one memorable evening? "Oh," she said again. "That's different. Let me take a look."

Secretly, she was thrilled at the thought of the gossamer-fine material with the rows of tiny pearls stretched up her legs. She felt tingly merely thinking about it. And the fact that Reed Malloy's face kept entering her mind had nothing to do with it, she told herself firmly.

"I'll take them. But what about you, Lily?"

The little girl didn't answer. Her gaze had gone past Charlotte, and her mouth and eyes had opened wide. "Ooh," she murmured, her voice barely audible.

Charlotte turned to see what had captured Lily's attention, and her own breath caught in her throat. Who would have thought, right here in Spring City in Webster's store? There stood Anna, holding the most beautiful dress Charlotte had ever seen, in the most captivating shade of vivid emerald green, trimmed with darker green lace.

She knew in an instant why Mr. Webster had thought of that dress for her. Charlotte remembered when she was little, her mother had bought her a dress in nearly the same color to set off the red tones in her hair. Her father had called her "his angel girl," and everyone in town had raved over how pretty she looked. That was about the last time Charlotte could remember such a thing happening.

Wordlessly, she took it from Anna and held it up against her body, turning to take in her reflection in the full-length mirror Mr. Webster kept by the dress rack.

The dress made the reds and paler shades of caramel in her hair come out in warm dazzling highlights, and her skin took on a clear, delicate glow. Even more surprising to her was that her eyes matched the sparkling green shade of the dress, and she'd always thought of them as ordinary grass green.

It was Mr. Webster who finally spoke. "Do you want to try it on?"

Charlotte nodded.

"Anna," he continued, "absquatulate yourself out of here, and tell Beatrice we'll need her sewing services. She can make any adjustments before Miss Sanborn leaves town today."

Charlotte was well aware that Beatrice had the first and sole sewing machine in Spring City. As it turned out, however, little in the way of alterations were needed. They picked out a pair of white stockings for Lily with one flower sewn on either ankle—slightly daring for a little girl, but Charlotte thought it wouldn't hurt. Then they thanked Mr. Webster and headed out to purchase shoes for Charlotte.

They were relaxing over a cup of tea and a glass of lemonade in the dining room of Fuller Hotel when Lily exclaimed, "Uncle Reed's tie!"

"Oh dear, it wouldn't do to go home without that, now would it?" Charlotte said.

After their refreshments, they headed over to the only men's clothing store in town.

After bypassing the overalls, flannel shirts, and denims, they came to the smaller section of the store that contained the fine cotton shirts and worsted wool pants, doctor's clothes, bang-ups, and Hessians. There, to Lily's delight, was a very small selection of silk ties.

"I'll leave this entirely to your judgment, Lily. I haven't a clue," Charlotte admitted, and she didn't want to be blamed for whatever they chose.

Coward, she told herself, but Reed Malloy seemed to be an exacting man who would rather stand naked than let a female choose his clothing. She still wondered why he'd given in so quickly.

As it turned out, Lily had as excellent taste in men's cravats as in women's stockings, and Charlotte wondered just what the little girl's life had been like in Boston. Could she have already been in high society at the tender age of eight? Was all this boring and provincial to her young cousin?

And what about Reed Malloy? Would he find the barn dance as tame as she feared? Charlotte almost reconsidered the purchase of the dress, except that Lily was so enthusiastic when they went to pick it up.

Her singular black cloud was running into Eliza Prentice, who was purchasing a bolt of lace to add to the dress her housekeeper was finishing for her. Mrs. Longwood was known far and wide as an excellent seamstress.

In school, although two years younger, Eliza had been a torment to Charlotte, who had always been painfully shy except when reading aloud, and their relationship hadn't improved as they'd grown up. Even now, Eliza had to raise her eyebrows at the idea of Charlotte attending a dance and practically demanded to see what she'd bought.

Charlotte closely hugged the large box wrapped in brown paper and tied with string, noting Eliza's smirk. Evidently, she'd already looked through the rack at Webster's and thought she knew exactly what it contained.

Charlotte was almost goaded into showing her, but it was Lily who brought her to her senses, saying it would be better as a surprise.

Of course, the little girl was right, a devastating, hopefully nasty surprise to Eliza. And not the only one, Charlotte thought, as they said their farewells, thinking how proud she'd be to show up with Reed and the two children.

For the sake of all that lived, wasn't Eliza happy with having already caught and become engaged to the most handsome young man in Spring City? Everyone knew as soon as her fiancé obtained his medical license, Eliza would be a doctor's wife. What more could she want?

Charlotte didn't have long to wonder why Reed had let them go so easily. He had been busy at her home, she saw, planting rose bushes in the front. It took Charlotte's breath away as they rounded the corner, Lily perched on her knee holding the reins.

Reed and Thomas were nowhere in sight, so the two females scrambled down from the wagon. It had been a splendid day, and Charlotte was already in a good mood, savoring the feeling of contentment at going home to a full house. But then to see what Reed had accomplished in such a short time!

"It's magic," Lily exclaimed.

They paused long enough to unhook Alfred from the wagon and lead him around to the stable where Reed's horse stood. Here, too, there were changes. Reed had tilled the ground where her mother used to grow vegetables, and he'd turned over the topsoil, ready for planting. A pile of weeds lay a few feet away.

Charlotte shook her head in wonder as she turned Alfred free in the small paddock. It was second nature for her to check his water and fill his food trough, and then she and Lily hurried toward the door.

They burst into the kitchen and stopped short. A veritable feast was obviously being prepared. Thomas sat on the stool, snapping off the ends of runner beans, while Reed attended to something in the oven that smelled heavenly. As he stood up and turned around, Charlotte's eyes raced over him.

She had grown slightly accustomed to his presence but not to the downright raw handsomeness of the man. Now, dressed in well-worn dungarees, a light blue cotton shirt, a handkerchief tied at his neck to catch the sweat, and comfortable looking cowboy boots, he appeared as the epitome of a westerner.

"Yes, Miss Sanborn?" There was downright pleasure dancing in his eyes.

She pretended to be serious as she frowned and shook her head at him in mock amazement.

"I didn't know eastern lawyers could dirty up so well."

He laughed aloud at that.

"Well, you can take over with dinner now that you're here."

He laughed again at her genuine look of terror. "Or at least Lily can take over and you can help her. I've got to go take a bath. I'm not fit to sit down to dinner with two such beautiful ladies."

Lily giggled at this while her little brother snorted his disgust. Charlotte kept silent, a smile crinkling the corners of her eyes.

"Have you got packages in the wagon?" he asked as an afterthought.

"Uh, yes," Charlotte replied, nervously remembering her dress. But Lily gave the warning as she followed Reed to the door.

"No peeking, Uncle Reed," she called after him.

Charlotte set to helping with whatever odds and ends needing doing, but had difficulty keeping her mind off the man in the room above them. After he'd heated enough water, Reed disappeared upstairs.

She thought of him removing his work clothes and then sinking his body into the steaming water, first his feet, then his well-shaped calves and hard thighs, and then . . .

"Sugar!" she exclaimed, shocked by her own thoughts.

"What is it?" Lily asked.

Her cheeks warm, Charlotte merely shrugged. "Nothing at all."

Over dinner, she thought more about the dance than she did of the succulent roast chicken.

"Excuse me?" she asked, realizing that Reed had just asked her a question.

"I asked what you're currently writing about."

She answered him, while all the time her mind was imagining them dancing in the candlelight of Drake's barn in town. She smiled at him directly through her reverie, and he smiled back broadly before she caught hold of herself, feeling a sudden hot flush at the stupid expression she must be wearing.

It was much later that night, after the unexpected treat of hearing Reed play the old, untuned piano in the parlor, when Charlotte finally sat down to her work. She still felt dreamy as she searched for the right words to end her article on barbed wire.

Who cares about barbed wire?

The knock at the door made her jump guiltily as if Reed Malloy had known she was in there thinking of him. She kept telling herself that it was natural for her to be interested in the only male to darken her doorstep since . . . well, the *only* male to darken her doorstep. And such an incredibly male one at that!

Then all of a sudden, his head appeared around the door.

CHAPTER SEVEN

"**F**ancy a nightcap and some conversation?"

Charlotte nodded wordlessly before she caught herself. Reed pushed the door open with his shoulder, and she could see he carried two glasses in one hand and a bottle of brandy in the other. Now where did *that* come from?

"Are you sure I'm not disturbing you?"

"Oh no," Charlotte said quickly. "I wasn't getting any work done anyway." She immediately wished she hadn't said that as he honed in on the remark like the well-trained lawyer he was.

"Why is that, Miss Sanborn?" He settled in the chair on the other side of her desk and, after attempting to clear a place on the little Pembroke table, finally set the glasses on top of the nearest pile of books.

He didn't look at her as he poured, but she was well aware that he awaited her answer. To give herself time, she moved around the front of her desk and leaned against it.

"Naturally the events of the past weeks have caused a bit of turmoil in my head."

"Yes, of course." His remark was toneless as he handed her a glass. "And I suppose the sooner it is all over with, the better for your career?"

"My feelings have not changed any, if that is what you're asking. I maintain that I am not well-suited to be their full-time caregiver." She couldn't believe they were at this again within seconds of starting a conversation.

He narrowed his eyes, taking a sip of the brandy. "I see." He stared into the rich amber liquid, and Charlotte wondered just what it was he saw.

She looked at his dark, thick hair, the now familiar lock of it hanging rakishly over his forehead. He appeared to be anything but her idea of a stuffy city lawyer. Her gaze went to his mouth, to his firm, well-defined lips that she had seen both smiling at her and held in a grim straight line. She preferred the gentle curve of his smile.

His eyes flickered to hers, and their gazes locked. Charlotte was unable to look away from his intense blue stare.

"How about a compromise, Miss Sanborn?"

She didn't say anything, mesmerized by his sensual gleam that didn't waver.

"What if you were a part-time guardian?"

Charlotte frowned. "And how would that be?"

"I'm not entirely sure, but an idea is coming to me. What if you were to move east with the children, have them live with you, and let their grandmother look after them whenever you were too busy."

Charlotte stared at him for a full five seconds. She was utterly flabbergasted that he could expect her to rearrange her whole life and move thousands of miles from her home in order to make easier his duty as executor. What made him think she had no roots here, no friends, no stake in her homestead? *Of all the unmitigated gall!*

"You're gurgling."

"That's because I can barely frame a civil word to you, Mr. Malloy. How dare you presume to move me and the children about to suit your liking, as though we're pawns?" She looked down at her glass and took a sip of brandy.

He had hit a nerve with that one, and she freely admitted—to herself alone, of course—that moving was one thing that terrified her. This home, and Spring City, were all she'd ever known.

His eyes widened in surprise at this reproachful utterance. He leaned forward, looking earnest. "I believe you're making excuses, if you'll pardon my saying so. As for the children, they're young and completely unaffected by all this traveling. They find it exciting. As for you," he paused, and she stared into dark sapphires and was mesmerized once again.

"As for you," he continued, "I don't presume, but I can suggest. I believe your writing career can only benefit from being in the midst of a large city as opposed to being stifled out here. Besides, many great writers and thinkers have come out of New England. Longfellow, Whittier, Hawthorne."

"Thoreau, Emerson," she added, with an involuntary grimace. "All men. If I were to move anywhere, Mr. Malloy, I would be better off moving to Wyoming. At least there, I could vote and have a say in the laws that you so aptly use in the defense of your clients."

He smiled at her. "I assure you, the Woman's Suffrage Association is active in Boston. The women of Massachusetts already have a great deal of power, Miss Sanborn. Perhaps you heard about the 1860 strike parade of shoe workers? That was led by eight hundred women."

She wasn't convinced. The issue was not, after all, her being a woman in Boston. The issue was her own terror at facing the unknown, with two small children in tow.

"In fact," he continued, "you would not merely fit well into our fair city, you would be welcomed as another literary light if you chose to write under your own name. Frankly, I would be extremely pleased to have you as an addition to my circle of friends and to help acclimate you to your new surroundings."

This last bit of news interested her the most. The idea of being escorted around Boston by Reed Malloy held great appeal.

But Charlotte was taken aback by this sudden insistence that she move east.

"My career isn't stifled," she said finally, latching on to his earliest point as the sole part of his speech she could debate. "After all, *you* had heard of me in Boston."

"Only because your cousin brought you to my attention."

She took another sip of her brandy.

"I will . . . take it into consideration, Mr. Malloy. It had not occurred to me that I could share the responsibility of the children."

She lied. It *had* occurred to her, but as a ridiculous daydream of sharing them right here in her own home with this handsome man whose very voice seemed to strum a chord within her. Something in that must have shown in her expression, for his own face took on a bemused look.

He tilted his head to one side, considering, and then he smiled. And something about the sheer sensuality of watching his mouth caused her stomach to clench. He stood up, setting his glass down in a slow movement and letting his gaze come rest on her again.

"It would make it easier on both of us," he told her, and he seemed to lean in closer, until Charlotte could smell the clean male scent of him, a sandalwood fragrance, and the warm aroma of brandy.

Her heart started to thump somewhat painfully in the base of her throat. His interests seemed to be shifting from their discussion to something more personal, as his hand reached down and took one of hers in a firm, warm grasp.

The jolt that went through her at his touch was as strong as it had been the first day they'd met, and she sucked in her breath as he lifted it to his lips. His eyes left her own wary green gaze only once, noticing the telltale heartbeat throbbing at the side of her throat, and she watched his pupils dilate.

Gently, he kissed the back of her hand. Then to her amazement, indeed almost to her undoing, he turned her hand over and branded her palm with another soft kiss. She gasped and yanked her hand away as if she'd been burnt. His sudden inclination was clear to her, and the most frightening part was that she wanted to go along with whatever this improper Bostonian wanted to do.

"I'd best be getting to bed," she heard herself say before flaming up in embarrassment, hoping he didn't think she had that on her mind. Silently, she cursed. That was the second time she'd embarrassed herself in the same way. In truth, his eyebrows shot up devilishly as if he knew exactly what she was thinking.

"What I mean to say," she added, stepping away from him and heading for the door, "is that it's late."

He was grinning like a cat with a canary in easy reach, but she heard him bid her good night as she slipped out the door. It wasn't till she was on the stairs that she realized she'd fled her own study!

When the tap came at her door the following evening, she was not as surprised. He was gracious enough to leave her to her work during the day, but it seemed even he longed for some adult company at night. She had told herself if he came again, she would not let herself be scared off, no matter the turn of events.

Charlotte took a deep breath, smoothed her hair, tugged absently at her white cotton blouse where it tucked into her skirt's waistband, and beckoned him to enter.

This time, he had two cups of coffee, but her first sip told her there was whiskey in the cup. It slid warmly down her throat, and she smiled.

"I appreciate your thoughtfulness. It is a real treat to be waited on in my own home, and it has been a long time since I have had nightcaps."

He coughed at that, then crossed one denim-clad calf over the other, stretching his long legs out in front of him.

"What is it?" she asked, seeing his amused look.

"It's just that you don't seem old enough to have had a nightcap a long time ago unless it was the knitted type, and you wore it to bed."

She blushed at this. He had caught her out, but she laughed good-humoredly at the image of her in a knitted cap.

"Well, you're right, Mr. Malloy. This study has not seen nightcaps of the liquid variety since my father's day. But I do, on occasion, have a glass of wine at Fuller's restaurant in town."

He sipped thoughtfully. "You mentioned that your father was a writer, too, didn't you?"

Charlotte found it easy to tell Reed about her family. Her stories of childhood were similar to the fantastical stories she told the children at bedtime, except these were of a family from the past. It seemed so long ago when she was a little girl with parents. She told him of her father's love of history and his work chronicling the lives of the early settlers there, those who came even before the rich veins of gold were discovered.

"I have read much history, Miss Sanborn, but I apologize, I have never heard of your father's work."

She wrinkled up her nose. "That is because my father's manuscripts lie right here in the drawer of this desk, still unpublished. One day, perhaps I'll remedy that." She shrugged.

"Anyway, he continued to work on them until he died, although to earn a living, he had to turn to the more practical field of teaching. He was the schoolteacher in Spring City for many years. But what he wanted was to strike it rich in one of the mines, and then . . . then I'm not sure what he would have done."

She spoke with such sangfroid that Reed asked, "Weren't you close to him?"

"Not particularly. He didn't see that I had similar interests, but then he wasn't close to anyone except my mother. He was extremely engrossed in his work. I guess I get that from him. And Mother, who saw that I was more similar to him than not, probably wished for a normal little girl. I know she missed her old life and all the social niceties of the city. But I'm sure you know more about that than I do."

"Some women live for it," he said obliquely.

Charlotte had the notion he was not talking about her mother at that moment, but she nodded. "Fortunately, I've never known any other way than my life here, so I am content."

"What about your brother?" Reed asked, sipping his coffee.

"Thaddeus was seventeen when he left." She bit her bottom lip. "I confess, that was not a happy day for me, coming inside this house after he rode off the first time. I see him about once a year, but I am not sure where he is now."

While Charlotte talked, she came around her desk and settled down on the floor in front of the fire. It was odd to her now to think of her younger years. Sometimes, it seemed as if she'd arrived there, fully grown, to look after Teddy and then to live out her quiet life without ever really connecting with anyone. She shook her head.

"What is it?" Reed asked, coming to sit cross-legged beside her on the floor. "What are you thinking?"

"I was just wondering what it would have been like to have had a more normal upbringing. Would it have shaped me differently? Certainly, my nature was already fixed as my mother pointed out to me time and again." Charlotte smiled wryly.

"But I wonder now, knowing Lily and Thomas, if the tone of the household, with Father so preoccupied and Mother so restless, must have had something to do with Thaddeus being rootless and with my being somewhat of a stick in the mud now." *Never mind the many moments lately when she'd felt more akin to the wildflower Reed had mentioned.*

"For the most part, there was no place here for children, not in my parents' lives." She sipped at her coffee again.

"And now?" he asked.

"Not now either," she continued. "I think if I had been more attached to people as a child, I would feel the need for company as an adult and would find this solitary existence more of a burden than I do. Once I got used to Teddy being gone, this lifestyle turned out to be a blessing. I can do as I please." She smiled wryly. "But then, there is not that much trouble I can get into as a single woman in Spring City anyway."

She held her cup in both hands and breathed in the rich smell of the coffee, wondering why she was being so talkative. Normally, she went weeks hardly speaking to another soul, yet she was unburdening her thoughts on Reed Malloy, who seemed to be studying her intently and listening carefully.

"Oh, I'm talking bunkum," she finished.

"No, I believe there's something to what you're saying." His eyes remained fixed on hers. "I have always been outgoing and have enjoyed public oration since I was a youngster. I'm sure the confidence and security instilled in me as a child partially led to my following my father into the practice of law."

Reed looked into the fire a moment, smiling at something far away in his thoughts.

"And the good-natured teasing of my sisters kept me humble, no matter my achievements."

But his confirmation of her notion worried Charlotte, especially in light of how they each had turned out. She was frowning, as she considered the place of parents, a large family, and a secure home. He reached up and touched the deep furrow between her brows, but she was too distracted to be alarmed at this intimate gesture.

"What about Lily and Thomas?" she asked abruptly. "Do you still believe that I am best for them? Don't they deserve a normal home?"

He sighed, and instead of replying with more reasons why she should take the children, he shrugged.

"Ann Connors wanted you to raise her children. I've never been a father and can't possibly say what's best. I trust her instincts that you would be a more vibrant influence than living solely with their grandmother. It is not simply her age." He took another sip of his drink before he continued.

"Alicia Randall has old-fashioned ideas of raising children, leaning strongly toward their being little seen and rarely heard. Of course, she loves her grandchildren, but her society is closed, stuffy even, and entirely made up of adults. Quite old adults. The children would live on a busy street in the heart of the city, in a fastidious residence. Would they get to be children? That's my question."

She stared at his concerned face. He obviously cared for them a great deal. It was not hard to do, given their sweet natures. Having heard his description of Alicia, Charlotte could see how her own home, with its open meadows, and her easygoing way of letting the children do whatever it was that children wanted to do would seem preferable.

They might be even more isolated with their grandmother than with her. But what about sharing the children? In truth, she had given some thought to his suggestion that she move to Boston. However, the very notion raised in her such an overwhelming feeling of fright that she had dismissed it quickly.

His eyes returned to her serious face. "I understand how this was a surprise to you, but I know, given your personality, that you're keeping an open mind."

She smiled at that. "Have you gleaned my personality, Mr. Malloy, from my writing or from the wonderful hospitality and domestic ability I have demonstrated since you came to my house?"

"As you told me on the day we met, you have more important things on your mind than domesticity, and I don't fault you for a lack of culinary skills. You have more than enough positive traits to make up for that."

"Do I?" she asked before lowering her eyelashes. Goodness, she was flirting, leading him on to compliment her. Taking a gulp of the steaming drink to cover her embarrassment, she choked as the whiskey burned her throat.

He patted her on the back, but as she waved him away, holding her handkerchief up to her mouth, she felt his hand making warm circles against the thin cotton cloth of her blouse. He pushed her long chestnut-colored hair, gleaming with firelit streaks of gold, over her shoulder. It felt delightful to be touched, to be comforted, even for something as silly as drinking too quickly.

He looked at her with a dark, interested gaze that set on fire the nerve endings where his palm rested.

"I guess delicate sipping isn't one of my good traits," she said, trying to make light, but her voice had a huskiness that sounded strange to her ears.

He said nothing. His hand was still upon her. Reed slid his palm down to the small of her back and then upward, resting it on the nape of her neck. Slowly, he massaged her muscles, grown stiff from leaning over her desk all day.

She bent her head up and then down, unable to stop herself from closing her eyes and relaxing under his touch. It was heavenly, this feeling of her muscles unknotting under his gentle kneading. She felt as if, in another instant, she would be purring like a cat.

Then to Charlotte's amazement, she thought she felt his lips touch her hair, brushing the crown of her head. It must have been her imagination, she told herself, smiling anyway, her lips parting in a sigh.

But she wasn't imagining the groan she heard next, making her eyes fly open. Reed leaned toward her upturned face, his gaze on her lips. Watching the flicker of firelight play across his tense features, she was certain he was going to kiss her. Every part of her was ready for it, some parts were aching for it. And then abruptly, he pulled away.

She could have cried out in frustration. The man seemed unable to keep his hands off of her, yet at the same time, he was restraining himself, although noticeably with greater and greater difficulty.

He stood up abruptly, towering over her, looking anything but relaxed and comfortable.

"Is something wrong, Mr. Malloy?"

He grimaced. "You are without a doubt the most captivating woman I have ever met. You are also extremely frustrating to a man, being as naive as you are. But, saying that, I wouldn't change a thing about you. Now, if you'll excuse me, I will retire."

He went to the door, then turned to her just before he disappeared. "I'm looking forward to dancing with you on Saturday."

Charlotte did not have time to respond. It occurred to her that this night, he had been the one to pull foot—and swiftly too—from her study, leaving his coffee cup behind in his haste. Sitting in front of the fire a while longer, she unraveled his words, sipping her coffee, and finally deciding he had been complimenting her in a strange fashion. She had never considered herself naive, but then, she had never dealt with such a situation.

And she, too, was looking forward to the dance on Saturday and most especially to finally being held in his arms.

CHAPTER EIGHT

Charlotte was determined to get all her work done before Saturday so she could spend all day getting ready for the dance if need be. With only a couple of days to go, she was filled with a mixture of abject terror and thrilling anticipation.

In the morning light, she grimaced at herself in the mirror hanging over her chamber set, while she dried her face and combed her hair. It probably *would* take all Saturday. And what would she do with her hair? What would Reed think of her dress? A thousand such questions knotted her stomach.

Reed had occupied Lily and Thomas with an early outing that morning, even taking a pic-nic breakfast, so she could work in absolute peace, but she simply didn't want to work. She had wanted to go on the outing, too, but it seemed she was to stay cooped up inside the Sanborn house till she died—a shriveled old maid, a spinster.

Charlotte fled her reflection at that thought and headed downstairs. The house seemed so empty with them gone. Her footsteps echoed in the silence in a way they had not done for the past few weeks. It reminded her painfully of when Teddy left, and she hugged herself tightly as she went down the hall into the kitchen.

Skipping breakfast, she made herself a strong pot of tea to take with her into the study. She hadn't had to fend for herself in days as Reed always made sure she took an occasional break or asked her if she wanted a beverage in the afternoon.

Charlotte stoked the fire in the stove until it blazed.

This is how it will be when they're gone, for all the rest of your days.

So what? It will be just as it was before they came.

But you've tasted companionship, and now it'll be so much harder.

It won't take as long to get over them as when Teddy left.

Maybe. Maybe not.

She tried to halt the conversation in her head as she poured the boiling water over the tea leaves in the pot, and then waited to pour the thin tawny liquid into her favorite cup. But the dreadful thoughts continued until Charlotte fairly ran to her study for sanctuary.

As she entered, the image of Reed in front of the glowing fire came unbidden. He had looked mysterious and inviting, both at the same time, and he'd taken her breath away with his eyes, his touch. Then he'd left, and she'd given up trying to write, no longer feeling satisfied working late at night while everyone else slumbered peacefully above her.

Today, instead of sitting straightaway at her typewriter, she opened the bottom drawer of her father's old desk and pulled out some of his manuscript, about half of the nearly one thousand pages written in his neat script. It had been a long time since she read it, a long time since she wondered how her life would be if he and her mother had lived. She flipped the pages, causing a breeze to lift wisps of hair curling by her cheeks.

Suddenly, she snapped the pages down on her desk. This was getting her nowhere. She worked steadily for an hour, then two. Eventually, she lifted her head and stretched. Her neck ached. What she needed was a bath, perhaps a cool one with some of her mother's best scented salts, to clear her head while she had a moment's quiet time. No children screaming and running through the house . . . or laughing or playing.

It took the usual ten minutes of hauling water to fill the claw foot tub. But as she eased herself into the soothing, aromatic liquid, only half-heated, she sighed and judged it to be well worth the effort.

Ever since Reed had brought her pulse to racing two nights in a row, she'd felt hot at the mere thought of him. She needed to wash his touch right away, or she'd never be able to concentrate on her work for the rest of the day.

She lingered in the fragrant water until it was cool and her skin began to feel chilled. By now, the sun was high in the painfully bright Colorado sky. Pulling her banyan around her damp body, she went downstairs and carried a porch chair into the yard, setting it in the full sunshine between the new rose bushes.

Pulling the comb from her pocket, Charlotte began to work the tangles out. She didn't notice the door open to her right. She didn't notice the man staring at her, fixed to the spot by the sight of her, perched on her chair, one creamy-skinned leg exposed where her silken robe fell open, her hair gleaming like a copper waterfall. But then she heard his footsteps.

Charlotte couldn't help the gasp that escaped her as she looked up to see Reed standing right in front of her, his head framed by the bright light as though a sun god in the flesh.

At first, because of the angle, she couldn't make out his features. But when she shielded her eyes with her hand, she caught her breath at the expression upon his face, pausing with the comb still in her other hand.

"Reed?" She heard the unfamiliar word from her own lips and blushed, realizing how inappropriately intimate that sounded. "Are the children all right?"

"We stopped at the Cuthins' home with Sarah's baskets and her dishes, and she wants to teach them how to make butter. Apparently, it will take them a while." He trailed off and still hadn't moved.

"Is something the matter?" Charlotte asked, catching sight of her own exposed leg, which she hastily covered.

"You." His voice was low and rough, and it brought her eyes directly to his once more. "Do you have any idea what a portrait of beauty you make sitting out here in your front yard?"

She gulped aloud. If she could have blushed any more than she already was, she would have.

"Oh, Mr. Malloy, I am not . . . I mean . . . really!" She dropped her gaze away from his face.

Unexpectedly, he laughed. "You are truly refreshing." He crouched down beside her on his haunches, and she nearly fell off her chair. His hand came up to take hold of a shimmering lock of her hair, still damp and gently curling.

"You seem to have no notion of precisely how appealing you are," he continued. "Not only your fine face," he said, touching her cheek with his other hand, "or your glorious hair," he added, twisting it around his finger, "but coupled with your admirable intellect, Miss Sanborn, I must believe the reason you've not been plucked off the tree of single womanhood by now is that you've hidden yourself in this backward place."

She opened her mouth to defend Spring City as best she could, but she could not think a complete thought with him kneeling beside her in the grass. She could hear nothing more for the blood was pounding in her ears, and she could feel her heart beating an excited tattoo in her chest. She was silent, watching this man with his tousled hair, whose handsome face looked so earnest.

"I'm wondering, Charlotte Sanborn, if right now you'd mind being kissed because at this moment, I have an incredibly strong urge—no, a compulsion—to kiss you."

For a long moment, she could not find her voice, staring into his blue eyes, which had become so familiar, whether engaging her across the dining room table or flickering intelligently as they conversed in her study at night.

There was a falling in the pit of her stomach as if she were sailing high on the rope swing she'd shared with her brother as a child.

Reed Malloy was not smiling now. In fact, he looked extremely serious and that, too, made her tremble. In fact, at that moment, she did want desperately for him to kiss her. But she was ashamed to tell him that she had never been kissed before, that she didn't know how or what he expected of her.

Yet when she opened her mouth to tell him such, all she said was, "Yes."

A fire lit in his eyes, and the expression on his face turned sensuous at her acquiescence, anticipating what would come next. With him on his knees and her on the chair, they were face-to-face. He had merely to lean forward, and he did.

Charlotte held her breath a moment, relishing the warm smell of him, the softly spicy sandalwood that always clung to his clothes and the male scent that she recognized as his alone. Her palms felt moist, and she dropped the comb as his face came closer.

She locked her gaze on his until the last moment when she closed her eyes. She gave herself over entirely to feeling, both her hearing and sight lost in the sensation of his mouth pressing against her own.

His lips were a sweet surprise, firm but gentle, slightly rough, and the roughness was an unexpected delight. His hands did not touch her at all, but enclosed her by resting on the arms of her chair. She felt enveloped but not trapped. His shirt brushed her arm as he leaned closer, and she delighted in her skin's sensitivity.

She wanted this moment to last and last as his kiss grew firmer. He didn't hold her head, but she kissed him in fervent response, as if pressed from behind.

For just a moment, she felt his tongue against her lips, and it sent shivers through her, heading directly to her most feminine parts.

Then slowly, lingeringly, he pulled away, resting his forehead against hers as her eyes opened in wonder. She inhaled deeply to draw air into her starved lungs.

"Oh," she said, still breathing heavily. He sat back on his heels with a mystified look lurking in his glittering eyes, and she noticed his own chest rising and falling rapidly.

"Thank you for the honor, Miss Sanborn." His voice was honey thick and low, as if it stuck in his throat. Then, in a quick, fluid motion, he was on his feet and walking toward the house.

Charlotte sat in her chair, stunned by what had happened. It was as if she'd conjured him with all her thoughts that morning. But she half-suspected that he'd hurried off to hide his own turbulent emotions.

She took in a deep breath and released it. How wonderfully welcome that kiss had been. She bent down to retrieve her comb from the grass, seeing the indentation where his knees had been.

Had he really been there, a moment ago, kissing her? It was incredible. And in another day, she would be going to the dance on his arm. She knew there was nothing she could think of that would be any better . . . except another kiss. How had her life swiftly become so exciting?

She paused as a dark slash of loneliness cut through her thoughts, hinting at what was to come when he and the children finally left. *Am I being a fool, playing with fire?* She knew she was growing ever more attached to her new family, and soon they would be gone. Everything would be as it was before.

She looked across at the house as it was now, silent and shaded, yet she could will herself to hear Lily's voice and Thomas's laughter as she'd heard them so often in the past few weeks, drifting down from the upstairs window.

Yes, everything would be as it was before, everything except herself. Her heart would be torn. She knew it as surely as she knew she was falling in love with Reed.

When he left Spring City, her heart would ache, but she closed her eyes and smiled into the warm sun. Without a doubt, the pain was worth it. She would hold nothing back and cherish every moment of their stay. She jumped up and hurried inside.

After a few moments, she found Reed in her study, staring hard at the books on her shelves. She didn't think he'd noticed her at first. Then, without looking at her, he said evenly, "This is becoming intolerable!" before snatching a book off the shelf at eye level.

Charlotte had expected anything but that. Since she didn't know to what he was referring, she moved into familiar territory. "Will Sarah bring the children home?"

"Yes, later, or they may walk." He seemed to be scanning Ramsay's *Life of George Washington* with great earnestness, as Charlotte moved closer. He still didn't look at her. "It seems they needed a change from playing with 'Uncle Reed.'"

She laughed, hoping to break the tension in his voice. "You've done an excellent job with—"

"The hell I have," he cut in, finally swinging his sharp gaze toward her. She thought she saw him flinch as he took in the sight of her, still clad outrageously in nothing but the garish banyan. Then his eyes met hers, and she saw all the pent-up passion barely hinted at in their kiss. It was there, sparkling in his eyes, and it almost seemed to be paining him.

"Reed," she stepped forward, not thinking of the impropriety of using his given name, allowing her strong feelings for this man to guide her. She took the book from his hand and put it down on the desk. "What is intolerable?"

"I can't stay here any longer. A decision must be made. That's why I came back here alone, to talk about—" Then he shook his head. "I'm lying. You know that, don't you? I came back to be alone with you."

His eyes were raking over her face, and she could see the war he was waging. "I'm supposed to be a professional, handling the execution of my client's last will and testament. I knew you weren't 'Charles' Sanborn. I just didn't expect . . ." He reached out and ran his knuckles along her jawline. "I didn't expect you to be so irresistible."

She felt a flush creep up her neck and spread quickly over her already heated cheeks.

"Damn," Reed swore softly, taking a step back from her as if his life depended on it, but coming up against the shelves so hard, he made all of their contents rattle. He shook his head, trapped. "None of the women blush in Boston's social circles, Charlotte. They aren't able to anymore."

She put her own hands up to her cheeks, hoping to cool them. She knew what he was saying without quite saying it. He wanted to be a man and woman together, but the proper, honorable Reed Malloy was warring with the freer spirit he'd found in himself here in the West.

Her own inner battle was more easily resolved. He had already established a place in her heart, and she had no one to whom she had to answer or be held accountable. No worried relatives, no gossiping friends. No one who would ever care if she gave in to the feelings that had sprung up between them so strongly over the past weeks.

She took another step toward him. It was her choice to break out of her insulated world, to reach out to Reed, to all of the feelings she'd been denying herself capable of for so long.

He groaned, reading the look in her eyes. And Charlotte could tell instantly that he was lost to the feelings, in the same way as she was. His hands reached for her, gripping her around her slender waist and pulling her against him.

Charlotte expelled the breath she didn't know she'd been holding. It was a physical and mental relief to finally find herself in his arms, against his broad chest, and she gave in to the desire to touch his thick hair.

She slid her arms up over his chest and laced her fingers around the back of his neck for a moment before entwining them in the waves just above his collar. One of his hands was still on her waist, holding her tightly, while the other roamed over her body, dipping low to gently sweep her bottom.

She gasped at the heat that coursed through her woman's core at the feel of his hand through her robe.

Then he was lacing his fingers through a handful of her shining hair as she was doing to him. His other hand moved upward over her rib cage, to lightly trace the underswell of her breast.

Charlotte caught the breath in her lungs and held it as Reed's hand moved farther up, splaying across her collar bone. He paused there a moment, before let his fingers travel down to the deep plunging neckline of her robe. Then he halted.

She looked up, meeting his gaze. His eyes seemed on fire with blue flame. She thought she would melt if she stared into them too long.

"Charlotte, I have a life in Boston. There is so much you don't know. Do you understand? Do you want me to stop?" he asked, his voice a raspy whisper that made her tremble.

His hand still rested at the opening of her robe. She could feel it shake slightly. It was knowing that he was as much in need as she was that calmed her fears.

She couldn't speak. She tried, then licked her lower lip with the edge of her moist tongue. He swallowed as if his own throat was dry. Then ever so slightly, in response to his last question, she shook her head.

He bent down, lowering his lips to meet hers, and the kiss was more fervent than what they had shared outside, less like the gentle stream of desire that had flowed between them before and more like a rushing river, swollen after the rains.

As his mouth claimed hers, enticing her lips open with his tongue, his hand behind her head held her against him. It was carnal and powerful, and the excitement she felt was heightened almost beyond bearing.

Charlotte knew she wanted to be wholly joined with this man, to assuage the madness that was coursing through her veins on account of him. She wondered how women survived such an encounter without fainting.

Reed's kiss continued, even as he began to push her robe aside, slipping his fingers inside the neckline to ease it open.

"I want to make love to you," he breathed against her mouth.

"I thought you already were," she told him, gasping a moment later as he swept her up into his arms.

"Not here," he told her, "not among musty old books with reminders of barbed wire and farmers' meetings."

He carried her up the stairs two at a time, down the hall into his room. His was smaller than the other bedrooms, the light dim due to the pulled curtains, and Charlotte felt safe and secure as he set her down and slipped her banyan off one shoulder, then the other. She felt it slide down her burning skin and pool at her feet.

"You're exquisite," he told her, as he pulled her close again, out of the peacock blue puddle of cloth and toward the bed.

This was right, Charlotte thought to herself. This was what she'd lain awake at night wanting ever since Reed had entered her life.

"Stop looking at me that way," he fairly growled as he began unbuttoning his shirt "or you'll be my undoing."

She laughed at the sight of him struggling with his shirt buttons and then sobered up quickly as he began to unfasten the snug denim trousers that had been driving her wild. Suddenly, a noise that was unmistakably a horse's whinnying sounded outside the window. She froze. He froze.

She started to stand up, but Reed paused a moment to glance between the curtains before climbing onto the bed beside her. He gathered her close and then eased her down onto his pillow. Once again, she breathed in the delicious sandalwood scent of him as it wafted from his bedding and filled her senses.

"Only Alfred and my horse moving about," he said.

Charlotte had already forgotten, too distracted by the rough feeling of his denims against her bare skin. It was heaven. As she raised her lower body, eager to press against him, Reed looked down between them, realizing what she was doing, and his mouth curved.

"You are so sensual," he breathed against her hair and treated her to a grinding of his hips against hers, deftly holding her in place. "Is that what you want?"

But she could not answer. Her eyes closed, her lips parted, and it seemed a struggle to remember how to breathe. Her body, low between her hips, was on fire and dampened at the same time by the identical moist heat that seemed to be pulsing through her veins.

She felt the hard ridge of his desire straining against his trousers as he pressed deeply between her legs, brushing the silken flesh of her woman's core.

"Ohh," she breathed, gripping his shoulders with tense fingers, knowing that there was more, that she should be patient and let him remove all his clothes. Instead, she shuddered, knowing instinctively she was already so far along a path, there was no stopping.

She didn't want the pressure on her mound or the rasping between her thighs to stop. She thought she said that, even though she heard her own voice, breathy and thick, pleading something.

Then there was only Reed, speaking softly, reassuringly, continuing the gentle assault on her body and heightening it with the increasing urgency of his hips. Then he lowered his head, and he touched her left breast with his lips. She felt as though she was shattering.

Crying out, she tilted her hips and grasped his bent head, as he nibbled on her breast. She was far away, light as a fall leaf, lifted on a breeze, and she thought she would keep drifting endlessly farther on the ripples of pleasure when finally, they ceased, and she began to settle back into herself.

She opened her eyes at the sound of his voice.

"Are you all right?" he asked her.

What a question! "But I . . . ," she stumbled over her words, feeling a momentary pang of selfishness. "I did nothing but take from you. I didn't even let you finish getting undressed."

He laughed then, a raspy male sound that made her shiver. "You have no idea how intoxicating it is to watch a woman as she discovers the sensuality inside her. I've never experienced anything like it before."

She digested his words: Was that what she had just done? *Discovered her own sensuality, and in Reed's arms?* She stretched and felt as if she could purr. He had never experienced that before. She didn't want to ask what he meant, though he had hinted at the jaded and cynical women of his acquaintance.

Could it be true that she was the first innocent he'd ever bedded? It seemed to her as if virgins would be lining up for the privilege of having Reed Malloy deflower them. Then she remembered she hadn't even been deflowered yet, and she decided to offer him that gift if he would accept it.

He bent to kiss her again. Then they both heard the unmistakable sound of a wolf's howl. They froze.

"The horses," she began. "Alfred—"

"They should be able to take care of themselves," Reed assured her, but he was already kneeling on the bed and throwing open the curtains. The sunlight streamed in and he scanned the meadow beside the house. "Have you seen any wolves around lately?"

"No, only during hard winters, not usually this late in the spring."

She sat up beside him on the bed, grabbing at the blankets to cover herself. "If they can't find deer, they go after livestock. But we don't have a lot of cattle around here, so they typically pass through."

Then they heard it again, a lone cry that made the hair stand up on Charlotte's neck.

"I don't know much about them," Reed said, "but I'm a little worried about—"

"The children!" Charlotte was off the bed in a flash and heading down the hall to her bedroom. She heard Reed go down the stairs moments later, as she hastened into her chemise, skirt and blouse, before running to catch up with him. He was in her front parlor, taking the gun down from above the fireplace.

"An old Sharps," he muttered, looking over the single-shot rifle. "Does it work?" he asked as she stopped in the doorway.

"It used to. My father used it. I know Thaddeus did, too." She closed her mouth, realizing she was babbling with fear. "The bullets are on the whatnot." She hurried over to the corner shelves and reached up to the highest one. "I've got them." She handed the small box to Reed.

"Let's get going," he said.

Charlotte watched him change from the passionate lover of a moment ago to the steely, collected man who had first knocked at her door, ready to slay dragons for these two children.

CHAPTER NINE

As they hastily saddled and mounted their horses, there was no embarrassment. It was almost as if the intimacy between them had never happened. They rode toward the Cuthins' homestead, less than a mile away. Charlotte, tense, leaned forward, looking ahead for any signs of a timber wolf pack, while Reed scanned from side to side.

They heard the wolf howl again, nearer now. Fear raced down Charlotte's spine and caused Reed to urge his horse to a gallop.

And then loudly, plainly, bloodcurdlingly, they heard Lily scream. Charlotte felt her heart jump into her mouth and stay there. Terrified, neither of them spoke. There was no point, no time. They simply headed for the sound, and then they heard it again.

"It's good," Reed called to her above the sound of the galloping hooves. "Lily's voice will keep the beast at bay. Thomas should call out, too."

She knew they shared the same concern. *What if something had happened and Thomas wasn't able to yell anymore?* She shuddered at the thought, but they were close, and she trusted that Reed was a capable, intelligent man. Everything would be all right.

She caught herself at that instant, unable to believe she was relying on someone else. Such a foolish reliance at that! Reed could no more guarantee the children's safety than could she, but it was comforting to share the responsibility, nonetheless.

"There," he yelled. "Over by those pines."

Charlotte looked to where Reed gestured. Sure enough, there was Lily, her back against a tall tree, a small branch in her hands, and a lone gray wolf, with its broad head and long body, crouching nearby. Thomas was nowhere to be seen.

She'd never seen anything similar before, never feared for her safety in all these years. Why now? Charlotte sent up a silent prayer that they would all get out of this safely.

Reed halted his horse and, in quick succession, slid off, braced himself, his feet slightly apart, and fired the rifle up in the air. The wolf barely took a second to look their way before it took off at a dead run.

Charlotte kicked Alfred forward, riding straight for Lily and was on the ground at a stumbling run before her horse even came to a standstill. She knelt down, gathering the little girl into her arms, tears coursing down Lily's pale face.

"It's all right, honey," she said, cradling Lily, who wrapped her arms tightly around Charlotte's neck.

Charlotte heard Reed's horse approach, and he was beside them in an instant, joining them on the ground and reaching out to touch Lily's arm.

"Sweetheart, where's Thomas?" he asked, his voice remaining steady.

"He . . . he fell in the ground," Lily said between sobs, "we were together and then I don't know," she wailed.

"Sshh," Charlotte hugged her tightly again and stroked her hair, trying to quieten her.

"What do you mean?" Reed asked. "Did the wolf chase him?" Charlotte could hear the tension in his voice as he struggled not to frighten Lily with the urgency of finding her brother. "Think, Lily, which way did he go?"

Charlotte felt the little girl stiffen in her arms. "One question at a time," Charlotte cautioned, trying to keep Reed from overwhelming the eight-year-old.

But Lily visibly gathered herself together, straightening her shoulders and looking around her. "We went to look for gold," she said, "over there." She pointed toward the foothills. Charlotte went cold all over.

"The mines," she said. "Reed, they went to the old mines." She had told the children about the abandoned mining camp one night as a bedtime story. Reed rose to his feet slowly.

Lily continued. "Doctor Cuthins got called away, so Mrs. Cuthins, said we could walk straight home. But we didn't." She started crying again. "I know you said not to, Aunt Charlotte, but we just wanted to take a look." She gulped for air. "You made it sound so exciting."

Charlotte had always known the mines had to be particularly dangerous for it was the one place her easygoing father forbade them to go. Nevertheless, Thaddeus had explored the passages thoroughly.

She looked up at Reed. "There are deep shafts. They're boarded up of course, but the wood is very old."

She didn't have to say more. She could see in his face he understood the danger.

"We'll need a lantern and rope," Reed said. "Lily, when he fell in, could you still see him?"

"No, but I could hear him. He was crying, and I told him I'd get you. Then I saw the wolf."

"I'll get supplies," Charlotte said. She let Reed give her a helping hoist onto Alfred. "I'll be quick, I know where everything is. And I'll take Lily home." She reached her arms out so Reed could hand her the little girl.

"No," Lily said. "I'm not going without my brother." She ended on a hiccupping sob.

Reed and Charlotte looked at each other. Then Reed lifted Lily easily onto his horse and swung up behind her. "Tell me which way to go."

"Due west," Charlotte pointed, "directly over that hill. Not far at all. You'll see the old water tank. And there's a shack, but it's all fallen down."

He nodded. Charlotte could see by the creases in his brow that he was already focused on finding the little boy.

"We'll meet you there," he told her and urged his horse forward.

For a second, she wished she was taking Lily with her. She wanted her safely at home. But where in the world could be safer than Reed's embrace? He was no longer touching her, yet still she felt his strength and took comfort.

"Come on, boy," she said to Alfred and rode home as fast as he could carry her.

Charlotte had run at breakneck speed into her barn to gather the supplies, but still she felt increasingly frustrated by the amount of time she had taken. As she approached the mines, she wished fervently that Thaddeus were around to help find Thomas.

The afternoon sun was already going down when she crested a foothill and spied Reed's horse tied to a tree in front of one of the mine shafts. Lily sat beside the tree, but there was no sign of Reed.

"Where is Mr. Malloy?" she asked Lily as she dismounted and tethered Alfred.

"I don't know. He told me to stay put."

"And you're being a very good girl. You keep watch on the horses." She walked a few feet away.

"Reed," she called out, breaking the tranquility of the setting.

Her voice seemed to echo in the silence of the hills, and she waited for an answer. Nothing. Her skin became clammy. What if he were in trouble, too?

"Reed," she cried out again, hearing the slight panic in her own voice.

"Over here."

She could have cried with relief at the sound of his deep voice, and she ran toward it recklessly.

"Be careful," he called out as she stumbled over the cover of one mine and nearly landed in the open hole of another.

"Those are air shafts," he told her, seemingly rising out of nowhere in front of her, but she could see upon closer inspection he was in the entrance to one of the old tunnels.

"Have you found him?" she asked, feeling better already at the sight of him.

But he shook his head. "I thought I heard a sound a few minutes ago, but now, nothing. Obviously, no one's done anything out here in years. It's a death trap."

She nodded. "Where should we start?"

"Wherever a five-year-old would start," Reed said, looking around. "Probably—"

"Help!"

The voice was small and sounded far away. It turned Charlotte's blood to ice and confirmed her greatest fears. There was no doubt now. Thomas was underground.

"Help!" They heard him again.

He was perhaps only yards away, down below their feet. "We're here, Thomas, right here," she called to him.

Reed said nothing, just scanning. "There," he said, walking carefully but purposefully to cover the distance between the calls for help and the air shaft. "He must have fallen right in here."

Charlotte came up beside him. It was nothing more than a black hole in the ground—a terrifying hole that had swallowed a child. She dropped to her knees in the dirt. What if they couldn't reach him? What if he were injured?

"Thomas, we're here, honey. Are you all right?" There was no answer at first. She tried to clamp down her fears. She'd be no help if she panicked. Then he called out again, "Help."

Reed stood up and looked at her, seemingly examining her from head to toe.

"It's too small for me to fit in there," came his quiet words.

She took a deep breath, knowing what he was saying, and she didn't hesitate. "I'll go in. You can lower me down easily."

"Can you handle it?"

Fear of being lowered into the darkness, of crawling creatures, of suffocating, of being buried alive, and a million other nameless dreads swirled through her head, making her want to flee.

Instead, she did what she'd done before jumping into their game of tag. Tucking her skirt into her waistband, she then rolled up her sleeves.

"You'd better tie your hair up, too. It might catch on something."

Quickly, efficiently, but with shaking hands, Charlotte twisted the length of her hair into a knot and tugged it tightly against her neck.

"Did you get a lantern?"

"It's over by Lily."

Reed hurried there and back in a flash, leading his horse. He had the lantern in one hand, and rope in his other hand. "Only one of the ropes is long enough to do us any good. I'll have to lower you down first, then the lantern."

She nodded.

"We'll go slowly," he told her, not waiting for her consent before beginning to tie the rope around her. He threaded it around her thighs and created a harness of sorts. As he fastened a secure knot in front, his fingers working deftly, his eyes caught hers and held them. "If I could do this, I would."

"I know." She wished her voice hadn't come out as a feeble whisper. At that moment, Thomas called out again.

"Hurry," Charlotte added, almost desperate to begin her part in the rescue. As he finished securing the rope to his own horse's saddle, he returned to where she stood by the dark hole. For some reason, she whispered his name, "Reed."

Without warning, he lowered his head and kissed her. It was quick and hot and fervent, and it gave her the courage she needed.

"Not a dull moment since we arrived, eh?" he said, checking the rope.

"There's a lot to be said for dull." Charlotte couldn't believe she was joking with him as she stepped toward the air shaft, but she got to her knees and stuck her head down. *Yup, pitch black and musty.*

"Feet first," he told her, and she sat on the edge of the darkness, dangling her legs into the dank air.

"Here goes." She didn't hesitate anymore, but allowed Reed to help her in.

For a moment, she wondered if she'd be able to get her hips into the hole, but she pushed and all at once, she was in, her shoulders slipping easily through where Reed's would have stuck fast. Then there was nothing.

Dangling in the darkness, with the rope cutting into her legs and only her skirt for padding, she thought she might scream. She did, but it was Thomas's name that came out of her frightened lips. For a moment, nothing, and then she heard him.

"I'm here, Aun' Charlie."

He didn't sound so far away after all. Reed was lowering her steadily down, and then her leg brushed against something. She flung her hand out in a panic and winced as something cut deep into her hand.

"Try not to swing," he called to her, sounding strained, and Charlotte forced herself to keep still as she went ever deeper into the darkness.

"Are you all right?" Reed called down. She looked up, able to make out the shape of his head framed by the light above him.

"I think so. I'm almost at the—" her feet touched down, "the bottom. I made it."

"Untie the rope and I'll lower down the lantern."

It seemed to take her fingers forever to work. Her hands were shaking, but she breathed deeply, trying not give in to the terror of the utter blackness. Reed was right there above her, and Thomas was somewhere close by. It was merely the thought of creeping crawlies and slithering creatures that made her skin prickle with fear.

"It's loose. Take it," she called up to him, and the last tangible contact to Reed disappeared from her grasp. She waited, thankful that he kept up a steady stream of commentary as he told her exactly what he was doing. Suddenly, she felt something brush against her foot, and she couldn't help the shrill scream that erupted from her.

"Hang on, Charlotte. The lantern's coming down now." He'd already lit it and the bright light was descending like a beacon. She could now see wooden structures around her, with at least some of the posts standing straight, and prayed the dirt wasn't going to cave in on them.

Soon, the lantern was dangling beside her, shining light all around.

It was not as bad as she'd expected once the oil lamp chased the darkness down the passages to the right and left of her. There were cobwebs strung from the wooden beams that lined the passages, and a ladder with broken rungs against the cavernous wall, but nothing scary in sight. Then she saw what it was that had touched her as a long pink tail disappeared out of sight. She shuddered.

"Thomas, where are you?"

"Here," he said. She headed toward his voice. As it turned out, he had not crawled far in the darkness. Relief was immediate but so was her sense that something was wrong.

"My arm hurts."

Charlotte set the lantern down and crouched beside him. Thomas cradled his left arm in his lap. His dirty face showed the streaks of tears, but he looked so good to her, she could have sat down and cried herself. Gathering him against her, she tried not to put any pressure on his arm.

"Does everything else feel all right? How's your head and your tummy?"

"I'm hungry," Thomas said, and Charlotte smiled. That was an excellent sign.

"We'll be eating soon and having cherry pie for dessert. But first we have to get out of here."

She felt him nod against her chest as she stooped to hook the lantern over her wrist and keep him secure at the same time.

"Charlotte," Reed's voice called anxiously from above.

"I've got him," she called back. "He's going to be fine."

It was late when they sat down together like a family, eating cherry pie as Charlotte had promised, all four of them at the kitchen table. Thomas scooped up forkfuls of pie with his right hand. His broken arm, which Doctor Cuthins had set, was in a sling.

"The color's returning to his cheeks," Charlotte remarked, glad that the boy was rapidly regaining his spirits after his ordeal. Sarah had practically needed smelling salts when Reed went to fetch her husband, so upset was she at having let the children walk home.

It had taken all Reed's convincing, he later told Charlotte, to reassure Sarah it wasn't her fault. Just bad luck and disobedient children.

"Wasn't it terribly scary?" Lily asked for the umpteenth time since she'd laid eyes on her brother. Her brown eyes moved from Thomas to Charlotte. "I couldn't stand being in a hole."

"Not a hole," Thomas scoffed. "It's a tunnel."

"He's right, but it's a dangerous one, at that." Reed was not through with the incident yet. He had been strangely quiet since the rescue. "I'm going to talk to your . . . sheriff?" he looked at Charlotte.

"Mayor," she said helpfully, standing up to start heating water for dishes. "Mayor Lang. You can find him most any day . . . sleeping at the City Hall."

"Sleeping?" three voices spoke in unison.

Charlotte nodded. "Mayor Lang was old when I was Lily's age. Now he's ancient. But everyone loves him, and he's always getting reelected, so . . ."

"I think I understand," Reed said, as he moved to pour himself a cup of coffee. "If you want something done, you do it yourself."

Charlotte shrugged. "Otherwise, you'd have to send word to the governor, but that can take months. Besides you won't be here long enough to be able to do anything about it."

She wished she hadn't said that as it put a quick damper on the little flame of joviality they'd been trying for that night. The children became silent at her remark, but when Reed answered, his tone was matter-of-fact.

"It won't take all that long to do what I intend if I can get my hands on the right tools and enough lumber."

Not that long, she thought. That was all the time they had left. She sunk her hands into the hot soapy water and hissed.

"What is it?" Reed was beside her in an instant.

"I forgot about the splinter," she admitted, turning her hand over to show a long dark line under her skin where the wood had broken off. The skin around it was red and irritated.

"That looks painful," Reed commented. "You should have said something earlier when Doctor Cuthins was here."

Charlotte struggled not to feel hurt by the harshness of his tone. "In light of Thomas's arm, it hardly seemed—"

"It's okay to ask for help," he cut in, his voice rough with irritation. "It doesn't mean you'll lose your independence. Do you have a needle?"

Minutes later, he was poking at the deep splinter with a needle sterilized over a candle flame. The children looked on fascinated. Charlotte bit her bottom lip and held her breath as Reed worked efficiently but painfully. After everything else that had happened today, she would be damned if she would cry now.

"Almost there," he said, looking up from his ministrations to see her pale face. He looked over her head and addressed the children. "Why don't you two head upstairs and get ready for bed. Lily, you can help your brother get his clothes off, can't you?"

When it was only the two of them, Reed gave her a smile. "Come on, lady writer," he added, his voice gentler now. "I've seen how full of grit you can be. Don't get all soft on me now."

When it was over, Charlotte accepted a glass of brandy, wondering if some mention should be made of what had passed between them so many hours earlier. The absolute quiet in the kitchen seemed tangible until Reed took over the dishes.

She took a small sip of the soothing liquid, certain he could hear her swallow. *But what to say?*

"Charlotte."

"Reed."

Spoken together, their names were blurred. Reed was unmoving, leaning against the counter with a dripping dish in one hand. Then he smiled a crooked smile that made her want to shed her clothes and her inhibitions.

"I think," he began, but she was not to learn what it was Reed thought as Lily called down the stairs for her. It seemed they turned to her more and more as time passed.

"I'd best see what she wants," Charlotte told him, a bit relieved by the interruption but chastising herself for cowardice at the same time.

He simply nodded. By the time the children were settled and sleeping, she could barely keep her own eyes open. Sitting on her bed, Charlotte intended to rest a moment, knowing that Reed was probably waiting downstairs or out on the porch. Instead, however, she fell almost immediately into a deep sleep.

CHAPTER TEN

Reed took off in the wagon right after breakfast and was gone all the next day. In his absence, Charlotte finished her article and began weeding her new garden late into the afternoon. She began to fret over the incident in his bedroom the day before.

They had barely had a moment alone together since the wolf had howled, and the longer the time dragged on, the more self-conscious she felt over melting in his arms. Did he think her wanton now?

She was still absentmindedly thinking of him when he came into view, driving the wagon at a slow pace. Even from a distance, she could see he was tired from his day's work, and as he came closer, she could also see he was dirty from the top of his raven black hair, now covered with dust, downward. She dashed inside to start heating water.

Before she knew it, it was supper. The children were brimming over with excitement about the dance, so much so that Reed could barely get a word in edgewise to tell her about the crude carpentry he'd done. With the help of two men from town—Dan, who ran the feedstore, and Ely, the barber—they'd nailed boards over every hole they could find.

Lily was already humming and tapping along with her toes. And Thomas, despite his broken arm, hadn't slowed down any, plainly determined not to let his injury ruin his fun. In any case, Charlotte didn't have the heart to suggest they stay home because of it. Truthfully, she didn't think she could bear the thought of missing the opportunity to dance with Reed.

After the meal, they all scattered to various tasks, and then it was time to bathe the children. Later in the evening, Charlotte sought refuge in the parlor.

"Are you avoiding me?" Reed asked, entering the room so silently she hadn't time to arrange her skirts or her thoughts.

"Of course not," she scoffed, putting down the book she'd been staring at for ten minutes without reading a word. She hadn't secretly been fearing this meeting, had she?

"So, you're not hiding in here?" he asked as he sat down and leaned his head back against the sofa. He wasn't even looking at her. His question seemed to be for conversation's sake, not because he believed what he was asking.

It was true that she rarely came into the parlor. But it had taken on a different air since the children started using it as a place to play, losing the dreary mustiness of years of disuse. Tonight, though, with Thomas and Lily in bed, Charlotte was simply appreciating the peacefulness.

"You haven't answered my question?" His head turned in her direction, his eyes a warm blue tonight, reflecting a man with a hard day's work behind him.

"What do I have to hide out from?" she asked.

Reed smiled at her before closing his eyes. "A counter question. Hmm. As far as I'm concerned, nothing. Last night, I could barely sleep. I kept having hellish fantasies about what could have happened if we hadn't got to Lily and Thomas in time. I still can barely believe how lucky we were. I just couldn't bear the thought of—"

He broke off abruptly, and she watched him run his palm over his eyes. It was obvious his weariness was making him say more than he'd intended, but she filed the small kernel of information away for another time when he was more up to discussing it.

Charlotte touched his shoulder, almost without meaning to, and watched him smile again, his eyes still closed. Then, taking a deep breath, he continued, "There were other reasons I found it hard to sleep."

She felt an abrupt rush of blood to her face, glad that he was not looking at her.

"While I was at the mines today, I kept wondering what you might be thinking and feeling."

"I was thinking of you," she told him truthfully, "and wondering the same."

Without lifting his head, he reached out and took hold of her hand, pulling it over to rest on his leg and keeping his own hand firmly on top.

"We should discuss . . . everything. There's a lot to talk about and," he paused to yawn broadly, "and something I need to tell you."

She took a deep breath, forcing her mind to quash the immediate influx of wild ideas. *Let him tell me before I jump to some unfounded fear,* she scolded herself. And as his hand relaxed its hold on hers, she calmed herself. Clearly, it was nothing serious. Still, he was silent.

"Reed?" she prompted.

The sound of his first deep snore reached her ears.

On Saturday, there was an undercurrent of excitement in Charlotte's house. Before lunch, Reed had prepared his Aunt Maya's pear crisps for the potluck supper, and Lily had wanted her bath early, then sat on her bed reading to keep clean. Wisely, Charlotte kept Thomas out of his party clothes until the last moment. Finally, at dusk, everyone was nearly ready.

Charlotte's fondest memory of the day, she thought as she finished dressing, was of Reed beside the kitchen table, fussing over his two pie plates, covered from head to foot with a mix of what appeared to be oats and cinnamon.

He had looked up at her as she'd entered the kitchen, with raccoon eyes in a flour-dusted face. And against all odds, this Boston lawyer had smiled and looked more appealing to her than ever.

After one last look in the oval mirror that stood in its maple frame in the corner of her room, Charlotte headed for the stairs. It seemed remarkable to her that all four of them had managed to get ready on time.

She heard Reed pull the wagon around front. The first to greet her, though, was Thomas, standing at the door with wide eyes. Then Lily came out of the parlor.

"You look lovely, Aunt Charlotte."

She thanked them both, silently blessing the little girl, for her words were the vote of confidence Charlotte needed. Now, only Reed was left to see—

The front door opened, and Charlotte turned slowly, feeling all tingly with anticipation. She wanted to bowl the man over. She appeared to succeed. His jaw actually dropped for an instant as he took in the sight of her, and his eyes widened as Thomas's had.

Taking her in with one glance, he whistled, long and steady, bringing an immediate flush to her cheeks. Then he let his gaze slowly travel the length of her. He started with her shining chestnut hair. She'd used a black velvet clasp to pull it elegantly away from her face, allowing it to cascade down her back in loose coppery curls.

Then his eyes halted at the deep neckline of her dress, where the gentle swell of her breasts rose above the dark lace chemisette. The pale color of her skin contrasted tantalizingly with the shimmering green of the fabric.

The cut of the dress accentuated her small waist, dipping to a deep V-shape before swelling out in a bell of emerald silk. The only thing he couldn't see were the sheer stockings, and Charlotte had the daring thought of showing them to him later. But for now, she had to break the spell.

Looking Reed up and down in turn, she nodded approvingly. He looked fine, indeed, in dark gray trousers that snugly fit his well-shaped thighs and a freshly boiled shirt that showed off the expanse of his shoulders. As he promised Lily, he was wearing his new silk tie, deep green with small black stripes.

Charlotte put her hands on her hips and whistled right back at him, making the children giggle.

"You, sir, look a huckleberry above most people's persimmons."

Reed laughed out loud at that as he reached for his charcoal frock coat, hung over her office door out of reach of little grabbing hands.

"Let's collect your pear crisps and get under way," Charlotte added, striding past him to the kitchen.

"Where have you been hiding?" he called after her.

"It's Aun' Charlie," Thomas said delightedly, trying to solve Reed's confusion.

"I think you're right, Thomas," she heard him say. "And I think Aunt Charlotte will make every head turn at the dance tonight."

Oh, she was fairly certain that every head would turn. *Charlotte Sanborn at a dance! With a man!* Still, she treasured his words, not to mention his heated glance that had started her butterflies fluttering once more. She wanted more than all the world for him to take her in his arms again, to kiss her, and to go on with what they'd started.

She handed each of the children a pie and told them to head outside. Reed paused to pick up her black shawl from the hall stand.

"You clean up really well for a western writer. A sweet, delectable huckleberry," he murmured into her ear, making her knees quiver. "Isn't that what you said?"

Then he draped her wrap around her shoulders before tucking her arm under his.

"Your carriage," he said, using the word loosely, referring to her old wagon, "awaits you, my lady. And may I tell you, your beauty is wasted on a barn dance. You would dazzle all of Boston society. Think about it."

She did, for about half a second, and then doubt crept into her thoughts. Was he trying to get her to agree to move east so he could fulfill his duties as executor of her cousin's will?

She tried to shake off that disappointing thought, but he seemed such a practiced and smooth attorney. Certainly, it wouldn't be beyond his abilities to manipulate her feelings. Yet the kisses had been real. The intimacy they'd shared had been magical.

Reed helped her onto the front seat, as the children clambered onto the clean blanket lining the rear. "No rips or tears, Thomas," Charlotte warned. "And Lily, dear, be careful of those stockings."

"You sound almost motherly," Reed said, climbing up beside her taking the reins. "But then," he dipped his head to her ear so Lily and Thomas couldn't hear, "you look anything but that tonight. More like a temptress."

She shivered at his words and the timbre of his voice. For a few minutes, she forgot her anxiety. But all too quickly the lights of the town appeared before them, and she bit her lip. Showing up was, for her, a momentous occasion that would draw stares and whispers, but showing up with a handsome man and two sweet children would bring about an utter flurry of gossip and speculation.

Reed drove them along the main street to Drake's barn. By the number of wagons and traps and horses, Charlotte knew most of the townspeople had already arrived. Reed circled around the enormous wooden building until he found a place in the back where Alfred could graze, and then he unhitched him and tied him to the rear of the wagon.

"Here we go," Reed said turning to the children, who started to run toward the barn before Charlotte had even climbed down.

"Halt," Reed called after them.

Charlotte watched them freeze in their tracks, barely containing their excitement over the bright lights and music and voices emanating from the building before them.

"My lady." Reed held his hand up to her.

She took it, standing up and placing one green satin shoe on the running board. But in an instant, he released her hand and took her around the waist. She gasped as he lifted her and set her down gently on the grass. His hands lingered a moment, and she looked up into his face.

He smiled, and she swallowed hard, feeling her heart pounding in her throat—nervous over the dance and sweetly terrified over her own strong reactions to Reed. Then his thumbs caressed her through the satin dress, and she lost the feeling of terror altogether.

"Remember," he said, looking into her clear, green eyes, "you've known these people all your life. They just haven't known you." He released her, took her arm through his, and started toward the well-lit barn. The children seemed to take this as permission to go ahead and ran toward the large open doors.

At the entrance, Charlotte gasped at the transformation of the normally plain and practical barn. So, this was what she'd been missing! It was a fairy world of oil lanterns, tables laden with food all around the perimeter, the fresh smell of beeswax, and even a platform of wood and fresh, pungent hay to support the musicians.

Right then, Anna Webster passed by with a pie and a greeting.

"That dress is absolutely perfect on you, Charlotte," she said. "And your man?"

Charlotte blushed. *Yes, he's perfect, too,* she thought.

"Anna, this is Mr. Malloy from Boston. Mr. Malloy, this is Miss Webster. Her father owns the piece goods store."

"Enchanted," Reed said.

"Likewise." Anna was all smiles. "I hope you'll try my pie later."

"Oh," Charlotte exclaimed, remembering the pear crisps. In their excitement, the children had left them in the wagon.

"The dessert," she exclaimed, about to go get them herself, but Reed stopped her.

"No, you don't. I get the feeling if I let you go, you won't come back. Why don't you pour us some punch, and I'll retrieve the pies."

Blazes! He was leaving her alone. The children had vanished into the crowd, and Anna had already disappeared in the direction of the food tables. Charlotte thought she'd heard her name murmured somewhere close by, and imagined she saw heads turn and fans go up over whispering mouths.

Her palms started to dampen, and she turned a sickly smile on the revelers. Luckily, the next person she focused on was Sarah, who gave her a cheerful wave. She waved back, determined to head over.

"Is that Charlotte Sanborn?" said a loud voice in her ear, followed by a tug on her arm. It was Jessie Hollander, the waitress from Fuller's restaurant. "Girl, you're all slicked up something fine."

"Why, don't that beat the Dutch?" said another. "Ruth, come over here and take a gander at Charlotte Sanborn."

"Charlotte, here?" came an equally loud voice. By this time, other people had started to form around her, and she felt as if she were the latest display at a traveling show.

"How . . . how nice to see you all," she managed. Then, pushing through the crowd straight toward her was Eliza Prentice, dressed in a cool blue color that matched her eyes and set off her blond hair.

"Where did you get that dress?" the girl practically hissed, right in front of everyone.

"Why, in town, of course. But yours is a homespun delight." Charlotte saw that barb reach home as Eliza's eyes widened and her nostrils flared.

But the pretty blond collected herself. "Wait until you all meet the magnificent man I met in town," she said conspiratorially to the other ladies. "I invited him here myself," she added with a simper.

Charlotte opened her mouth to explain about Reed Malloy, but before she could, she saw Eliza's gaze shoot past her. She knew who Eliza saw over her shoulder, as the young woman's hand immediately raised up to pat her hair.

It was too late. Reed chose that moment to appear, holding the pie plates stacked one on top of the other.

"There you are," he said, and Eliza turned a brilliant smile upon him. It died as he went directly to Charlotte's side. "I could barely see you through your throng of friends. Good evening, ladies, and . . . um . . . Miss Prentice, isn't it?" Reed nodded his head to each one in turn.

"Now, Miss Sanborn, where's our punch? And the children?" Reed handed her the pear crisps and propelled her away from the awe struck, momentarily silent group, a firm hand on her back.

"That was wicked," she told him with a smile, placing their offering on the end of the table with the other cakes and sweetmeats. "But I'm grateful."

"I love to rescue a lady in distress," he told her handing her a cup of punch, "especially one as beautiful as you."

She smiled at him and sipped at the fruity drink. "This has to be one of the most exciting nights of my life. And to think, I never would have had the opportunity if not for you."

He smiled down at her. "Then let's make the most of it. Shall we dance?"

She set down her cup. "Believe it or not, that's one thing I *can* do. My mother insisted I learn, bless her, although it has been a while."

Reed led her onto the swept floor as a new tune started up. It was slow and sweet, and Charlotte was relaxing into Reed's strong arms as they danced.

Surely, this was a little bit of heaven, far away from editorial deadlines and her cluttered study. The pressure of his hands, one resting on her waist and the other holding her hand securely in his, made her feel like . . . like a full-fledged woman. She slanted her head to look at him, their eyes meeting.

"Your mother taught you well," he said, gently squeezing her hand.

"And where did you learn to dance, Mr. Malloy?"

"I picked it up here and there. And it's time to be Reed and Charlotte now, don't you think?"

She nodded. The intimacy of first names in public sent another shiver down her spine. *What would Eliza think of that?*

"Tomorrow," he added, looking around them at the other dancers, "we need to talk."

"Tomorrow," she repeated, and his blue eyes met hers. Tonight, however, there was no need for words. The next tune picked up the tempo, and Charlotte was soon whirling around the dance floor.

"Everyone is so fine-looking," she observed as he drew her in close, "like freshly picked flowers, don't you think?"

Reed shook his head.

"You have no idea that you're the most radiant woman here."

She stopped still for a moment, looking up at his handsome face, now grown dear to her. He tightened his hold on her hand and led her off the dance floor, stopping at a quiet spot, next to one of the empty stalls.

"There's something so vibrant about you, Charlotte, so different from anyone I've ever known. I can't help but wonder what it would be like to keep company with you at home. In Boston, I mean."

He cocked his head at her, and daringly, she rested her palm on his chest, feeling his heart beating fast from the dancing. "Would you become the same as all the women I've known in the endlessly tedious drawing rooms of Boston?"

She shrugged, unwilling to break his lighthearted musings and at a loss as to how those other women had behaved.

He continued, "I doubt that any environment could change the honest reactions of one Charlotte Sanborn. You could never be other than a head full of strong opinions, with the intelligence to garner respect, and the beauty that encourages men's admiration and women's envy."

"Oh, my," she laughed. "I sound like a paragon, indeed." If he was trying to persuade her, he was nearly succeeding. She was about ready to pack her trunks.

"Not too much of a paragon, I hope," he said softly, changing the mood. His gaze dropped to her full lips for a moment, then to her own hungry glance, making her want desperately to be kissed, wishing they were alone.

"What are you thinking?" he asked her, leaning his head even closer. She didn't care that they were against the rough wooden wall in Drake's, with every person she'd ever known a few feet away. She didn't care that he'd put his hand on her waist in public or that his leg was close amongst her skirts. She wanted desperately for him to kiss her right then.

"I'm only imagining how it would be—"

She was interrupted by Lily and Thomas and three other children whom Charlotte recognized from town. They were all chattering at the same time as she and Reed moved quickly apart. Reed was able to speak before she was.

"Silence, please." His voice was not stern or loud, just commanding, and they obeyed him instantly.

"All right then, what's this all about? One at a time," he ordered as they all opened their mouths again. "Lily?"

"The late train has come in from the east, and they say," she gestured toward a group of gossiping women, including Eliza, "that there were people on it from home."

"From home?" Reed and Charlotte said at once.

"From Bos'n," Thomas added.

Charlotte felt a clenching in her stomach. Could it be the children's grandmother coming to get them?

Alarmed at the surge of protectiveness and possessiveness that welled up, she determined that she didn't want to let the children go, and that the feeling was unrelated to Reed.

She fervently hoped these strangers had nothing to do with the Lily and Thomas or their lawyer. Things were going so well, and all she wanted was a little more time.

The station was nearly deserted when the last train pulled in. Only two occupants got off at Spring City, and they went directly to the hotel, securing two separate rooms. Because nearly the whole town was at the barn dance, the travelers freshened up and wandered down to the end of the street where the bright lights of Drake's barn welcomed them.

It was here that Helen Belgrave sought her fiancé and John Trelaine looked for his law partner—one and the same, Reed Malloy.

CHAPTER ELEVEN

Charlotte felt Reed stiffen and followed his gaze across the room to where the doors were standing open. If her own unexpected appearance had caused a stir, the arrival of out-of-towners caused an absolute maelstrom of murmurs to course around the room. It was easy to follow the wave of whispers and stares to see where Reed was looking.

A few feet inside the entrance, searching the crowd, stood an impeccably clad woman accompanied by an equally well-groomed gentleman about the same age as Reed and dressed similarly in darkest charcoal.

The stunning female was undoubtedly used to the attention, paying it no mind as she dipped her head to confer with the man. Her night-black hair was swept up in a smooth chignon and she wore a sophisticated cream-colored gown trimmed with black satin.

Immediately, Charlotte saw the great contrast this pair made with every other person in the room. Except Reed. Everyone looked downright provincial in the shadow of their polished demeanor. Even herself, she realized, acutely aware of the outdated fashion of her crinoline in contrast to the dark-haired woman's sleek gown with its shapely bustle, pleated skirts, and elegant train.

Charlotte already knew the answer but asked anyway. "Do you know them?"

He nodded, not taking his eyes off them until they finally saw him, and the man waved. The woman, even from this distance, seemed to greet him with her eyes, her whole expression, and even the way her body relaxed toward him.

Reed lifted up his hand in greeting, and the pair started toward them. Only then did he look at Charlotte.

"It appears as though we've run out of time," he voiced her thoughts. "My life in Boston seems to have been unable to wait any longer." By then, the two strangers were upon them.

"Reed, we've been looking all over for you." The man spoke first, obviously relieved. The woman glanced from Reed to Charlotte, and back again.

"You found me," Reed said, stiffly. "John, I'd like you to meet Charlotte Sanborn, Ann Connors' cousin. Miss Sanborn, this is my partner, John Trelaine."

"How pleased I am to meet you," the man told her, taking her hand and bowing over it.

Charlotte instantly liked his kind brown eyes. She wondered what had brought another lawyer all the way across the country to the middle of Colorado. In the next moment, she understood.

"Reed, I insisted John bring me out here. I was worried about you." The woman leaned over and gave his cheek a quick brush with her flawless red lips. And Charlotte felt a mix of emotions running the gamut from hot anger to shattered sadness.

"You needn't have worried, Helen, and you shouldn't have bothered John." Reed's voice was steady, but Charlotte detected a note of irritation. "Helen, this is Miss Sanborn."

Charlotte was painfully aware that the intimate use of first names had given way to formalities again. Now, it was *this* woman who was so obviously on familiar terms with Reed.

Helen Belgrave's eyes slid over to her. They were unfathomable pools of darkness. But her words were courteous.

"You are Charles Sanborn's . . . sister?" Her tone was smooth as her raven hair.

John Trelaine cleared his throat slightly. It was obvious to Charlotte that he knew.

Reed simply drew in a deep breath as if girding himself for battle.

"Charlotte Sanborn *is* Charles Sanborn," he told her.

The woman's mouth dropped open for the briefest of seconds and then snapped shut, as the color rose in her lovely face. It appeared as if trouble were brewing.

"It is a pleasure to meet you," Charlotte began, "although I'm afraid you have the advantage." She looked questioningly at Reed, who was staring hard at her now, his wary expression a puzzle to her.

"Miss Sanborn," he said at last, "this is Mrs. Belgrave."

"His fiancée," the beauty added, placing her gloved hand on his arm.

John Trelaine coughed at that moment as if he were choking. Charlotte was thankful it covered her slight gasp. Her gaze flew to Reed's face. He had not stopped staring at her. And now she knew why he'd watched her so carefully. He had been waiting for her reaction to the disclosure he was certain she would hear.

Reed's jaw clenched. His lips were a straight line that matched his eyebrows, and he looked downright grim. Charlotte could tell he was a man who did not like to be caught holding back the truth . . . even if, apparently, he didn't mind holding it back in the first place.

"His fiancée," Charlotte repeated aloud in what she hoped was a light and gay voice. "Why, Mr. Malloy, you should have told me. I'm sure I wouldn't have let you stay so long in this backward place" she bit out the words, "when you had Mrs. Belgrave awaiting your return."

"I assure you, Miss Sanborn," he said evenly, his eyes never leaving hers, "I do not let anyone make me do anything I don't want to do."

"Reed does get caught up in his work," Helen Belgrave said, apparently having recovered from her surprise at finding out that "Charles" was a female. Her words were placid enough, even though her tone was unamused.

Charlotte felt a distinct lack of amusement, as well, and wondered if the kisses she and Reed had shared, not to mention their passionate interlude in his bedroom, were written across her face.

Seemingly not, for Mrs. Belgrave continued, "My Reed is quite thorough at whatever he does. His work ethic demands that he accomplish his business affairs ahead of most anything else."

My Reed. Charlotte thought she was going to be sick. She squashed the image of Reed and Helen Belgrave in some expensive restaurant in Boston, having a romantic dinner, before going together to his home to . . .

"Helen," Reed said, his voice sounding more like a warning than a lover's address, "what *are* you doing here?"

Charlotte barely listened to her answer. She was pondering why he had dallied with her in the first place. Had he been so intent on getting her to accept the children that he would trifle with her? She just didn't know. How could she? After all, she'd only known him a few weeks. *How stupid she'd been to think she knew him at all.*

Helen Belgrave was still talking, and John looked about as uncomfortable as Charlotte felt. As for Reed, she couldn't even look him in the eye at that moment, so she boldly addressed his law partner.

"Mr. Trelaine, you must be thirsty after your long trip. Would you care for some refreshment?" Taking his arm, she led him away almost before he'd replied with an enthusiastic affirmative. Turning, she nearly tripped over the children who had all stayed to listen and to watch.

"Come along, Lily, Thomas. Mr. Malloy needs some time alone with his," she almost choked, "fiancée."

The children ran off with the other three and disappeared into the crowd, probably to tell everything they'd heard.

"The word sort of sticks in your throat, doesn't it?" Reed's partner asked.

She looked up at John Trelaine, blushing furiously. Could he tell she had feelings for Reed?

"Sticks in mine, anyway," he told her, not waiting for a reply. "And I've had a lot longer to get used to the idea. That woman jabbered at me across eight states, and I can't say when I've been happier that it was the brevity of train travel versus a lengthy journey by coach. Still, three days escorting Mrs. Belgrave goes beyond my duty as partner and friend."

"It's understandable that she should be worried about Mr. Malloy," Charlotte offered, trying to sound gracious when she felt like spitting nails. "She must love him very much to come all this way."

They stopped at the punch table, and John Trelaine handed her a cup before taking one for himself, adding a little something extra from a silver flask he kept in his coat pocket.

"Would you care for some *sustenance?*" He gestured to the flask.

"Yes, I would," Charlotte allowed, letting him pour a generous portion of the clear liquid into her cup. "Thank you." They both turned to look at the handsome couple whom they'd left on the edge of the dance floor.

"Oh, don't let this dramatic little trip out west fool you." He paused and looked at her directly.

Charlotte confirmed her first impression. Mr. Trelaine did have kind eyes, but there was a hint of annoyance now in his gaze.

"If I may be so frank, Miss Sanborn, there is only one thing Mrs. Belgrave loves and that is Mrs. Belgrave."

Charlotte didn't know how to respond to this, so she sipped her punch and coughed once as the doctored liquid slipped searingly down her throat. She looked over to where Reed still conversed with the raven-haired beauty.

It did, certainly, look like anything but a lover's *tête-a-tête.* Reed was somber, his mouth in a straight, hard line whenever his fiancée spoke.

Helen, in turn, appeared stone-faced, speaking in short clipped words. Her breeding and manners dictated that she remain cool and her face emotionless. When someone passed closely, she immediately flashed a dazzling smile that died just as quickly when she looked at Reed. Eventually, her eyes met Charlotte's across the room, and the mask slipped to reveal unadulterated wrath.

Charlotte shivered and turned to John Trelaine. "She is a widow?"

"Yes, for about four years. Her husband was a Boston blue blood, as they say. About as old as Methuselah," he added, taking another swallow of punch.

"Well, sometimes love makes its appearance in unexpected forms," Charlotte surmised.

John Trelaine's eyes were sharp as he looked at her. "You are an intelligent woman, Miss Sanborn. I have read your work. I think you're forward-thinking, too, on social issues. Am I right?"

She nodded, although she couldn't imagine to what he was referring.

"Thus, I don't think it will shock you to hear that I believe theirs," he glanced toward Reed and Helen, "is a loveless union, but perhaps I could shock you by telling you they have been a couple of convenience for going on three years. And still, no marriage banns have been read out in the church, no announcement in the papers, and no ring on her finger. I believe the convenience is all on Reed's side."

Charlotte's puzzled brow made him smile. "He keeps her close to keep others away. No woman in Boston would dare cross the path of Helen Belgrave. But you—"

"Me?" Charlotte was startled into interrupting him. Undeniably, this lawyer was as perceptive as his partner. She took another gulp of her punch.

"Mrs. Belgrave is no fool. She knows as well as I that Reed could have sent one of our junior associates to carry out this task. He didn't. Instead, he came more than two thousand miles to meet you, having first read all of your work he could get his hands on."

She blushed, unable to help herself from looking over at Reed again, this time with a more thoughtful gaze. Perhaps he didn't love the striking woman beside him, but how could Charlotte ever think he'd be interested in her, in *that way?* Still, he had come, if John were right, intent on meeting her, and not solely because of the children.

"Ah, I see he didn't tell you that he is an admirer."

"Mr. Malloy did mention my cousin had introduced him to my work. But I assumed he'd *had* to come himself, to carry out the duties of executor."

John Trelaine was silent a moment. Then he said pointedly, "But Mrs. Belgrave knew otherwise. And she didn't like that—even less now she's found out you are a woman and that Reed knew all along of your fairer sex."

Charlotte mulled it over a moment. So, Reed had an interest in her as a writer, and out of curiosity he'd handled her cousin's wishes personally. But was there any more to what had occurred between them? It made her head ache to think about it, about him in her house, about their brief flirtation, about the way she'd felt when held in his arms, dancing.

She looked up at John Trelaine, with his intelligent eyes and gentle expression, and she flashed him her own most dazzling smile before looking toward the dance floor. Those who were not still standing around gossiping and staring at the newcomers were dancing up a storm.

He took the hint and relieved her of her empty cup. "What say we drop discussion of the tribulations of my law partner and the indomitable Mrs. Belgrave and take up the more pleasurable task of dancing?"

"I would love that, if you are not too worn out from your trip."

"Your company is refreshing my constitution every minute," he murmured, escorting her to the center of the room.

Despite everything, Charlotte was having a pleasant time, even if the magic of the first few dances with Reed was gone forever. The warmth of imbibing the whiskey combined with an attentive dance partner served to alleviate the initial upset Charlotte had suffered. She danced with John Trelaine for the rest of the evening and avoided meeting Reed's glance.

Charlotte couldn't help but notice that he did not dance with Mrs. Belgrave—whether by his fiancée's choice or his own, she couldn't tell. Neither seemed to be having a good time, and that made Charlotte's evening more bearable. She and John Trelaine ate supper together on the long low wooden tables that had been placed around the perimeter.

She heard him sigh. "Such a grist of food has crossed our plates and disappeared, I don't think I can stand up," he said good-humoredly, but it didn't stop him from perusing the desserts. Later in the evening, Charlotte stifled a yawn as they sat on a bale of hay, eating Brown Betty in companionable silence.

"I think I have room for one more helping of something," Mr. Trelaine observed, getting up to see what was left. Charlotte groaned at the thought.

At that moment, Eliza Prentice strolled over, planting herself squarely in front of her.

"It looks as though your Mr. Malloy goes through women about as quickly as his friend goes through desserts."

"He is not *my* Mr. Malloy," Charlotte said, hoping she sounded suitably disinterested as she looked anywhere but up at Eliza.

"No, of course not. He's made that evident tonight, despite all your high-falutin' slicking yourself up. On the other hand, word has it that he has been staying with you, *in your house*."

Charlotte said nothing in reply, still not looking at the petite blond.

"Just the two of you, *alone*," Eliza prodded once more, and Charlotte could tell the woman was dying to pile on the agony.

"On the contrary," Charlotte said at last, standing up, "the children are there with us. And where's your young doctor this evening? Away studying? Unable to accompany you, as usual?" Charlotte asked, sounding as catty as she felt. Eliza had far too much time on her hands and spent it concerning herself with other people's business.

"It seems to me you'd best be worrying about your own man, Eliza, and how many young ladies he might be meeting while at that school in San Francisco."

Pushing past her, Charlotte hurried out of the barn's side door, not wanting to hear any more of Eliza's petty comments. There was no doubt if there was an eligible bachelor in town, Eliza would have only to beckon her finger, what with her shining blond curls and periwinkle blue eyes. What on earth was the woman trying to prove?

All Charlotte had ever wanted to do was stay out of everyone's way. The world had come knocking at her door, not the other way around. And even for that, she was paying a price.

She came to a halt by the large oak tree that overshadowed the barn and the town livery. No one knew how old it was, but everyone in Spring City had at one time or another climbed its branches as a child or sat in its shade as an adult. Charlotte now rested against it, closing her eyes and feeling comforted by its solidity at her back.

And then suddenly Reed was there. She sensed it even before she opened her eyes and saw him approaching, already mere yards away. No doubt he'd followed her. She sighed.

Everything had changed. *Everything!* And she could not in good conscience meet him here alone by this tree while his fiancée was nearby. Charlotte tried to walk away, but he was too quick, gripping her arm and backing her up against the tree.

"Let me go! For goodness sake, Mrs. Belgrave is on the other side of that wall."

He didn't release her and she tried again, "For the sake of my reputation."

Reed dropped her arm immediately. "You are keeping close company with John," he muttered into the silence.

"Blazes!" she swore with exasperation. "Do not try to tell me you're feeling jealous over my dancing with your associate while you're spending the evening with your fiancée!" She moved past him, realizing her primary feeling was one of betrayal. "This whole thing is preposterous."

"Will you listen a moment?" His hand touched her shoulder again.

"No, I don't think I will," she told him. She was as angry as a cornered badger and felt like a fool, to boot. The last thing she wanted to do was chat. But as she moved, he reached for her again, pulling her toward him.

She struggled for a few seconds, hating her treacherous body that still clamored for his touch and seemed to burn where his hands held her upper arms. She pressed her hands against his shoulders and pushed.

"If you don't stay still and listen, Charlotte, I'll kiss you."

It was the oddest threat she'd ever heard, but it bespoke how well he already knew her, or at least knew how she reacted to him. For it stilled her. She stared up at him, wanting even then the fiery heat of his mouth, knowing how her nerve endings would jangle in response and that she would feel as if she was flying. It was humiliating.

Her salvation came from an unlikely source. Helen Belgrave appeared at the door. Reed saw the look on Charlotte's face as she caught sight of the woman over his shoulder. He turned to see his fiancée's face contorted with rage, but when his gaze returned to Charlotte, his expression was impassive.

"You will hear me out later," he vowed before dropping his hold on her and allowing her to step away from the tree.

Charlotte took this opportunity to flee. She ignored Mrs. Belgrave's frosty glare and slipped around behind the building to reach her wagon. She had already hitched Alfred by the time John Trelaine came upon her.

"Excuse my rudeness, sir, but I am done for the evening." She had seen Reed leave without a backward glance, his hand on Helen Belgrave's elbow, no doubt escorting her to the hotel.

"May I see you home?" John asked.

She returned a grateful smile to his pleasant but weary face. He had been an impeccable escort all evening despite his lengthy journey.

"I assure you that I am perfectly able to get myself and the children home."

After extracting a promise that she would drive at a steady pace straight home, he'd bid her good night and headed to the hotel. By the time she had corralled the children into the wagon, Thomas was yawning broadly, already closing his eyes, and Lily, curled up next to him, was about to join him in slumber.

Holding on to the side rail, Charlotte lifted her skirts and placed one satin-clad foot on the running board when, abruptly, strong hands at her waist lifted her as if she weighed no more than a feather. For a second, she thought Mr. Trelaine had returned, but then she knew, even before she took her seat and turned to face him.

Reed looked up at her.

"Ready to go?"

With her mouth slightly open, she stared down at him. Then she closed it with a snap. He looked at her, waiting for her to move over or to speak. She chose the latter.

"Have you taken leave of your senses? Or are you just completely dense?" Her own voice sounded loud and shrill in the gathering darkness, but she was at the end of her rope.

"Neither. I brought you here and I'm taking you home. And may I remind you that the children are sleeping."

She lowered her voice. "I have been driving myself from home to town and home again for over a decade. I believe I can manage without your assistance. I urge you to go to the hotel and to your fiancée, *Mr. Malloy.*"

After all, she thought, that's what this is all about. It didn't matter that John Trelaine had told her Reed purposefully came all the way to Spring City to meet her. He had misled her in more than one instance.

"Mrs. Belgrave is safely ensconced in Fuller's finest accommodations, *Miss Sanborn,* and now I intend to see you safely home, as well."

"Besides," he added, "all of my things are at your house."

Charlotte was tempted to say, "Hard luck," and drive off, but she didn't. She would never know why she moved over to let him onto the seat beside her, but she did. He swung himself up, and Charlotte scooted sideways even farther when his warm thigh touched hers. There wasn't much room to move, but she intended to keep as much distance as possible between her and the man who had too easily touched her heart.

"I thought perhaps I'd be too late, that John would have seen you home," he said evenly, as they started out of town.

"He offered," Charlotte returned, her voice equally steady, while sitting ramrod straight. "But I declined. He was extremely tired after escorting your worried fiancée halfway across the world to find you."

That closed the conversation for the ride home. Eight minutes of pure, hellacious silence. Charlotte couldn't help but glance up at the windows of the hotel as they passed, and wondered if Reed had given Mrs. Belgrave a good night kiss when he'd taken her to her room.

Still, she thought with some small satisfaction, he could have stayed with his fiancée, if he'd wanted. No one in Boston would ever have known about that breach of propriety out here in the untamed west.

If he'd wanted, she repeated to herself and felt better despite the strained stillness between them that she enforced by turning her face away.

Now, she only wanted to get home and remove the ridiculous party dress and silk stockings that had not even put her in Helen Belgrave's league. Then, with the covers pulled up over her head, she would try to forget the entire evening.

CHAPTER TWELVE

However, Reed was not going to let her slip quietly away to her room. After they'd tucked the children into bed, he half invited, half dragged Charlotte out onto the front porch into the cool night air. He sat on the swing and pulled her down beside him, her dress billowing about both their legs before settling.

"I'm sorry this happened," he blurted out, and it was the first time Charlotte had ever seen Reed less than composed, except at the mines.

"You're sorry for what exactly?" she asked, her voice low with weariness. In truth, she was not up to the anger she'd felt earlier. She was as tired as the children, although for different reasons.

"Perhaps you're sorry your fiancée arrived before you finished what you came here to do. Or are you sorry you didn't tell me you *had* a fiancée before you got caught in a deception?"

She felt rather than heard him take a deep breath.

"I'm deeply sorry you are hurt. I never meant to mislead you."

She laughed then, leaning her head against the swing and looking up at the stars.

"No, I mean it, Charlotte. I was going to tell you about my situation with Helen the other night," he paused, "and, of course, we were going to talk tomorrow, but we ran out of time."

His situation with Helen. What an odd way to describe an engagement. although according to John Trelaine, it wasn't a traditional engagement at all.

Charlotte closed her eyes against the winking stars, remembering Reed saying there was something he wanted to tell her, right before he fell asleep on the sofa the night before. But he should have told her before the very first kiss out on the grass.

"We have run out of time," Charlotte agreed.

She felt him take her hand from where it rested upon her lap, and as he had done before on her porch, Reed caressed her palm ever so gently with his thumb.

She drew it slowly back, clasping her hands firmly together on her skirt.

"You are spoken for," she said, not looking at him. "Everything is different now."

"Is it?" He turned her to face him with a strong hand under her chin. She squeezed her eyes tightly shut. "I don't feel any differently about you. Nothing has changed for me," he vowed.

She was still as a statue. She could feel the rough rasp of his thumb along her jaw, and she wanted to turn her head ever so slightly and touch her lips to it. Instead, she held her breath.

"Charlotte, look at me."

"No," she said. If she opened her eyes and saw his familiar face and deep blue gaze, she would be lost.

"Charlotte."

Nothing.

Then she felt his lips touch her own. First, only a soft caress, then another more insistent kiss.

"Charlotte, the situation is not what it seems."

She knew he was talking about Helen Belgrave, and she wanted to believe him.

He kissed her again, deeply, thoroughly, and as he pulled away, his teeth caught at her lower lip for the briefest instant, making her stomach do a pleasant little flip.

"You know how I feel about you. There has been no pretense as far as that is concerned."

She needed to believe him. The trembling deep inside her, like coiled tigers ready to spring, was becoming a passion quite untamable. A passion ready to erupt.

"Please look at me, Charlotte." It was the husky tone to his voice that nearly got her. Then she felt the slightest nibble on her right earlobe, next to her pearl earring. It was all she could bear. The flames of desire roared through her.

Why not? she asked herself, keeping her eyes closed but snaking her arms around his neck. *Why shouldn't she feel this way, just for one night?* And then Helen Belgrave could have him back.

She shuddered. She could never do that, could she? But now he was kissing his way down the column of her neck. He reached the hollow of her throat, and she moaned softly and then felt him pull away.

Finally, Charlotte opened her eyes, and there was his fine face, his warm lips slightly open, his blue eyes gazing into her own. She licked her lips and heard him groan before his mouth crushed hers again beneath a kiss so fierce it would have frightened her if she hadn't been intent on returning it with equal ardor.

His arms came around her, gripping her to him, so tightly that the fine fabric of her dress was crushed against him where it strained across her instantly taut nipples. His hand cupped the back of her head, his fingers in the locks of her hair, compelling her lips against his as his tongue entered her mouth, plundering her sweetness. He tasted like fruit punch.

When he lifted his mouth from hers, the thunder in her head quieted a little until she opened her eyes again and looked into his. The desire she saw didn't alarm her. After all, it reflected her own burning need, which he'd so easily aroused. There was no denying the silky heat building in her core.

Charlotte was tired of hiding in her home, away from the life she only knew through books. Now she wanted to live it—to taste the excitement of being with a man, not as she had done the other day, but fully and completely, watching Reed take his pleasure as well. She had never felt more certain.

He brushed his knuckle ever so lightly against her dress, across her full aching breasts, perked expectantly under his gaze, and she was lost. The roar returned like a wind over the mountains.

"Reed," was all she could manage.

"God, help me, Charlotte," his voice was hoarse, and he punctuated the words by dropping kisses on her face, first her lips, then her temples, and stroking the sensitive skin along her neck. "I want you so much I won't be able to stop myself in another moment. You'd better run."

She didn't. She raised her hand to touch his cheek, before tracing the line of his sensual, strong lips.

He closed his eyes a moment, still fighting, but then he hesitated no longer. Standing, Reed pulled her with him. He was in the house in three long strides, pulling her along behind him.

At the bottom of the stairs, he swept her up in his arms, heading directly into her room at the other end of the hall from the children. Charlotte didn't even mind that she lost both her green slippers on the stairs.

He stood her down in the middle of her room where she'd dressed for the dance a few hours earlier. It seemed eons ago. The moonlight streamed through the paned window, illuminating her grandmother's oval mirror and her own four-poster bed.

She stared at it a moment and then went to draw the curtains, but Reed halted her.

"In this light, you're an emerald, a precious jewel."

Charlotte shivered at his tone and at his touch as he started to take out the clip that held her hair.

"Your hair is your crowning glory, and I want to feel it on my chest when I have you on top of me."

That did it! Her knees went weak, and she swayed toward him. By God, he was magnetic and she couldn't resist his intense pull.

He kissed her again, his fingers moving through her silken tresses that tumbled over her shoulders, softly scented with lavender perfume. And she returned his kiss with all her strength. She lost track of time as they simply devoured one another.

When his hands roamed up and down her back, she hummed her pleasure, until he paused, leaning his forehead against her own.

"Your gown is the loveliest creation I have ever seen, but I'm going to have to rip it off you if you don't stand still. Better yet, turn around."

With that, Reed spun her in his arms and lifted her hair over her shoulder. Having free access to her gown, he swiftly unhooked the fasteners, and she was soon standing in her petticoats, corset, and stockings. Another moment and her petticoats were also at her feet.

She stepped out of the green pool and turned slowly. Reed Malloy looked to be a man momentarily astounded, and Charlotte felt thrilled that she had inspired such an expression. His eyes lingered on the swell of her breasts, which were pushed up halfway above the trim white corset and the sleeveless chemise underneath.

"Lily picked out my stockings," she whispered, feeling instantly foolish. But then his gaze dropped to her white lace drawers and the sheerest white gossamer stockings.

"She has impeccable taste." His voice sounded thick with desire, as his intense gaze raised up to meet her own. "But then, I think you would look lovely wearing nothing at all."

Slowly, as he spoke, he slipped the suspenders over his broad shoulders, and then took off his collar and his white shirt. Both landed on the floor. Unlike two days earlier, Charlotte had time to notice the muscles that moved across his chest and that sculpted his upper arms. Then her eyes dropped to the trim line of his waist and below.

Swallowing, her mouth suddenly dry, she brought her gaze back from that path to his face. He didn't smile, kicking his shoes off toward the closed door. Only his trousers remained . . .

Charlotte held her breath. There was delicious terror and there was desperate anticipation warring within her. She was glad she had waited and not taken the tumble offered her by a neighboring boy when she was seventeen. But, by God, there had been a lot of years in between then and now when she had wished for a man to touch her.

She took a step forward, and Reed pulled her to him, sweeping her up against his body and letting her feel the hot hardness of his desire, before he lowered her gently to the bed.

The most handsome man I have ever seen evidently wants me the way I want him.

As he removed his black trousers and drawers, Charlotte shamelessly watched him. She'd had no idea!

"Man alive," she murmured at the sight of his manhood, proudly erect, and of Reed himself, unembarrassed by her frank stares. He joined her on the bed.

She tore her gaze from the mystery that she longed to fully understand and looked him in the eye.

"I'm a little frightened," she confessed.

He shook his dark head. "Just let me adore you."

She nodded, and he began to untie the ribbons that held up her stockings. He pushed the sheer fabric down her long, slim legs with sensual ease, one at a time.

For a moment, she had goose bumps from ankle to shoulder. Then he let his hands slide up her legs, pausing at the lace-trimmed drawers.

"Your corset," he said with grim determination and an audible sigh. His skilled hands loosened the laces and unfastened the hooks, before tossing the garment aside, and finally her breasts were loose against her hip-length cotton chemise. He drew it up above her navel.

Charlotte gasped as he tilted his head to kiss her smooth stomach, right above her lacey drawers.

"These have to go," he said. Untying the drawstring, he pushed them down over her slim hips.

"Reed," she exclaimed, feeling her face hot with embarrassment and excitement.

She heard his throaty laugh as he whisked away her chemise, baring her body to his gaze and his touch. She sighed when his hands closed over her breasts, relieving somewhat the building tension in her body. His mouth plucked tenderly at first one nipple and then the other.

This must be what heaven feels like, Charlotte thought. But the throbbing between her legs and the trembling in the pit of her stomach told her there was something more she needed.

Reed already seemed to know that, as without warning and with his mouth still teasing one breast, his hand slipped downward over her stomach and lower. When the warm palm of his hand closed over her woman's mound, her eyes flew open and her body arched against him of its own volition.

Reed lifted his head to kiss her lips, and while he touched the tip of her tongue with his own, he slipped his finger between the moist, hot petals at her core and touched the small bud that throbbed there.

She whimpered against his lips. The feel of his fingers and the scent of his warm skin overwhelmed all her senses. She was drugged by the heady sensations, unable to move even if she'd wanted to.

Not lifting his mouth from hers, Reed murmured, "You're exquisite, Charlotte Sanborn, and tonight, you're going to be mine." He kissed the edge of her lips and along her jaw, then moved to nibble on her earlobe.

"All mine," she heard him add, his voice husky with, she assumed, the same desire that kept her helpless under his touch.

Soon, she could think no more as the practiced rhythm of Reed's fingers and the scorching of his mouth on her skin drove all coherent thought out of her brain. She squeezed her eyes tightly closed and clenched his shoulders with her hands as he drove her wild.

Charlotte felt as if she were flying higher and higher. If he stopped the steady movement that echoed the imaginary beating of her spirit's wings, then she would collapse in agony.

He didn't stop, and there was a moment of fright as she thought she might disintegrate with the powerful shudders that wracked her. When it was over, she felt diffused with warmth washing over her limbs, which had gone liquid with the exertion of her own relaxing muscles.

Charlotte lifted her lids to find Reed looking at her with eyes blazing moonlit fire. She reached for him, both arms around his neck, and pulled him down. She kissed him gratefully, thoroughly.

He groaned against her lips, then was silent.

"Reed?" she queried, but she already had an inkling of what was causing him discomfort, for there had been moments in the last few minutes when the pleasure was something very close to pain, and if he had stopped before she'd finished . . .

She looked at him steadily before grasping hold of the firm protrusion—like flint encased in velvet—that pressed against her body. He shuddered and leaned down to kiss the damp tendril at her temple. Holding onto his throbbing shaft even more tightly, she stroked it cautiously. Once up, once down.

He actually growled. Raising himself on his hands, one muscled arm on either side of her, Reed parted her thighs with his knee and settled himself between them.

Resting on his forearms, his face mere inches above hers, his eyes held captive her own green gaze. Charlotte saw the query waiting there and smiled slightly. With that response, she felt Reed press against her warm cleft, where she was still damp and swollen with pleasure. Amazingly, although she'd thought herself satisfied mere moments before, she felt the wanting stir again.

"You've been there alone," he said softly, and she felt the tip of him enter her. "Now let's go there together."

She bit back her apprehensiveness as his arousal slid inside her a little farther. It was thrilling and fearsome at the same time. She felt a mild discomfort when he continued to press into her, and a flash of pain, like a bee sting, sent dazzling colors swirling before her eyes making her squirm.

"Christ!" he exclaimed, looking to Charlotte like a man restraining himself with great difficulty. "Don't move, woman, or I'll—"

But she continued to writhe involuntarily away from the burning discomfort.

He broke off his words, looked her straight in the eye, and embedded his shaft into her as a sword in its sheath, right up to the hilt. She cried out, unable to help herself, and he froze, the sweat now breaking out on his forehead.

"Are you all right?"

"I think so," she told him, the stinging already dissipating as her body adjusted and closed around his erection. "Will it hurt anymore?" she asked, feeling a little less enthusiastic.

"No," he fairly croaked, "I don't believe so." He rocked his hips, then stopped.

"All right?"

"All right," she answered, awed by the new sensation of being intimately joined to Reed. It was incredibly sensual, this hot fullness, this feeling of being stretched to the limit by his potent manhood. "More than all right," she whispered.

With that, he gave in to the passion between them, stroking slowly at first until she held on to his shoulders, urging him, demanding more. He increased the intensity, quickening his motion as the tension built for both of them.

Her body understood the ancient ritual better than her mind, for she was matching his rhythm with an easy lifting of her hips. Her hands roamed over his broad back, and she felt the sheen of dampness on his skin.

His hands were alternately in her hair, on her breasts, or wickedly, under her buttocks, squeezing and separating them as he rocked in and out. And then again, she started to soar, climbing higher and higher with each long stroke of him, deep insider her. Only this time, Reed was sharing the pleasure, locked together, as one.

When her quivering release came, it was answered by the shuddering of his own muscled frame, as he pressed into her again and again, filling her up with liquid heat. His mouth was against the damp skin of her neck, murmuring primitive words of passion.

Finally, he collapsed on top of her, spent and seemingly exhausted, before he rolled to the side.

When she returned to earth, her body calming for the second time, he was holding her in his strong arms, her head pillowed on his expansive chest. She felt him kiss the top of her head gently as she drifted into blackness.

CHAPTER THIRTEEN

Her eyes still closed, Charlotte stretched out her hand to touch Reed as she had done more than once in the night. This time, he was gone. Hearing the children outside, playing in the yard, she stretched and smiled and felt . . . tender . . . all over. Except her toes. She wiggled them. Nope, not sore. Then she listened for Reed's voice.

Creeping downstairs, feeling a little embarrassed, a little awkward, especially when she saw her green satin shoes lined up neatly in the front hall, she started to heat water. Still no Reed. Ten minutes later, she sank into a hot bath with relief. But Charlotte didn't linger too long.

Washing away the traces of their night diminished none of the memory that was burned into her brain. It had been a wonderful night. She looked at her naked reflection in her grandmother's mirror. *And I don't regret it for a moment. I am an unrepentant sinner.*

Her body looked different to her that morning as she considered it through Reed's eyes, a thing of beauty and pleasure.

"Perhaps he doesn't find Mrs. Belgrave to be so desirable," she told her reflection.

After dressing with care in her best day frock, she made her way down the stairs once again. Her office, empty. Parlor, empty. She proceeded to the dining room and the kitchen in turn, both empty. Then she went outside, learning from Lily that Reed had come downstairs full chisel and pulled foot for the stables. That was nearly an hour earlier.

He'd gone straight to town. *To Helen Belgrave*, her mind concluded.

Charlotte felt a slight sickness in her stomach. He'd gone straight from her bed to his fiancée without even a good-bye. Had he taken his possessions already? She turned hurriedly toward the house.

"Aunt Charlotte," Lily's voice stopped her, "wasn't his friend beautiful?"

She nodded and tried to smile normally. Then Thomas piped up, borrowing Lily's word from the night before, "A pincess."

"That's *princess*, Thomas, with an 'r.' Have you had your breakfast?" Charlotte asked, wondering if her voice sounded as strained as she felt.

They had, so she was free to run upstairs and check his room. Astoundingly, his belongings were still there. So, he *was* coming back.

While cursing herself for being a silly romantic, she couldn't deny she was relieved he hadn't simply ridden out of her life for good. Although it wouldn't be any less than she deserved if he had. She had behaved outrageously, like an adventuress from one of Denver's infamous brothels.

Charlotte stood a moment at the top of the stairs. *What to do? How to pass the time until he returned?* While she made tea, she cut a thick slice of bread and buttered it absently.

Let me adore you, he'd said. Perhaps he had meant more than the physical act. Perhaps he hadn't. Reed had wanted her beyond reason, past the ability to stop. He must not feel that way about Helen Belgrave, or he would have spent the night with her.

However, it was hard to hold onto that belief as she sat in the dining room listening to the ticking of the clock on the mantle, trying to quell the uneasy feelings inside her—the guilt mixed with happiness mixed with wonder mixed with sadness.

So much for no regret, she thought.

And then there was the nagging fear that what they'd done would have long-reaching effects. She hadn't even considered the delicate matter of protection, but then, it seemed, neither had he.

And thus, she waited, stirring her now cold tea, unable to think about working, unable to stop thinking about their night together. Her ears strained at every noise, waiting to hear the sound of his horse's hooves. And finally, it came.

She heard Reed greet the children, and she got to her feet. She heard him on the back steps and then coming along the passageway, and she sat down again. Then he halted at her study, obviously looking for her, and finally, he appeared at the dining room doorway.

"Hello," he said, sounding normal, yet he stood there hesitantly and said nothing else.

For her part, Charlotte found she'd lost her voice at the sight of him.

"May I come in?"

She must have nodded for he came in the room slowly and sat across from her.

"Reed."

"Charlotte."

They both spoke at once. He smiled at her. She blushed at their first prolonged eye contact, and her skin seemed to prickle in every spot that he had touched or kissed. She set down her spoon.

"I know that you have a life far from my homestead," she began slowly, "a life to which you must return. I knew you would, sooner or later. Return to your life, that is." She knew she was beginning to babble and stopped herself, trying hard to focus on the important issue at hand.

She'd reached a decision. She'd had all morning to consider and to reconsider as she'd sat waiting for Reed. Perhaps her choice had been determined by the fear she'd felt at the dance when she thought someone had come by train to take Thomas and Lily away.

Perhaps she'd made her choice even sooner but had been too scared to admit it. In any case, Charlotte knew that, with some alteration to her life, she could become an adequate mother to her cousins.

"I've decided to go whole hog and keep the children. Thomas and Lily may stay with me. Your duty is done as executor of my cousin's will. You can go." It came out all in a rush and sounded imperious even to her own ears, but once said, she took a steadying sip of lukewarm tea.

Reed stared at her. "Do you honestly want the children, or are you saying that to get rid of me?"

What an odd question, she thought. Why would *she* want to get rid of *him?* Then she realized he was smiling. She took a deep breath and relaxed.

"I have come to love my cousin's children, and I will give them a good home." As it turned out, her love had come as easily as breathing, both for Thomas and Lily . . . and for Reed.

"I'm glad you feel that way."

However, he didn't sound as she had imagined he would. This meant the end of his business here. He could return to Boston, knowing he'd fulfilled his commitment to Ann Connors.

"I believe you and the children are good for each other," he added. "If you raise them to be anything like yourself, then you'll be doing just fine."

She nodded, accepting the compliment and acknowledging that she would enjoy having a purpose to living, other than her writing. But still, her heart ached a little, knowing nothing would be the same when it was only the three of them. She *could* live without Reed Malloy. Clearly, she would have to. And the sooner she started, the better.

"I went to town this morning. I didn't want to awaken you," Reed continued, his voice lowering.

Even so, she looked nervously over her shoulder, fearing Lily or Thomas might hear him.

"I went to see John . . . and Helen."

Charlotte abruptly pushed her chair away from the table, knocking over what was left of her tea as she did. *It was all too civilized.* First, discussing the children as if they were livestock instead of people. And now, chatting about his fiancée when he had recently deflowered Charlotte and given her the most incredible night of her life. She wasn't worldly by half to handle this.

"I'll get a towel," she pronounced over her shoulder as she dashed out of the room.

"Charlotte," he called after her, but she was practically running. The tea stain be damned, she decided, and kept on going, down the hall and out the back door. She didn't slow her pace until she was out of the yard and heading across the adjoining field of wildflowers.

It struck her that she'd done exactly what Reed had told her to do—shed her wallflower façade and experience a little more out of life. But at what cost?

Hearing him call her name again, she knew he was coming after her. She also knew it was useless. She didn't want to face what they'd done the previous night . . . willingly . . . and more than once. And she didn't want Reed to tell her whatever he'd discussed with his fiancée that morning.

He was close behind her now, and with the sun on her face and her lungs gasping, she finally stopped and stood completely still except for the rising and falling of her chest.

"Charlotte," he said again. She didn't turn completely, but she could tell he was out of breath, too, by the way he was bent over with his hands on his knees. She wanted to touch him and say, "You're it, Mr. Malloy." But this was no game.

When he reached out to touch her, she let him. But as soon as Reed's fingers closed on her arm, she felt her body react. A simple touch and she wanted to kiss him. Instead, she jerked her arm free.

"Do I have to hear about your morning trot into town to be with Helen Belgrave? I hope you took your fiancée to Mrs. Cassidy's. It's the best breakfast in town. And I hope she choked on her eggs."

"She's gone."

"I thought I could handle one night with you, and the good Lord knows what you think of me now! What kind of woman does what I did, knowing there is no future for us? Or maybe that's normal for some women of your acquaintance, and you expected it. But it's not normal for me, and it's certainly not customary for me to meet a man's fiancée and then let him in my bed, but I—"

"I said she's gone." His voice was quiet, but this time she heard him. She stopped mid-sentence with her mouth open. His words made no sense.

"What do you mean 'gone'? Your fiancée came all the way across the country, filled with worry for you—"

"I thought you wanted her to choke on her eggs."

Was he finding amusement in all this?

"You sent her away after one night! And you didn't even spend it with her. If you were my fiancé, I would not put up with it. Not with your flirting with idiot girls in the country, nor dancing with them, not to mention kissing and bedding them. And as for your going off for weeks and then sending me packing, why if I was your fiancée—"

"If *you* were my fiancée, you would not have to worry about my going off for weeks or dallying with other women. Because I would be right beside you, like this." He took her in his arms and pulled her close.

"And I would not be kissing anyone but you, like this." With his hand on her chin, he tilted her head slightly, taking her mouth under his with a firm pressure, before tugging on her lower lip with his teeth.

Unable to stop the moan that escaped her, Charlotte responded without even considering the matter. She had no conscience, no morals, no shame! Then Reed's gentle laugh invaded her senses, and she pushed him away, undoubtedly wearing an indignant expression on her face while gasping for the air her lungs needed.

"Oh, beautiful Charlotte, I'm not laughing at you," he promised. "I'm absolutely delighted and deeply honored I was the one to discover what's underneath the aloofness you project to the world." He reached for her again.

"You are such a warm, vivacious woman who flares up at my touch and inflames my own passions. All I want to do now is lay you down on the grass, pull your dress up around your waist, spread your silken thighs and—"

"Stop, Reed, please." She was beet red from her toes to the roots of her hair. "What about Mrs. Belgrave?" Charlotte hated to bring her up again, especially since the woman's name was as ice water on a blazing fire. Reed shrugged and dropped his hand from her arm.

"Helen and I will talk more later. And besides, she's not my fiancée."

Charlotte's mouth was open again. The infernal man had her head spinning.

"*Not* your fiancée?"

"Not really."

"How is someone *not really* your fiancée?"

"No formal engagement was ever made," he admitted. "I've never asked for her hand. I tried to explain to you last night, first at the dance and then on your porch. She and I had an understanding." He ran his hand through his hair.

"At least, I thought we did, although it is becoming increasingly less understandable by the moment. I told her last night at the hotel that she shouldn't have come and that our arrangement is over."

She blinked up at him. *Last night.* Charlotte made a mental note that she had not gone to bed with a betrothed man, even though she hadn't known that at the time.

"This morning, we talked," he said hesitantly, and Charlotte couldn't believe that conversation transpired without heartbreak and hullabaloo. "In the end, I put her on the train to St. Louis. Helen has a sister there whom she intends to visit on the way home."

Home, Boston, close to Reed. Charlotte doubted that Mrs. Belgrave would simply bow quietly out of his life. She could probably be quite convincing when she put her mind to it, especially if her reputation were at stake.

"She is known as your fiancée? I mean, in Boston? She introduced herself as such, and John confirmed it."

"Yes, we're acknowledged as a couple," he admitted. "I suppose it's assumed we will marry eventually. She favors the lifestyle I keep, and the society I move in. Truthfully, over the past year or so, I believe she preferred our lifestyle far more than I did. But Helen knew we were a pragmatic couple at best, useful to each other."

"Useful?" Charlotte repeated, thinking of many uses Reed could have for a woman such as Helen.

"No, you goose," he said, plainly reading her thoughts. "Having Helen on my arm kept every mother with a girl of marriageable age from calling at my door, leaving cards, sending invitations, and assaulting me at functions. She has played her part perfectly and warned off any number of women—"

"You have been much burdened by pursuit," Charlotte said, her voice dripping with the sarcasm she felt.

Reed's sigh was audible. "For many men, it wouldn't be the worst encumbrance, I know, but for a previously confirmed bachelor." He shrugged.

"Why a bachelor, Reed?"

Her quick blunt question caught him off guard. She could see it in the vulnerable expression overtaking his features. Then he visibly relaxed. "Why? Because no woman ever measured up to the first female I loved, besides my mother, of course."

Charlotte's eyes opened wide. She had not expected that. "Was it very painful? When you broke up, I mean?"

He looked grave. "It was always painful. She used to pummel me mercilessly, lecture me, demonstrate my lesser intelligence by constantly showing me up in front of my father. But we have never broken up."

Charlotte gasped just before she realized he was jesting. He laughed. "I speak of my oldest sister, Elise, now married and with two babes of her own."

She did not miss for an instant how he had quickly sidestepped the issue of why he preferred bachelorhood.

"So, this . . . relationship with Mrs. Belgrave is a platonic one?" Charlotte asked, willing now to know the whole truth. She'd come this far, and all his answers had been less painful than she'd anticipated.

While looking directly at her without guilt, still, he had the grace to flush slightly with embarrassment. "I am a grown man, Charlotte, and Helen is not without her charms."

Charlotte cringed at that, having seen precisely how physically charming Helen was, and not wanting to think of Reed doing with her what they had done.

"The answer to your rather indelicate question," he continued, "is that I have not been a monk, and Helen Belgrave has not minded an occasional tryst, not that she seems to gain the same pleasure from my touch as you do."

Oh, God, he was comparing them! She covered her ears with her hands. "How can you say such things aloud?"

"Well, how can you ask such things?" he sounded angry now. "I am not a young boy. I am a man with desires and urges like every man. I am not in love with Helen Belgrave, nor have I ever been. And although I have taken her to my bed," he added, "I did not take her innocence."

"Obviously not," Charlotte snapped. "She was a widow." He raised his eyebrow and she remembered what John Trelaine had said about the aged Mr. Belgrave. It was possible that Helen Belgrave had come out of her marriage as pure as she'd gone into it, however pure that was.

Charlotte shook her head. It made no difference to her if Mrs. Belgrave had gone to her marriage bed already deflowered or if Reed had made her a merry widow. Indeed, if Charlotte were to marry tomorrow, she would no longer be the exemplification of innocence either.

"I should not be discussing the lady in question," Reed said, "and I wouldn't with anyone but you. She has been a good diversion at times, even a companion. However, despite our supposed engagement, when it comes down to it, she is not the kind of woman with whom I want to spend my life."

Reed frowned. "Not her or any of her kind. However, I am sure there are many men who would be happy to have her. And now," he said pointedly, "I don't wish to discuss her further." He crossed his arms.

Charlotte looked up at him. Suddenly, she wanted to be alone in her quiet study to consider his words, improper though they'd been for him to utter. The idea that he would ever discuss her virginity with anyone was beyond bearing, but she trusted he wouldn't.

As for the rest of it, she had known he was an intelligent man from the first few moments they met. She'd even sensed he could be persuasive, if not downright manipulative, and that he used those powers in his profession. However, she hadn't before thought of him as coldly calculating. Yet, surely he would have to be exactly that in order to maintain a relationship with a woman for three years merely to keep others away, and then to dismiss her so quickly and so callously.

He had a hard look about him now, staring at her with those sapphire-blue eyes and considering. When he took a step closer, she retreated.

"The children," she said lamely, turning toward the house. Good Lord, she'd almost forgotten about them, playing so close by in the front yard. So far, she did not rate her mothering skills very highly for the day. Her brain felt as if it was made of oatmeal.

"Yes, the children." His tone turned serious, as he fell into step beside her. "As I said, I'm relieved you'll be raising them. I know, after seeing you with them, that it's for the best. However, John and I had a talk this morning over breakfast. He confirmed what I feared—their grandmother has threatened to contest the will."

Charlotte started to protest, but he interrupted. "For now, they are yours as specified by their mother, and you should act accordingly. I don't believe a judge will override Ann's wishes in any case, given Alicia's age. However," he paused and made her stop beside him.

"What?" she queried, not liking the seriousness of his expression.

"It would be best if it did not become known that a single man was staying with you. Morally, you must be above question."

She should have been angry. She should have told him that it seemed a bit late for his consideration along those lines. After all, it would be no thanks to him if anyone did question her morals.

Instead, she asked the question uppermost in her mind, "You'll be leaving soon, then?"

He nodded. "On tomorrow morning's train with John. I'll stay at the hotel tonight," he added, glancing away from her. But then he faced her. "I have to return to my law practice before clients begin to wonder whether I still represent them or not. As John reminded me this morning, I've got responsibilities elsewhere."

Breathe normally, keep calm, she told herself, fighting to quell the desperate sadness that seized hold of her like a fist squeezing her heart. Not even one more night with him. She put her hand up in pretense of shielding her eyes from the sun. In reality, she couldn't meet his gaze for fear he would see the emotions there.

What if he pitied her? Soon, it would be exactly as before. No man's razor on the washstand, no male laughter, no one to lean on when she felt the need, no warm touch. But she would have two wonderful children.

"We'd better return, or Lily and Thomas will wonder where we've gone." She started to walk again.

"Charlotte," he grabbed her hand and held on. "I don't know when we'll have a private moment again, and I want to address what you said earlier about what I think of you."

She lowered her gaze to the ground, feeling the heat creep up her neck once more. He raised her chin with his other hand and looked into her verdant eyes.

"What happened between us was unusual, not only for you, but for me, too. In fact, it was extraordinary."

When he had brought a timid smile to her face, he continued, "I have never for a moment thought of you as anything less than the most intelligent, most upstanding lady I have ever met. I also know you are keeping a passionate spirit held tightly in check, and I wish I could stay to coax her out again."

"As do I," she said, with complete honesty. "But you have a life in Boston, and I knew that from the beginning."

"And I asked you to consider coming there," he reminded her.

She could not lie at that moment. "This is all I have ever known, Reed. I would be lost. Nothing much scares me these days," *except being haunted by the thought of your touch for the rest of my life,* she thought. "But starting over in the city seems overwhelmingly frightening. I have never used my sex as an excuse, but I am sure it would not be easy for a woman alone."

"You are all of twenty-four, let me remind you, not seventy-four. Your own life is just starting. However, I understand your desire to stay where your family raised you. You must have close ties to this land. I would feel the same about being asked to leave New England. But if you ever change your mind, I would be more than happy to . . . ," he trailed off.

She sensed he was battling with something more he wanted to say. She watched him take a deep breath and run his hand through his thick hair. Then in a quick movement, Reed brushed his thumb over her slightly parted lips. "I would be happy to help you settle there and to introduce you into Boston's social circles."

It was not the impassioned plea she might have hoped for, nor was it liable to change her mind.

Later, she sat on the porch swing where he had kissed her so fervently the night before, and she replayed his words. If he'd said them differently, if he'd asked her to move east for his own sake, she would probably do it—and full chisel at that, confessing how little love she felt for this house where she'd known so much loneliness since she was young.

Indeed, if he'd made it sound as though she would hold a special place in his life and not merely be someone he would introduce to others in order to make her feel welcome, she would not have hesitated. If only . . .

She shook her head at her own romantic notions. Hadn't he kept company with Helen Belgrave specifically to ward off marriage seekers? Why would she fancy he could want to tie himself down now to a wife and children?

Reed had dropped her hand as they'd approached the house. It had not taken him long to pack. Both Thomas and Lily cried. Since their mother's death, he had been their sole constant. He hugged both the children long and hard and promised to write to them.

"Mind your Aunt Charlotte, both of you," he said, his gaze going over their heads, locked on hers.

Charlotte couldn't speak with the lump of tears balled in her throat. She could only listen carefully to his words, noticing the mistiness in his own blue eyes as he ruffled Thomas's hair and squeezed Lily's small hand.

She was surprised when, in front of the children, he hugged her—it was firm and quick—and then he was gone. He'd given no intimation he would return, even for a visit. After all, she reminded herself, ultimately, this was simply business.

Although Reed Malloy had let it get personal, she had a feeling he would now consider the entire adventure to be a task accomplished. He had disappeared down the road in the vehicle he'd rented from Spring City's livery, leaving her and the children in a cloud of gloom.

Charlotte realized she would have to do something and fast. "You know what this means?" They shook their heads, looking morose. "Well," she said, taking each one by the hand. "You each get your own room. And we're going to start rearranging them right now, precisely how you want them."

Their trunks would be arriving in less than a week, thanks to Reed's promise to wire Boston before he left. He would also deposit a sum of money in Charlotte's account for their upkeep. Money would arrive at regular intervals, and she was to send him a telegraph message if there was an emergency.

It all seemed to have worked out so perfectly, except her heart was on the train heading east with a man who hadn't asked for it.

Gently, she swung and closed her eyes, laying her hands over her stomach. She had found, after Reed left, a package on her bed containing one pre-filled syringe containing a solution marketed to "married ladies." She knew what it was for, knew what it contained, mostly vinegar and lemon juice. She should use it as soon as possible, just in case, but so far, she'd done nothing but put the note that accompanied it into her jewelry box:

Charlotte, I didn't intend to be careless. Please forgive me. If anything should occur, let me know immediately.
Yours, Reed

Continuing to rock, she looked up at the stars. For the time being, her passionate spirit, as Reed had called it, was doomed to stay hidden from the rest of the world, for the one man whom she cared to share it with would soon be thousands of miles away.

CHAPTER FOURTEEN

1884, Boston, Massachusetts

*D*earest Charlotte,

I find myself with the unpleasant task of once more writing to you for other than a joyful purpose. I hope this matter will not turn out to be as serious as the death of my dearly beloved daughter, Ann.

While you are by birth a Sanborn, as your mother's daughter, I have always considered you a Randall. Thus, I take for granted that you hold a virtuous life in the highest esteem. It is, therefore, unthinkable to me that certain sordid allegations, which I shall not set down in writing, are anything other than balderdash.

However, as these contentions come from a seemingly reliable source, I have no other recourse, Charlotte, but to request that you and my grandchildren come at once to Boston for at least a temporary visitation.

During that time, I am convinced this matter can be resolved. How could I rest if I did otherwise than to make sure my grandchildren are situated in a household of the highest morality?

I should not like to be forced to use legal measures to defy my daughter's last wishes, however ill-advised I think them to be, nor do I want our family thrust into the public eye. Nevertheless, I shall do what is necessary on behalf of my only grandchildren. I look forward to your timely response.

Yrs. with all due love,
Alicia Winifred Elms Randall

Charlotte lowered the letter to the cloth-covered table in the train's dining car. She had read and reread Alicia Randall's words, but the result was still the same. She and the children were on the long journey to Boston.

She hadn't given herself time to think about what she was doing, or to change her mind. Precisely three days after receiving the letter, with an excited child holding each of her hands, she boarded the train heading east. They eagerly looked forward to returning "home," as they still referred to Boston, even though it had been a month since Reed left. And Charlotte felt she could not delay the trip. Everything had to be settled when school started in the fall.

Before leaving Spring City, she had sent two telegrams, one to her aunt telling her she was coming for the requested visit, and one to Reed explaining she would be arriving in Boston and why. She didn't want him to think she was following him for any reason other than the children. Still, her heart grew lighter knowing they would soon be in the same city.

Folding up the letter, she returned it to her bag. Charlotte's first emotion had been anger that her aunt would listen to rumors, especially when she realized the only possible source had to be Helen Belgrave. No one else with eastern connections, except possibly John Trelaine, knew where Reed had stayed during his visit to Spring City, and no one else would particularly care.

She alone had grappled with the worry after her uninhibited night with Reed, until two weeks after his departure when she'd received her monthly flow. At least then, the only serious repercussion of their union was her own melancholy.

As she watched the children finish their meals, Charlotte knew that going east to face her aunt was the right decision.

Even though Ann Connors had thought her cousin's life suitable for her own children, perhaps she'd been under the misconception Charlotte lived a more interesting existence, more in touch with the centers of advancement and learning, in a real city even. Not a small, dried up town that had outlived its usefulness as a miner's haven.

Perhaps Alicia Randall *could* give the children a better start in life. Or perhaps Charlotte could do that herself . . . in Boston, if she could prove to her aunt she was fit to raise them.

However, when she ran into Reed Malloy, as she surely would, it was going to be far harder to maintain a semblance of propriety where he was concerned. And what if she liked it there? Then, Charlotte supposed, she would put down new roots and stay.

As she chewed on a buttered roll, she hoped she wasn't fooling herself, using Alicia Randall's threat as an excuse to follow a certain attractive lawyer. After all, he had warned her that her aunt might contest the will. He'd also thought, in all likelihood, the older woman would lose. Charlotte knew she really should have nothing to worry about. But had Reed taken into account the possibility of their brief impropriety reaching Alicia's ears, not to mention a judge's?

Charlotte went over and over the questions in her head, for three long days. They took the Topeka & Santa Fe railroad to St. Louis, seeing Dodge City, the capital of the cattle industry, and Kansas City along the way.

At St. Louis, Charlotte might have rested a day, but all she could think about was Helen Belgrave having stopped in that town to see her sister. Now, the woman was spreading malicious tales, albeit true, possibly all over Boston.

She and the children kept moving, switching to the Baltimore & Ohio railroad to the east coast. They chugged through Baltimore, Philadelphia, and New York.

By the time they reached Boston's Providence Railroad depot, Charlotte felt ready to take on Reed Malloy, Helen Belgrave, and Aunt Alicia Randall, all at once. Unfortunately, none of the three appeared to meet them at the station.

She chided herself for not getting confirmation of her telegram. *What if no one knew they were here?* She'd be forced to make her way with the children and their trunks all the way across town to Beacon Hill. She didn't even know how to secure a brougham or how much it would cost.

Just as her fears were mounting, she spotted the familiar figure of John Trelaine coming toward them through the bustling crowd like an answer to her prayers.

"Thank goodness I didn't miss you, Miss Sanborn," he said, taking the carpet bag she was carrying. "I was held up in traffic. I have my coach waiting."

"That is most kind of you, Mr. Trelaine. I was not expecting you to meet us." Since she did not want to say whom she was expecting, she closed her mouth.

"How was your journey?" he asked politely.

"Long and tiring. We couldn't get a hotel car on such short notice but we did secure a sleeper. It was an adventure, to say the least." She looked down at her charges. They resembled how they'd looked the day Reed first showed up on her doorstep, weary and slightly dusty, yet without that desperately lost look. Instead, they were bolstered by their enthusiasm for having returned to the city they knew.

"I assume you've got baggage?" John's voice broke into her thoughts.

"Yes, a fair amount, I'm afraid." The children giggled at this. They had insisted on bringing much of what had been sent out to Spring City a few weeks earlier, not wanting to be without many of their belongings again.

"I'll speak with the porter, and we'll get it all sent to your aunt's. That is where you intend to stay, is it not?"

She assured him he was correct, and in a flash, he had sorted everything out with the porter. Another vehicle was procured to take their trunks straight to Alicia's residence on Chestnut Street.

"Mrs. Randall contacted my office and apologized for not coming herself, but she is not up to all the commotion."

"Oh, that's quite all right, Mr. Trelaine." She smiled at him, "We'll be under her scrutiny soon enough."

He offered her a sympathetic glance. They were traveling at a slow pace through the city, passing parks and long avenues. The streets were all cobblestone. *Not a dirt road in sight,* thought Charlotte. *And the sidewalks were solid granite!* From the train window, she felt she'd seen enough wonders to last a lifetime, but now, the whole city was a new and exciting adventure for her to explore at her leisure. That brought to mind the man who was never far from her thoughts, the one who'd offered to show her his home town.

"I half expected Mr. Malloy to meet us, given his interest in the children," she mentioned, hoping not to sound too disappointed.

John looked uncomfortable, appearing to be exceptionally interested in their route. He pointed out the dome of the State House as they approached Beacon Hill.

"Recently covered in gold leaf," he added proudly, as the sun struck it, momentarily dazzling them. Charlotte was already so overwhelmed by the height of the buildings—many of them over five stories—that she merely put her hand up to shield her eyes as she gawked at this new wonder. Then he cleared his throat.

"The truth is Miss Sanborn, Reed never received your telegram. He had already left town when it arrived."

"Oh, well, in that case, I appreciate even more your coming to the station." Undeniably, Boston had lost a little of its appeal now she knew Reed was away.

"Miss Sanborn—" he began.

"Please, call me Charlotte."

"Only if you will call me John."

The children, sitting quietly on the seat opposite laughed at this exchange, and Reed's partner flushed. He started again.

"Charlotte, there is more. Reed was on his way to Spring City."

His words echoed in her head until they finally made sense, except they didn't. Not a bit.

"Whatever for?" she asked, as the absurd image of their trains passing each other on the open prairie popped into her head. Moreover, her heart started to beat a little faster. Anything to do with business, Reed would have handled by telegraph or regular correspondence.

"I'm afraid there is nothing more I can tell you. Reed will explain when he returns, I'm sure."

Charlotte opened her mouth to speak but was startled by a harsh voice in her ear: "Scissors to grind!" Her head snapped to her right to see a small man with gnarled hands and a portable grinder on the pavement, very close to the carriage, plying his trade of blade sharpening. She took a deep breath, but John didn't let her speak.

"Please don't ask me any questions. I know it would not sit well with Reed were I to say anything more. Not that I know anything more." He was silent again as his driver maneuvered their carriage through the traffic.

"I have endeavored to reach Reed by leaving messages at stations along the route, and he is probably already on his way back." The coach made another swift turn onto a small street that sloped gently upward.

"Grandma's," Lily burst out, recognizing her surroundings as the two horses pulled them steadily up Chestnut Street, and there wasn't time for any more questions.

Charlotte looked along the discreetly elegant road with all the homes pressed closely together. It had brick sidewalks and gaslights at every corner.

About halfway up the incline, their carriage halted, and she gazed at the narrow but imposing four-story brick structure that Lily pointed out as Alicia Randall's. At a second-story window, Charlotte was certain she saw the heavy rose-colored curtains move aside and then close once more.

Knowing that her family had never been welcome there after her mother married her father, Charlotte wondered what her reception would be now. Alicia was her mother's older sister by twelve years, but she was also a stranger. Still, after coming all that way, it was hardly the time to hesitate.

Moments later, she climbed the six steps to the arched front door, which opened before they had time to knock. They were ushered into the pink marble foyer by a stooped and grizzled man with enormous white eyebrows.

To him, Charlotte said a quiet, "Good day."

Beyond the butler, coming down the stairs was Alicia Randall, short in stature, slightly broad around her waist and hips, and dressed in matte black crape, in mourning for her daughter. She looked nearly exactly as Charlotte had expected— except for her gray-streaked hair styled high upon her head, with ringlets and curls that were clearly not her own, spiraling down the sides. The impression was at odds with the conservative Bostonian Charlotte had envisioned from her aunt's letters.

As she got closer, it was Alicia's eyes that captured Charlotte's attention, flashing in the same vivid green as her own and as her mother's.

"Charlotte, dear," her aunt said, extending a hand.

Charlotte grasped it in both her own as her aunt leaned forward to kiss the air between them.

"You do have the look of my sister, poor sweet girl that she was. I have never forgiven your father for taking Regina away to that barbaric Colorado territory."

It didn't seem to be an auspicious opening, and Charlotte braced herself before replying, "It was her choice to marry my father, and her choice to go." She tried not to sound disrespectful, but she wanted to make it firmly known from the start that she would not tolerate hearing her father abused. She knew he had tried his best and had loved her mother dearly.

"He always spoke highly of you, Aunt Alicia," she added, stretching the truth like warm caramel.

"Yes, well, he knew a good woman when he saw one," her aunt said, mollified. "Let me see these children." They moved shyly forward and stood in front of her, lined up as they had apparently been taught to do.

"Hm. Lillian, I think you have grown."

Charlotte almost laughed. The older lady's tone bordered on disapproval as if the girl had done so without permission.

"Thomas, you are the spitting image of your father." That was sweet Charlotte thought, until Alicia added, "I don't know how I shall bear it."

"Are you all famished? I've held up the mid-day meal for you. Everyone, upstairs to wash and change." Alicia clapped her hands together as she discharged her orders. "We'll be eating in the dining room in fifteen minutes. Gerald, show my niece and my grandchildren to their rooms," she added, turning to the old man.

Charlotte let herself be ordered around for the moment, only wishing John had stayed for the meal instead of begging off with pressing business. She walked behind the shuffling Gerald, up the gently curving stairs at the end of the foyer and along a hallway, lined on one side by paintings. On the other side was the staircase to the next level.

Insisting on seeing the children's rooms before her own, she climbed to the third floor. Reed had been correct about her aunt's lack of understanding for childlike frivolity. If the rooms in Spring City had been basic at best, Alicia Randall's idea of a child's room was downright grim. The dark furniture with heavy bed hangings, even heavier curtains, and dark-patterned wallpaper did nothing to inspire youthful joy, nor to chase away the melancholy over being left as orphans.

As soon as they unpacked their trunks after lunch, their own things would brighten up the staid rooms, Charlotte assured herself.

Gerald was standing at the bottom of the stairs when she descended. He led her along the hallway, opening the door to her room and gesturing her inside with his gloved hand.

"Miss," he said, with a slight bow.

She stepped inside and turned to thank him, but the door was already clicking closed. She surveyed her surroundings and whistled, sounding as Reed had done when seeing her in her emerald green dress.

To say it was grand would be an understatement. Unlike Thomas who had hurled himself into the middle of his large canopied bed, Charlotte was afraid to sit on the silk cover that had nary a wrinkle.

Placing her best bonnet and her mantelet across the heart-shaped chair by one window, she went out onto the private balcony that led off her bedroom through paned-glass doors.

She was glad to see she was at the rear of the house, overlooking the small garden and the brick stables and carriage house. What a peaceful place it seemed, although right then, there was no time to linger.

Going back inside, she looked at herself in the mirror above the mahogany dresser. Alicia had said to change, but her clothes were still packed away, her trunk not even yet in the room. However, she spied an ivory-handled comb, which she used to tidy stray wisps of hair that had come down from her inelegant topknot.

There was cool water in the chamber set's pretty flowered pitcher, and she poured some into the large bowl residing on its own mahogany stand. After washing her face and hands, she patted her hair once more, this time with damp palms, before going downstairs.

Directed by Bridget, her aunt's personal maid who greeted her at the foot of the stairs, Charlotte headed to the dining room. She could hear the children had got there before her, already regaling their grandmother with tales of the West.

As she entered the room, with its enormous fireplace and huge crystal chandelier, Charlotte cringed to hear them talking about Reed and her dancing.

"How interesting," Alicia said, her eyes fixed on Charlotte, who took a seat next to Thomas at the highly polished table with its lace runner and thick placemats.

Charlotte returned the older woman's gaze without flickering. If this was to be a test of wills, she would not bow, not even to her imperious aunt, who was seated so regally at the head of the table. Lily sat opposite Charlotte on her grandmother's left, and a young woman of about sixteen years was busy serving the food.

As they began to eat, out of politeness, they fell silent for a few minutes, enjoying the full fare of vegetable soup, roast chicken, cutlets, potatoes and green beans with gravy. It was a welcome change from the train and hotel food they'd been eating.

"I've invited a new acquaintance of mine to tea tomorrow afternoon," Alicia said, when their appetites were nearly sated.

Charlotte smiled politely, wiping gravy off Thomas's chin, while a serving girl filled her coffee cup. "Thank you, ah . . . ?"

"I'm Lacey, miss," the girl responded, her thick Irish brogue sounding exotic to Charlotte's ears.

"Yes, I believe you've met her," Alicia continued as if her servant hadn't spoken.

It was the way she said *her* that gained Charlotte's undivided attention and clued her in as to whom the guest might be. Inwardly. she groaned, but outwardly, she continued to fuss with Thomas, letting nothing of her agitation show.

Alicia looked peeved when Charlotte didn't ask her acquaintance's identity, but that didn't stop her aunt from saying in a triumphant voice, "Yes, a Mrs. Helen Belgrave, a congenial woman who recently came calling. I believe she is a friend of my late daughter's lawyer."

"Yes, I believe so," was all Charlotte said. So, the inquisition would start almost immediately, and Alicia was bringing in the star witness.

Despite a sinking feeling, she managed to drink her coffee, finish her last bite of potatoes, and push a few runner beans around her plate. Lily and Thomas resumed their tales of Spring City, the train ride, and every thought that popped into their heads.

"The children should probably have a rest and then we can unpack," Charlotte said, pushing out her chair. "Tomorrow, they're going to show me their city. Isn't that right, Lily?"

The little girl agreed, although her grandmother looked as if she would make some protest. Charlotte leveled her gaze on her.

After all, she was their legal guardian, at least for the time being. Nevertheless, she could be kind about it.

"Would you care to accompany us?"

"Oh no, dear. Nothing out there I haven't seen before. We'll find something else we can do together, perhaps a carriage ride or an evening at the opera. I do want to spend time with you, dear," Alicia added, "and really get to know you."

And dig into my personal life as much as possible, Charlotte silently concluded, standing up and taking Thomas's hand.

"As for tomorrow's sightseeing," Alicia continued, "I must insist you postpone it, at least for a day. We have much to do. First, we need to outfit you with a whole new wardrobe, appropriate for the city, posthaste by the look of it," she added with a glance over Charlotte from head to foot.

"And you'll need all sorts of accoutrements. At the end of the week, we're going to a little party at the Tremont House."

"A little party?" Charlotte repeated. The thought of being thrust so soon into Boston's society drove out of her head any question about what *accoutrements* she could possibly need.

"Well, I confess," Alicia said, "it's more of a ball. You do dance, don't you? Of course you do," she added pointedly, no doubt reminded that her niece and grandchildren had been dancing in a barn. Then more wistfully, she added, "My sister was an excellent dancer."

Then her aunt gave Charlotte a small smile. "It is a special occasion, having Regina's oldest child finally come home after all these years. My friends are dying to meet you, and this is a splendid opportunity. Of course, I shall maintain my mourning and not dance, but that needn't stop you from entering society."

Charlotte thought her aunt's welcome would be lukewarm at best. Instead, Alicia seemed to be rolling out a royal red carpet. And Charlotte could perfectly well imagine herself falling flat on that carpet, in front of all of Boston.

"Aunt Alicia, I don't think this is such a good idea. At least, not so soon."

"Balderdash," the older lady insisted, then her green eyes narrowed. "Unless you have some good reason for not wanting to go out in genteel society."

"Of course not," Charlotte said through gritted teeth. "However, the new clothes. I can hardly afford such an expense."

"Nonsense. It is my gift to you for all the missed years. You won't begrudge me the pleasure of doing this for my only sister's child."

Charlotte could hardly fight her on that. Besides, Alicia was batting her eyelids beseechingly. She sighed. "I suppose a new gown—"

"Good," Alicia cut in. "Now get going, you three. Bridget will get you settled. Your trunks should be in your rooms by now. Take your naps. Lacey, you may clear." Having completed her orders, Alicia dismissed them all with a clap of her hands.

With a child on either side of her, Charlotte climbed the stairs. *From mistress of my own house to jumping at Alicia's orders.* And she was to be shown off at a party as though she was the latest spectacle from the mysterious Orient.

Lily yawned, and Charlotte squeezed her hand encouragingly as they started up the second staircase behind Bridget. Regardless of what Alicia put her through, Charlotte was certain in her heart that keeping the children was the right thing to do, whatever that took.

CHAPTER FIFTEEN

The next morning, Charlotte was awakened by Thomas as he jumped right into the middle of her bed.

Lily was tugging at the covers. "Come on, Aunt Charlotte, Thomas and I want to go out."

"Good gracious," Charlotte exclaimed, looking at the mantle clock. "It's already eight!" Her first morning in the city, and she had overslept. Carriages and whistles, boat horns, and loud voices had kept her lying awake when she'd first gone to bed the night before, and now she felt a little wool-headed.

"Wait till you see the shops. Grandma says we're going to as many as it takes."

"As many as it takes to what?" Charlotte asked, trying to wrestle Thomas into stillness.

"To outfit you appropriately for Boston," Lily said, doing a good impersonation of her grandmother.

Charlotte grumbled inwardly. It was her day to be outfitted. *I will go along with this,* she promised herself, *if only so as not to embarrass myself in front of Alicia's acquaintances. Or Reed's,* she added, remembering how sleek Helen had looked at the Spring City dance.

Freshly washed and dressed, Charlotte descended to the foyer. She could hear any number of carriages passing outside, as well as street vendors. Apparently, the milkman had already delivered because Lacey was letting Thomas carry a bottle.

"Careful, Master Thomas. Don't slop it."

Oh, my Lord, I'm in Boston. Charlotte wanted to throw the front door open and head out into the heart of it. Why had she ever thought she'd be afraid? People were people, no matter where they lived, and she had studied people from the confines of her study.

She knew why artists went abroad for inspiration and why farmers stayed put to plow their land. She knew why politicians made promises and broke them as easily. She knew why some investment bankers became rich while their investors went broke. And here was a wide swath of folks she'd written about. There were simply so many more of them in one place than she'd ever dreamed.

"Charlotte, what on earth are you doing? Close that door."

She had, indeed, opened the front door and stood looking out like a grinning fool. She closed it guiltily, glad that her aunt had been unable to see her face.

"Good morning, Aunt. I was just checking the weather. What a day! And how glad I am to be here with you."

"Are you?" Alicia asked, coming forward, still in black, once again with her hair piled high. Even higher, Charlotte noted, with an extra layer of ringlets. "I'm so happy to hear you say that, my dear. I feared you might be angry at me for asking you to come all this way."

"No," Charlotte said. *Well, not anymore.* "I may've done the same thing in your shoes."

The older lady tucked Charlotte's arm under her own. "Come, have some breakfast. We have a busy, busy day."

Not long after, they were driving along the length of Boston Common in Alicia's white open-air barouche. Children played on the grass, people crossed and re-crossed the pond on paddleboats, and women pushed their babies in the fanciest perambulators Charlotte had ever seen, with fine lace hangings and painted sides.

"We'll go for the worst first and save the best for last," Alicia said.

"The worst?" Charlotte asked.

"Oak Hall, my dear." Alicia's nose fairly wrinkled up as she said the words. "It isn't in the nicest part of town, you know, but it is the largest clothing store for *prêt-à-porter*, and it's the best place to start when you need everything."

Charlotte pulled her mantelet around her more tightly, feeling for all the world as if she were wearing nothing more than rags.

She saw a sign for North Street as their driver turned the corner, and then before them was a large wooden building with nine gaslight globes attached to its exterior, ten towering pinnacles, and a huge American flag. To Charlotte, it was nearly as impressive as Boston's gold-domed State House.

"Oh my," she exclaimed as she alighted from the coach.

"What is it, my dear?"

"The aromas," Charlotte replied, "so many of them."

She spun around, taking in the busy street around her, so different from the sophisticated atmosphere of her aunt's residential Beacon Hill. Alicia merely stared at her blankly, as did the children.

"Don't you smell them?" she asked, looking at the three of them. "The leather and the . . . what is that? Linen? And tea and coffee, and somewhere—" She raised her head to catch the scent. "Why, we must be very close to the sea!"

Her three relatives looked at one another with varying degrees of smiles. "That's the ship chandlers you can smell, too," Alicia added. "Rope and tar and salt air. But there's no time for dawdling or smelling things." She made a tut-tut sound.

They were in and out of Oak Hall in less than two hours, with packages of every shape and size—all for Charlotte— containing several pairs of shoes, an assortment of bonnets and matching drawstring reticules, a blue-gray pelisse, several pairs of silk pantalets and cotton bloomers.

"Onward to more exclusive shops," Alicia ordered.

They headed across town, back toward the Common where Thomas immediately spotted a confectionary shop. With a small bag of candy each, the children were fortified once again.

Alicia talked incessantly about the various couturiers that she patronized, and soon they had arrived at the doorstep of the first.

Before Charlotte knew it, she was in a dressing room with a shop girl who was pinning and fitting her with a linen Dolly Varden dress. A pink-and-mauve flowered overskirt, attached to the bodice and draped up elegantly behind her at the bustle, was left open from her waist down to show off the light pink underskirt.

This outfit was approved by her aunt and then Charlotte was stripped down and redressed in a simple cream bodice and skirt.

"This is a surprise," she said turning to her aunt, thinking the simplicity was much more her style, when with a flourish, the shop girl presented her with a turquoise blue silk-satin jacket.

"I'm not sure," Charlotte protested but then stood back and looked in the mirror at the neat vertical pleats and fitted waist. She touched the deep aqua-colored glass buttons marching down the front. The long tight sleeves with their puffed shoulders and matching grosgrain ribbons and bows at the cuff showed exquisite workmanship. And the color set off her coppery hair to perfection.

What could top this? she wondered. She found out in another minute, dressed in a jacket bodice and matching skirt in the softest chocolate brown satin. It was the latest fashion for daytime, and her aunt nodded approvingly. She was made to try on a similar ensemble in dove gray.

"One more shop," Alicia said.

Charlotte blanched. "I think I have more than enough."

"For day time, perhaps, but now you need more formal wear, dear."

Alicia was greeted by Madame Merrianne, the owner, with a dazzling smile and a soft chair. Charlotte gaped at her collection:

satin ball gowns, daringly cut, and gossamer silk princess dresses hung on every available dressmaker's dummy.

While Charlotte and Lily looked wonderingly at a gown covered in peacock feathers of the brightest hues, Alicia consulted with Madame Merrianne, who then ushered Charlotte into a fitting room. She liked everything she put on, and soon her aunt had chosen two of the loveliest creations, one in black satin and one in a warm amber organdie that complimented Charlotte's hair.

"One more," said her aunt.

When Charlotte put on the last gown, she smiled at the image of herself in the mirror. The indigo satin, shot through with golden threads, clung all the way down over her slim hips. Turning sideways, she gave a wiggle and watched the folds of fabric hooked to the shapely bustle sway suggestively. It was different, with no bows and little adornment.

She thought this one the best, and judging by the nod of her aunt and the "ooh" from Lily as she walked out into the shop, they did, too.

At last, they were done. She was deeply in her aunt's debt, but so be it. Imagining Reed's face when he saw her looking every inch as stylish as Helen Belgrave made it quite worthwhile.

Home on Chestnut Street, Charlotte watched Gerald and the driver staggering under the load of her parcels. Some of the outfits had come home with her, while others had remained at the couturier's for slight alterations. Nevertheless, Bridget's eyes were gleaming, and Charlotte knew the maid couldn't wait to see the new attire.

"We'll get all this put away," Charlotte said, gesturing for Bridget to come with her.

Alicia paused on her way to the kitchen intent on ordering pound cake and lemon puffs from the cook. "You will come down for tea."

It was not a question.

"Before then, I expect." Charlotte had not forgotten the dreaded tea with Helen Belgrave, not for a moment all day, but she was determined to keep her nervousness in check.

Letting Bridget try on her new bonnet when they were alone, they were soon laughing and wondering aloud at how all the new clothes were ever going to fit in the wardrobe and chest of drawers.

"I think we have a spare wardrobe with double doors up in the attic," Bridget suggested with the same Irish cadence as Lacey. "I can ask Gerald to bring it down."

They looked at each other, imagining the aged butler doing such a task, and grinned.

"I wouldn't want to be the cause of him sustaining an injury," Charlotte protested, thinking it might be better if she and Bridget and Lacey tried to move it themselves.

They were still rolling stockings and discussing the outrageous price of silk when Bridget heard the bell before she did.

"That'll be your company, miss," the maid said.

"Not *my* company," Charlotte muttered, putting down the new reticule with amber and mauve beading. She thought she now knew what it felt like to be a lamb going to slaughter. Except worse, because she knew what awaited her.

Taking a look at herself in the mirror, she was relieved when Bridget said, "You look fine, miss."

"I should have taken the time to change into something new," Charlotte said, smoothing down her tan skirt and matching bodice. "Never mind now. Thank you for all your help, Bridget."

The girl fairly turned pink with pleasure and rushed out ahead of Charlotte.

Going down the stairs more slowly than Bridget, she could tell Thomas and Lily had come in from the garden and beat her to the parlor.

"The princess!" she heard Thomas exclaim and quickened her steps. Too late. She entered the doorway in time to see him bound onto the sofa where Helen Belgrave was seated, stylishly draped in a figure-fitting, burgundy gown of the finest brushed cotton.

"Stop that," Helen scolded, an expression of horror marring her attractive features as he touched the sleeve of her dress with muddied fingers, fresh from digging up some treasure.

Charlotte caught the frown that crossed her aunt's face. Evidently, they were both realizing that Helen Belgrave did not care for children.

However, the elegant woman managed to rearrange her features into a neutral mask, as Lily stepped forward and took her brother by the hand, hauling him off the sofa.

"Children," Charlotte called them to her, sincerely hoping she hadn't had Helen's horrified expression upon her own face when Reed first presented her to Thomas and Lily. "Say good day to Mr. Malloy's friend and then go get washed up. I'm sure cook will have a treat for you in the kitchen."

They barely mumbled their goodbyes before they ran down the passage.

"So energetic," Mrs. Belgrave said, brushing at her sleeve before taking a cup of tea from the tray Lacey had placed on the low table in front of the sofa.

"Mm," Charlotte smiled, taking a seat at the other end of the sofa and helping herself to a lemon puff. "Isn't it wonderful?"

"I must say," Alicia added, "that I had only my Ann to raise, and she was rather less enthusiastic than Thomas, but I do love having my family in the house again."

To Charlotte, her aunt's smile seemed completely genuine, and she couldn't help but feel warmth toward her.

"That reminds me," Alicia continued, "I've contacted the children's former governess whom Ann used. You can tell them that they'll see Mrs. Hunnewell by the end of the week."

Charlotte would certainly ask them if they *wanted* to see Mrs. Hunnewell, but she intended to examine the woman and her lessons carefully, for she would brook no ill-tempered, closed-minded educator for Lily and Thomas.

"Back to you, Miss Sanborn," Helen Belgrave remarked, turning to face Charlotte rather abruptly, "you must take it all as an enormous disruption to the quiet literary life you had. It seems that life suited you perfectly."

Charlotte picked up a cup and saucer. Was this a trap? What game was Helen playing?

"I like my life in Spring City," she said carefully, "but I am also thoroughly enjoying Boston. Of course, I've only been here a day."

"And raising the children doesn't give you pause?" Helen continued.

Charlotte frowned. She thought they'd be talking about her unseemly behavior, dancing in the barn and letting Reed stay in her house. This was too easy.

"I wondered initially if I was up to the task," she turned to take in her aunt, "even though their mother had chosen me. Naturally, I was flattered but nervous."

Alicia nodded, as if she understood how that would be.

"But after spending even a small amount of time with my cousin's children, they totally captured my heart. How could they not?"

Again, Alicia nodded in agreement. "My grandchildren are wonderful, indeed."

Helen, who seemed to be shaking her head in disagreement on the wonders of children, swiftly turned it into a nod of agreement.

"Well, then, we must get to the heart of the matter," she said with a sigh, as if it pained her to bring it up. "About your being a fit guardian, about your *behavior*," Helen started, but Charlotte cut her off.

"I know what you're going to say, Mrs. Belgrave. I know you have already mentioned to my aunt your concerns."

Helen had the grace to look discomfited, and Alicia gazed down at her tea and stirred absently.

"But things are different in Spring City," Charlotte continued.

"Morals are morals everywhere," Alicia piped in.

"Of course," Charlotte agreed. "And I consider myself a highly moral individual, raised by decent parents."

"There can be no doubt that my sister was above reproach in that area," Alicia agreed.

"Why then—?" Charlotte began.

"Your father, however," Alicia continued, "was not known to my parents. His parents were dead when he met my sister, and the Sanborns were not a Boston family. Indeed, they have all died out."

"Except for me," Charlotte said, "and my brother. We are Sanborns," she insisted.

"I didn't know you had a brother," Helen said, and Charlotte could just about see the wheels turning in her head. Perhaps she intended to try to dig up some dirt on Thaddeus, too.

"To the topic at hand," Charlotte said, glancing at Alicia, "my father was a good man, a quiet man, who neither drank nor smoked nor gambled. And he loved my mother."

"Your parents aside," Helen interrupted this list of virtues, "it is *your* suitability to raise children that is in question."

"Really? By you?" Charlotte asked, amazed at her gall.

"Of course not." Helen appeared flustered. "It has nothing to do with me. I was merely making certain Mrs. Randall, who is beloved by all on Beacon Hill, knew the situation her grandchildren were in." She sipped her tea again, having regained her composure as Alicia thanked her for her kindness.

Charlotte, on the other hand, wondered how eager Helen would be to finish her cup of tea and skedaddle if her questionable arrangement of *convenience* with Reed was brought up. Aunt Alicia surely wouldn't approve of that. However, Helen was not yet finished trying to discredit Charlotte.

"I believe I saw behavior more appropriate for a single woman than for a mother," Helen added.

"For example?" *Go on,* Charlotte thought, *I dare you.*

"Well," Helen said, pursing her lips as if it were distasteful, "I could not help but notice that you had allowed a single gentleman to stay with you."

She dared!

Alicia set her teacup and saucer down with a clank. Apparently, they had gone beyond whether Charlotte had danced indiscriminately at Drake's barn and moved right on to the crux of the matter. Helen was jealous of Reed's time with Charlotte. Rather than feeling guilty, though, her rancor blossomed.

"Let's not play games, Mrs. Belgrave," Charlotte said more plainly than she had at first intended. But, good God, she would not be brought down by one such as Helen Belgrave, who didn't mind sharing her favors with a single man on the pretense of some vague understanding, and dressing it up with a bow of duplicity as a bona fide engagement.

At least Charlotte had given herself to the man to whom she'd also given her heart, no matter how rash that might have been.

"Aunt Alicia, the only man ever to stay in my house since my brother left was Mr. Reed Malloy."

Alicia gave a notably loud gasp, and Charlotte hurried on. "But it was out of necessity. He would not leave those children with me unless he was sure I was capable."

"Why didn't he stay at a hotel?" her aunt asked.

"Yes, why?" echoed Helen. "The accommodations, while rustic, were adequate." She looked at Charlotte over the top of her teacup and added, "They fulfilled all my needs."

Charlotte coughed, but her thoughts were searching quickly for an answer—a good one. "Because Thomas was having nightmares," she said, not untruthfully. "And with my being a stranger to them both, Mr. Malloy was not comfortable abandoning his charges. Besides, the children were there to chaperone, and my neighbor, a doctor's wife, dropped by regularly," she added for good measure. "In any case, Mrs. Belgrave, while you and I are unknown to each other, can you truly be questioning the behavior of your own fiancé? You are engaged to Mr. Malloy, aren't you?"

Charlotte saw Helen curl her left hand into a ball in her lap, hiding the lack of a ring. But she didn't have to answer before Alicia stepped in.

"It was wrong of you, Charlotte. No matter the character of the man, you must think of your own reputation. I am sure my sister would not have approved." With a cluck of her tongue, she shook her head. "It's actually worse than I thought. I believed the sole concern was an unchaperoned dance and of your spirited display with not one but two men."

Alicia looked to Helen for confirmation. Helen barely nodded, subdued by the course of the discussion.

Charlotte addressed her aunt. "I wish you wouldn't trouble yourself so. Spring City is not Boston. It is much more," she considered the correct word, "informal. In any case, Aunt, I can tell you this, I would never do anything to harm Lily and Thomas. And what's done is done."

"What's done is done," Helen repeated softly before looking straight into Charlotte's eyes.

Charlotte, for her part, couldn't help blushing, and she was certain, in that instant, Helen knew for sure what she and Reed had done.

The widow stood abruptly. "Thank you for an interesting afternoon, Mrs. Randall. I hope it was not too stressful for you."

"No, my dear. We shall do it again, I'm sure," Alicia said, sounding perfectly happy. She nodded toward Charlotte, who stood as well, unsure of the protocol. Should she be the one to show Helen to the door? Where was Gerald?

With a shrug, Charlotte followed their guest into the foyer. At the door, Helen paused to adjust her hat and slip on her gloves.

"When are you returning to Colorado?" she asked without preamble.

"At present, I have made no plans to return."

"Well, I suggest you make some." And Helen yanked the door open, striding smoothly down the front steps.

Charlotte watched the widow's swaying bustle as she sashayed to her carriage and was helped in by her driver. *Blazes!* It seemed as if she'd just made a more serious enemy out of the woman than she had before. While Charlotte had dealt with Eliza Prentice and her sharp barbs all her life, Helen's arsenal of weapons might be of an entirely different caliber.

Swallowing sharply, feeling a thread of trepidation wind itself around her, Charlotte closed the door.

CHAPTER SIXTEEN

When the calling card first arrived, embossed with a large gold *F*, Charlotte thought nothing of it. A number of them had been dropped off the previous day. At least superficially, people were interested in the long-lost branch of the Randall family.

Charlotte chalked it up to social boredom, but she also felt the tiniest bit flattered at being the object of so much curiosity.

Still no word from Reed, however. She tossed the latest card down on the table in the hall and went in to breakfast. It was only when Gerald brought the cards to Alicia on a silver tray after the meal that Charlotte learned to whom the single burnished letter belonged.

"Jason Farnsworth, III" Alicia exclaimed. "My word. What an honor to have a Farnsworth asking for an introduction, and the eldest son at that." She fingered the card thoughtfully. "We must respond at once, Charlotte, then you will have an undeniably acceptable escort for the ball."

Charlotte could hardly voice her desire that she hoped Reed Malloy would escort her, especially when her aunt lowered her voice a notch, as if the two squabbling children were even the least bit interested in the adult chatter, and added, "and we can put all the unpleasant business of your previous indiscretions behind us."

Charlotte could see the merit in having a proper, respectable Bostonian at her side. What's more, now that her aunt knew Reed had been her houseguest, the next time their paths crossed, Alicia would be watching with extreme vigilance. They would have to be careful to give no hint of impropriety.

If all it took were a few respectable outings with Mr. Farnsworth to clear her in the eyes of her aunt, Charlotte thought it was, indeed, worth it.

"And how do I go about meeting Mr. Farnsworth?"

"Oh, no, dear." Alicia looked aghast. "I will handle it all. Be prepared for some afternoon sightseeing, chaperoned of course, and maybe with the children along. Do wear the gray outfit for this first encounter."

Charlotte was calmer than she'd anticipated for her introduction to Boston's highest echelon. Something in the relationship she'd begun with Reed had given her confidence in herself and in her ability to hold her own in a conversation with a man. Surely, she could pull off an afternoon with a stranger for whom she cared nothing.

"Miss Sanborn, I am charmed, quite," the tall, fair-haired man said, after Gerald showed him into the parlor and vanished.

Unsure of how she could possibly be charming when she had yet to speak, Charlotte stood up to greet him, meeting him in the middle of the brightly colored oriental rug. He touched her hand to his lips before releasing it.

"It is kind of you to come by," she said.

He smiled broadly at that, and she thought he should do so often, for it gave him a winsome set of dimples.

"Mrs. Randall," Mr. Farnsworth greeted her aunt, approaching Alicia's winged chair. "I appreciate your giving me the opportunity to enter your lovely home and to acquaint myself with your niece."

It was a good start that only got better. Jason Farnsworth met the children with a boiled sweet for each of them. When they were all sufficiently satiated by tea and sandwiches, Jason invited Charlotte to go for a stroll. They started out along the length of the Common toward the business district, with Bridget walking discreetly behind with Lily and Thomas.

Charlotte marveled over the hundreds of suited businessmen, who seemed to be hurrying from place to place. Jason pointed out where the Farnsworths had offices.

"I understand from my aunt that your family is in import and export," Charlotte remarked, finding it easy to converse with her jovial new acquaintance. There was no undercurrent of tension, no feeling that she would sizzle if his arm brushed hers, merely relaxed company.

"For as long as Boston has had a harbor," Jason replied, launching into a family history upon which Charlotte was devoting all her attention until she saw the street sign for Court Street. *Scollay Square was nearby.*

Without intending to, she'd been searching for that street sign and the place where she knew the offices of Malloy and Associates were located, where Reed had practiced his profession for nearly a decade. *Was he there now?* She longed to know if she was truly within a hundred yards of the man who had so changed her life.

On his way back to Spring City. John's phrase had replayed in her brain again and again. Whatever was Reed up to? He had her head spinning, and he wasn't even there. She allowed Jason to direct her steps through the financial district until they were directly in front of Faneuil Hall.

"The Cradle of Liberty," she remarked, referring to the meetings that took place there in the previous century.

Jason arched an eyebrow. "Are you interested in history?"

"Much more so than in shopping," said Charlotte.

He looked surprised. "I don't think I know many women who take an interest in this sort of thing," he said. "Pardon me, that sounded rude."

"Not at all," she said. It was probably unladylike of her to want to tromp through the building, but she couldn't pass up the opportunity. If there was no meeting going on, they could wander around at their leisure.

"Shall we go in?"

"As you wish," Jason said, holding the door for her.

"I've spent many pleasurable hours reading the speeches of James Otis and Samuel Adams," she explained, as they entered the great auditorium where the so-called Sons of Liberty met. In her mind, Charlotte conjured an image of the room filled to overflowing, the balconies lined with concerned faces, as voices debated the fate of a new country.

A shiver went down her spine. She was in the heart of a city that had shaped her nation. After a short while, however, Thomas yawned so broadly, Charlotte thought his face would split.

"Time to leave," she said, making sure Bridget and the children were following.

"You must be smart as a steel trap after reading so much," Jason remarked when they exited, and Charlotte couldn't tell if he was being condescending. She decided to give him the benefit of the doubt and smiled. After all, who could take offense or be cross when stepping out into the middle of Quincy Market. Street vendors were everywhere and Charlotte marveled at their liveliness.

"Hot corn," called out one woman. "Fresh apples," yelled another. She couldn't resist letting Jason purchase shaved lemon ice for each of the children. But she turned away with a shudder when a boy, not much older than Lily, screamed out, "'Nother murder! Get your *Gazette*!"

"How about we take a ride now?" Jason offered, smiling at her while gesturing in the air to his driver with a casual hand over his shoulder. Immediately, the vehicle that had been trailing them all afternoon was right beside them.

Charlotte arranged her skirts on the black, morocco-leather seat of the stylish carriage with the large gold "F" emblazoned on its plum-colored side. Lily sat next to her, with Thomas opposite, positioned firmly between Alicia's maid and Jason Farnsworth.

Charlotte couldn't help it. Tossing decorum aside, she discreetly removed one glove so she could brush her palms against the soft, goat leather seat. What a luxury! Relaxing, she would have closed her eyes if Jason hadn't been there, as the unaccustomed ruckus of Boston after dark had kept her from falling easily asleep each night. But that would be beyond rude, and so far, she'd managed to be on her best behavior, doing nothing her aunt could quibble about.

Still, for a moment, despite Jason's friendly society, the coziness of his carriage reminded her of her peaceful study, her own comfortable chair, and her solitude. She sighed.

"What is it, Miss Sanborn?" Jason's soft tones seemed to match the upholstery of his plush vehicle.

She laughed at her own foolishness. "I don't want to sound provincial, but I cannot believe all that has happened in such a short time. If you could see where I was merely a week ago and now, I'm strolling through Faneuil Hall."

"You could never be provincial," he returned, making her blush, "but I expect our lively city is, without a doubt, a vast change from . . . Spring City, was it?"

"Yes, where—"

"You and Thaddeus grew up."

She closed her mouth quickly with a snap, as his words caught her by complete surprise. "How did you . . . ? That is, do you know my brother?" she asked, her heart suddenly pounding at the thought of seeing Teddy.

"I met him on a trip along the northwest passage." Her companion regaled her with a story that made her almost wish she were a man. It seemed he'd met her brother soon after Thaddeus had left home, two young men from very different backgrounds, both searching for their purpose.

Charlotte was astounded. "Why didn't you tell me this from the beginning? And how on earth did you know I was here, Mr. Farnsworth?" she asked.

"Please, call me Jason. How did I know?" He tapped the side of his black bowler with his ivory handled cane. "I know my city, Charlotte. I keep my ear to its workings and know what's what." He looked out the window a moment as if contemplating those workings.

"Thaddeus talked a spell of wonder about his older sister, the renowned 'Charles Sanborn.' So, when it came to my attention that one Miss Sanborn was coming to stay with her aunt, I thought to myself, could it be? Thaddeus's older sister lives in Colorado, nigh two thousand miles from here, but sure enough, it was you. I sent over my card as soon as I knew you had arrived."

She ignored the liberty he had taken in using her first name, and the fact that he hadn't told her aunt outright that he knew her family. After all, he was a friend of her brother's, and she decided then and there she liked him, despite his slightly dandified ways.

Uppermost in her mind, however, was one question, and she asked him directly, "Do you know where my brother is now?"

Jason Farnsworth shook his blond head. "Not a clue. Thaddeus Sanborn comes and he goes, always a wanderer, but he's sure to show up sometime, no doubt when you least expect it."

That was true. He showed up out of the blue, stayed a week—two, at the most—and then left, sometimes only once or twice a year.

Although they always had a great deal of affection for each other, Teddy never hid his dislike of the humdrum of daily living in Spring City. And Charlotte tried not to let her heart break each time he left her behind.

At the top of Alicia's front steps, Jason paused. "I hope you will allow me to take you out in the evening to see the brighter, sparkling side of Boston. Perhaps without your young charges," he added, gesturing after the children who had already run inside with Bridget.

Intrigued, Charlotte could think of no reason to decline. So, this was how it felt to simply be with a member of the opposite sex, without the searing desire that overtook her whenever Reed was near. This was nice, a little tame by comparison, but also less draining. They'd been on an even keel all afternoon.

But what about Reed? He was supposed to be the one showing her his birthplace, and she wanted more than anything to share it with him. She would hate to be busy when he returned from his trip. On the other hand, Jason had been more than kind.

Surely, an evening out with him would be a welcome distraction while she awaited Reed's return. Looking up into Jason's dancing felt-brown eyes, she nodded.

"I would like that," Charlotte told him, then remembering how Alicia preferred to handle her social engagements, not to mention having no idea whether it would be acceptable for her to go out with Jason unchaperoned, she added, "but I couldn't possibly say when."

"I wouldn't think of pinning you down, Charlotte," he said, leaning against the doorway to the annoyance of Gerald who was waiting to close it, "to a date, that is."

Charlotte knew he was teasing her and smiled. It would be agreeable to spend more time with one of Thaddeus's friends.

"Oh, what a dazzling smile," Jason added. "It pierced me right through my heart." He held his chest melodramatically. "Don't worry about saying when. I'll leave my card again and hope that our plans coincide for an evening. The sightseeing was delightful, as are you." He took her hand and kissed it again.

As his carriage pulled away, Charlotte basked in his flattery for a moment, even though it was obvious he was a shameless flirt. She barely got in the door before her aunt emerged from the parlor.

"On a first name basis, are we?" Alicia didn't look entirely displeased. It seemed one could be familiar with a man if she considered him the right sort of man and in the right situation.

"He turns out to be an old friend of Thaddeus's," Charlotte remarked. "I didn't even know my brother had been to half the places Jason mentioned."

"Well," Aunt Alicia sniffed, "if he's been to Boston, he certainly hasn't contacted me."

"Mr. Farnsworth didn't say Thaddeus had ever been here," Charlotte said, trying to soothe the older woman. They were getting along so well, despite Helen Belgrave, that Charlotte hated to have anything break the peace.

It seemed that the issue of her questionable behavior would dissipate if she remained under Alicia's roof and allowed her aunt to keep an eye on her. Naturally, Charlotte would behave impeccably at the ball. Would Reed show up? The hope of dancing again in his arms was far too thrilling to renounce for the sake of decorum.

Unfortunately, when the night of the ball arrived, Reed had not. Over the course of the week, Charlotte had made the acquaintance of two ladies who came calling to meet Alicia Randall's niece, but Charlotte had received neither a visit from Reed, nor any word that he was once more in Boston.

Instead, with her aunt's approval, it was Jason Farnsworth who had taken her on a daytime outing the day before and who now escorted her to the Tremont House. She wore her new gown of midnight blue and allowed Bridget to do her hair as Alicia had suggested, styling it in an elegant chignon that showed off the graceful curve of Charlotte's neck.

As she descended from Jason's carriage to join him and her aunt on the pavement, she couldn't help wishing she were in Spring City at Drake's barn with Reed and the children and the sweet smell of hay. But the children were home with Bridget, Reed was nowhere to be seen, and the smell of women's perfume thickly infused the night air.

With Aunt Alicia in front of her, Charlotte walked between the four Doric columns of the hotel's entrance with her hand on Jason's arm and a tentative smile on her face.

"I can see at a glance you are the loveliest woman here," Jason murmured in her ear as they descended the grand steps to the ballroom. "That is, I could, if I could take my eyes off of you."

Charlotte was already used to Jason's free-flowing compliments, thinking them less substantial than dandelion puffs. Nevertheless, she was now extremely pleased to be with at least one familiar face.

As for the rest of the glittering crowd, there was not a person whom she recognized, until she saw John Trelaine across the room.

A few women sat in a semi-circle with the men hovering around them as bees to sweet flowers. John handed a drink to a pretty round-cheeked woman and then looked up, catching Charlotte's eye.

She felt a pang of guilt as she watched him take in her male companion, but she shook that off as a ridiculous notion. After all, John could not know with certainty that anything had occurred between her and Reed, not unless Reed had confided in his friend. She doubted he would have openly compromised her in such a way. Before she could approach John, she heard her aunt's voice.

"They have a table reserved for us, Charlotte," Alicia said, leading the way to an honored position atop a dais at one end. Not only did it give her a commanding view of the entire room, it gave the other guests a perfect chance to ogle the newcomer from the West.

Charlotte approached the dais next to a set of large French doors leading to an expansive wraparound terrace. The doors stood open now to let in the cool night air. It was Jason who spoke first.

"As you promised, Aunt Alicia, your party is obviously the talk of Beacon Hill tonight."

Alicia looked at Jason carefully. There was a glint in her eye, as she admonished him.

"First of all, I am not your aunt, nor have I given you leave to address me as such. Second, this is not *my* party, although I do believe it might not have come about if not for my participation." She gave a small smile of satisfaction, then looked at her niece.

"You must meet the hosts, my good friend Amelia and her husband, Oliver. I have already spotted them over by the violinists."

Hearing the name Oliver made Charlotte startle, recalling it was Reed's father's name, wondering if everything about Boston would make her think of him until the man himself finally put in an appearance.

"In that case, Mrs. Randall," Jason amended, with a kiss to Alicia's gloved hand, "allow me to begin the rounds. I know practically everyone and will see to it that Charlotte does, as well. Of course, as you say, we'll start with the esteemed Mr. and Mrs. Wendell Holmes and work our way back to you."

"It seems that I have nothing to say in the matter," Charlotte said, "but am to be trundled around like a carthorse." And then the import of his words sunk in. "I am to meet Mr. Oliver Wendell Holmes, the fireside poet?" Her head whipped around as she searched for one of America's greatest writers, who had a place on her bookshelf along with Longfellow, Whittier, Lowell, and Bryant. *Goodness!* Reed had been entirely correct about the opportunities in Boston.

Alicia only laughed, and Charlotte allowed Jason to begin the introductions.

"It won't be so bad," he promised, thinking her reluctant, "I'll steer you clear of any tigers."

An hour and a half later, it did seem to Charlotte as if Jason knew everyone, and now, so did she. Or at least, she knew their faces, even if she couldn't recall all their names, except for those famous ones already known to her. Her excitement at having shaken Holmes's hand and that of his gracious wife was keeping her in a constant state of exhilaration.

"Mr. Charles Greene," Jason said, and Charlotte turned to greet one more guest, "may I present Charles Sanborn."

She gasped at his use of her pen name and started to protest, but then Jason added, "Charlotte, this is Mr. Greene of the *Boston Post.*"

"Oh, sir, it is an honor to meet you." Ten minutes went by in which they spoke of editors they both knew and writers they admired, and then it was nearly time for the dancing to begin.

"If you'll excuse me a minute, Mr. Greene, Mr. Farnsworth." Charlotte took leave of them and headed to where she'd seen other ladies going to check their hair. As she left the powder room, to her unwelcome surprise, she met with a familiar face.

Helen Belgrave looked more like a wolf hunting her meal than an invited guest.

"We ought to have a *tête-à-tête*, don't you agree, Miss Sanborn? You like the intimacy of one-on-one, I believe."

There was a tone to her voice that Charlotte was not going to put up with.

"You will kindly be civil, or we will not have this discussion at all."

Helen narrowed her dark eyes until they were merely slits. "Just what in the devil's name are you really doing in Boston?"

Charlotte raised her eyebrows. So much for pleasantries in the cultured city.

"I would have thought that was obvious. After all, you were the one who spoke to the children's grandmother about my suitability as their guardian."

"Oh!" Helen sounded peeved and exasperated at the same time. "As if I had dreamed that would bring you hundreds of miles. What *does* he see in a picayune creature like you?"

Charlotte blanched at this indirect mention of Reed. It was odd, indeed, to have a stranger discuss her private affairs. But Helen was only getting started.

"You are a mousy spinster from the middle of nowhere, a bookworm at that! When he came to St. Louis—"

"Reed went to—?" Charlotte interrupted herself, abashed that she had admitted to an interest in his comings and goings.

It was too late. Helen seized on her slip of the tongue like a cat on a mouse.

"*Reed*," she sneered. "By what right do you call my lover by his Christian name?"

Charlotte knew that Helen spoke the truth. Reed and Helen *had been* lovers. He'd admitted that much, but she also noted that Helen had dropped the pretense of being engaged. In any case, Charlotte could think of no response. She could hardly say, "Well, we were lovers, too, so I am allowed to take that liberty." She blushed at her own thoughts.

Helen noticed Charlotte's high coloring. "Even the word *lover* is too much for such a prim, dried-up oddity as yourself." Smoothing her satin skirts, she shot Charlotte another direct glance and smiled. It was a terrible expression, lacking any warmth or friendliness.

"I guess he didn't tell you when he sent me off to St. Louis that he would be joining me on his way to Boston. Reed has always loved that city, and it was the perfect place for us to make up from our little quarrel."

"I understand you have a sister living there," Charlotte remarked, keeping her voice calmly neutral. The notion that Reed had left her in Spring City, after their emotional conversation, to go straight to the awaiting Helen was a devastating blow, but she had to find out if any of what he'd said had been true.

"Yes, I do." Helen looked surprised that Charlotte had that information, but she smiled again, another sly grin, making the hair raise on Charlotte's neck. "She is a modern woman, my sister Isabel, a suffragette. And as I am a widow, I am unrestricted under her roof. I come and go as I please, and with whom I please."

Helen seemed to feel she had gained an advantage, for she continued, "Reed and I cannot easily be intimate here in Boston where everyone who is anyone knows us. But when we travel, we are freer to indulge." She cocked her head and tilted her chin up. "Reed is a man of great passion."

"It is my understanding, however, that you are *not*," Charlotte quipped. "Of great passion, that is, according to Reed."

She didn't know how those words escaped her lips, but she'd been unable to stop herself from saying them. And why shouldn't she speak her mind? She couldn't stand there defenseless while Helen insulted her unchecked.

Charlotte was satisfied to see how well her words hit home. Helen looked as if she'd been slapped. Her eyes were wide with shock.

"How could you know . . . ? He wouldn't . . . he wouldn't tell you that."

Charlotte chose to retreat to safer conversational territory. After all, any mention of Reed should be couched only in terms of his being her deceased cousin's lawyer.

"We had many discussions while we settled the children's affairs."

"The children!" Helen hissed, sounding as if she blamed them as the impetus for all her perceived problems with the handsome Mr. Malloy. "Bawling, dirty, loud little creatures, always upsetting furniture or tearing clothing. I thought you, of all people, would understand." She looked at Charlotte with a frown.

"When I found out in that filthy barn that the learned 'Charles Sanborn' was actually a woman, I thought I understood you. You were living a life of freedom, albeit in isolation. I thought you would detest the unwelcome intrusion of those little brutes." She shook her head slowly, as if she couldn't fathom Charlotte at all.

It was painful that Helen could have pegged her so well, at least the old Charlotte. But Helen didn't know of the love that had crept into Charlotte's heart or of the sheer joy she felt at sharing a hug and a smile with Lily and Thomas. And then it dawned on her.

"You didn't think I would fight for them," she said musingly, and it made sense. When Helen whispered her scandalous secrets into Alicia Randall's ear, she hadn't intended to make Charlotte come to Boston to face a moral inquisition. Rather,

Helen thought Charlotte would welcome the excuse to give up her cousin's children, thereby severing all ties to Reed, including legal obligations.

It was becoming apparent that Helen's spitefulness had more to do with trying to keep hold of Reed, than with getting revenge on Charlotte. Seemingly, Helen thought if Charlotte fell from Reed's favor by sending Lily and Thomas back to Boston, his approving gaze would fall once more upon the shapely widow.

"You're not fond of children, Mrs. Belgrave," Charlotte said at last.

"Fortunately, my husband already had grown daughters when I married him. Children get on one's nerves so, and I imagine long exposure to them would damage my delicate constitution irreversibly." Helen sniffed. "I think it is apparent to anyone who knows me how I feel."

Including Reed, Charlotte thought, and Reed liked children. Very much. *She is not the kind of woman with whom I want to spend my life,* he had told Charlotte in the meadow. And he had obviously been pleased to see how she'd warmed to her young cousins.

"Whatever is that foolish smile for?" Helen cut into her thoughts. "Your coming here was a mistake. There is nothing for you here."

Charlotte considered the overwrought woman in front of her. It was clear to her now that Reed admired a woman who offered more than stunning good looks, but whether admiration could be translated into something more, she wasn't sure.

Besides, the idea that Reed had stopped off in St. Louis on his way home shattered all Charlotte's certainties that he had been absolutely truthful with her. It would be too easy for him to continue the convenient association he had with Helen.

At her continuing silence, the dark-haired beauty stamped her foot.

Charlotte sighed. "You could tell my aunt you were mistaken and retract your accusations concerning my morality. After all, the barn dance was entirely innocent. Then, I might take the children and return to Colorado."

Helen looked as if she were considering the possibility.

"However," Charlotte continued, "I quite like Boston, and for Lily and Thomas, it is home after all. In all probability, now that we are here, we shall stay, regardless of what you say to my aunt."

Helen Belgrave blanched white with fury. "If you think I will let a mudsill such as you make a laughingstock of me in my own town, you are mistaken. If you stay, I swear I will shred your reputation until every whoremonger in Boston comes scratching at your door, and I won't care what the consequences are to Alicia Randall."

In a swirl of claret red skirts, Helen was gone. Only then did Charlotte notice that Jason was watching from across the parquet floor. She approached him slowly.

"What was that?" he asked, his usually complacent smile replaced by genuine curiosity.

"One of the tigers, I'm afraid," Charlotte murmured, wishing the woman didn't have the ability to make her feel so shaken. But until she could talk to Reed about Helen's threats, she would have to handle them as best she could. Fortunately, there wasn't time to explain anything to Jason as her aunt beckoned her with an imperious wave.

"It's time to dance, my dear. Come now, Mr. Farnsworth, you must do your duty with my niece."

Before she knew it, Charlotte was whirling on the dance floor in Jason's arms. He was as good a dancer as he was a conversationalist, and a horseman, as she had discovered firsthand the day before when they'd taken a ride, with Bridget along as chaperone. And, if his words were true, he was also an excellent marksman and hunter.

"We look divine together," he told her, leaning close to speak into her ear. "Not a couple in the place looks as good as we do. Beyond doubt, no woman looks as graceful, and I don't mind saying no man looks as dashing."

He was outrageous, but she couldn't help smiling at him.

"Your self-confidence would seem impossibly boastful and boorish in most men, but somehow, with you, it is an endearing trait."

"Yes, I am singular," Jason admitted.

At that, her smile became a genuine laugh.

"Singularly full of yourself," she added, but he didn't look the least chagrined. With perfect timing, he spun her out and drew her back in. "It wouldn't surprise me—" she began.

Charlotte broke off as Reed's face came into view, unsmiling, handsome, and exceedingly angry.

CHAPTER SEVENTEEN

Reed knew the exact moment Charlotte noticed him. He watched the words die on her full lips, as surprise widened her shimmering green eyes.

"Ah, Mr. Malloy," Alicia Randall intoned, holding out her hand to him, and he dragged his attention back to Charlotte's aunt. "I am so glad you made it to the party. I have not had the chance to thank you for handling Ann's affairs so smoothly. The aftermath of my daughter's death was made somewhat easier by your capable assistance."

"That's gracious of you to say, Mrs. Randall." Reed released her hand. "I know not all of Ann's decisions were to your liking. In the end, however," he couldn't help letting his gaze travel back to where Charlotte was dancing in a swirling blue gown that left his chest feeling tight, "it seems it all worked out for the best."

She looked to her niece on the arm of the rich and eligible Jason Farnsworth, III. "I believe so, Mr. Malloy. I had some apprehensions, as you know, and I understand you had concerns, too." She paused and eyed him sharply. "So much so that you felt the need to stay in my niece's home to set your mind at rest."

Reed was momentarily shocked that Alicia Randall had such information, but he returned her gaze with aplomb. Having perfected his guileless stare in the courtroom, he used it now to protect Charlotte as best he could.

"Naturally, I couldn't simply drop off your grandchildren in the middle of what until recently was a territory, with a woman whom their mother barely knew. I did my duty as I saw fit," he added, unable to believe his own audacity.

"Hm," murmured Alicia, apparently satisfied for the moment. "Your diligence, while admirable, was irresponsible where my niece is concerned. I wouldn't want word of it to spread here or any hint of a connection between you and my niece prior to her arrival in Boston. Do you agree?"

Reed nodded, his face grim. Clearly, he wasn't going to get to dance with Charlotte that night, after all.

"Oh, Mr. Malloy, why so sullen?" Alicia continued. "I am enjoying having my grandchildren with me, and Charlotte, too, of course. That is, when I see her at all. She is taken with young Mr. Farnsworth," Alicia pointed out, "and he with her. They do make a handsome couple, wouldn't you say?"

What Reed wanted to say, he couldn't. Not aloud. Not in polite society. And what he wanted to do would get him thrown out of the Tremont. If he could, he would walk onto the dance floor, land his fist squarely in Farnsworth's soppy face, and throw Charlotte over his shoulder.

Once he had her away from the ball, he would kiss her until she couldn't remember being in the arms of another man, and then he would undress her and—

"Mr. Malloy, are you all right?"

He returned his gaze to Alicia Randall, realizing he had been staring like an idiot at the most captivating woman in the room.

"Quite," he said, unable to keep from glancing toward the dance floor again. He had missed seeing Charlotte more than he cared to admit. Suddenly, a beautiful face blocked his view.

"Good evening, Reed."

"Helen." He gave her a courteous nod.

"I was starting to wonder where you were keeping yourself." She put her hand on his arm before turning to Alicia. "Mrs. Randall, your hairstyle is exquisite."

"Why, thank you, Mrs. Belgrave," Alicia said, squeezing the younger woman's hand.

"I wasn't aware you two were acquainted," Reed said, feeling a headache begin to pound right in the middle of his forehead. It intensified when Helen gave him her most feline smile.

"We are newly acquainted."

"Mrs. Belgrave was, shall we say, instrumental in getting my niece to come to Boston, where she and my grandchildren belong."

"Yes, well, some consequences are utterly unforeseen," Helen said, looking pointedly at Reed. "But I fear that Mrs. Randall hasn't seen that much of Charlotte. Her head has been turned by Jason Farnsworth. Everyone has seen them about the city. Why, only yesterday, I believe I saw them riding through the Common. Isn't that right, Mrs. Randall?"

"If you ladies will excuse me," Reed nodded his head to each, "I'm going to get something to drink. I've had a long day and an even longer journey."

He moved away before Helen could offer to accompany him. He wanted to strangle her, knowing somehow, she was the cause of his having gone halfway across the United States to learn that Charlotte was in his own front yard.

His mood had not improved when finding out Charlotte had been in Boston for over a week, spending much of that time in the company of one of its most eligible bachelors, who was also a lazy gadabout, riding the coattails of his family's money.

That thought didn't do much to lessen the green mist of jealousy swimming before his eyes, the very color of Charlotte's own sparkling gaze. Reed downed a large scotch and felt fortified.

After all, he was home and Charlotte was here. He looked over to where she still swayed on the dance floor and was rewarded with her craning her neck, searching for him. She might be dancing with Farnsworth, but he could tell her thoughts were on him. *Good!*

Having spent a hellish month away from her, he'd finally come to terms with the realization he had to have her in his life, and he'd been determined to get her. Hence, his fruitless trip back to Colorado. He simply hadn't expected to see her looking as if she belonged so well in the ballroom of the Tremont. She certainly hadn't owned that dress in Spring City.

"Careful, Reed, you're practically drooling."

He stiffened as Helen leaned against him, watching the dancing couple.

"If you keep looking like that, her dear aunt might think you're intending to corrupt her niece, and then you'll find yourself minus one lucrative family account, not to mention snubbed by Alicia Randall's circle. Besides, it appears Jason got there ahead of you."

"Just what part of this did you have a hand in?"

She blinked at him, but couldn't hide her self-satisfied gleam. "Relax, Reed, and enjoy the party. You look a little frustrated. Perhaps, if you're very good, we can enjoy each other later."

He looked directly at her, taking in her clear pale skin, dark eyes, and ruby-stained lips. Every hair was in place, every detail of her wardrobe carefully planned for optimal effect. The low-cut décolletage of her gown displayed enough to entice but not to be vulgar.

And he felt nothing.

"I thought I'd made my position unquestionably clear in St. Louis."

Looking over to where Charlotte was being escorted from the dance floor after that interminable waltz, he couldn't deny he was, indeed, frustrated. And only a certain auburn-haired woman with eyes like emeralds could satisfy his need.

Watching every movement she made, Reed noticed how she touched Farnsworth on the arm, how he held her elbow. It took every ounce of restraint he had to return his attention to his longtime paramour. "I've always been honest with you, Helen, have I not?"

She was glowering at him now. "Maybe, maybe not, but are you being honest with yourself? What is it you think you've found in Miss Sanborn that you couldn't find here in Boston? Look at her now, Reed. Is she really any different from the rest of us?"

Helen had hit on the point that had been gnawing at him since he'd walked into the room. He looked at Charlotte. She seemed as if she were in her element, confident, gorgeous, and on the arm of one of the established Brahmins.

She didn't look out of place or awkward or like a woman fresh from Colorado. *Where was her simple knotted bun that was always coming down?* When had her bright green party dress been replaced by this sophisticated, alluring gown?

Charlotte was talking animatedly with Charles Greene, the head of the city's most influential paper. And he was obviously eating up her words. Feeling a lump of jealousy rise in his throat, Reed knew he was being selfish. He'd promised her that her writing would have new opportunities and outlets. At the time, however, he had thought *he* would be the one to introduce her to those avenues.

"She looks every bit as if she grew up in our parlors and ballrooms, doesn't she, Reed?"

He felt the muscle in his jaw clench. What did he least want in this world? A society miss? He ordered another scotch from a passing waiter and didn't even mind when Helen took hold of his arm.

"Forget about Charlotte Sanborn for a moment. She's obviously occupied. Have you eaten?"

He looked at Helen. A couple of months earlier, he would have said she was easily the most beautiful woman in the room, and he would have probably taken her to his bed when the incessantly boring round of social niceties was over. She was not the most passionate creature once undressed, but at least she'd never made a moral fuss in the dawn's light.

Now, the woman he wanted was across the room, encircled by admirers, and even if she could break away, she wouldn't. She couldn't come to him under the watchful eye of her aunt. He understood that.

Like hell he did!

Would a passing greeting bring down the wrath of Alicia Randall on Charlotte's pretty neck? He doubted it. But he dared not approach her, not given her aunt's veiled warning and not here, while much of Boston watched and would no doubt wonder. Someone, such as Alicia Randall or even Farnsworth, would have to bring him to her or her to him. Clearly, that was not going to happen.

The second drink had burned its way down the back of his throat and settled into his empty stomach, leaving him feeling a little raw and infinitely tired. This was getting him nowhere. It was torture to have been the only man to get close to her, now to watch while she attracted men as a magnet drew iron filings. He'd be damned if he was going to go begging for the favor of a greeting.

"You're right, I suppose. Supper, somewhere away from here, is exactly what I need." He let Helen accompany him toward the door. "As long as you understand this doesn't change what we discussed in St. Louis. We've known each other three years, and I would like to think we can still be friendly."

"Friendly," Helen agreed, slanting up at him one of her brightest smiles. "Of course."

Charlotte watched them leave together, and her hopes left with them, her heart sinking into the soles of her lovely new dancing slippers. She'd had a near-perfect evening, despite her initial concerns, and she'd even been asked to lunch by Charles Greene with the promise of an assignment. To cap the climax, Reed had returned to Boston. So why, suddenly, did she want to go home and cry?

She hadn't completely believed Helen about their romantic reunion in St. Louis, but she had seen with her own eyes when they'd walked arm in arm out of the ballroom. And Reed had never even come over to speak with her. Not even to say hello, after all the time apart. Actually, he'd looked downright forbidding.

The assumptions she'd been making about Reed's return trip to Spring City had to be wrong, for he definitely didn't act like a man who'd traveled across the Plains to be with her. He had looked as though he wanted to wring her neck.

"You appear a little tired, Charlotte. It's a lot to take in for one evening. Are you ready to go home?" Jason asked.

"Yes." The whole event had lost its rosy glow. "I'll just go see if it's acceptable to my aunt."

"Of course, dear, you may go," Alicia confirmed a few moments later. "But I must accompany you. It wouldn't do for you to be alone with Mr. Farnsworth, especially now you've danced."

Charlotte wanted to roll her eyes at such a silly notion. After all, she was a grown woman, who'd looked after herself for years.

But Jason nodded, looking solemn. "Quite right," he agreed.

Alicia frowned. "Although I had hoped to speak to Mrs. Peabody about the Blue Blood Society. I was going to invite Mrs. Belgrave to join, but she left. Did you see, Mr. Malloy, Charlotte?"

"Yes," she said, blushing despite herself.

"They went off without a by-your-leave," her aunt huffed. "Breach of etiquette, in my book," Alicia added, with a cluck of her tongue. "But he has been away, I understand, and they looked as if they wanted time to catch up."

She looked pointedly at Charlotte, as if to remind her of how improper it had been to let the family lawyer sleep under her roof.

"We may have a fall wedding to attend," Jason offered, causing Charlotte's already wan face to pale further.

"My, but you do look exhausted, my dear." Alicia turned to Jason. "I believe you've been running my niece off her feet. Perhaps I will allow you to take her home immediately, and I'll say my goodbyes properly."

Charlotte couldn't believe her aunt was going to let her get into a carriage alone with a man. She wasn't. Her aunt snagged a passing waiter.

"Please bring one of the female servers here at once."

And with that, it was quickly determined a perfect stranger, as long as she was female, would be paid by her aunt to accompany Charlotte home. One of Alicia's own staff would then have to bring the girl back to the hotel since she, too, couldn't be in the sole company of Jason.

It was a complicated operation, but apparently preferable to one's reputation being tainted.

"Mind that you take the short route, no dallying" Alicia added, as Jason kissed the older woman's hand once again.

Alicia kissed Charlotte on the cheek. "I'll be along directly, dear."

"The short route, it is," Jason agreed as they left. And true to his word, she was on her aunt's doorstep only minutes later.

Charlotte assumed Gerald had already retired when she had to use her key to open the front door. The house was silent. Bridget had put the children to bed hours earlier and was probably in the kitchen, waiting for her mistress to come home.

Ushering in the hotel worker, she directed the young woman to the parlor to wait for her.

Suddenly, she and Jason were alone. Strangely, Charlotte had a moment's anxiety, looking past the glow from the gaslight chandelier in the foyer, down the darkened hallway, and feeling Jason close behind her. Quelling her fears with a silent admonishment, she reminded herself he was a member of high society and turned to face him.

Jason leaned against the door jam, looking handsome and even a little rakish. His eyelids drooped lazily as he watched her. "I had a grand evening. I hope you did, as well."

"Oh, I did," Charlotte said, not being completely truthful. After all, it wasn't Jason's fault that misery had closed in around her after Reed departed the Tremont. "Thank you for all your effort in introducing me to your friends and acquaintances. I felt extremely welcome."

"Then why the sudden long face?" he asked, his voice having dropped a notch as he reached up to stroke her cheek. She didn't pull away as her instincts told her to do. That would be rude. And as far as she knew, he was harmless, if a tad forward.

"I guess, occasionally, I feel a little homesick," she lied. No one in Boston could ever know of her ardent feelings for Reed. The chance that she could lose the children was too great.

Jason smiled. "I thought it might be some such thing. Please, let me know if there is anything I can do to make you feel more at home here."

He leaned forward suggestively, and she realized with dismay he was going to kiss her. Stepping back involuntarily, she bumped into a large form, making her gasp. All of a sudden, Gerald was there at her side, unsmiling but not unknowing. She took a deep, relieved breath, glad for the butler's presence.

"I am grateful for that," she told Jason. "Goodnight."

She let Gerald begin to close the door, forcing Jason to step off the threshold. Heading toward the parlor so she could dispatch the serving girl, Charlotte assured herself the last view she'd seen of him—with a hostile, even malevolent look on his face—had been nothing more than the play of nighttime shadows.

CHAPTER EIGHTEEN

Barely able to sleep after the excitement and the disappointment of the party, Charlotte eventually dreamed of Reed, as she had done so many times over the past month. Thus, it was with a fanciful feeling when she awoke the following morning, momentarily confused by her surroundings but certain she'd heard his deep, rich voice.

Realizing where she was and how real the possibility that she'd actually heard him, she jumped out of bed, pausing at the sight of her ball gown draped over the Hepplewhite chair. The memory of Reed leaving with Helen returned unbidden. *Had he even noticed her dress?*

Charlotte washed her face and brushed out her hair, which kept a gentle wave from the style of the previous night. Her aunt would have a fit, however, if she were to appear in company with it flowing loosely around her shoulders. Taking the time to draw back her hair, she used the many pins scattered across her bureau to secure it in a tidy bun. Next, she dressed in her new peach-colored, combed-cotton gown with indigo ribbons that reminded her of Reed's gorgeous eyes.

Descending the stairs, she headed toward the sound of laughter—warm, male laughter!—and children's giggles, coming from the drawing room.

She felt a little breathless when she entered, seeing Reed with Thomas on his right hip and Lily stretching up for a hug. Her heart skipped a beat, and she was instantly filled with happiness. Thomas was talking about a grasshopper, and Charlotte knew he was relating their trip to Faneuil Hall with its whimsical, green grasshopper weathervane.

Hearing footsteps, Reed turned and saw her, standing in the doorway. An expression crossed over his striking face that was close to what she felt inside. Even so, the smile he gave her was guarded.

Charlotte had imagined their first meeting many times, but she had pictured them alone, without spectators. It had involved his arms around her, a kiss, and words of love, and certainly not the fresh memory of him with Helen Belgrave. Still, he was there, only feet away.

Reed placed a quick kiss on Thomas's forehead and set him down before taking a step toward her, then he stopped.

"You're looking well, Charlotte." His tone, as his smile, seemed restrained.

Before she could answer, Lily ran forward. "How was the ball, Aunt Charlotte? Grandma wouldn't let us wake you up this morning. She said you were out late."

Irrationally, Charlotte felt guilty and stole a glance at Reed, whose own face was abruptly an emotionless mask.

"Not that late," she said, then stopped herself. She had done nothing wrong! *He* was the one who had walked out of the Tremont with the woman who was no longer supposed to have a place in his life.

"About as late as Mr. Malloy," she added.

"You were there, too?" Lily asked, turning to Reed.

"And your princess?" asked Thomas.

Reed frowned slightly. "My princess?"

"He's referring to Mrs. Belgrave," Charlotte explained sweetly, watching Reed carefully. "Yes, Thomas, Uncle Reed's princess was there, too. In fact, we had a rather interesting conversation."

"I didn't know the two of you had spoken," Reed said, crossing his arms over his chest.

"More than once," Charlotte said, frustrated that they were spending the first few minutes of their reunion discussing Helen.

It seemed to be putting Reed in an equally dispirited mood, judging by the way his eyebrows had knitted together.

Absently, she put her hands up to pull on the knot of her hair before realizing the secure bun was in no danger of coming down. Making a pretense of smoothing it instead, she felt out of place and awkward.

Her misery must have shown on her face, for Reed cleared his features of any grim traces and flashed her a much more familiar smile. Again, he moved toward her.

Charlotte stepped back in alarm for his eyes bespoke an intention of which there could be no mistake. He intended to embrace her. She reached out and grabbed his hands in her own before he could sweep his arms around her. *Lord, was the man insane?*

"Reed," she protested, as he stopped short.

"Charlotte, I—"

"Mm, hm."

Behind her, Charlotte heard the unmistakable sound of Alicia Randall clearing her throat. Feeling Reed stiffen, she swore one of her brother's curses under her breath. He released her hands so slowly it seemed as if she'd never be free to turn around and face her aunt, but it was probably better than springing apart with guilt.

In Reed's presence barely five minutes, and she was already compromised!

Moving another step away from him, she turned to face the sobering view of her aunt, wearing a gardening apron over her silk day dress, clutching a basket of roses in her right hand and clippers in her left.

Alicia looked anything but idyllic, however. She looked downright sour.

"Mr. Malloy," Alicia Randall greeted, without even nodding her head. "Gerald said you were here. And what a display you are making with my niece in front of the children. Thomas, Lily, upstairs. It's time for your music lessons, and Mrs. Hunnewell is waiting."

Charlotte watched the children go with mournful faces, Lily dragging Thomas along by the hand. It turned out they loved Mrs. Hunnewell, but they seemed to adore being with Reed even more.

"My apologies," Reed said immediately after they'd gone. His voice was smooth as cream sherry. "Miss Sanborn and I didn't get a chance to exchange a greeting at the ball last night, and after all we went through in Colorado, I consider her a solid acquaintance."

Charlotte's eyes opened widely. *What on earth was he saying?* Her aunt was liable to toss her out on the street at any moment over such a remark. In fact, her aunt was staring from Charlotte to Reed, and back again.

"All you went through?" Alicia repeated, her voice rising.

"You did tell her about the mine shaft, and the wolf, didn't you?" Reed asked.

Charlotte gasped. "I . . . that is, I . . ."

"No, she did not," Alicia cut in. "She most definitely did not mention a wolf."

"I didn't think it was important," Charlotte began. "I mean, you're not liable to meet any here in the city."

In truth, Charlotte hadn't wanted to give Alicia any reason to think Spring City was an unsuitable place to raise the children, in case she should she end up returning there. She had cautioned the children on how upsetting it would be to their grandmother if she found out about the terrifying incidents, and they'd been good as gold not to mention that horrible day.

Now all at once, Reed was making her home sound as though it was little more than a deathtrap. He seemed utterly undaunted by Alicia's disapproving gaze.

"Miss Sanborn was a hero, Mrs. Randall, displaying some truly outstanding qualities. Evidently, she takes after you."

Charlotte could only stare at him. He was laying it on a bit thickly, she thought. But Alicia smiled.

"Why, thank you, Mr. Malloy." The older woman's tone had softened measurably, and Charlotte could tell he had succeeded in distracting her aunt from the compromising position in which she had discovered them.

Setting her roses and clipping shears down on the table beside her, Alicia asked, "Did you come here to tell me about the wolf?"

He laughed. "I'll let Miss Sanborn do that later. I came to offer my assistance in selling her homestead."

That was the last thing Charlotte had expected him to say. She hadn't even given a thought to that transaction or if it even should occur. And she couldn't help the wave of disappointment she felt, having assumed he had come over purely to see her.

"That is most appreciated," Alicia responded. "Is it not, Charlotte?"

She barely nodded. "Of course, I will enlist the services of Malloy and Associates when the time comes," she said. "But for now—"

"For now," Alicia interrupted, "you two will have to get along without me. I'm afraid I must get ready for my meeting. I'm responsible for the decorations," she added, pointing to the roses. "I'll send Gerald in." Reed bowed, and Alicia glided out with a backward wave of her hand.

"Her meeting of women suffragists or free love with Victoria Woodhull?" Reed asked, his face deadpan.

Charlotte stifled a laugh, envisioning her aunt rallying for the right to vote, never mind the right to dally with a man outside of wedlock.

"Hardly," she made a face. "Christian Science with Mary Baker Eddy." But the reference to suffragists reminded her of Helen's mention of her sister. Before she could ask Reed about his mysterious trip out west, a voice in her ear caused her to jump.

"Tea in the garden, Miss Charlotte." Gerald had entered the room on silent butler feet.

"Thank you, Gerald," Charlotte replied, trying to appear as if she were used to being waited on. She turned to him, but the extremely efficient Gerald was already disappearing through the doorway, and she found herself speaking to an empty space.

The amused look on Reed's face proved she was failing at pretending to be a practiced lady of leisure.

"Can you stay?" she asked him, her heart pounding.

For an answer, he gestured for her to lead the way to the garden.

Outside on the brick patio, amidst the small lawn and the flower beds, Lacey had set the table for tea and was already pouring. Wordlessly, Charlotte sat down, unsure where to start. They waited for Lacey to go inside.

They were finally alone.

"It's hard to believe you're really here in Boston," Reed said as soon as she was gone.

"I could say the same thing of you. It never occurred to me you might be away when I arrived." She waited, hoping he would enlighten her.

"What did John tell you of my trip?" he asked, not looking her directly in the eyes but fiddling with his teacup.

"Nothing, only . . . nothing," she finished, realizing it was the truth. Reed would have to be the one to explain if he wanted to.

"It's not important now," Reed said, putting further distance between them. If he had returned to Spring City to invite her to come eastward once more, then why didn't he simply tell her?

She bent her head to hide her confusion and breathed in the rich aroma of the roses her aunt cultivated. They reminded her of the roses Reed had planted for her outside her house.

"Did you really come here to help me sell my home?"

He gave her a wry smile and shook his head, dislodging a lock of hair that she very much wanted to touch. But touching him was what got her in trouble in the first place.

"You've read the telegram I sent?" she asked. "You know what my aunt is threatening and why?"

Charlotte wondered if he knew instinctively, as she had, that Helen was the source of the rumors.

He nodded. "I warned you this could happen. It looks, however, as if you're winning your aunt over."

Charlotte shrugged. "She is a decent woman who loves her grandchildren." Looking into his handsome face, one she'd missed so desperately, she hoped he would put things right. "Reed, you do know that Helen has spoken to my aunt?"

"I am aware they know each other," he admitted.

"She hinted to Alicia that I had acted questionably at the dance."

He nodded. "I believe she said more than that. She told her I'd stayed in your house."

Charlotte bit her lip a moment. "No, actually, I did that."

His mouth fell open, and he shook his head, apparently baffled. Before he could speak, she sought to explain herself.

"It was only a matter of time before Helen said it, so I said it for her."

Reed sighed, and Charlotte thought he might be disappointed in her.

"Helen didn't know anything for certain," he said. "She didn't know what occurred before she arrived or even if I slept in a room at Fuller's the night of the dance. You may have given her a dangerous weapon."

"I didn't exactly give it to her," she protested. But the lady in question was undoubtedly going to use it. "But you're right. Helen has as good as told me if I don't leave Boston, she'll try to destroy my reputation any way she can."

He looked unconcerned. "She has tried with your aunt. I fail to see what else she can do."

Charlotte sighed, realizing he was going to sweep Helen's participation under the rug. For old time's sake or for the present's sake? His next words were on a completely different tack entirely.

"I wish I had been here when you arrived, but it seems you have amused yourself and been kept entertained."

She shook off her thoughts of his paramour for the moment and, instead, remembered her shopping trip and taking the children on their daily expeditions. She nodded, not realizing how her eyes were sparkling with the pleasure of her exciting new life. "Indeed, I have been having a wonderful time."

"Farnsworth knows his way around the city," Reed commented, looking somewhat stern. "I'm sure he's been an adequate guide."

She thought of Jason and how many times over the past few days she'd wished her companion had been Reed. "He has been very kind."

It sounded to her as if Reed snorted. It was such an odd sound and so unlike anything she'd heard from him that she stared into his blue eyes. "Is something wrong?"

"No." The word was clipped.

"Jason knows Thaddeus," she added.

"Your brother? Is he here?"

"No. No one knows where he is."

"I see." Reed stirred his tea once more.

She lapsed into miserable silence. Where was the fluid conversation she'd so delighted in over a brandy in her study? Why was she unexpectedly feeling awkward, and why was Reed looking as though his collar was a few sizes too small? She tried another topic altogether.

"I met Charles Greene at the party last night."

"The *Post*'s editor? Yes, I saw you talking to him."

He had, indeed, been watching her, even when she thought he was deeply engrossed in conversation with Helen.

"I'm hoping to get an assignment. It would give me great confidence to know I can support myself here. Then if I decide to stay, I will begin inquiries regarding housing in the city. I think it best to get out from under my aunt's roof. Then I would have to sell my parents' home, as you suggested. Jason says he knows of some fairly reasonably priced residences a few streets over, on the other side of the Common."

She wasn't mistaken this time as a blunt look of scorn crossed Reed's face. It occurred to her that he didn't care for Jason Farnsworth, III. Not one bit. Almost as little as she cared for Helen.

She resolved to be utterly frank. "I was surprised to see you with Helen last night after we . . . after all you said to me in Spring."

"Last night held a few surprises for both of us, then," he answered cryptically, standing up again and starting to pace the patio. She could see by the closed expression on his face she should let the matter drop, but she couldn't.

"Reed, I must ask you something."

"Ask me what, Charlotte?"

She swallowed. "Did you stop in St. Louis after you left Spring City?"

He paused a moment, obviously surprised by the question. Then he nodded.

"I did."

That was it? That was all he was going to say? Her temper began to rise.

"Is there anything about that visit you think I ought to know?"

"No." His penetrating blue eyes never left her own glittering gaze.

"I see."

She, too, stood up slowly. This was getting her nowhere.

Then he sighed, sounding exasperated. "What I mean, Charlotte, is that when we parted in Spring City, I told you I planned to speak with Helen further. There is nothing new to tell you. As far as I'm concerned, my prior arrangement with Helen is over. She knows that, and people will come to realize it."

"Not if you carry on as you did last night," she bit out, immediately regretting how jealous she sounded. In any case, Reed didn't look the least bit guilty. She crossed her arms.

"You were otherwise occupied," he pointed out, "and I was hungry. That was the end of it."

Hungry, for what exactly? And how convenient, Charlotte thought. When Reed needed a dining companion, he had no problem being with Mrs. Belgrave. And when he wanted to end something, he deemed it finished. Damn the consequences or the untidy leftovers for that matter, such as Helen throwing threats around the way a duck shook off water.

"Is there anything else about last night you wish to discuss?" he asked when she did nothing but stare quietly.

"No, nothing," Charlotte finished.

He cocked his head to one side, and she thought perhaps he had something more to ask, but all he said was, "I'd best be getting to my office."

She didn't know how to react to this distant stranger, who was not at all the playful, loving man who'd taken such a firm hold of her affections. Perhaps this was how he had to be in the city.

It saddened her, making her truly homesick for the first time. Leaving the tea untouched, she passed by him to lead the way inside.

"Charlotte."

Halting, she turned expectantly.

Without another word, he gripped her upper arms and brought her up against him. Before she could register what was happening, Reed's lips were upon hers, firm and insistent.

Prepared or not, her reactions were immediate and unrestrained. She returned his kiss thoroughly, breathing in his familiar scent and remembering all about this man who held her closely against his chest.

He was no stranger after all. He could make all the nerve endings in her body sizzle, and he was kissing her with a possessiveness that thrilled her. Knowing her aunt might still be at home and looking out one of the rear windows only fleetingly entered her thoughts.

"It seems a lifetime since I tasted you," he said when at last he let her come up for air, the intensity in his voice touching Charlotte's heart. Here was the Reed she loved, his eyes glittering like sunlight on a clear blue Colorado lake.

As he pressed his mouth against hers once more, she felt his tongue slide across her lower lip. Another instant and she let him slip his tongue inside. A small moan escaped her.

She wanted to tell him then how much she loved him. She wanted to see him smile at her words, take them inside his heart, and then give them back to her with equal passion.

Later, Charlotte was not sure whether, if circumstances hadn't intervened, she would have told him or not in that instant, and whether she could have avoided so much hurt that came after.

"In the garden, you say," came a familiar male voice through the door.

Charlotte pulled away from Reed as if stung. If Jason saw them together and mentioned it to her aunt—or to anyone, for that matter—Alicia would surely know what had occurred between them in Spring City. Their indiscretion would be obvious.

Reed, however, didn't seem to want to let her go. She managed to yank her hands out of his, just before Jason stepped onto the stone walk. Reed looked black daggers from her, with the red blush creeping up her face, to Jason who was sauntering into the garden as if he owned the place.

"I believe you gentlemen know each other," she managed into the thundering silence.

CHAPTER NINETEEN

"Why, yes." Jason was the first to speak, after looking curiously from Charlotte's red face to Reed's annoyed expression. "Mr. Malloy has been handling my family's affairs since . . . why forever."

"I assure you," Reed said, "it only seems to you to be forever. My father handled your family's accounts long before I became a lawyer. But then you are too young to remember that."

Jason colored at the insinuation he was still wet behind the ears. Charlotte had seen in the short time she'd known Jason that he cultivated a worldly image. Unfortunately, next to Reed, Jason's worldliness seemed exactly that, *an image*, while Reed exuded natural sophistication and unquestionable authority.

At the moment, though, Reed was exuding natural irritation and unquestionable annoyance over Jason having interrupted their kiss.

"Mr. Malloy handles my aunt's family's affairs as well," Charlotte began. "I guess that means my family's affairs. Not that I knew any such thing until a few months ago, but that's how we met."

It was her turn to blush with embarrassment as she realized she was prattling to relieve the tension blooming more strongly in the garden than even her aunt's flourishing roses. "He brought my cousin's children to me in Colorado."

"Yes," Jason responded, "you mentioned that when we were out riding, I believe. It was above and beyond the call of duty, I'd say, to go all the way out there in person. I would think your firm large enough to have underlings who can handle such dusty matters."

Charlotte saw Reed's jaw work a moment before he took in a deep breath.

"I give your concern over the running of my firm all the respect it's due, Mr. Farnsworth. However, you know as little about it as you do your own family's business. You have to work at something to get to know it intimately," he continued, glancing over at Charlotte. "As for my going to Colorado, it was unarguably in my best interest. And what's in my interest is good for my business. Speaking of which, I must return to it."

Jason stood in stunned silence as did Charlotte, until Reed took her hand. He brushed it lightly against his lips in a parody of what had occurred before Jason had come into the garden.

"I bid you good day, Charlotte. I will see you again soon, I hope."

What could she do but nod her agreement, realizing Reed had intentionally used her first name in front of the other man. She was more than a little alarmed at the thought of Jason figuring out there was something between her and her family's lawyer. For his part, Jason barely managed a curt nod as Reed pushed past him.

"How rude," Jason muttered.

Charlotte felt responsible for the inexplicably nasty encounter. "I am sorry. He's usually not that way." Jason's eyes opened a little wider. "I mean," she hurriedly amended, "in my dealings with Mr. Malloy, I've always found him to be both pleasant and amicable."

"Really?" Jason looked her over a little too perceptively. She didn't like it.

"What are you doing here?" she asked, then smiled to soften the tone of her words.

He seemed not the least put off. "I thought to surprise you, to make sure you had fully recovered from last night."

"As you can see, I am fine."

"Indeed, I can see that you are positively perfect." He had returned to his ridiculously flattering, endearing self.

"Good," she returned. "Then you must go. For thanks to you, I'm having lunch with Mr. Greene, and I have to get ready."

Jason pretended to sulk. "But when will I see you again? How can you banish me from your sight?"

She threw up her hands. "Good lord. We've seen each other nearly each day since I arrived, and in all honesty, I don't want to give you the wrong impression. I enjoy your company, but right off the reel, I must tell you—"

"Give me the wrong impression?" He laughed. "Never! The impression you make is always right. That is, it's always one of beauty and sweetness. And as long as you find my company agreeable, I am a happy man. I'll leave you to your morning constitutional. All the best of luck to you with Charles Greene."

He kissed her hand, much as Reed had done, although lingering a little too long, and then he was gone without letting her explain that she, in fact, wanted to see him less.

Trailing slowly behind him into the house, she considered her new life. A few months ago, she was alone. Today, she had visited with two men in the garden and had another one waiting for her at lunch. She smiled. When it rained, it certainly poured.

"I was extremely pleased you agreed to meet with me, Miss Sanborn," Charles Greene said, as they awaited their meal.

"I am the one who is extremely pleased, sir," Charlotte returned, "and I am honored." Hoping to present herself as worldly to this well-known editor, she had dressed the part wearing her new chocolate brown outfit with its long, straight skirt and elegant jacket over a cream-colored blouse with small, lacy ruffles.

After Jason's departure, she'd spent the rest of the morning arranging the newspaper clippings of her articles in an orderly fashion and pacing the parlor. Finally, at 12:30, she'd stepped into her aunt's carriage. Not too many minutes later, she'd been looking up at the gaily striped awnings of Boston's most famous fish restaurant.

Taking a deep, calming breath, she'd wrinkled up her nose.

"*Hm*, fishy," she said aloud, before telling herself to relax. How frightening could it possibly be to discuss her writing career over haddock and coffee? She hurried inside.

"Honestly, I didn't expect to have an assignment so soon after arriving here," Charlotte told the bespectacled, gray-haired man after he'd looked through her portfolio, "but I am eager to start writing again. I'm not used to having so much time on my hands."

"At the party, it looked to me as if Farnsworth would be happy to take up some of that time," Mr. Greene said good-humoredly, leaning back in his chair and pushing his blued-steel wire glasses farther up his nose.

When Charlotte only smiled politely, he coughed. "To tell you the truth, I had a letter from Frank Hudson and would have sought you out even if we hadn't had the fortuitous circumstance of being introduced at the Tremont. Hud and I have known each other for many years. I understand you did some excellent work for his paper recently."

By the time they finished lunch—oysters, which Charlotte moved around on her plate dubiously without being able to eat a single one, and thin buttery chowder with parsley on top, which she finished down to the last delicious drop—she had an assignment that would keep her busy over the next few weeks.

Her first instinct as she parted from Charles Greene was to locate Reed and tell him of her good fortune. Instead, she directed the driver back toward her aunt's house. Alicia greeted her with the news that Jason had sent a supper invitation.

"Anything else?" Charlotte asked as she removed her hat and gloves.

"What more do you want the boy to do?" Alicia asked. "Issue a marriage proposal after knowing you barely more than a week? Not that it would be the first time that has happened to a Randall."

"Oh, good gracious, no," Charlotte protested. A marriage proposal was the last thing she wanted, at least from Jason.

"No, I meant is there nothing from anyone else?"

"No, dear," Alicia answered, then looked at her with a shrewd gaze. "Were you expecting someone else's card?"

Charlotte was treading into dangerous territory. "Of course not. But I expect after last night's party, there will be other people with whom I can socialize. I don't want to spend an excessive amount of time with Mr. Farnsworth. It will give people the wrong impression."

"Precisely so." Alicia smiled approvingly. "But Mr. Farnsworth is known as one of the best sort. Or at least his family is, so I don't see any harm. Why don't you tell me all about your luncheon with Mr. Greene?"

Charlotte was of two minds all afternoon: should she go out with Jason again that evening or decline his invitation? She hated to encourage him, and he seemed to think their friendship was progressing along toward something more. She didn't, however, want to make Alicia suspicious, particularly after the compromising scene her aunt had walked in on that morning with Reed holding her hands.

Besides, Reed knew where she was staying. He could have extended an invitation if he so chose. If he began to court her slowly, then Alicia would have no complaints, but for the time being, it looked as if he wasn't going to court her at all.

Charlotte sank into a hot bath after sending an acceptance along to Jason at the last possible minute. It was partly out of spite, she was sure. As she lathered herself all over with her aunt's best-smelling soap, she could not deny that she hoped Reed would somehow discover she was going out again and with whom.

She sighed. Why was she playing games? What she truly wanted was to be with Reed, not trying to make him jealous, if that were even possible.

Letting Alicia choose, Charlotte was soon dressed in her new black gown. "The palatine cape will be ideal," Alicia added, taking the black satin out of Charlotte's wardrobe just as there was a light tap at the door.

"Come in," they both said at once.

"Mr. Farnsworth is here," Bridget said in her Irish lilt. Then she gasped. "Oh, miss, don't you look lovely!"

Charlotte could not get used to having a servant. She would love to be able to tell Bridget all about her strong feelings for a certain lawyer, but she knew it was impossible. Charlotte could only let the girl finish her hair before following her aunt down the stairs.

Jason's carriage at night, with its five lamps shining brightly on the polished exterior, was impressive, no matter how many times Charlotte saw it. In gentlemanly fashion, after he assisted her in, he also gave Lacey, acting as chaperone, a helping hand to clamber inside. The girl scooted to the far side and tried to disappear.

With such trouble having been taken simply so she could go out for the evening, she decided to have a splendid evening and not think of Reed or what he might be doing.

Besides Jason was an easy companion, quick to laugh, although somewhat cynical in his jokes and remarks. Oddly enough, what Charlotte found most acceptable about his company was how she felt nothing for him at all.

It answered a question that had been nagging at her—whether she had latched onto Reed purely because he was the first man to pay her any attention.

But here was a fine-looking man, both attentive and interesting, paying her all kinds of compliments. Yet for all his gallantry and dashing good looks, Jason caused no flutter in the pit of her stomach, no tingling across her skin.

"First stop," Jason said, "the Gaiety Theatre."

"Oh, the ballet," Charlotte exclaimed. "It's my first time."

"I hope we can share many firsts," he told her.

While not sharing his hope, she let him take her hand as she climbed out of his carriage. Inside the theatre, the women looked like jewels, and Charlotte could barely contain her excitement when they were escorted to the Farnsworth family's box seats. There was plenty of room both for the two of them and for Lacey to sit two rows behind.

As the curtain rose for the first time, Jason glanced at her then touched her hand. "Charlotte, are you all right?"

She let out her breath in a rush, then gasped for more. "I was holding my breath," she told him, "I am so excited."

Hours later, Charlotte felt as if the music were still playing in her head while they ate a late-night supper. The sole shadow upon the evening was having Lacey seated nearby but alone. Charlotte wished she could call the young woman over, as if they were at Mrs. Cassidy's café in Spring City.

"I can't thank you enough for this evening," she told Jason. "What superb dancers they were."

"The night is not finished yet, dear Charlotte."

Next, over drinks at the Parker House, Jason introduced Charlotte to some of his friends. She was again reminded of Reed's promise to show her around Boston and felt another twinge of guilt.

Any remorse vanished seconds later when, to her astonishment, Reed entered the lounge with a stunning woman, dark-haired like Helen yet more freshly beautiful and far less artful.

It made Charlotte's heart sink. Why, they didn't even have a chaperone like the now-yawning Lacey who sat nearby, looking bored. For a moment, Charlotte couldn't take her eyes off the striking couple. Seemingly, Boston was full of good-looking women. And Reed probably knew all of them.

Jason broke off the conversation he was having with a man to his left and said to her, "Reed Malloy. Twice in one day. Do you know that woman accompanying him?"

She didn't bother to deny where her interest and her glance were wandering. She merely shook her head. Jason smiled, as if he were about to partake of a particularly delectable meal.

"It is my understanding that Mr. Malloy is engaged to the widow Belgrave. You remember her, from the party? A striking woman, though too brittle for my taste. Akin to embracing marble, I should think. Considered a snob, too."

He looked over at Reed and his companion again. "Still, the woman probably has feelings that could be hurt, if only she knew."

Charlotte didn't want to hear anything more. Naturally, Jason assumed Reed was being unfaithful to Helen, and it made her blood boil. If he was going to be unfaithful, he was supposed to do so with her! Suddenly, she felt foolish indeed, comparing herself to the woman with whom he was deep in conversation.

They were laughing and speaking earnestly. It reminded her of how it used to be between them in Spring City, in her study, on her porch, in her bed. Her thoughts turned to escape, immediately and without Reed seeing her.

"Jason, I'm fatigued, especially after last night. We retire much earlier where I'm from."

He glanced down at her pale face. "How thoughtless of me, dear lady. Come along, I'll get you home in a snap. Gentleman, ladies," he addressed the small group with whom they'd been sitting. "You will excuse us while I take my charming companion home."

Charlotte was glad to see her aunt's doorway, probably almost as much as Lacey, who ran ahead and hurried inside, obviously considering her duty to be concluded. As Jason walked her up the steps, she gave him the promise he always demanded to see him again soon.

"Are you all right, Charlotte? You seem too quiet, not your normal self, ever since we left my friends."

"I'm just weary." It wasn't a lie. She'd been burning her candle at both ends of the day, up early and up late. "It's not every day I have such an important luncheon meeting and then follow it up with the ballet and supper out. What a life I'm leading."

"There are more evenings such as this in your future if I have anything to do with it." He took her slender hand in his. "You are a most interesting woman, and I would be happy to take you to the ballet and have you at my supper table for the rest of my days."

Jason's tone sounded serious, too serious, and utterly unlike his usual over-the-top style. And then, he leaned down, and it didn't look as if he were aiming for her cheek.

She started to move into the open doorway, but his other hand reached out to stop her. There was no Gerald coming to her rescue tonight, it seemed, and Aunt Alicia had to be deeply asleep by then, as well.

His lips came down on hers seconds later, before she even had time to protest. His kiss was hard and wet, and the feeling that went through her was one of alarm, not pleasure. She froze.

He lifted his head after a moment, and she drew a breath.

"Jason, you have overstepped yourself, but I fear it is my own fault. You have misunderstood my—"

"I meant no offense," he said hurriedly, and instantly, she was looking into the contrite face of the jovial man she'd come to think of as a friend. "I merely wanted to express my deep regard for you, Charlotte."

"That's . . . that's quite all right." But she had to fight off the urge to wipe her mouth.

"Please, don't think ill of me," he beseeched.

"No, no, of course not."

"Dear God! If I've ruined the attachment between us—" He broke off, looking distraught and ran a hand through his hair. "It's only that I feel so strongly for you."

She could see now that he was genuinely sorry for taking such a liberty with her.

"It's fine," she assured him.

"I will never do it again, until you give me permission."

"I'll see you again, soon, Jason."

He reminded her of her promise to do exactly that, and then he was gone.

Relieved to shut and lock the door behind her, she didn't fight the impulse any longer but rubbed her gloved hand across her lips. It had been nothing like Reed's kiss, nothing at all. And she'd known it wouldn't be, even before it happened. In her heart, Charlotte was certain no other man's kiss could make her feel the way Reed's did.

The house was quiet as she tiptoed up the stairs. She'd paused a moment on the landing, considering checking on the sleeping children, when the first scream rent the night's silence. Dashing up the second staircase, Charlotte reached the nursery before any of the other adults, reacting to the sound as familiar to her as it now was to Bridget, Lacey, and Aunt Alicia, too.

"Thomas," she said, then again, more loudly, as she reached his bed. He was thrashing from side to side, but she knew what to do. With a little shaking, she awakened him, bleary eyed with his lower lip beginning to quiver.

"I had a bad dream," he told her as Bridget came in at a run, still pulling her wrap around her slender shoulders.

"I know," Charlotte told him, gently stroking his forehead. "But remember, it was only a dream. And whenever you have it again, someone who loves you will be here straightaway to bring you out of it. Isn't that right, Bridget?"

"Yes, miss."

At that instant, Lily's small form appeared, silhouetted in the open doorway. She came right in and climbed into bed with her brother. "I'm glad you're home, Aunt Charlotte," Lily said. "I was worried."

Charlotte felt a lump in her throat. How could she ever have thought of these two children as a burden?

"Do you want to sleep with Thomas?" Charlotte asked. Lily nodded.

"Would you like that?" she asked the little boy. Thomas smiled in answer as his sister hugged him. "All right then, but no talking. I want you both to go straight to sleep."

She needn't have issued her dire warning, Charlotte realized. They were asleep before she even closed the door.

"Poor little guy," Bridget said, yawning widely. "Good night, miss." And she headed down the hall to her room. Charlotte dimmed all the lights on the third floor and went back downstairs.

In her own room, she removed her cape and put it carefully in the wardrobe. Her head was spinning. She should have felt nothing but excitement at seeing her first ballet. Instead, all she could think about was Reed, out on the town with another woman.

She recognized a bone-deep jealousy that frightened her. *Would it have been better if it had been Helen? At least, she was not a mystery.*

Lighting one low lamp, she sat for a while in the chair by the window and thought how, in such a short span of time, her whole world had changed. If it all fell apart tomorrow, could she see herself returning to Spring City, living alone in her parents' old house, and never again feeling the way she felt when she was with Reed?

It made her shudder to imagine the loneliness and emptiness that awaited her there. She heaved a deep sigh and got up.

Undressing as quickly as her layers allowed, Charlotte put on a clean white chemise, noticing while she did that Lacey had turned down her bed. It was pure bliss, she thought, falling into the puffy down mattress.

Leaning over to put out the lamp, she heard a noise on the balcony, which stayed her hand. She was not a fainthearted soul by nature, but all her fears of Boston came rushing back as the evils of the city seemed to be suddenly at her door.

CHAPTER TWENTY

Charlotte could see the silhouette of a dark shape on her balcony, just as the handle started to turn. With a small cry, she jumped out of bed and was nearly at her door when she heard a familiar voice.

"Shh, Charlotte," Reed hushed her, slipping into her room, leaving the door slightly ajar to the moonlit night. The gentle breeze from the garden carried with it the scent of roses, mingled with his aroma of sandalwood. She leaned against the closed door to the hallway, her heart still pounding from the jolt of fear.

"By the horn spoons! If my aunt were to catch you," she whispered, and trailed off, thinking of the terrible and irrevocable consequences.

"She won't," he whispered back, approaching her calmly as if they were meeting for tea in broad daylight.

Had he completely lost his faculties? She thought of the last place she'd seen him, at the lounge with an attractive woman, and of the things a man might do when buoyed up with a little liquor . . . or maybe a lot.

"Do you have a brick in your hat?"

He froze in his tracks. "I would answer that if I had any idea what it meant."

She sighed, "Did you drink too much at the Parker House?"

"I could ask you the same thing." *So, he had seen her!*

"You could," she said, as quietly as possible, "except I'm not the one creeping into your bedroom at night like a fox in a hen house."

He smiled, his eyes taking in every inch of her from head to foot, as the evening breeze tickled her skin. She wished for her old gaping banyan, unflattering or not! Unfortunately, Alicia had banished it.

Even in the dimness of her room, she saw the flare of desire in his eyes as he took in her sleeveless chemise and the sight of her long slender legs visible beneath the hem. Then his gaze moved upward to her nipples, which stood out like dusky moons against the virgin white fabric.

Charlotte thought he would grab her to him right then, and she wanted him to. All her female modesty and her aunt-enforced morality aside, she wanted Reed to gather her in his arms and kiss her soundly.

"Perhaps I'm here simply to be certain you made it home safely." He moved forward, close enough to reach out one finger and stroke it down the bare flesh of her arm, and then, equally slowly, he brushed it across the taut fabric covering one nipple.

She gasped and pressed herself flatter against the hard grain of the wooden door, even while she felt the passion spiral low in her hips. She wasn't sure about *this* Reed. He seemed somehow dangerous. Shivering, she hugged herself tightly.

"I made it home just fine."

"Evidently." His eyebrows slanted up. "You've been busy. Out with two men in one day." His tone was cool.

Her anger flared as quickly as her desire had.

"You've been spying on me?" she accused incredulously, hugging herself more snugly.

Perhaps he had forgotten he was dealing with a woman who had done for herself and been independent since she was fourteen.

"I won't stand for it, Reed. Besides, you looked rather busy yourself."

"Are you jealous?" he asked, the slightest of smiles playing at his lips.

She narrowed her eyes at him. *Was he playing a game with her?*

"I am disconcerted that you were out with Helen last night, kissing me in the garden today, and out with another woman tonight. Do your passions run so fickle, Mr. Malloy?"

He actually laughed softly in the pale light. *The infernal man!*

"I assure you, Miss Sanborn," he spoke her name as a caress, while uncoiling her left arm from across her slender frame, capturing her hand in his own and planting it firmly next to her head on the paneled door behind her. "You have entirely engaged my passions and have no need to worry about fickleness *on my part.*"

Clearly, he wasn't pleased with her outings. Indeed, it was becoming obvious he was equally jealous of her evening's companion as she was of his. He bent to kiss her exposed neck.

"Reed," she said, her voice husky with warning, as she leaned away from him, pushing against his chest with her free hand. She might as well have pushed against a brick wall. He merely smiled again and, taking her hand in his, pressed it against the door on the right side of her head.

"The woman I was with," he continued, as his thumb stroked her wrist absently, causing her mouth to go completely dry, "is someone I've mentioned to you before." He paused, looking at her lips before turning his head to drop a kiss on her shoulder. "My oldest sister, Elise, whom I will gladly introduce to you someday soon."

His sister! Charlotte would have thought Jason was acquainted with all the Malloys, yet he had not seemed to know her.

Before she could think on this, Reed had nudged her legs apart, straining the fabric of her chemise tightly as his thigh pressed against her woman's core. She bit her lip and saw his gaze rest a moment on her mouth, his pupils dilating.

"Had you stayed any longer in the lounge, you would have seen Elise's husband join us. I don't need to spy on you, Charlotte. This city is small enough for me to know practically everyone. When you have lunch with the city's most important editor, then I learn about it from John Trelaine over lunch at Ladd's an hour later."

He lowered his head and to her amazement lightly grazed her nipple through the cotton.

Gasping, she interrupted him and tried to pull her hands away from his grip but couldn't. If she hadn't trusted him completely to do her no harm, she would have struggled. As it was, she wanted him to release her so she could wrap her arms around his neck.

"If you go to the ballet," Reed continued, "then have supper at one of the most expensive restaurants in Boston, and after that, go for drinks at the Parker House, all with damned Farnsworth," he paused to suck her other nipple into his mouth, fabric and all, and she held her breath at the sensation.

When he raised his head, he continued, "Then I happen upon the very same place and have half a dozen of his friends sing your praises the moment you leave."

He looked directly into her eyes. "I don't need those foppish pups to tell me how fetching you are. Right now, the moonlight has bathed you in a heavenly light, and you look like an angel."

That silenced any retort she was about to say.

He released one of her hands so he could stroke his thumb across her pale-pink lips. "My thoughts, however, are anything but angelic."

She swallowed hard at the thick feeling in her throat. Her pulse was racing, and she rested her free hand on his shoulder, noticing her palm was damp.

He snaked his hand around her waist, locking the door behind her before releasing her other hand and pulling her to him.

"Are you afraid of me, Charlotte?"

Her lips parted, whether to protest, to encourage, or to receive his kiss, she didn't know. But he didn't kiss her yet, although his gaze lingered another moment on her lips before fixing once more on her wide green eyes.

"It occurred to me tonight, lady writer, that with your lack of experience in some areas," he pulled her with him to the bed, "you might not understand how extraordinary this feeling between us truly is."

He lowered her to the bed, leaving her with no doubt what area of experience he meant.

"Reed," she began, and for a moment, she did feel a flash of apprehension. *Was he really angry that she'd been out with Jason?*

"If this is part of the new life you want to explore further while you're in Boston, I'll tell you right now, Charlotte, I won't allow it."

She had no intention of "exploring" anything with any other man, but that didn't matter. How dare he give her orders? "You won't *allow* it," she repeated incredulously.

"Not with Farnsworth, not with anyone . . . except me." He pressed her against the downy mattress, and at last, he kissed her.

Finally! she thought. How she loved kissing this man.

"Mm," she sighed against his lips, grasping his hair between her fingers before clasping her hands together behind his neck. He was thorough when he wanted to be, making her curl her toes as he bit her lower lip and pulled it into his own mouth. But after a moment, he pulled back and looked down at her darkened eyes, his own blazing.

"This passion is not to be had with just anyone," he continued, capturing her chin with his thumb and forefinger while she blushed under his scrutiny and tried to turn away.

His voice was low and rough. "If you think you'll react to *him*—"

She started to shake her head, but he went on, "If you think Farnsworth can make you moan as I can, you're mistaken."

Speechless, she was thinking of the very same conclusion she'd come to regarding that exact topic earlier in the evening. Jason left her cold with his unwelcome kiss. Charlotte put her hand involuntarily to her lips.

Reed seemed to see in her eyes, and in her gesture, something of what had occurred. He fairly growled at her—this refined, urban man who had scaled her aunt's house and climbed into her bedroom, who now, fully clothed in his evening suit, pushed himself up on his hands on either side of her.

"I have had the pleasure of knowing a few women, Charlotte."

She closed her eyes and wished she could close her ears, not wanting to hear about his lovers.

"Look at me," he said, his voice gruff.

She opened her eyes and stared into his. Reed's eyes were nearly all black, his consuming desire obliterating the civilized blue.

"I have never before felt the *electricity* that springs between us. Do you know the word?"

She nodded, having written about magneto-electricity and how it pertained to machines, but never considered it in relation to people. At that moment, it made perfect sense.

He continued, "I feel drawn to you at every moment you're near. It is exceedingly different from anything I have ever experienced. You don't feel this way with Farnsworth?"

It was half a statement, half a question, but he didn't pause for her response.

"I thought to wait until . . . ," he stopped himself. "It's no matter. I have the urgent need to remind you exactly how rare it is between us."

"I already know—" she began, but he was not going to listen.

Reed silenced her with another kiss, one that held all the pent-up longing of nearly two months of separation. It deepened with a strong surge of his tongue until Charlotte had to press against his shoulders with her palms to make him let her take in a gulp of air.

His breathing was as ragged as her own. Leaning on his elbows, he cupped her pale face with both hands before tracing her now red lips with his thumbs.

The civilized man returned momentarily. "Do you want me to leave?" he whispered. "I'll do whatever you want."

Slowly, in response, she parted her lips, allowing one of his thumbs to slip inside her mouth. Then she did what her unleashed sensual nature demanded. Charlotte sucked its roughness while his other hand moved down to slide up under her nightdress. Her eyes widened, but she didn't stop her tongue's carnal exploration of his thumb.

As his hand caressed her thigh and then halted at the hot cleft between her legs, she moaned as he'd said she would. Reed cupped her a moment before dipping his finger between the soft folds of her already-swollen flesh, stroking the small nubbin that stood erect, like an island in a sea of moist heat.

Charlotte gasped, closing her eyes at the heady sensation and letting her head arch with the pleasure of his touch.

With his free hand tangled in the thick strands of her coppery hair, his mouth descended again continuing his sensory assault. His tongue slipped in and out in a perfect mimicry of how his finger now danced into the slick passage between her legs.

"Christ," he said against her lips. "I just want to be inside you, Charlotte."

She nodded, unable to speak, but her eyes opened as he began to unbutton her chemise. She felt his hands tremble, and it matched the trembling in her slender body.

When he'd undone the ten pearl buttons, Reed slid the sheer cotton down over her shoulders and left it bunched at her waist. As he kissed her smooth shoulder, her limbs turned to jelly.

Then the cool air rushed over her as Reed stood up to undress.

Watching with fascination, she anticipated every inch of him as it came into view, nearly faint with lust for his touch, his lips, his straining manhood. But she also felt something akin to an ache in her heart—a love so intense, so big inside her, she would swear it physically hurt.

He rejoined her on her soft bed, but it could have been the hard earth for all either of them cared. He came into her without hesitation, and she relished the feel of her body clasping his pulsing shaft deep inside her.

When he moved, she moved with him, until the instinctual rhythm of their bodies took over, and she could think no more. Charlotte could only hold on as they rode the waves of passion as if they were on a steed of purest pleasure.

Her head was filled with the smell of him, masculine and clean with a hint of brandy. Her mouth was filled with the taste of him, as she kissed whatever part of his skin came within her reach—his straining shoulders, the column of his neck, his firm lips, all the while rubbing her upturned breasts against the dark hair that dusted his chest.

He responded with kisses dropped on her eyelids, her forehead, her lips, her chin, before he bent to nibble the sensitive skin of her neck, and finally to give a last searing kiss to her dusky nipple before she cried out, muffling the sound against his shoulder.

In turn, Reed stifled a groan against her tangled hair as his body shuddered with his final hard thrusts.

They both lay spent, entangled in bed clothes and sweaty limbs. Charlotte thought of it as utter abandonment to pleasure, feeling even more love for this man than she would have thought possible.

However, as the haze of desire lifted, they both were acutely aware of their perilous situation.

Reed stroked her arm, and with a grimace, he said, "I ought to leave immediately."

"I know." She touched the side of his face, so dear to her.

"I don't want to," he added.

"I know."

"May I escort you somewhere tomorrow?" he asked.

Yes, to church, to be married, her heart cried. "Mid-day meal?"

He grimaced. "I was thinking of an evening event. I want to see you in that blue gown again, and then I want to take it off you."

She responded by settling in her bed and pulling the sheets up higher to cover herself.

"I would love that," she admitted honestly, unable to stop the effusive blush, "but I promised Aunt Alicia we'd spend a quiet evening talking. It wouldn't do for me to be out two nights in a row."

"And you wasted your night out with Farnsworth?" Reed rolled on top of her and planted a hand deep in the pillow on either side of her head, "The worst example of codfish aristocracy."

She could see now he was teasing, and she grabbed hold of his wrists, steady as two tree trunks. "I can honestly say the best part of the evening was spent with you, Mr. Malloy. Are you going to have lunch with me or not?"

He lowered his weight onto her hips again, and she experienced how quickly desire could flare up, when only moments before she thought them both sated.

How heavenly it would be if they could spend a whole night together and wake up to take breakfast without shame. *As husband and wife.* She stared up into the face of the man she loved with all her heart.

Reed lowered his head and kissed her thoroughly with the promise to return by one o'clock the next day. He was almost off the bed when he turned to her.

"Just let me . . ." He didn't finish his words but kissed her again, working his way down her throat, tugging at the sheet, until his tongue was circling the hollow between her breasts.

She arched. He grunted. His lips closed on her nipple again, lathing the bud, tugging it, then moving to the other. Her fingers gripped his shoulders. *Good Lord!* She wanted him again.

"Charlotte," he breathed against her skin. "I—"

"Yes," she nodded.

"I should leave now," he whispered.

"Mm," she agreed, grabbing the back of his head and holding his mouth against her breast.

But then he went lower. Trailing kisses down her flat stomach. She held her breath.

"Reed?"

He blew gently at the soft copper curls between her legs.

"I . . . that is, . . ." She didn't know what she wanted to say.

He blew again, then dipped his head and kissed her there.

She was mortified. She felt his tongue. She was ecstatic!

"Ohh," she cried out. He moved up and across her body in a second and silenced her by catching the rest of the animal sound in his own mouth.

A second later, as his ready shaft entered her, she let her thighs fall to either side in abandonment, taking him into her ready and yielding body as far as she could.

"Reed," she breathed against his lips.

And they said no more as he rocked in and out, the climax building more slowly this time. She fought to stay silent, her eyes closed, her head arched on the pillow, her lips parted, her throat exposed to his mouth as they came together, in long pulsing waves.

Minutes later, she watched him slip away, closing the balcony door behind him with a quiet click. Charlotte got up to retrieve her chemise from where it had ended up abandoned on the floor and to unlock her door in case one of the children tried to come in before she awoke.

Inexplicably, tears pricked her eyes. She would like to have heard from him the words she hadn't heard anyone tell her since she was a girl.

Her heart felt heavy with uncertainty. *What part of love was this overwhelming desire she felt? If Reed felt it, too, did that mean he loved her?* She touched her lips. For now, she could not deny him or herself the exquisite passion that flared between them.

What had he called it? *Electricity.* Eventually, Charlotte knew, the flame of his desire would vanish without the love necessary to keep it burning forever.

It was only as she climbed once more under the disheveled bedclothes that she recalled Reed still hadn't told her about his reason for going out west. And then, she sat bolt upright in bed.

"Dear God!" she exclaimed in a whisper. They had done it again . . . and then again! And he had spent inside her both times.

She was usually such a careful person, too, and she assumed Reed was meticulous as befitted a successful lawyer. Tossing herself back onto the rumpled sheets, she considered how one went about procuring *protection* in Boston. Life was becoming so much more complicated outside of Spring City. And here she was, playing with fire.

Punching her pillow, Charlotte sighed. She would worry about it later. After all, one couldn't think about saving the horses after carelessly leaving the barn door wide open. Tonight, she had to sleep. Tomorrow, she was beginning the research for her article with a visit to police headquarters.

CHAPTER TWENTY-ONE

Walking toward the public library, Charlotte found herself smiling distractedly, as she had been doing all morning during the quiet moments. She'd dressed in a hurry, not allowing herself to indulge in sweet remembrances of her night with Reed.

Now, however, she was certain she wore the same smile of satisfaction that had prompted her aunt to tell her she looked "particularly well" at breakfast.

She'd fairly sailed out the door to the police department located at the domed City Hall to begin her work. An hour and a half later, she was armed with notes from her visit with the Boston police and on her way along the Common to the library.

"The best library in the country," she'd been told by absolutely everyone. It was alleged to have 100,000 volumes, which she could scarcely believe.

Relishing the resources at her disposal, Charlotte silently thanked Alicia for causing her to come east. She couldn't quite bring herself to thank Helen, however. Still, Charlotte could see whole worlds of possibilities opening up to her.

"I'm writing for the *Post*," she reminded herself, trying to slow her excited footsteps as she entered the imposing building of brick and sandstone with its huge arched windows.

In front of her, she saw two large staircases, one on the right and one on the left, which together embraced a vaulted hallway leading between them to the rear of the building. People were coming and going up and down the stairs, and a sign on the right announced a coat room at the top, so up she went.

"Man alive," she murmured, at the sight that greeted her as she ascended the stairs. Directly in front was a large semi-circular desk with a librarian, who looked up briefly to nod at her. Beyond the desk, Corinthian columns reached upward for three more stories, effortlessly supporting the expansive roof overhead.

Turning in a complete circle, she felt her feet slide on the smooth black-and-white tiled floor as she let her gaze follow the line of columns, standing like soldiers around the perimeter. Behind them, in the alcoves lining the reading room, were floor-to-ceiling book shelves, with two more floors of shelving looming above the room on two sides. Given all those shelves, she was surprised to see more books stacked on the floor.

"Sweet Jesus." Charlotte almost laughed when she remembered how proud she'd been of her father's library. The thought brought with it a pang of sadness at how it now sat unused, with only Sarah Cuthins stopping in to dust. She would have to decide on many things . . . and soon.

A man came up the stairs and brushed past her, heading directly to the librarian's desk. She watched him fill out a card and hand it to a woman in black with a white apron, who glanced at it with glasses perched on the end of her nose before she headed off to the stacks to retrieve his request.

Still craning her head up and round to take it all in, Charlotte headed toward the coat room and handed her mantle to another woman in black and white. She tugged down her shirtwaist. She was ready.

Instead of being a solemn and grave place, the library was a hive of activity as people came and went, and women in aprons flitted about carrying books. There were more people reading books than she had ever seen before, than she could ever have imagined seeing.

In between the columns were rows and rows of small drawers filled with cards listing each book that waited to be discovered. It didn't take Charlotte long to figure out the system, and with trembling hands, she filled out three cards, turned them in, and then sat down patiently at one of the oval tables.

Most tables had two or three people seated and books scattered across the dark mahogany surfaces. Her table, next to a gleaming marble statue, had one other occupant, a man with his head buried in a thick tome.

Fighting the overwhelming urge to hum, so thrilled was she, Charlotte sat quietly, curbing her desire to talk to the stranger, to ask him questions, to ascertain what he was reading.

Within a few minutes, her three books arrived at her table and were placed directly in front of her. It reminded her of a Christmas from childhood, as she opened the first one with reverence.

Hours later, Charlotte was hidden behind a mountain of books and newspaper articles, along with a stack of the *National Police Gazette* and the *Illustrated Police News*. All at once, she let out a small cry, clamping her hand over her mouth to stifle it.

Reed! She suddenly remembered their agreement to meet mid-day. And then she thought of it only because her stomach gave a particularly loud rumble.

Charlotte glanced at the large grandfather clock at one end of the room. It was already well past one o'clock, the appointed time when she was to meet him at his office. It was unthinkable to simply disappear, especially after their night together. Briefly drumming her fingers on the table, she made a decision.

Putting her stack of reading material to one side and leaving a piece of paper with her name on top, Charlotte dashed down the stairs and out of the library. The library's doorman hailed a cabriolet, and she was on her way.

Fumbling in her reticule a moment, she drew out her compact mirror. With her handkerchief, she blotted the shine from her nose, checked her hair, and shrugged. She would have to make do with her appearance. In under ten minutes, she was at Malloy and Associates.

A doorman let her in, and the pervading scent of beeswax polish reminded her of her aunt's home, both with the same understated elegance. Just inside, a second man rose from his desk, introducing himself as the secretary. He took her name before escorting her to a seat in the waiting area, where a coat rack reminded Charlotte she'd forgotten her mantle in her haste.

Assuring her that Mr. Malloy was in the building, the secretary disappeared upstairs to notify him of her arrival.

Preferring to stand, Charlotte paced the thick oriental rug surveying the art on the walls. There were newspapers in dark cherry-wood racks and more strewn across the tables on either side of the settees, but she didn't have time to peruse them for she heard a familiar voice in the doorway.

"Charlotte," John Trelaine greeted her, clasping her hand warmly. "I heard you were here. Reed will be with you shortly. He had a client drop by unexpectedly, and they're finishing their meeting."

"Oh, that's quite all right. I am late—" She broke off as it occurred to Charlotte that John presented a golden opportunity to learn more about Reed. The flame of investigation sparked by her writing assignment had gripped her, along with plain old curiosity.

"Would you sit with me while I wait. That is, if you're not too busy." She smiled up at him.

"Not too busy at all," he replied.

They sat down on the long plush settee. "How are you liking Boston, so far? I understand that the local intelligentsia have found you already."

"You are referring to Mr. Greene. I'm thrilled to be working again. I suppose you and Mr. Malloy have worked together for many years?" Charlotte felt brazen in her question, but he didn't seem to think her shift in interest too peculiar.

"We graduated together from Harvard, Dane Law School, about ten years ago," John told her. "I very much respected

Reed's father, and have always found his son to be equally skilled. When the opportunity arose, I became a partner."

Charlotte adroitly steered the conversation to the more personal aspects of Reed's life. "Knowing him so long, you must also be acquainted with his family. He has spoken to me of his eldest sister, Elise, I believe?"

"Yes, she's a lovely woman, although I get the distinct feeling she would like to see her brother settled, as would all of the Malloy family," John admitted.

That couldn't have happened more easily, Charlotte congratulated herself, as she grabbed at the opening John offered.

"That seems so easily accomplished," she pointed out. "To continue along the lines of our brief conversation in Spring City, yet Reed seems to have gone out of his way to put up a barrier to keep eligible young women at bay."

"You mean Mrs. Belgrave," John offered.

"She is certainly a formidable barrier," Charlotte said, then offered a wry smile. "I must admit I'm puzzled why a thoughtful man who has had success in his professional life and comes from a happy family wouldn't want to know that same happiness himself."

She had to push on and ask, "I know he is trying to fend off marriage-minded females, but why?"

"Hasn't he told you?" John Trelaine looked surprised. "Well, it's no secret, I guess. He—"

"He what?" Reed asked, startling them both from the waiting room doorway.

John stood up first, looking far more composed than Charlotte felt. She was sure it appeared to Reed as if she were snooping which, of course, she was. And she realized with chagrin that John, who must be as shrewd a lawyer as Reed, had known exactly what she was doing, too.

"He should probably tell you about Celia himself," John finished, ignoring Reed's withering look. John pressed her hand once more before taking his leave.

Charlotte couldn't help but notice that he had a slightly smug look, knowing he'd opened Pandora's box with one simple, mysterious word.

Reed's annoyance seemed to vanish along with his associate. He took Charlotte's hand and with his gaze holding hers for a long moment, he brushed it lightly with his lips, raising memories of the night before.

"I was starting to doubt I'd be seeing you. I didn't expect to find you here in our lounge, deep in conversation with John."

"I apologize for my belatedness," Charlotte told him, trying to regain her composure that slipped the moment he touched her. "I was caught up in my research and lost track of time."

Thinking of the library, she nearly bounced with excitement. "I've been at the library for hours. Oh, Reed, it is . . . well, it's some pumpkins!"

"On the contrary, Miss Sanborn, you are some pumpkins!" His eyes were smiling. "Besides, late or not, you must eat, as must I. We can still do that together, no matter the time."

Her stomach rumbled again loudly. Mortified, she winced but acquiesced gracefully. "I guess my stomach has overruled my brain, which was inclined to skip a meal altogether and keep working."

"We'll leave the grand tour of my establishment for next time," Reed said, wryly, ushering her toward the door, "when your appetite is less demanding."

"Did you want to invite John to join us?" Charlotte asked, as he hailed his driver. She nearly bit her tongue as soon as the words were out of her mouth, for she couldn't wait to follow up on the mysterious "Celia" over lunch. It occurred to her that Reed knew so much more about her than she about him.

"No, I'm sure he's busy," Reed replied, a bit too quickly. "You will have to settle for my company alone."

Charlotte tried not to look too relieved, especially given the way he'd said *alone*, tickling her fancy. She soon found out that, in truth, he meant it.

When they alighted from his clarence, it was not in front of an eating establishment but a private residence. She looked at him questioningly.

"Lunch," he offered, "by the best cook I know."

"You?" she asked. He laughed.

"Hardly, I'm not so deluded about my cooking abilities as to believe they outshine the best restaurants in Boston. But those of my cook's do. You'll see."

That was not the only surprise. Reed's home was a former sea captain's, built almost on the pilings of India wharf.

"It's marvelous," Charlotte told him, stepping inside and gazing around the eighteenth-century home. She couldn't imagine what he had thought of her landlocked little house.

"It's not as archaic as it looks. I've modernized it with the latest in indoor plumbing and gas lighting. Still, the good people of Beacon Hill consider me to live on the wrong side of Atlantic Avenue."

She shrugged. The wrong or right side meant nothing to her. All she knew was that the wide pine floors covered in richly colored oriental carpets and the gleaming brass fixtures catching the light throughout the downstairs seemed quintessentially Reed.

His home was masculine but not stark, and Charlotte thought it suited him perfectly. Right down to the impressive view of the ocean from the parlor at the rear of the house. Sailing ships of every size filled the harbor, and there was even a large steamship with flags flying.

"Think about it. All of our great nation is at our backs," she said. "We're simply perched on the edge of the continent." Charlotte looked out at the sea, which reminded her of Reed's eyes, going from deep blue to gray blue depending on the sunlight. "It's breathtaking," she added.

"As are you," he said, close behind, slipping his arms around her waist and resting his chin on top of her head. "The view is even better from upstairs."

"Really!" she admonished, but the touch of his hands and the heat of his body against hers had instantly lit the flicker of fire.

She had to resist the urge to press against him, although she could vividly envision how thrilling it would be to make love to Reed with the magnificent view of the ocean before them.

"Monsieur Malloy." The male voice startled her, and she felt Reed jump, apparently equally distracted by the heady sensations making her feel as if they were the only two people in the world.

Reed recovered first. "Pierre, this is Miss Charlotte Sanborn. I have already told her of your magical powers in the kitchen."

Pierre greeted her with a nod and a smile. "We are ready," he said.

"I've never met a Frenchman before," Charlotte told Reed's cook, as they entered the formal dining room, which also had a splendid view.

"Then I am honored," he said, as Reed drew out her chair for her.

The table was set for an intimate lunch, with both place settings at one end of a large maple table. Pierre brought out the first course, the enticing aroma of baked cheese and pungent spices drifting out of the kitchen behind him.

"Where is Jeanine?" Reed asked as he sat down, and Pierre clucked affectionately.

"She went on errands, at the wrong time once again." Pierre left them with two small quiches and salad.

"Jeanine is Pierre's wife, my only other domestic. They came as a pair," he added. "She's a mystery of female competence and makes my life easy so I ask no questions."

Charlotte didn't know whether to be envious of this seemingly phenomenal woman or enlist her services for private tutoring, but she longed to hear Reed speak in the same admiring tones over something she had done.

As if on cue, he said, "Since you haven't yet volunteered the information, I'll be bold and ask what it is you're working on for the *Post*."

"I'm working on an article about criminal reform. Mr. Greene decided to try me at a little investigative reporting."

Reed's jovial expression disappeared. "Is it dangerous?"

She studied his concerned face. "No more than my being here alone with you."

"But you're not alone," he pointed out. "There is Pierre, and Jeanine will return soon."

"And will they come if I call?" she asked, teasing him.

"Not if they know what's good for them," he said with a wolfish grin. "They are to remain out of sight and out of hearing distance, except while bringing food."

"Do you do this often?" She tried to keep her tone light as she thought of him having *tête-à-têtes* with Helen in the afternoons.

"You mean eat lunch?" he asked innocently.

She made to smack him with her free hand, and he seized it, bringing it to his lips for a gentle kiss.

"You are a special case, and I told them so this morning."

"This morning?"

"Yes. I told Pierre and Jeanine 'Charlotte Sanborn is extremely special to me.'"

"Oh, Reed, you didn't say anything that would . . . ," she trailed off and was blushing furiously, trying to hide it by taking another bite of the creamy quiche.

"Of course not." He offered her a rueful smile. "I am honestly trying not to compromise your reputation, at least not for the remainder of the day."

It seemed to her as if he had been the sole source of attempts to compromise her since she'd met him, and she had gone along willingly. The previous night, though, in the emptiness after he left, Charlotte had experienced the lingering doubt that perhaps he hadn't used protection on purpose, knowing she was too intoxicated by the headiness of their lovemaking to consider it. The perplexing question was, *why would he take such a risk?*

She wasn't sure how to bring it up, or what motive she could attach to such an action. Before she could broach the subject, Pierre reappeared with roasted pheasant and red potatoes, which he followed with a chocolate soufflé.

"Pierre," she said, catching Reed's cook before he returned to the kitchen the third time, "you are a huckleberry above most people's persimmons."

The Frenchman frowned and looked to Reed. "I am a berry?"

Reed couldn't help the smile. "Just take it as a compliment, Pierre."

"But it is," Charlotte assured the man as he smiled at her uncertainly and left the room. "Oh, dear. I hope he wasn't offended."

"He wasn't. But I'm sure it isn't every day he's called a fruit."

"You'll explain it to him, won't you?" she asked.

"I'll try. Now, my lady writer, has your hunger been satiated?"

She groaned in mock pain as they walked to the parlor. "If this is what you eat for lunch, I can scarcely imagine the extravagance of your dinner."

"Five courses," Reed admitted. "That's why I keep busy from morning until night to work off all the food."

She laughed. Their conversation was back to being easy as it had always been, as if their night of lovemaking had broken down the wall between them.

Charlotte again felt the unusual paradox of being utterly relaxed with this man and on edge at the same time, anticipating his hand touching her skin while enjoying the play of ideas that flowed between them.

During the meal, she hadn't wanted to disturb the agreeable atmosphere, but now, she thought, it was as good a time as any to broach the subject of Celia, whomever she may be.

As far as she could tell, John had given her some kind of key, and it was time to see what it would unlock. She opened her mouth, the question ready, but before she could ask it, Reed took her hand.

"Charlotte Sanborn, I would like to marry you."

CHAPTER TWENTY-TWO

The look of stunned surprise on her face must have been absolute, for Reed laughed and took her other hand, keeping them both captured between his own.

"I'm sorry. That was stupidly clumsy of me. Not at all how I meant it to come out. But now, it's out. I suppose, seeing as Alicia Randall is your oldest living relative," he added, "I should have asked her permission first, but you've been independent so long, perhaps we could overlook that formality."

"Consider it overlooked," Charlotte muttered, not caring at this point if Reed was handling the situation somewhat unconventionally, or that he seemed to have picked up her habit of nervous babbling. Her mind felt almost frozen by his words: *I would like to marry you.*

His blue eyes turned dark as a Colorado winter sky capturing her own in the intensity of his gaze.

"It seems I had no choice from the moment I met you," he said. "When you offered me your delicate hand to shake, our union was inevitable. However, it was after I made the mistake of leaving you behind that I discovered the absolute necessity of our being together."

"May I assume this is why you were on a train to Spring City when I arrived in Boston?" She was amazed how a whole sensible sentence had come out of her mouth.

His face shadowed over and those familiar eyebrows assumed their straight line. "I thought you told me John had said nothing."

"Well," she admitted, "he did say you'd gone back there."

Reed's eyes narrowed. "He shouldn't have told you anything at all. Isn't it a man's right to surprise a woman when he asks for her hand in marriage?" he grumbled.

"I don't know, Reed. I've never had a man actually *ask* me," she told him pointedly.

He flashed her the smile that always melted her stormy thoughts like butter near a hot stove.

"The weeks we were apart dragged with all the ease of Sisyphus pushing that damnable rock. I was unable to concentrate to any degree that was useful to my clients. I tried throwing myself into the social rounds, but believe it or not, they seemed tame compared to Spring City and the evenings spent with you."

He brought both her hands up to his lips, first one then the other, kissing each before he continued.

"I could think of nothing and no one except the beautiful lady writer I'd left behind. And when I could stand it no longer, when I knew I had to have you here in my life, filling it with your honesty and your intelligent conversation, not to mention your sweetness and," he paused, giving her a wicked smile, "your shapely body—"

"My what? Reed, really!" But she wasn't the least bit upset with his words so far, except for a lingering sense of disappointment. She could not get around the fact he hadn't yet mentioned love, the love that had taken up residence in her heart since their first days together.

Still, he had gone all that way back to Spring to get her, and that couldn't have been for her mind and body alone, could it? He must want her heart, too. His wanting to marry her surely explained why he hadn't bothered with protection the previous night.

His expression turned serious as he pulled her toward the sofa, pressing her to sit and then, astounding her further, by going down on one knee beside her.

"Reed, honestly, you don't—"

"Ssh," he told her, placing a finger across her lips, "I can see by your expression I've gone about this all wrong, but then I've had no experience." His eyes glimmered. "Now be silent, woman, and let me do this properly. You deserve that."

She let him take her hand and waited, trembling slightly, as his playful demeanor gave way once more to a serious expression. Now, she was sure he would say the words.

"Charlotte Sanborn, you are an extraordinary woman. I took the children out west myself, for the specific purpose of meeting you."

She started to tell him she already knew that, but he hushed her with one shake of his dark head, causing a lock of hair to fall over his forehead in the way she loved.

"When I met you, you turned out to be nothing that I expected, except for your being smart, of course. You resembled a little girl lost in that house of yours. Yet you had such a no-nonsense demeanor as if you'd never been a child. You are charming and frustrating and refreshing and infuriating, all at once."

He bowed his head, weighing his next words, then looked up at her again. "Charlotte, I have known many women." She frowned at this. It sounded similar to what he'd said in her bedroom the evening before.

"I mean to say, I have been in the *company* of many women," he corrected, "in every parlor and ballroom in this city from the time I first grew whiskers. And they all bored me or lied to me or were just plain silly. I had it set in my head all women would ever be thus and was determined never to tie myself to one."

He squeezed her hands. "It merely took a little while for it to sink in that I could, indeed, change my mind once I found a woman who would never bore me or lie to me, a woman who would only be silly when I coaxed it out of her, when she was naked and in my bed," he finished, ruining the romantic speech with his excursion into the erotic.

She didn't mind but was unable to stop the heated flush that quickly colored her cheeks.

"I must add to my credit, I am from a fine family," Reed continued. "I make a good living, and my house, though in an unfashionable part of town, is comfortable." He paused, looking as if he wanted to add one last thing to his weighty list of reasons why she should marry him.

Then he smiled sheepishly and added, "And I am able to cook, as you already know. So, Miss Sanborn, will you do me the honor of becoming my wife and letting me assist you in raising Lily and Thomas and any other children we are blessed to have together?"

He certainly stated his case with all the ability she would expect from a seasoned lawyer. She possessed all the qualities he desired, and he was a suitable mate with many desirable traits. And now he waited for the answer he was already certain she would give.

Yet what was lacking in Reed's speech was so apparent she couldn't help but focus on the single, terrible oversight. He had still made no mention of love. Charlotte had waited this long in her life—had been already called a spinster by at least three people she could recall—and she could wait a little longer for his love. And if it never came, she knew she could manage quite well without a husband.

After all, she was a woman of the world now, a cross-continental traveler, a writer exploring a stimulating city. And for the first time, she'd found out she could love freely and wholly and even *need* someone without fear. Reed and the children had taught her that and in such a short time.

When she looked at Reed's handsome face and into his intense eyes, however, her stomach clenched. *What was it about this man that was holding him back from love?* She loved him completely, and most definitely did not want to be without him.

Wasn't that enough to make their marriage a happy one? Even if he wasn't head over heels in love with her?

Reed was obviously impatient with her silence. "If you are waiting for my permission to speak, you have it now," he urged.

"Thank you, Mr. Malloy, for your permission and for your kind offer." She felt him caressing her hand with his thumb. Most likely, he was certain of her answer, and this irked her.

Was she supposed to be so grateful to have finally been plucked from the tree of single womanhood, as he'd once described it, that she should settle for a loveless union? Wouldn't he grow tired of her, as he'd done with Helen, within a couple years if there was no love to hold them together? She swallowed and removed her hand from his.

"I'm afraid, as things stand now, I shall have to turn you down."

His expression thunderstruck, he rose immediately to his feet.

"Charlotte," he started quietly, "you're not the type of woman to play games. Tell me what's wrong, and I'll fix it."

She smiled softly at that, and rising from the sofa, she touched his cheek in a gentle caress. It was a dear thing for him to say, despite how it ran against her nature to rely on someone else to fix anything.

Previously, his statement would even have made her angry, but at that moment, she was too embarrassed to tell him what was wrong or to ask him outright: *By the way, do you think you will come to love me for I need to hear those words once before I die?* It would be more than a little humiliating to remind the man who wanted to marry her that he was supposed to declare his love first.

Deep in her heart, Charlotte believed love followed attraction and passion, as inevitably as day followed night. Yet she didn't want to make the mistake of marrying first and then waiting for love to occur, in case it never happened.

With a newfound confidence, she decided she would make herself eminently lovable, and soon, he would succumb. All they needed was a little time, and the match would be as ideal as he'd described it. Meanwhile, she had to give him a reason.

"I have so recently arrived in Boston. As far as society is concerned, it would look highly suspicious, extremely improper, for us to be engaged so quickly."

"Damn society—" he began, but she shook her head at his violent oath.

"It's not purely for appearance. With Lily and Thomas at stake, I cannot do otherwise. It is exactly as you said it would be. I *do* feel liberated here. I want to experience my new life and make sure I like it enough to stay. Everything is happening a little too quickly," she finished, turning away slightly, feeling she was coming uncomfortably close to telling him a lie.

He took her chin in his hand and made her look directly at him. "I am a reasonable man, Charlotte. I understand your hesitations and respect them, but I would prefer you experienced the city under the aegis of being my fiancée than as an unchaperoned single woman."

"Then you shall chaperone me whenever you wish." She smiled tremulously. By spending more time together, either Reed would fall in love with her or he would withdraw his proposition.

He tried one more time to understand her hesitation, "Does your refusal have anything to do with my past association with Helen, or anything she may have said?"

Charlotte considered her answer. She ventured to ask him the question that had bothered her for days. "Are you sure all your associations with Helen are in the past? I saw you leave the ball with her."

"And I know you left the ball with Jason. Should I be worried?"

"That's not the same thing. I am trying to protect myself from any hint of scandal where you're concerned. No thanks to Mrs. Belgrave. Have you forgotten she has threatened me? She would love for Aunt Alicia to send me packing with or without the children."

"I think Helen is bluffing," he said. "She has nothing to gain by making you lose the children or by making you leave."

Charlotte raised her eyebrow. "Does she know that? Are you confident she understands you don't want what she offers anymore? Because I believe she thinks she has a lot to gain from riding me out of town on a rail."

"I have told her, in no uncertain terms, she has no future with me."

"When you joined her in St. Louis?"

He expelled his breath in a loud puff. "We've been over this. I stopped there to speak with her so that she completely understood the situation before either one of us returned to Boston."

He looked directly into her eyes. "If you're still wondering in that overly busy brain of yours, the answer is no, Charlotte, I didn't go to bed with Helen in St. Louis. I have not touched her since I met you."

She looked at her feet. "Well, that is nice to hear."

"And Farnsworth?" Reed continued. "Is he merely for appearances' sake?"

"Not exactly," Charlotte admitted, truthfully. "He has been gracious about showing me around and making sure I don't feel as though I'm an outsider. But mostly, yes, I'll admit that my keeping company with Jason is helping to convince my aunt I am not a moral pariah."

Reed remained quiet, and Charlotte rushed in to fill the silence. "Just by association with him, Alicia sees me as a respectable young woman with one of Boston's finest gentlemen courting me, and he doesn't even know how useful he is."

Reed looked grim. "You are learning how to survive here very quickly. Using people for your own ends is undeniably the first lesson."

She felt as if she'd been slapped. *Was that truly how he saw it?*

"I set much store by your opinion," she said slowly. "If your treatment of Mrs. Belgrave is any indication, you are certainly the master where manipulation is concerned. Now, if you'll excuse me, I must—"

Charlotte was interrupted by the entrance of a lady, petite and brown-haired, bearing a tray with a silver coffee urn and two china cups sitting on matching blue and gold saucers. The aroma of rich coffee blended with the subtle flowery fragrance of the woman herself.

"Good afternoon, Jeanine. This is Miss Sanborn," Reed introduced, his voice having lost the lighthearted tone he'd used in introducing her to Pierre.

The lady smiled at her and nodded, then set down the tray. She didn't say a word before she left the room.

Reed shrugged. "Her English is not as fluent as her husband's, which makes her a bit shy around strangers."

Charlotte was thankful for the interruption. It forced her to calm down and remember their unpleasant exchange had arisen from the fact that Reed had asked for her hand.

In truth, she would love to be able to accept his proposal, if only she were certain she could win his whole heart and not simply captivate his desires. As if reading her changing emotions, Reed took her hand and pulled her down next to him onto the sofa once more.

"Of course, I have trouble thinking of you as a stranger." His voice was even again, and it seemed he, too, had regained his good humor. The feeling of his thigh pressed against her own ignited the quick passion that seemed never far from the surface when they were together.

He leaned toward her, and she closed her eyes. A moment later, his lips were on hers, tenderly at first, then more insistently. She wrapped her arms around his neck and held him closely.

"Marry me, Charlotte," he whispered against her mouth.

She shook her head, and he pulled away. Gazing at her, he searched her face from her earnest eyes to her kissable lips. Then Reed sighed.

"Coffee?" he offered half-heartedly.

She nearly laughed, so surprised by the trivial question. "No," she said, feeling drained by the mountains and valleys of their conversation. "I should return to the library, before someone disturbs my research materials."

"Tell me what time you'll be finished, and I'll give you a ride in my carriage." He stopped her when she started to protest. "I know, you said last night the evening is promised to Alicia, but I can at least see you safely home. Use the library's public telephone to reach me at my office when you're ready."

Her expression told it all.

"I didn't think you had remembered," he said, unable to keep from smiling as she held her blushing cheeks. "I'm sure the library has a telephone, and of course, we've had one at my office for a few years. Next time you are behind schedule, lady writer, you might try it."

Of all the stupidity, she muttered to herself, letting him help her into his carriage a few minutes later. But reconsidering, Charlotte was glad she hadn't thought about using the telephone. She might have cancelled their meeting outright since she was running late. And then she would have missed out on an extraordinary afternoon with the man she was falling so deeply in love with, the man who had asked her to marry him, the man with whom she could not assume anything. And, of course, there was still the mysterious Celia.

Back at her table in the library, she tried to outline her article as she scanned her notes. Criminal reform, mental health institutions, the court system. Her talent was in gathering what was usually right in front of people's noses and synthesizing the facts so they clearly and comprehensively explained the overall story from beginning to end.

Charlotte found, however, it was now impossible for her to concentrate on anything except Reed's oddly pragmatic proposal. She carefully made a list of her sources and then left the library. She needed solitude, but she had one more place to go before her work was done for the day.

Despite a swift carriage ride down Pleasant Street and across the Port Point Channel into South Boston, it was nearly four o'clock when she arrived at the Lunatic Hospital, Boston's sole institution for the insane within the city limits.

Taking in the size of the building, Charlotte decided the best she could do, given the late hour, was to set up an appointment with the head doctor and perhaps get an idea of which, if any, criminals they housed there.

However, after she gave her name and her reason for visiting, she was met not by a doctor but by the institution's superintendent, Mr. Mason.

Squat of stature and thick of neck, the man with hard black eyes neither invited her into his office, nor even offered her a chair. Instead, he started walking her down the long, tiled hallway that smelled strongly of lye. Charlotte put her gloved hand to her nose and hurried after him.

"I'm afraid it's impossible for you to come in here and talk to anyone," the superintendent said, his voice as grating as an unoiled wagon wheel. She practically had to run to keep up with him, as his heels clicked at a fast pace along the cheerless corridor.

"I don't understand," she said. "Why is that so?"

He seemed to sneer as she tried her best to maintain professional neutrality.

"What is unclear to you, Miss Sanborn?"

"This hospital has a reputation as the hub of reform and experimental cures. Furthermore, it is a public institution, run by the state. The courts commit people here to be cured of their insanity and return to their regular lives in the midst of all of Boston's citizens. I don't see how you can say it is off limits to journalists."

"I am in charge here," he said. "I can answer any questions you have about the inmates. But not today. You'll have to return another time. In any case, you don't need to see the head doctor. He's a busy man." They reached the large double doors at the side of the building. Charlotte stopped dead in her tracks, refusing to be put off.

"Is that what you call them, Mr. Mason?"

"What?" he looked bored and distracted.

"Inmates. I'd assumed they'd be considered patients."

He shrugged. That nearly destroyed the last of Charlotte's professionalism. She felt a surge of annoyance. "Is there a problem with my finding out the answers to a few questions?"

"Such as?" Mason's impatient look was changing to one of irritation.

Charlotte pulled out her notebook and quickly scanned her list of questions. "I'll need to know about the types of patients, the general length of their stay, and how many are consigned here by the courts for violent crimes, as opposed to, say, intemperance. And if there are any voluntary admissions or placements by concerned family members."

The superintendent seemed to think the idea of voluntary institutionalization rather humorous and showed his yellowed teeth in his version of a smile. It made Charlotte cringe to think of being under this man's control for any length of stay.

"Now, why would a pretty lady like yourself want to know all about such downright depressing things? Some of them are here for unspeakable, vile reasons." He showed his teeth again at her shocked face. "Why, I bet there are plenty of other subjects you could be writing about, such as—"

"Mr. Mason," she interrupted, unwilling to listen to him roll off his version of suitable topics. "I'm going to have to insist on an appointment with the head doctor. If you think it would be useful for me to ask you a few questions, then I'd be pleased to speak with you in a separate interview." She glanced at her pocket watch as if assessing its accuracy.

"In any case, I'll be back at ten o'clock sharp tomorrow morning. And I assure you, if you turn me away, I'll return the following day and the day after and the day after that, as well. The good people of Boston will hear about it if you persist in putting me off."

His yellow sneer became more of a grimace. "There's no need to get in a pucker, Miss Sanborn. I didn't realize how important this was to you. You simply caught me by surprise. But not tomorrow," he repeated, looking thoughtful.

"The inmates are exercised and given all manner of treatment on Wednesday. There wouldn't be any time for you to speak with the doctor. But the following day." He stroked his chin. "Yes, Thursday will be fine." He turned on his heel and headed back along the hallway without even a good day.

Charlotte stood still and watched him go. What an oaf! Then she let her shoulders droop. It had been quite a day. She could take the cabriolet straight home and send word to Reed, or she could stop at the library and use the telephone as promised. She smiled to herself. As if there was any choice when she could spend a few more minutes with Reed.

The driver returned her to the library where she was surprised but relieved to spot Reed's black clarence out front. She was more than ready to have a quiet ride home. She paused beside the carriage, but Reed was nowhere to be seen, and his driver, Forbes, was dozing on top. Perhaps she would climb inside to wait and surprise him.

Charlotte opened the door and then stepped back in astonishment. For lounging inside was none other than Helen Belgrave.

CHAPTER TWENTY-THREE

"You!" came a petulant tone from the depths of the clarence, and then Helen Belgrave exited the carriage, dressed in a form-fitting pink-and-white striped dress. Her parasol matched the outfit, as did her hat. To Charlotte, she looked like a peppermint sweet.

"What do you mean by throwing open the door to Reed's carriage? Don't you know that personal, private activities go on inside?"

Charlotte didn't bother to respond to that. Instead, she asked, "Where's Reed?"

"Not even the pretense of 'Mr. Malloy'?" Helen remarked, adjusting her hat with one hand. "Really, you're going to give it all away, my dear Charlotte, and one day, it will be in front of the wrong person. One day . . . ," she ended with a small pout on her lips and a shrug.

Thinly veiled threats again, Charlotte thought. "Helen, this is becoming tiresome. Did you ride over with Reed, or not?"

Helen smiled. She was obviously not going to give away anything. Charlotte turned on her heel.

"Fine. Tell Reed I have made other arrangements to get home." She walked off. *Now, why did she bother to say that to Helen?* She knew the woman wasn't going to pass on any message from her, not even to save her own life.

Charlotte started off at a brisk pace but soon slowed as she realized her feet were aching. It had been a long day, and to top it off by encountering Helen in Reed's carriage . . . well, it was enough to make her savage as a meat ax. Yet, she had to believe what he'd told her earlier. There was an explanation as to why Helen was there in his carriage, but it was irksome in any case.

By the time she caught sight of Jason's carriage dogging her steps, she would have welcomed a ride from the devil himself.

"You are out walking late, dear Charlotte," Jason called out the window to her, before making his driver halt the horses. She turned a weary smile toward him.

"Yes, and I've had a fairly full day." She gratefully took hold of his hand and stepped up into the plum-colored coach. "Heaven must have sent you to rescue my feet."

She didn't care if it was proper as she rested her balmoral-clad feet on the seat opposite while Jason's driver secured the door. Her savior cast an eye on her shoes beside him before bestowing a friendly glance upon her.

"Heaven, apparently, has put *you* in my path," he agreed. "Unfortunately, other rescuers were sent as well."

She raised her eyebrows, uncomprehendingly. He sighed, looking older than she had seen before.

"I believe I spotted the ever-present Mr. Malloy, scoping from his vehicle probably for your very person. Were you expecting a ride from him?"

"I was, yes," Charlotte admitted, sitting up straighter in her seat. Reed had seen her get into Jason's carriage. That would annoy him. Then she thought of Helen reclining on Reed's black leather seat like a candy waiting to be tasted, and she added, "But his carriage was a little too crowded."

She couldn't help the venom in her voice. Helen Belgrave was as bothersome as a wasp in summer. If Reed was annoyed, so be it.

Jason made no comment. He simply cocked his head to one side and tapped the carriage's ceiling with his walking stick.

As they began to roll, he smiled. "Nevertheless, we were seen, so I suppose I have to take you home after all."

"Well, of course," Charlotte said, although something about Jason seemed odd. "Where else would you take me?"

She started to remove her feet from the seat, but he put a restraining hand over her skirts, and she was forced to leave her legs where they were.

He smiled. "Yes, where else indeed?"

She was beyond happy to get home. Charlotte meant it when she told Alicia there was no place she would prefer to be than in their parlor, her feet up on an overstuffed tuffet, and drinking a cup of very strong tea.

"How about a glass of wine instead?" Alicia asked.

Charlotte smiled. "Even better." Everything was perfect. She could hear the children playing in the garden, and momentarily, they would all go in to dinner. Yes, it was perfect, except for the specter of Reed in her head asking her to marry him. And for every reason except the one she longed to hear.

Seriously! Marry him without a declaration of love? The man needed a good shaking.

"What is it, my girl? You seem preoccupied."

"It was an eventful day, Aunt. But I don't want to think about it. I'm trying hard not to, in fact." She paused, looking at Alicia's lined face. There was something so familiar in it. "Tell me about my mother," she said at last.

"Tell you what, dear?"

"Anything, something distracting. Some story of when you were young girls together, something I don't know."

And they passed a pleasant evening. When she climbed into bed that night, she kept an eye on her balcony door, half expecting Reed to show up. After all, whatever else was between them—or in the case of love, perhaps *not* between them—there was one thing they did flawlessly and without misunderstanding, without even needing to speak. Eventually, despite the noises of the city, she fell asleep.

Unable to return to the Lunatic Hospital the next day, Charlotte was at a loose end. She brushed Lily's hair and let Lacey teach her how to braid it. She taught Thomas to play cat's cradle, and even showed Bridget how to perform a western jig, which turned out to be similar to the maid's own Irish folk dancing.

After their mid-day meal, she had to get outside. She took a walk up one side of the Common and down the other, unintentionally ending up near the business district. She hesitated on the corner of Scollay Square. Part of her wanted to go to Reed's office, maybe to see him for only a moment, maybe to have a heart-to-heart talk. Part of her wanted to run and hide.

She exhaled slowly. Her overwhelming feeling was confusion. *How could he be so intelligent and yet so dimwitted at the same time?* Did he truly want her, Charlotte Sanborn from Spring City, as his bride? Or was he merely fond of the idea that she was not from Boston and, therefore, not the same as the other women he professed to know?

Unable to contain a big sigh, Charlotte returned the smile of an older lady who passed by, and then realized she must look a veritable simpleton, standing still and staring into the distance.

"I am a ninny," she said to herself, turning around and heading past Boston's oldest burial ground where the rich and famous enjoyed their eternal slumber. With her head down, feeling as though she wanted to turn off her brain for a little while, she had barely gone five steps when she bumped into the very man himself.

"One thing I should tell you about living in the city," Reed said, crossing his arms as he stopped to look at her flustered face, "is that you have to look where you're going."

She thought of his proposal. She thought of Helen. She thought of the unknown Celia. She touched her bonnet to make sure it was still in place, giving her a moment to stay the words that wanted to start bubbling out of her mouth like water from a fountain.

"I apologize for treading on your foot, Reed."

He didn't smile. "I've sustained no injury. But I'm surprised to see you walking. You have a penchant for riding in a certain ridiculous violet-colored vehicle, don't you?"

So, he *had* seen her get into Jason's carriage. And it had irritated him as she'd suspected it would. Charlotte blushed, wishing she could stop the guilty-looking color from rising to her cheeks.

"I needed a ride. Mr. Farnsworth was kind enough to give me one."

"I offered you a ride. Surely, you don't think your aunt would find it any less improper for you to be driving around unchaperoned with Farnsworth than she would with me."

"I guess that depends on the chaperone. And I didn't particularly care for the one you'd chosen."

Reed narrowed his eyes. "What are you talking about?"

"The ever-present Mrs. Belgrave." She wished she didn't sound so peevish whenever she mentioned that woman.

He shrugged. "You are talking in riddles. It is always back to Helen, no matter how many times I tell you she means nothing to me. I have not had the same assurance from you regarding Farnsworth. I know he has kissed you."

She blanched.

"Yes, that's the exact look that told me so. Was he familiar with you yesterday in his carriage?"

Her mind went immediately to Jason's hand across her ankles. Her eyes widened.

"Damnation, Charlotte," Reed swore. "I am not a man to give up, but I am being sorely tested."

He walked past her, not looking at her again. Not even saying goodbye. She watched his tall figure moving rigidly away, and she felt physically sick. Disregarding the other people strolling the path, she called out to him.

"Reed Malloy, don't you walk away from me." *Please.*

He stopped in his tracks but didn't turn around. Perhaps he was weighing his options. Was it worth it to turn and face her? Was she worth the trouble?

He had offered her his hand in marriage, Charlotte reminded herself. She could certainly take the first step. She took one, then another.

"Reed," she said again, more steadily.

He turned, but his face was still forbidding. She walked closer until she was only an arm's length away. She looked up earnestly into his blue gaze.

"Jason did not kiss me in his carriage yesterday. He took me by surprise one evening, perhaps he was a bit in his cups." She hesitated, remembering the feeling of repulsion. "I didn't like it, and I would never let him do that again."

"Does *he* know that?" Reed asked, his voice quiet, his tone flat.

"I … I think so," Charlotte returned. *What exactly had she said to Jason?*

"You think so! Yet you are exceedingly clear when telling me you cannot accept my proposal of marriage."

"Reed—"

"You are playing with a grown man."

She thought he meant himself, but then he added, "If you get into Farnsworth's carriage and ride alone with him, you are sending him a clear signal."

"Yours was otherwise occupied," she stated, but then added, "I'm starting to think you didn't know that."

His blank face confirmed her suspicions.

"Helen was in your carriage at the library."

It looked like dawn breaking over a rough ocean as he comprehended the situation.

"She was not in it by my invitation, Charlotte." He took her hand in his. "I swear it."

"I believe you." Truly, she had known this all along.

"I went into the library to find you. I looked upstairs and down, to no avail. When I came out, I thought you might be nearby and started toward your aunt's home in my carriage. By myself," he added. "Alone. Then I saw you disappear into the confines of Farnsworth's coach." His grip tightened.

"If my feet hadn't been hurting, I wouldn't have accepted a ride," she promised.

"If you get in his carriage, if you let him take you places, you're encouraging him to pursue you," Reed said, dropping her hand.

"That's not fair," she began but stopped her protests when he swore under his breath, looking to the heavens for patience.

"You don't understand how it works. You can't possibly, but I'm telling you, Charlotte, if others also saw you get into his carriage, your behavior would not be deemed appropriate, no matter how much your feet hurt.

She stared hard at him, but he was right. She looked down at the pavement. Her behavior was that of a bumpkin, someone who, as Reed had said, couldn't possibly know.

His hand raised her chin. "Look at me."

For some reason, the gentleness in his tone nearly brought her to tears, and she closed her eyes.

"Charlotte Sanborn. Look at me."

She swallowed and breathed evenly until the feeling passed. *What had she to cry about anyway?* When she finally looked up, she encountered an unquestionably sensual blue gaze.

"Will you come with me?"

"But you just said—"

"That doesn't apply to me, Charlotte. I *am* pursuing you." He smiled at her. "And you *are* encouraging me correct?"

She nodded and let him take her arm. "Where are we going?"

"You'll see," was all he said.

Inwardly, she felt a delicious tingle at the thought of a mystery.

Finally, she was alone with Reed in his bustling city. He was by her side, they were on friendly terms, and all seemed right with the world. She thought they were heading toward his office, but then he took a turn and they were on Washington Street.

"Almost there," he said, after they'd gone a block. And in the next minute, they arrived at the corner of School Street, and she gasped.

"Oh, Reed," she exclaimed, examining the building's signage, "it's incredible." It was not the interesting architecture that caused her reaction. For though the corner building was old, it was not particularly attractive. It was the sight of all the books for sale in the large, old bookstore.

"I am sure I could get that particular reaction out of one singular woman," Reed said, not taking his gaze off her brightened face. He escorted her inside.

"Tell me about this place," she beseeched, as she perused the first line of shelves.

When other men might whisper sweet nothings, he told her of the building's history. Erected in 1718, it had withstood much change and was a testimony to the ongoing value of the written word. Earlier in the century, the bookstore had the reputation as the most respectable bookselling and publishing house in America, and it was once the gathering place of Hawthorne, Emerson, and Thackeray, and even Charles Dickens had gone there.

Charlotte was enchanted, even more so by the fact that Reed had understood her enough to know how she would feel about such a place. They spent an hour lingering in the shop, picking up books and pointing out passages to each other, sharing their likes and dislikes.

"Choose something and let me buy it for you," he said, as she scanned a shelf of English classics. She considered his offer.

"In the first place," she said, running her hand over the spines of the books in front of her, "I am not sure I should take a gift from you. After all, I don't understand about how such things work."

She shot him a glance and saw he was smiling wryly. "And in the second place, I would never be able to choose one," she concluded with a helpless shrug that took in the hundreds of titles available.

"It works this way," he said, grasping her gloved hand. "You let me shower you with gifts as I see fit because it brings me extreme happiness. And if you can't decide, then I shall pick one for you," Reed countered, pulling her after him to stand by the clerk. "Stay right here," he told her. Then he strolled back through the shop, pausing a few moments until he finally settled on something, which he would not let her see.

"Patience," he said, as the shop clerk wrapped his choice in brown paper. Once outside, they walked a block to a coffeehouse and took seats outside. Only after ordering refreshments did Reed hand her the small package.

Charlotte opened the brown paper slowly, then she caught her breath as she withdrew a leather-bound copy of Ovid's *Ars amatoria*.

Staring at the elegant gold lettering on the cover, she read over the Latin words as her mind translated, "The Art of Love." For a moment, she tried to convince herself it was silly to attach meaning to the thin volume in her hand, but her heart raced anyway.

"Have you read it?" he asked finally, when it seemed she couldn't find any words.

"No, I have not."

"Truthfully, I haven't either," he admitted.

She laughed. "I would have thought his *Metamorphoses* might be more apropos given the change that has taken place in my life in the last few months."

His gaze never wavered from her face. "No, I chose the right book." Taking her hand in his, he seemed unmindful of passersby.

"Once again, Charlotte, I am asking you to marry me, but this time, I am going to do it correctly."

CHAPTER TWENTY-FOUR

Reed reached into his pocket and pulled out a small black velvet case. He placed it on the table, and before Charlotte had time to realize what he was doing, he opened it.

In front of her was a ring with a single, glittering diamond, rectangular in shape. It was so clear and sparkling, it looked almost blue.

"It's exquisite," she murmured, unable to stop herself from leaning forward and taking a closer look.

"I wasn't going to do this now, not today, not in this manner. But running into you has been fortuitous, and I cannot let the opportunity pass. Yesterday, when you gave me the mitten—"

"I did no such thing," she interrupted. "That is, I did turn down your proposal, but only because . . . ," she trailed off and sat back, with her mouth closed.

"Because?" Reed insisted. "Because why?"

Charlotte groaned inwardly. He thought she was being difficult, but how could she *ask* him to love her?

When his question met with silence, he continued, "As I said, when you turned me down, I spent the afternoon nearly deranged with frustration, especially when I'd seen for myself how easy it was for another man to take you away from me."

"It was nothing more than a ride home, Reed," she protested, but he wasn't listening.

"Then last night, I passed a jeweler and it hit me, like a wagonload of diamonds, I guess." He smiled wryly. "A man should never ask a woman for her hand without offering her something glorious to put on it."

Charlotte had been listening to his words with growing horror. At his conclusion, she rubbed her hands over her face and sighed.

"Is that what you think of me? That I would not agree to be your wife until I saw the size of the stone? Do you think I've been saying no in order to honey-fuggle the biggest diamond I can?"

"No, that's not what I meant. Yet I can think of no other reason." He looked exasperated. "Please, Charlotte, what *is* the problem?"

"The problem is," Charlotte began, thinking to tell him again that she simply needed more time. Then she narrowed her eyes at him. Maybe she wasn't using her head. Perhaps it was time to try the key John Trelaine had graciously given her.

"Would you care to tell me about Celia?"

"Celia!" He was obviously caught off guard. She could see it in the way he stared at her, surprised, just as he had done long ago on her front porch when she'd suggested *she* needed a wife. Then he shook his head.

"I wondered how long it would take before you'd ask. I admired your restraint through lunch yesterday." He sighed. "What a pity I interrupted you and John when I did. If I hadn't, you need not have bothered to ask me at all."

She refused to back down at this point.

"That's not fair, Reed. Until yesterday, I didn't know there was anything to ask about. Shouldn't I know about the past of the man who already knows practically everything about me?"

He stared at her a moment before settling more comfortably in his seat and sipping his coffee. When he put the cup down, he looked resigned to the ensuing discussion.

"Very well. But I'm telling you now, Celia has nothing to do with us, no more than Helen does. Do you understand that?"

Charlotte nodded. "Please continue."

Reed sighed. "I don't know why John mentioned her, of all people. She hasn't even lived in the States for over a decade." He shrugged as if this were all tedious. "She was the most beautiful girl in Boston when I was a green youth of eighteen."

Charlotte tried to conjure up the image of Reed being anything other than sophisticated, but failed.

"We moved in the same circles. Her father was a banker and her brother was at Dane Law School at Harvard, two years ahead of me. Naturally, I arranged to be where she was, to show up at the same parties, and always to play the gallant. What I was actually playing was the fool."

He said it as a recognized fact, without shame or humiliation or even bitterness. Charlotte remained silent, her hands clasped tightly in her lap, willing him to continue.

"For a year, I followed her around, thinking her the sweetest, most desirable female in the world. While there were other girls who showed an interest in me, and I'm sure some were quite nice, my eyes could see nothing but Celia. At times, I thought I was close to winning her." He smiled wryly at his youthful naiveté.

"She would dance all evening only with me or agree to go riding on the Common. The next day, she would be out with some other young man. I started to give up hope when all of a sudden, she came to me and said I was being far too slow at courting her. Needless to say, I was astounded . . . and ecstatic. A week later, I bedded her."

Charlotte gasped, and Reed locked eyes with her. "You wanted to know."

"Yes," she whispered through the abrupt pain that had no particular location in her body. It was an overall jealous ache at his wanting another woman so fervently. "Go on."

"It had been over a year of wanting her, after all. I took the opportunity she gave me, as a drowning man finally being thrown a rope. Believe me, no one was more surprised than I was." He paused, a sardonic look upon his face.

"Perhaps I should clarify, however. I believe *she* bedded me. For as it turned out, she was already *enceinte* and was looking for a suitable father on whom to pin the blame. Apparently, the one who planted his seed was from the wrong side of town."

"How horrible!" Charlotte exclaimed. "The woman you set upon a pedestal—"

"Turned out to be a conniving, manipulative bitch, playing every man off each other. Unfortunately, she concluded I presented her with the best choice for a husband, as I was doing well, particularly in moot court, and showing every promise of graduating early from law school."

Reed had a faraway expression as if recalling it in vivid detail. "When her father learned about her condition, he came looking for me. Even though I'd used every precaution, unlike when you and I were intimate. For some reason, I was able to keep my head about me with her. Not with you," he added, ruefully.

Charlotte felt the familiar warmth infuse her cheeks, thinking of their completely uninhibited passion that wiped the thought of protection out of both of their minds.

"He nearly succeeded in railroading me into the marriage, even when it became clear that there were other men in line for ownership of the babe blossoming inside her. Then he tried to buy me, as any wealthy banker would, I suppose. Finally, he threatened my career, and my father stepped in."

He paused, and Charlotte put her hand out to touch his, although he didn't seem to notice.

"My father was an excellent attorney in his day, not to mention a formidable man. He had a presence that commanded respect and in some cases, downright terror." Reed gave a wry smile, remembering.

"Before I knew it, Celia was on a boat to Europe. That was the end of that," he said firmly, before draining the last of his coffee in a quick gulp.

"And you soured on women," Charlotte finished, then thought of how he used Helen to keep marriageable women at arm's length, "and for a long time, on marriage, too." *And what about love?*

"I wasn't such a twit to believe that one woman represented all women, but I did start to notice a pattern in my social circles. Something along the lines of women on the hunt, bagging the most eligible man within their reach." Reed shrugged.

"I admit that Celia's betrayal caused a certain mistrust to grow in me, and it wasn't hard to notice how women often conveniently fall in love with the wealthiest or most influential man in the room. As I became more of both, I found myself being pursued by more women than I could have imagined, some who professed to love me, almost at first sight."

Charlotte wanted to defend her own fair sex but couldn't. He was probably accurate in his assessment of the young women of his acquaintance. She withdrew her hand from his and waited for him to continue.

"Then I soured, as you put it. I'll end this by saying that, at least with Helen, I knew exactly what I was getting."

And now? Had he changed his mind about women? "I assume your marriage proposal means with me, as with Helen, you know exactly what you're getting, except you find me more acceptable as a wife than you do her."

He looked straight into her eyes, sensing, perhaps, she was not entirely happy about being a creature who lacked any mystery.

"That seems a dispassionate way of looking at it," he said, "especially since you've been unconventional from the beginning. To tell you the truth, Charlotte, I'm never sure what will happen when it comes to you."

She merely shrugged and let him take her hand.

"To me," Reed said, "there is something incredibly appealing about an independent woman supporting herself, even spurning all company, seemingly so straitlaced but hiding an utterly passionate spirit."

She wished there was a way to keep herself from blushing constantly. She must appear like a barber's pole, but he continued, "And then, you traveled two thousand miles to fight for children who aren't even yours."

Reed ran his free hand through his thick, dark hair. "Yet, I would have to say you're correct. Through everything, I feel I know where I stand with you. Or at least I did until yesterday. I don't think you're one to play games. Thus, I'm at a loss, Charlotte."

His eyes searched over her face. "I know you to be an excellent companion, and I trust I can be the same to you. And our compatibility in certain areas," he continued, and she was in no doubt as to what he meant, "is obvious. I fail to see why you won't marry me?"

How could this man be so dimwitted and so intelligent at the same time? She simply could not ask out loud, *Do you love me?* He would, in all likelihood, answer in the affirmative regardless, and she would always wonder if she'd forced it out of him.

No, he would have to come to it on his own or not come to it at all.

"I've already told you," Charlotte said, referring to the myriad of trumped up reasons she'd given him the day before. Gently but firmly, she pushed the jewelry case toward him. Gathering her new book and her reticule as she glanced around at the long blue-gray shadows on the sidewalk, she added, "It's getting late. Aunt Alicia will be wondering how I could walk for so long."

His eyes narrowed and his face looked grim. "Your answer is still no."

"Yes," she said quickly. "That is, no. I mean, you are correct, my answer is still no."

He stood up silently, then reached for the velvet case and closed it with a loud snap. Pulling her chair out for her, he offered her his arm and they walked to his clarence. Still, he said nothing more. When the carriage door was closed behind them and they were moving, Charlotte lifted her head and searched out his gaze, but he was looking at the passing landscape.

"Reed," she began, but stopped as he turned to her, his piercing blue eyes locking with her own. She wasn't sure what she saw. Annoyance, anger, perhaps sadness.

Then he spoke. "I will not bother you again with my offer of marriage until you have had sufficient time to 'experience your new life.' That is how you put it yesterday, isn't it?"

She hadn't heard that tone from him before. It was clear she had hurt him, or perhaps wounded his pride. In either case, as things stood between them, Charlotte didn't know how to resolve the situation. If he distanced himself from her, how would he ever fall in love with her?

She leaned forward. "I have experienced far more since meeting you, and with you, than I ever have in my life. I have *seen the elephant*, as they say."

"And yet?" he prompted, his gaze staying steadily on hers.

She swallowed, trying to think of a way to phrase what she truly wanted from him.

He spoke before she could. "Yet you still think there may be something more out there, and you're not ready to settle for me."

Charlotte clutched at the book on her lap. *Settle for him?* How ridiculous! They both knew he could have any single woman in Boston, and probably many of the married ones, too. Still, she feared that by putting him off, *giving him the mitten*, as he'd said, she'd touched upon the old wound left by Celia, who had used him horrendously while trying to get what she wanted.

"You have been sheltered and closed off from relationships and society," Reed continued, warming to his hypothesis for why she was refusing him. "I've had more experience with the world than you, and so I'm able to ask you, with complete certainty, to share my life, despite the brevity of our acquaintance. The question is, how long shall I be willing to wait for you to do the same?"

She couldn't help but bristle at his veiled ultimatum. Plainly, he was telling her to hurry or risk having no marriage at all. He had no right to accuse her of being ignorant or naive. She knew her heart and had already decided he was all she would ever want. She paused before responding, collecting her emotions and reminding herself that he was hurt, after all.

"It is my hope," she said softly, daring to lay her gloved hand on his arm, "that you can wait until . . . until everything falls into place. I have faith the time will come sooner rather than later." Basically, she had to figure out how to make him fall head over heels in love with her and declare it.

Reed sighed then, and his face relaxed. "You are being cryptic, but I suppose not intentionally." He placed his hand over hers. "There's obviously too much going on in there," he said, half in earnest, tapping the side of her head with his index finger.

"Too much by far," he added. "Why couldn't I have chosen a simple woman?" His thumb moved down slowly to caress her cheek. The tingling began in her body at his touch, immediate and, as he'd said before, electric.

"Because you would be bored," she said, trying to regain her composure. Charlotte had to speak lightly, or she feared she would beg him to make love to her in the carriage. "Isn't that why you kept Mrs. Belgrave as your watchdog?"

The cloud that crossed his features passed over in the space of a candle flame's flicker, but she knew she'd seen it. There was something else, she was sure, that had caused him to retreat from the ranks of eligible bachelors—something in the way he'd put a quick end to the woeful tale of the beautiful Celia.

Moreover, his brief expression reminded her too well of the face that used to look back at her from her own oval mirror. It held fear such as she had once known. And while hers was a fear of loneliness after Teddy moved away, what Reed could be afraid of was unknown to her.

They drew up in front of her aunt's home. Charlotte realized, for the moment at least, they had come to a truce or a stalemate. She wasn't sure which. While she waited for Reed to help her down, she heard a loud crack followed by a man's warning cry.

Through the open carriage door, she saw Reed's horror-struck face as he looked down the street toward the noise. She barely had time to acknowledge the quick surge of alarm that raised the hairs on her neck when a bone jarring impact sent her flying.

CHAPTER TWENTY-FIVE

Reed caught her in midair as the clarence lurched forward. His team of horses spooked and ran a few yards, striking another carriage and a lamppost before Forbes could get them under control. Charlotte and Reed landed together ungracefully with her on his stomach at the foot of Alicia Randall's steps.

"Are you all right?" Charlotte asked, looking down at Reed sprawled on his back, his face barely visible underneath her skirts.

"I think I should be asking you that," he said as they began to untangle themselves.

"I'm fine, I think," she stammered.

Her aunt's door opened, and Gerald came into view followed by Alicia.

"Gracious! What happened?" her aunt asked, as Gerald came down the steps to assist Charlotte.

"It seemed to be a runaway carriage," Reed said, dusting himself off. He scanned the roadway. "But it's gone! Forbes," Reed called, as his driver returned with the shaken pair of Bays and the damaged carriage still attached. "What in God's name happened?"

"Don't rightly know, sir," the sandy-haired man answered. He, too, looked shaken. "I heard what sounded like a gunshot, then a man called out. I turned and sees the *whisky* coming straight for us, horse an' all. There weren't no one on the dickey as I could see."

"No driver!" exclaimed Alicia, grasping the seriousness of what had just occurred. "You could have been killed," she said, hugging Charlotte who still felt a bit dazed.

"Reed," Charlotte asked as her aunt released her, "how could there be no driver? I heard the noise, too. Was it a gunshot?"

He looked red-faced with anger. "It was some blamed fool out of control. Thankfully, it was a shay. Something heavier and we might not be here right now." He surveyed his clarence. One of the back wheels was cracked with the spokes sticking askew, and the rear axle was hanging at an odd angle.

Charlotte noticed he hadn't answered her questions and began to wonder if he suspected foul play. Horses ran away with their carriages all the time, but gunshots in the city were uncommon. One name popped into her head, along with her last unfinished threat. She knew Helen was capable of vicious slander and cruel manipulation, but had never thought bodily injury was in her repertoire. Still, the stakes, as Charlotte's father would have said, were very high.

"I think it's time to retire, don't you?" Alicia asked, looking pale.

Charlotte nodded. This wasn't the place or the time to discuss her suspicions regarding Helen with Reed.

"Thank you for the ride home, Mr. Malloy," she offered, "and for your quick reflexes."

"Are you certain you're—?" he began.

"I'm unharmed," she finished. "At least, nothing a hot bath won't fix. But what about your carriage?"

"Forbes will take one of the horses and fetch a wainwright. I'll ride the other home."

Charlotte wanted to smooth his eyebrows out of their severe straight rule, but she could do nothing in front of Alicia, who might already be suspicious about why she was spending so much time with the family attorney.

Glancing behind her, she made sure her aunt had mounted the steps and was out of earshot.

"You do make an excellent pillow," she added under her breath, trying to make Reed smile, but he didn't.

"How is your niece this morning?"

"Why, I'm fine," Charlotte answered Jason's query directed to her aunt, as she floated into the parlor on a wave of determination to breach the barriers of Boston's Lunatic Hospital in an hour. Seeing him there so early, however, breaching the polite etiquette she'd learned since coming East, caused her concern. He was behaving far too familiarly with her.

An array of emotions crossed Jason's face when he saw her, the last one seemed to be utmost happiness.

"I heard there was some trouble in the street here yesterday, and I was concerned."

Charlotte took a seat in the parlor as tea was brought in. The warm, familiar scent of it was reassuring. "There was a runaway curricle, but no one was hurt."

"I'm surprised word reached you already, Mr. Farnsworth," Alicia piped in. "Surely, the news of our little mishap hasn't been in the papers."

"No, rest assured, dear lady," Jason said, taking a seat. "I have other friends on this street and heard the news when taking coffee this morning. But I am relieved to see no harm has come to either one of you." He turned to Charlotte. "Are you up for some riding today?"

"I'm afraid my days of leisure have come to an end, thank goodness." She thought that sounded rude the moment it was out of her mouth. "Not that I haven't enjoyed the time we've spent together, but as I mentioned to you before, I'm used to being a working woman. And now that I have a task at hand, I am eager to accomplish it to the best of my abilities."

"Does that mean you're shutting me out of your busy new life altogether?" Jason asked, sipping the tea he had poured himself from the pot. "I don't think I could stand such banishment."

Charlotte smiled, but wished there was an easy way to disentangle herself from Jason, now that she knew it bothered Reed.

"It simply means you have to find some other amusement for the time being." And hopefully, his interest would wane.

"What about supper tonight? It seems as if it has been ages since we've eaten together."

Alicia coughed politely, and at Charlotte's glance, she nodded her approval. However, she hesitated. While Jason and her aunt were waiting for her to acquiesce, she had absolutely no desire to give him the wrong idea about their relationship, in case he was beginning to care for her.

More importantly, she didn't want to cause Reed a moment of jealousy, not after learning about Celia's dishonorable actions. It was certainly not the way to win his heart.

"We dined together recently, as I recall. Besides," Charlotte added as Jason started to brood, "I have other people to see, people who've left calling cards since the night of the party." In truth, she didn't intend to go out with anyone except Reed.

"Now, if you will excuse me, I must get ready for an appointment."

"May I give you a ride?" Jason asked, standing up with her.

"I've got my aunt's barouche," Charlotte told him and continued to resist even when he pushed the matter. "Besides I'm not ready to go yet," she explained.

"I can wait," he insisted.

She was beginning to get annoyed when he flashed a winsome smiled and shook his head.

"I meant no offense. I wanted to spend a few minutes more in your company. That's all. However, I can see I've overstayed my welcome. Not wanting to wear it out completely, I'll be off. I'll call on you again in a few days. The supper invitation still stands of course." And he was gone.

"Well, he pulled foot in a hurry," Charlotte remarked, relieved.

"Hm," Aunt Alicia agreed, "I wonder if you've finally offended the boy."

Charlotte was welcomed more warmly when she returned to the hospital. Superintendent Mason met her at the front door precisely at ten o'clock, ushering her into his office.

"My only rule, and this is for your safety," he added, showing his yellow teeth, "is that you stay with a staff member at all times." He promptly headed off to fetch the doctor.

She waited, feeling a little nervous, occasionally hearing footsteps along the corridor, until finally a man came striding through the office door.

"I'm Dr. Pridgen. I understand you wish to speak with me."

Charlotte assessed the man, in his mid-forties, slightly graying at the temples, with a kind face and active, intelligent eyes. Here, at last, was someone who would understand her project.

"I'm working on an article for the *Boston Post*," Charlotte responded, offering him her hand. "Thank you for taking the time to see me."

"Please, have a seat." He merely leaned on the edge of the superintendent's desk. "Mr. Mason is a little overprotective," he said, with a slight shrug, "but I can find the time to discuss my work with a pretty journalist."

Charlotte felt a blush creep up her face.

"I was hoping to gain your clinical perspective on how treatment is working for the criminally insane. Is there ever a possibility of recovery and release into society? Furthermore, I'd like to learn what type of criminals are sent here and what is the duration of their treatment. Are they sent again to prison after they are released, or do they go to trial? And are any ever sent home?" She stopped to take a deep breath.

"My, you do want to know a lot. I assume you have some paper handy."

With that, the good doctor launched into a long discussion of every aspect of the institution that he headed. Charlotte could barely keep up with him. Until finally, he offered her a tour of the facilities.

She wasn't entirely certain she wanted to see the patients, but knew it was her duty to observe how they lived if she was to write as thoroughly as she wanted. Closing her notebook, she picked up her reticule and preceded the doctor out the door.

"That's it," Dr. Pridgen said, about half an hour later, as they left the dining hall and the permanent wards behind, "You've seen it all."

"I have, indeed," Charlotte said.

Her mind was a-whirl with the sights and sounds of the hospital. The institution was terribly overcrowded, although the staff had no control over that and looked to be doing their best to make the patients comfortable.

She'd seen any number of treatments—men and women strapped in chairs and cuffed to their beds, patients shaved bald, others screaming, some quiet, some immersed in water up to their necks, and many who seemed utterly normal as they read books or played music or talked with each other.

However, as they headed down the last staircase, she noticed a wing in which they had not ventured.

"Just storage," Dr. Pridgen said. "I hardly ever go down there myself. Cleaning supplies, dry goods, etc. The superintendent handles all such things."

"Doctor!" A nurse came hurrying down the stairs after them. "We need your assistance immediately."

"I'm on my way." He looked at Charlotte, a flicker of doubt on his face. "Do you mind?"

"Not at all. You've been more than generous with your time. I'll make my own way to Mr. Mason's office."

"It's straight along there," he said pointing toward the front of the building.

Charlotte nodded and began heading in the direction he indicated as he hesitated a moment, watching her. She gave him a last smile and picked up her pace. Then she heard him go up the stairs with the nurse.

Later, she would attribute it to her writer's instinct or her woman's intuition, she wasn't sure which, but Charlotte knew she had to take a look down that last hallway. It simply didn't sit well with her not to see everything.

Quickly and quietly, she retraced her steps. There was a series of storage rooms as Dr. Pridgen had said, rooms that previously housed patients before the second and third stories were built. But at the far end, there was one room that had an old-style door with built-in bars at eye-level, resembling the enclosures from the House of Corrections nearby. The door was closed and visibly secured by a large padlock.

Scarumph. Charlotte thought she heard a noise inside, something scraping on the floor, and it made the hair on the nape of her neck stand up. She took a step forward, thinking to take a quick look through the bars, when a voice boomed out behind her.

"Here now, what are you doing down there?"

She froze, terror-stricken for a brief second. Then she took a deep breath and turned to face the unfamiliar voice, grateful at least that it wasn't the unpleasant countenance of Superintendent Mason.

"I'm Miss Sanborn, a reporter for the *Post.* Dr. Pridgen was giving me a tour when he was called away."

The man appeared to be a custodian, holding a pail in one hand and a mop in the other.

"Does Mr. Mason know you're here?"

"Yes, of course. In fact, I'm on my way to his office now. I guess I lost my way."

"You must be lost if you think the Superintendent would have a room such as that for his office." The man snickered at his own levity. Charlotte smiled. She knew how to handle him.

"If you tell me your name and what you do here, I'll put you in my article." She flipped open her notebook.

"In the paper and all?" The man's voice was awestruck.

Charlotte smiled before quickly jotting down his personal information. Then she gestured nonchalantly at the room beside them. "Can you tell me what this room is used for?"

He screwed up his face as if still debating whether to speak with her. Then he relaxed, obviously thinking a moment of fame was worth the risk.

"It's usually empty," he told her. "I was keeping my pails and brooms and the like in there until not long ago. Then Mr. Mason says to me to clear it out and toss in some bedding. And then we put in the latest bloke waiting to get the black gown."

"The black gown?" she asked.

"Yeah, to be sentenced, you know?"

Charlotte nodded, unable to repress a shiver. There was something odd about it. Dr. Pridgen had lied to her, unless he didn't know there was anyone in there. But he was the head doctor, how could he not know?

"Why is this patient here? How long is he staying?"

The man shrugged. "I asked the very same thing. I don't care for my storage room being taken over. Mr. Mason says to me, 'As for his length of stay, that's entirely up to him.'" The janitor gestured toward the room, indicating the person inside. "He's suffering from demen . . . demen—"

"Dementia?"

"That's it," the man said, setting down his bucket, "and Mr. Mason goes on, 'Until he remembers who he is, a criminal guilty of murder, then he can't be sentenced.' But it makes no never mind, he tells me."

"How is that?" Charlotte asked, curious now to see into the room, which she thought looked more like a prison cell than a hospital room, at least from the outside.

"Well, Mr. Mason says he can either spend the rest of his life in there," he hooked a thumb at the locked room once more, "pretending to be someone he's not—"

"You mean suffering from delusions," Charlotte offered.

The janitor shrugged. "Mr. Mason said 'pretend,' I'm sure of that. Or," he continued, "he can be cured of his dementia and return to the courts where he'll more than likely be bagged for life in the boarding school."

"The boarding school?" Charlotte asked.

"Ay, you know, the state penitentiary. That's if he's not the guest of honor at a necktie sociable, so to speak." He mimed a man being hanged, pretending to pull a noose up above his own head. "I guess the superintendent is right. It makes no difference. A cell is a cell."

With that, the janitor stepped aside, allowing her to look through the bars. She had to stand on her tiptoes and felt somewhat foolish, even ashamed, as though she was viewing an animal in a cage.

Peering into the gloominess inside the locked room, with the only light coming in from behind her, she could just make out a huddled form, leaning against the bare wall opposite. He rested on top of what appeared to be a crude straw mattress on the concrete floor. Murderer or not, the cell looked as though it wasn't fit for animals, let alone people.

As her shadow fell across the man, he turned, and Charlotte saw clearly the wretched and dirty face of her younger brother.

CHAPTER TWENTY-SIX

Charlotte fled the building and ran through the immaculately groomed gardens until she reached her aunt's carriage. Once inside, she tried to calm the panic, but she couldn't clear her head of the image of her brother, filthy, his hair matted, staring at her with incredulous eyes, and then inexplicably lifting one finger to silence her.

Clamping a hand across her mouth, she had stifled the cry that had been on her lips, and then she'd backed away. Shaking slightly with shock, she told the custodian she was feeling ill and left as if all the hounds of hell were after her. She had to find Reed at once. Then she thought about the telephone.

"Casey," she addressed her aunt's driver, "as soon as we cross the channel, please stop at the first large office building you see. Anywhere you think there will be a telephone."

The journey back to Boston proper seemed interminable, although it was only minutes. Casey pulled up on a commercial street, and Charlotte alighted from the carriage, recognizing nothing but heading toward the large stone facade of a bank. With little preliminary discussion, she demanded that they call Malloy and Associates.

It wasn't long before she had John Trelaine on the line. It was the oddest thing she had ever experienced, hearing his crackling, disembodied voice as he told her Reed was out but was expected to return momentarily.

"I'll be there shortly. If you see him, John, tell him it's an emergency. Tell him I found my brother in the Lunatic Hospital."

She closed her eyes, and all she could see was the image of Teddy. She prayed that Reed would have returned by the time she got to Scollay Square.

Charlotte paced the well-appointed lounge, unable to sit and starting at every sound. When she'd arrived ten minutes earlier, the doorman informed her John had left to search for Reed. And when she didn't think she could stand to wait any longer, she heard him enter.

The sound of a female voice halted her from running out of the lounge and throwing herself into his arms for comfort. She peered out of the waiting room. A lovely woman, dressed impeccably, had hold of his hand.

"I'm so glad I ran into you," she was saying, leaning close. "Paris was heavenly, but it would have been much more fun with you there." Then, in full view of anyone who cared to watch, Reed took her in his arms, spinning her around with her feet off the ground before setting her down and kissing her on both cheeks. He held her close a moment, possessively.

Charlotte felt sick to her stomach. She was still terrified and confused at seeing Thaddeus. Now, she was stunned at seeing Reed holding this woman in his arms. Nothing was as it should be, and she couldn't breathe properly, knowing exactly what it meant to feel lightheaded.

"Will I see you tonight?" she heard the woman ask.

Charlotte had been a fool and was continuing to play the fool. His words came back to her: *I have known many women. A week later, I bedded her. I'm a man, not a boy.*

Why didn't Reed simply acknowledge the corn? He was a philanderer! A veritable Don Juan! He might have used Helen to ward off the many girls eager to throw themselves at his feet for marriage, however that certainly didn't stop him from trifling with the women he chose for himself. Charlotte could hardly blame him for taking what she'd offered. Hadn't she readily behaved as loosely as any Jezebel?

She stepped forward, feeling desperate to escape. Reed's eyes darkened, seeing the signs of agitation plain upon her face. Moving away from the mysterious female, he blocked her path.

"Charlotte, what is it? Is it the children?"

She thought for a moment about telling him, about spilling her fears in front of this graceful stranger who was eyeing her with a curious glance, and then Charlotte felt a cold fury.

Why was she running to this man? All he had ever done was be the first to bed her and make her love him, and then abandon her the next day, precisely as everyone she loved had abandoned her.

Perhaps his marriage proposal was merely another way to gain a long-term fiancée, someone to replace Helen, whose only crime had been to become too routine. For the first time, Charlotte felt a little pity for the woman, just a little. In any case, she would not pin her hopes of helping Teddy on Reed.

"No. It was a mistake to come here." She ignored both their astonished faces, and pushed past them, heading for home.

"Charlotte," she heard him call after her, but she ran to her carriage, glad she had brought her aunt's closed-in brougham and not her open-air barouche.

"Hurry, Casey," she demanded, slamming the door shut behind her and twisting the lock. Once inside, she saw Reed, mere steps behind. Still, he made her jump when he banged on the carriage door the moment before they pulled away from the curb.

It was on the way home to Alicia when she thought of Jason. He was, after all, a member of one of Boston's wealthiest families. She spoke into the mouthpiece, a tube hanging down from the driver's seat and through the ceiling into the carriage, so her aunt didn't need to bang on the roof or speak out the window.

"Casey, do you know how to get to the Farnsworths' residence?"

It wasn't five minutes more and she was there, a couple of streets away from her aunt's home. The large plum-colored vehicle alongside the curb had never looked so welcoming. She hastened up the front steps of the house on Beacon Street, neither noticing nor caring about the furnishings when she was shown into a large parlor.

Charlotte counted exactly how many steps it took to cross the black and gold-patterned carpet—one way, then back the other—while she waited for the maid to take her message to Jason.

Hearing his footsteps, she turned as he entered. Jason crossed the room in long strides, taking both her hands in his.

"My dear Charlotte. Whatever is wrong?" Half of her wanted to sink into his arms and let him handle everything, but another part of her wanted to charge right over to the police station and demand the court rescind the order that had put her brother in the Boston Lunatic Hospital.

"It's my brother." She saw the play of emotions cross his fine features. She should have thought of Jason first. After all he knew Thaddeus. He would help her.

"Calm down," he said soothingly, pulling her down to sit beside him on the sofa. She filled him in as quickly as she could, wanting to hasten whatever process was necessary to make Teddy free again.

"You're certain it was he?" There was a tone of incredulity.

"Yes, of course."

After a thoughtful pause, Jason nodded. "In that case, your brother knows you're here now, and he realizes you'll be helping to free him. It must be a great relief to Thaddeus to know that he's no longer alone."

"I didn't think of that," Charlotte agreed, "but I can't forget how he looked, like a caged animal. It was awful. And then to have him gesture for me not to give any sign of recognition, it was downright frightening. I can't imagine why he did so."

"Perhaps he feared for your safety."

She frowned. "But why?"

Jason shrugged. "That's what I've got to find out."

"*We've* got to find out," she corrected. "Where are we going?" But he shook his head as he stood up.

"You, my dear one, are going to stay put. I don't need to be worrying about you as well as Thaddeus. Stay here and don't talk to anyone until I can determine if you're in danger. You haven't mentioned this to anyone yet, have you?"

She thought of Reed with that woman in his arms.

"No."

Jason seemed to consider that a moment. "I'm going to City Hall to see what I can discern. The Farnsworth name will open doors at the police station and get answers. Stay here, Charlotte, so I know you're safe." And with that, he was gone.

As he'd ordered her, she stayed put, but only until the minute hand on the mantle clock had passed seven minutes. Then, unable to sit and do nothing a moment longer, she rose to her feet. Glancing down, she saw she was clutching her hands together.

Good God, she thought, *I will not be reduced to a hand-wringing ninny.*

Grabbing up her reticule, she headed outside. Her aunt's carriage and driver were gone—another strange occurrence in an already baffling day. Hurrying along the street and turning the corner, she began to walk the few blocks to Alicia's.

In the front hall, as Charlotte tossed down her hat and gloves, Reed came rushing out of the parlor, Alicia in close pursuit.

"What the devil is going on?" he asked, his eyes blazing. "And why did you run out of my office?"

Charlotte eyed him warily. This was not the calm, collected man she'd seen handling everything from wolves to women.

"Everything is under control," she assured him. "Jason is helping me with the situation."

"Farnsworth?" He looked as if he were about to explode.

"Yes. You seemed too busy with your . . . your—"

"Sister," he finished for her, flatly.

"Oh, which one?" Alicia asked, seemingly oblivious to the war that had erupted in her entranceway.

"Sophie," Reed answered without taking his eyes off Charlotte, who was turning an ugly shade of red.

Alicia smiled. "The one who plays piano. A lovely girl, so refined. Please give her my regards next time you see her. Why, Charlotte, she would be an exceedingly suitable friend for you. The two of you must meet."

"Precisely what I was thinking," Reed agreed, looking pointedly at her.

Twice guilty of the same crime! Charlotte accepted the fact that her blinding jealousy had caused her to reach the wrong conclusion. Again! However, in her defense, she'd been overly distraught with panic and with the seemingly endless waiting. She only hoped she hadn't let her emotions get in the way of helping Teddy.

"What's all this about your brother being in the insane asylum?" Reed asked without preamble.

"How did you know?" Charlotte began.

"John arrived back as I was coming after you."

"It doesn't make any sense at all," Alicia interrupted. "Are you sure it was my nephew?"

Charlotte tried not to feel exasperated. "It has been exactly fourteen months since I last saw Teddy, and I don't believe even if it had been fourteen years, I could forget what my own brother looks like."

"But why didn't you explain to whoever was in charge that Thaddeus was not demented, or a killer, and then you could have brought him home for supper?"

Charlotte glanced at Reed, then tried to explain to her aunt about Thaddeus's silent warning, but the older woman would not understand.

Hearing a carriage, Charlotte raced to the window, thinking perhaps Jason had returned with news. Instead, the hall was soon filled with excited voices as Thomas and Lily came in from an outing with Bridget. They grabbed onto Reed and hugged him for all he was worth.

"That's enough, bub and sis," Alicia intoned. "Upstairs to the nursery and do so quietly please. Charlotte, why don't you explain the details to Mr. Malloy while I try to teach my grandchildren the civilized way to enter a house." She bustled up the stairs, shooing the children in front of her.

"Tell me what's going on, Charlotte," Reed asked as they stood facing one another in the parlor.

She filled him in on exactly what had occurred, and his expression grew more and more grave. Finally, he ran a hand roughly through his hair.

"I have contacts in the police department. I've been on the defense end of a few trials. At least, it should be easy to discern who charged your brother and for what."

She hated to bring up *his* name again, but she had to. "Jason has already headed to City Hall."

"I wish he'd go to hell!" Reed exclaimed, hands fisting at his sides. "Look, I'm not going to address this now, but as far as Farnsworth is concerned, I don't want you to share any more information with him, to go anywhere with him, even to speak to him, until I tell you otherwise."

"Blazes!" she said, pacing away from him and then returning swiftly in a swirl of skirts. "Ever since I arrived . . . no, ever since *you* returned to Boston and met Jason in Aunt Alicia's garden, you have done nothing but bully. I am a grown woman, and you have been overprotective and overbearing."

"Overprotective. Overbearing," he repeated her words, while she stood there quivering with anger. Slowly, he took a step forward, forcing her to step back if she did not want to be nose-to-chest with him.

"I suppose you do bring out in me a primal urge to protect you. But contrary to what you believe, I see you are making your way admirably in Boston, better than I could have hoped.

However, I will repeat myself only once. Stay away from Farnsworth. Contrary to what you believe, I know you to be ignorant of his true character."

"Explain yourself," Charlotte said, feeling as if she wanted to choke him.

"Shall I waste time talking about Farnsworth, or shall I go see about your brother?"

"But—"

"But me no buts, Charlotte. I don't want you even leaving this house until I tell you it is safe to do so."

Charlotte watched his tall, straight back retreat from the parlor. She heard the door close with the slightest of emphasis. And he was gone. *Blast the man!* Why did it annoy her so much more when Reed gave her orders than when Jason did?

Realizing she was once again wringing her hands, she dropped them to her sides. A moment later, however, she dashed upstairs to tell her aunt of her intention to go out. All she had to do, then, was find Alicia's carriage.

"This is absolutely not a good idea," Alicia said, standing in front of the door. "I can't possibly allow you to run off in the state you're in."

Charlotte pinned on her hat and adjusted her mantle before taking a deep breath. She was not going to shove her aunt aside. Unless she absolutely had to. On the other hand, she needed to get command of her emotions and deal with her rationally.

"I am perfectly calm, Aunt. I am level-headed, and I am determined. I simply cannot wait any longer. Mr. Farnsworth talked of his family's influence, and Mr. Malloy mentioned his police contacts. Well, as a writer for the *Boston Post,* I have influence, as well, and two days ago, I made contacts at the police station. I'm determined not to remain here helplessly while the men run around getting nowhere."

She knew Reed would not be happy. But this was *her* brother, and she had a right and a duty to take care of Teddy, just as she had done when they were children.

Alicia pursed her lips and gave her head another shake, her impossibly high curls springing around her pale face.

Charlotte tried again. "I appreciate your concern, and I will act with all due caution, but you cannot," she gentled her voice, "stop me."

Her aunt sniffed. "I have lost my sister and my daughter." The words came out without a waver in her voice. They were an undeniable fact that the older lady was relaying, not to seek pity but as a warning. "I am not inclined, Charlotte, to lose you."

"I know." Charlotte's voice broke. "I am not inclined to lose you either. Please, understand, I was not raised to sit idly by."

Alicia glanced at the floor a moment, then back at Charlotte's face. "Yes, I see that. You very much resemble my sister in manner and spirit. Well then, I expect you home by supper."

Charlotte felt a surge of warmth for the older woman. Family was so important. Hugging her aunt, who returned the embrace tightly, she stepped around her and out to the awaiting carriage.

The driver's mysterious disappearance had already been solved—Jason had dismissed Casey so Charlotte wouldn't leave his home. *Another overbearing man trying to wrap her in cotton swaddling!*

"Be discreet, be calm," Charlotte coached herself on the way to City Hall. What worried her greatly was that, undoubtedly, there had to be someone in authority, maybe more than one person, who already knew they had the wrong man in custody. If anyone found out she knew who Thaddeus was, she could, indeed, be in danger.

Charlotte was still counseling herself as she got out of the carriage. Before she had taken two steps, she was grabbed from behind with a vice-like grip clamped around her upper arm.

Closing her eyes, she would have shrieked, but the wind was knocked out of her as she was swung back against the side of the barouche.

"I should throttle you," came the menacing voice in her ear.

CHAPTER TWENTY-SEVEN

Charlotte opened her eyes at the sound of Reed's voice. She looked up at him, his deeply furrowed brow displaying how livid he really was.

"In front of the police station?" she asked softly, her heart beating so loudly she was sure he could hear it. He had come out of nowhere, surprising the breath out of her. "I could have you arrested for manhandling me," she added, trying to make light of the situation. She didn't succeed.

"You are going to climb right back into this carriage and return to your aunt's house. And when I get there—"

"I'm not going anywhere. And what have you accomplished? It's been nearly half an hour, and I've beaten you here. I'm going in there to speak calmly to some of the gentlemen I interviewed two days ago. I'm sure they'll help me."

"I stopped at the office to make some discreet phone calls. I had to confirm something about the carriage that nearly sent you flying the other day."

"The shay? What has that to do with my brother?"

"Maybe nothing, maybe everything. It belongs to—"

"Well, isn't this cozy?" It was Helen Belgrave, and all Charlotte's best intentions to stay calm and to be discreet were forgotten.

The dark-haired woman was walking along the street, her reticule swinging from her wrist, and her carriage following along to take any packages she purchased. But she didn't look as if she was in a shopping mood. In fact, Helen's mouth was tight with anger as she approached them.

"So, you are out in public now, groping on the street! Reed," she directed her gaze at him, "this is not to be borne. I won't stand for it. You will cease gallivanting with this country girl, at least until I've told people we are no longer together. I will not be humiliated by this guttersnipe. I have been patient, but I promise you, I'll shred her reputation and yours. Is that clear?"

Reed opened his mouth to speak, but Charlotte, in no mood to be polite, spoke first.

"No, Mrs. Belgrave. Let me make one thing unequivocally clear. Your threats are tedious and pointless, not to mention showing a general ill-breeding that I would think you ashamed to display. *You* have a reputation in this town to ruin. However, I do not, so I suggest you shut pan all together."

She took a step toward Helen, who stood open-mouthed as Charlotte continued.

"The mud you sling will be of no great shakes to me, but will be seen as the embittered ranting of a woman who didn't have the dignity in the first place to leave a relationship when she knew—and apparently the whole of Boston knew—she was utilitarian at best and a physical amusement only occasionally." Charlotte paused, her chest heaving as she looked back at Reed.

"You did say only occasionally, didn't you?" she asked him for confirmation.

Looking somewhat stunned, he nodded before leveling his azure gaze on Helen, who was now staring, white-faced, at the both of them.

"Helen, what the impassioned Miss Sanborn is trying to tell you is that you're fighting a losing war. I have explained the situation to you thoroughly more than once. We are finished."

His voice was firm but not harsh as he continued, "I truly believe you deserve better than I can give you, and I know I want more than what we had. Besides you can't hurt Miss Sanborn's reputation, since I've already asked her to marry me."

Without batting an eye, Charlotte let Reed escort her past the speechless widow and into the police station at City Hall. Once inside, however, they halted. Reed looked down at her.

"Are you quite collected?"

"Yes, although I feel as if I've whipped my weight in wild cats."

Charlotte smiled at the desk sergeant, the same one with whom she had spoken previously. He looked surprised to see her again, and even more surprised to see one of Boston's foremost lawyers by her side.

"Miss Sanborn has enlisted my professional help in her article," Reed explained. "As I have represented a number of defendants who ended up institutionalized instead of incarcerated, she thought I could give her some information on how the men behaved before treatment. I usually rely on you to keep the detailed records," he lied, "and I'm wondering, Sergeant, if we can have a look at some recent murder trial records."

The heavyset man considered the request. "As you know, sir, murderers hardly ever end up at the Lunatic Hospital," the officer replied. "However, I believe there were a few who have done so. Whether you represented them or some pettifogger did, I can't say."

Nodding Reed tried again, "Perhaps you could let us browse through the records of all the murderers who are now in the hospital. Even if I didn't handle the cases, I'll be able to give Miss Sanborn my professional opinion."

The sergeant sighed, looking at the pile of work on his desk. "It is rather late, almost my supper time. If you return tomorrow—"

"Perhaps, Sergeant," Charlotte piped up with the artifice that had worked so well on the custodian at the hospital, "you would be available for a quote or two, which I shall put in my article, something along the lines of 'the highly professional and cooperative police department doing such a splendid job of keeping the dangerous criminals off the street.'"

The man visibly swelled with pride. "I think I could arrange to say something quotable," he told her. "Why don't the two of you take a seat in that office, the captain's out today, and I'll bring in the records."

"Thank you, Sergeant," Reed said, escorting her to the office where they each took a seat. "That was very smooth, lady writer."

In moments, they had a pile in front of them, which they divided in two.

"I pulled records for six months," the sergeant told them. "As I said, there aren't many murderers allowed to rehabilitate. Most of them end up dead or in the state prison at Charlestown. Even the best of 'em," he added, gesturing to Reed and including all lawyers, "can't get some men out on hocus pocus. That wasn't, by the way, my official quote."

"Sergeant," Reed caught him before he left. "Did anyone else come in asking to see these records today?"

"Now why would anyone else be interested in examining what, if you ask me, is as boring as checkers?" he asked over his shoulder as he walked out the door.

Reed looked at her. She looked at him.

"Perhaps Jason simply didn't think of it," she offered lamely. Reed rolled his eyes but remained silent as they started to search, looking for descriptions of the defendants and immediately eliminating those who could not be Thaddeus Sanborn.

"I think I may have located his file," Reed said some ten minutes later. "Charged with murder, six feet one, brown hair, green eyes, a small scar on his right hand?" He raised his eyebrows, looking to Charlotte for confirmation.

Charlotte blanched and nodded. She vividly remembered the day Teddy had fallen out of the large tree in their front yard.

"He was all of seven years old," she said aloud, thinking of how he'd punctured his hand on a sharp rock. He hadn't cried then or when her mother cleaned and dressed the wound. "It's a crescent-shaped mark in the palm of his right hand."

"That scar and that hand now belong to one Jeremy Dawson," Reed announced.

"Who was he supposed to have murdered?" she asked, feeling a little dazed.

"It says here that he took the life of Arthur Harvey, a seaman, about three months ago. That explains why I didn't hear about the case," Reed added. "I was in Spring City. Harvey's body was discovered by the docks, on Rowe's Wharf. That's not too far from my house, coincidentally," Reed told her, thinking over what businesses were in that area.

"The murder went unsolved for one week, and then Jeremy Dawson, or rather, your brother, was deposited on the police station's doorstep with a nasty bump on his head and the murder weapon in his coat pocket. They also found papers on him indicating his identity."

"Good grief," Charlotte said. "What an obvious sham. *Someone* at the station must have wondered who'd hit my brother and left him on the steps. Of course, if no one knew him in town and if he had papers on him to indicate an identity, then they would not believe anything he told them."

"Especially with the murder weapon—it was a knife, incidentally—on his person, no doubt covered in his fingerprints and his alone. His motive was stated as 'petty larceny.'" He lay the open file down.

"I wonder why someone wanted your brother to be put away. It says here," Reed continued, "that the prosecuting attorney pressed for the death penalty, or, at the very least, a life sentence to Charlestown."

A surge of terror rushed through her, making her pulse race. How close her brother had come to hanging! "How did Teddy end up at the hospital?"

"The judge decided the bump on your brother's head and his unvarying story he was not Dawson but Thaddeus Sanborn from Colorado persuaded him to seek a psychiatric consultation."

"But why didn't they check out his story? They could easily have telegraphed to Spring City where I would have corroborated his identity, or what about our county clerk's office where our birth records are on file?"

"What about his own aunt living ten minutes away?" Reed added, continuing to leaf through the thin file. "Ah ha. It states here his entire story was checked, yet nothing and no one could confirm it."

"But that's impossible, unless—"

"Unless the officer assigned to check his story lied."

"And that officer is?" Charlotte asked.

"A Sergeant Sheffield. I've heard his name before around the courts, but nothing particular comes to mind. I'll check into it. Perhaps someone is paying him off."

"Either that," Charlotte said, "or he is the worst detective in the entire history of the police force. I've a notion to go find this Sergeant Sheffield and tell him exactly who I am and who my brother is."

Reed stood up. "You'll do no such thing. I believe whoever did this to your brother knows exactly who he is, and in that case, knows you, at least by name. Your presence in Boston, not to mention here at the police station, puts you in danger. Doubly so, if the culprit already knows you're working on an article that takes you anywhere near the hospital."

He took hold of her hands and fixed his gaze on her. "Charlotte, I don't want anything to happen to you."

"Neither do I," she told him, swallowing hard at the emotion on his face.

"Then be a smart woman and listen to me There is nothing more you can do today. I'm going to put you in your aunt's carriage and you're going to go home, and I want you to stay there until I come for you myself. Hopefully, with your brother. And whatever you do, Charlotte," he squeezed her arms, "don't go out with *anyone*, unless I'm with you. Especially Farnsworth. All right?"

His tone was scaring her into behaving in a less than independent way, but for the moment, she didn't mind Reed looking after things. If he could get Teddy out, she would comply with his requests.

"Reed." She wanted to ask him more about his plans, but his lips came down on hers and sealed off her words. The kiss was necessarily brief, but its impact reached clear to her toes.

"Don't fight me on this, Charlotte."

She shook her head. "I won't."

With a new feeling of trepidation, Charlotte watched Jason alight from his carriage, which pulled up outside Alicia's house just before supper. She already felt as drained as the empty teacup on the table beside her.

Although the children had wanted her to play with them, she'd been unable to leave the window seat in the front room, clinging to Reed's promise he would return should he learn anything else about her brother. And she was about to jump out of her skin with the waiting.

When Jason hesitated at the bottom of her aunt's steps, looking up at the front door, Charlotte barely paused before hurrying through the hall and opening it to meet him. It was possible, despite Reed's doubts, that Jason had learned something concerning Teddy. Why else would he have come?

Gerald was nowhere to be seen when she hurried down the front steps.

"Jason, thank goodness. Did you find out anything?"

To her relief, he nodded. "I did, but it's . . . confidential." He glanced around, then over Charlotte's head. "I think you'd better step into my carriage so we can discuss this in private."

She looked at the house, Reed's warning echoing in her ears. She thought she saw Alicia at the upstairs window but couldn't be sure it wasn't merely the play of the setting sunlight on the panes.

"Jason, come in and you can tell me over tea."

"There is no time for that. Your brother is not at the Lunatic Hospital any longer," he said, darting his glance to the great windows at the front of her aunt's house. "Thus, we must move quickly."

"Where is he?" she began.

"Please, Charlotte, climb into my carriage, and I will explain everything. It'll only take a moment."

Again, she felt unease. Her nerves were on edge, but this was Jason, after all. "As you wish, but I must warn you, I am not in the best frame of mind at the moment. And I don't appreciate the additional suspense."

"Oh, dear," his face fell with concern, but he took her hand and helped her inside.

The shock of his touch, reminded her she was without her gloves, hat, or mantle—practically naked in public!

Fidgeting on the seat, desperate for him to tell her his news, she realized she should have insisted he come into Alicia's parlor while she heard whatever he was about to tell her.

Before she could suggest this again, he seated himself opposite her and rapped on the roof with his cane. With a sudden lurch, the vehicle started to move.

"What on earth are you doing?" she exclaimed. "I am not in the mood for games."

"No games, Charlotte," he assured her before his face lost its veneer of gentlemanly good humor as quickly as one closed a window's shutter. "I'm taking you to your brother."

"My brother!" she exclaimed. "Jason, I don't understand."

He shook his head, his eyes bright, as he gazed at her, almost with mirth. His continued silence alarmed her.

"Jason, please. What's this all about? I demand you tell me at once." The prickling at the nape of her neck was a warning coming too late.

"You demand?" He laughed, but his amusement didn't resemble Reed's warm laughter. It sounded more like the harsh brakes of a railway car. "In case you haven't noticed, you are in no position to demand anything. But out of the kindness of my heart, I am taking you to him, then the two of you can perish together. It's the least I can do."

She wasn't certain if she'd heard him right. A moment later, as he fixed on her a stare that turned her blood to ice, she was certain. He was behind this whole mess and, like an idiot, she had walked out of her aunt's house and simply stepped into his carriage, despite Reed's warnings. Without even a struggle.

It occurred to her then that the carriage was not his usual gaily colored one, emblazoned with the family monogram. Of course, he would not use his own vehicle for whatever dastardly plan he had.

"Oh, I can see your thoughts tumbling as keenly as Swiss clockwork in your head," he said with a thin smile. "Fortunately for me, you didn't do a little more thinking first. I'm glad the shay incident didn't work. I regretted it almost as soon as I'd arranged it."

She realized with dawning horror that Jason had tried to kill her with the runaway carriage even before she'd made her discovery at the asylum, the very thing he'd hoped to prevent. And she had foolishly suspected Helen.

He grinned and nodded at her stunned expression. "Oh, but what a stroke of luck that your Mr. Malloy was there to catch you. Still, I cherished how you turned to me in your time of trouble, not knowing that, all the while, I could snuff you out at my will." There was little emotion in his words except the overtones of gloating.

"Your brother indicated you were somewhat reserved, despite being intellectually precocious, but I think you're a lively creature. In other circumstances," he leaned forward to caress her cheek, and she drew back as far as she could against the seat, "we could have had a wonderful time together, I'm sure."

Charlotte turned and bit him.

Without hesitation, he slapped her hard across her cheek. She didn't cry out but sat there, stunned. It was the first time violence had been perpetrated against her in her entire life. And it filled her with some fear, although mostly with anger.

She resolved then that, come what may, she would not let this brutish man destroy her life. Not when she had found such happiness with Reed and the children, and even with her Aunt Alicia. This was not the time to die.

"Don't make things unpleasant, Charlotte."

"Then don't touch me again." Her voice was as frosty as his gaze.

He stared hard at her through narrowed eyes, and then nodded. "There's not much time left anyway. We're almost there."

Where was there? she wondered. They hadn't gone far. She could smell the sea air strongly now, and it occurred to her that the Farnsworths were a merchant family—codfish aristocracy, as Reed had called them, knowing his contemptuous words had been for Jason alone and not his entire family. In any case, they most probably had a warehouse on the docks.

Her mind was whirling as she thought of the seaman's dead body on the docks and of her brother's innocence. Jason had sought her out as soon as she'd arrived in Boston, and then she'd gladly told him all about the article she was working on, including her intention of going to the Lunatic Hospital. And all the while . . .

"I'm certain your warehouse will be secluded at this time of the evening. Just as it was when you murdered Arthur Harvey," she said, watching his eyes open wide for the briefest instant. It made her feel better to unnerve him with even her small piece of the puzzle. Then he smiled lazily at her.

"I imagine it will be, and perhaps there will be time to indulge in our baser passions after all." Without warning, he prodded her skirt between her legs with the gold-headed cane he still held.

She shuddered and pushed it away. So much for unnerving him. Next time, she would keep her mouth shut. If there was a next time.

CHAPTER TWENTY-EIGHT

Jason's carriage drove between the open warehouse doors, which were then closed quickly behind them by two burly men. The buildings' windows had been blocked with boards on the inside, and hanging oil lamps were the sole source of light.

As Charlotte emerged from the coach, she watched those same men grab up Thaddeus from a chair, securing him between them.

"Teddy," she cried out, running toward him, as he struggled to free himself, a reddened bump on his temple evidence he'd been manhandled.

"Let him go," she demanded, feeling wild with anger and fear.

At Jason's nod, the men released his arms, which he wrapped around Charlotte as she held onto him tightly. She could scarcely believe he was real, his heart beating under her cheek.

"Charlie," he murmured into her hair. "I was beginning to think I'd only dreamt I'd seen you."

She had started to think the same thing and was so glad he was there in her arms and not locked in that dismal cell, until it dawned on her that Teddy would be safer if he were still at the hospital.

"Put them in the spice store until the ship arrives," Jason ordered.

The men were obviously stevedores, with their kerchiefs around their huge necks and muscles bulging under their thin shirts. One man grabbed her brother, already weakened by his head injury and his long incarceration, and hauled Thaddeus's arms behind him. The other one held Charlotte by her forearm.

They took their captives toward the rear of the warehouse, threading their way through crates and coiled ropes, before stopping at the open door of a small room. It smelled strongly of all manner of spices.

Charlotte felt a rough hand in the small of her back before she went flying into the windowless chamber, her hair spilling out of its knot as her hands and knees hit the hard floor. Thaddeus came tumbling into her before the door slammed shut. They were left without even a candle.

Holding on tightly to her brother in the absolute darkness, Charlotte wanted to ask him about all that had happened, but Jason's mention of a ship came into the forefront of her thoughts.

"If we don't get out of here soon, Teddy, we're going to be sailing away from Boston, never to be seen again."

"Perhaps that bastard Farnsworth is going to sell us as slaves," Thaddeus offered, and Charlotte felt him run an unsteady hand through his overgrown hair.

She blanched at the thought of ending up in some man's harem. Then she remembered Jason's words on the ride over.

"Jason said we would be perishing together. He means to kill us. The ship is a convenient way to get our bodies far out to sea. It wouldn't do to have your convicted and incarcerated corpse show up in the harbor."

"This is all my fault," Thaddeus began.

"I truly want to hear all about why I'm going to die, little brother," Charlotte told him, reaching for his face in the darkness and holding his cheeks in both her hands, "but I'd prefer to hear such a story when we're safely out of here. Any suggestions?"

Under her fingers, she felt him shake his head.

"You saw those two brutes. On a good day, I might be able to hold my own against them. Well, maybe *one* of them . . . for a while, at least," he said.

Charlotte could tell that her brother was, indeed, no longer the slender youth who weighed barely more than she did. He had certainly towered over her in the warehouse, and she was sure, when he wasn't exhausted and half-starved, he could defend himself quite well.

"But this isn't a good day," she finished for him.

He squeezed her in another close hug, and again, she felt his lopsided grin under her fingertips. They couldn't die now, she told herself. She had Lily and Thomas to think of. They'd already been orphaned once.

"Charlie, if we get out of this, it will be because we have a cunning plan that has nothing to do with physical strength, or . . . because you brought help?" he ended with a question.

She thought of Reed. Even if he'd already returned to her aunt's, how would he know for sure Jason had taken her, and how would he ever figure out where she was?

"I'm afraid it's up to us, Teddy, at least for a while, and I think I know where to start."

"Where?"

"With Jason, himself."

"That ruthless pig," Thaddeus spat out. "He'd sell his own mother for a profit. What good would it do to talk to him? Do you think he's going to suddenly see reason and let us go? He already has a policeman answering to him, and there's no doubt someone at that hellhole I was kept in was on the take."

Charlotte recalled how Superintendent Mason had put her off for a couple days, probably needing to check with Jason as to whether she should be allowed to talk to the doctor. And she still wondered if Dr. Pridgen had steered her clear of Thaddeus's cell on purpose.

"I'm wondering if we can try a little blackmail," Charlotte said. "If he thinks I've got something on him and have already told someone else, he might delay our demise until he checks out my story. I'm not totally alone in this rescue, Teddy. I believe I just need to gain us more time."

Then she remembered how close help could be. "Not to mention find a telephone!"

She didn't wait for her brother to offer an alternative plan or to dissuade her from the poor one she'd already formulated. Jumping up, she stumbled forward in the dark and banged on the thick wooden door until one of their beefy guards opened it, letting in a sliver of light.

"What is it?" he yelled at her without ceremony, and she almost lost her nerve.

"Tell Mr. Farnsworth I want to speak with him. Tell him I know about Sergeant Sheffield," she added, taking an educated guess that the policeman who'd failed to check Thaddeus's identity was corrupt.

He hesitated but then slammed the door. Charlotte listened to his footsteps and then silence. Thaddeus got to his feet and put his arms around her.

"I know we're damned if we do and damned if we don't, Charlie, but be careful. And I'm not letting you out of my sight, by the way."

"Don't worry. If the situation gets out of control, we'll simply retreat. Then we can die together," she added, with a touch of mockery. Oddly, she felt braver than she ever had, especially with Teddy beside her, and with all the upheaval she'd already weathered in a few short months.

The footsteps returned, and the door was wrenched open. One of the men grabbed her by her upper arm and dragged her out.

"She's a lady," her brother yelled at him, following closely behind. "Don't be so rough." He was stoutly punched in the stomach by the other man and shoved back into the store room.

Charlotte had time for one backward glance at her brother, doubled over on the floor, before the door swung shut.

You'll pay for that, too, Jason, she vowed silently.

"So, you know about Sheffield," Jason said, confirming her supposition. "The question is, what else do you know?"

"No," she said, taking the seat he offered in a small partitioned section of the warehouse that was serving as an office. Jason sat behind a large desk on the corner of which lay a pistol. One of the men remained blocking the door behind her. "The question is, whom have I told?"

He blinked once, twice, then he laughed in short barks. "Between mid-day when I told you to stay put and dinnertime? Since you've lived in Boston a relatively short time, Charlotte, and since I've monopolized nearly all of that time, I can't think who would believe your half-cocked story about seeing your brother. Except perhaps your doddering Aunt Alicia, and I do plan to deal with her soon."

The threat to her aunt sent a bolt of white-hot fury through her. The arrogance! That Jason should think himself free to harm people as he saw necessary for his own plans. And then the image of Reed, dangerously powerful but infinitely gentle, came unbidden to her mind.

He'd taken her at her word about Thaddeus, never once questioning whether she had actually seen her brother. What an extraordinary man who had come into her life. She would be damned if she'd allow Jason to ruin everything now. Her anger gave her the necessary courage.

She countered. "In my short time here, as you know, I *have* met people, including the *Post*'s editor. And it doesn't take long to pick up a telephone," she added, at the same time noticing there wasn't one in the warehouse office.

Jason shot her a narrow look.

"Is it Greene, then? What does he know?"

She didn't want to endanger Mr. Greene by saying anything more. If she didn't come through it alive, he would be next on the list after Alicia. Jason took her silence as evidence of not cooperating, and he gestured almost offhandedly to one of his men.

From behind her, large hands grabbed both her arms and held them around the back of the small wooden chair. Jason was quick then, moving toward her while she was still trying to figure out what there was to be afraid of in this new posture—until she saw the knife he held in his hand.

Charlotte opened her mouth as he reached toward her.

"Scream and I'll draw blood," he promised.

She stifled her voice along with her terror as he slit open the top of her gown where it strained over her breasts. Struggling to free her arms without impaling herself, it was like pulling against stone. This, she realized, was when she should retreat to the relative safety of the store room, but she hadn't accomplished anything yet.

"He will come. He was on his way to my aunt's house. When he learns I have been abducted, he will put it all together and find me."

Jason plainly thought she was still talking about Charles Greene, the slight, bespectacled editor with an unassuming manner. Laughing again, he wrenched down one side of her dress and caressed her shoulder.

Unflinching, Charlotte stared him squarely in the eye.

"So, this is how Jason Farnsworth has to get a woman," she sneered, feeling outraged by the liberties he was taking.

He slapped her for that, as he had done in the carriage, and her cheek stung with the blow. Undeterred, he cut away the strap of her chemisette. Below that was a corset, but he already had a full view down her gaping neckline.

"Not the only way, Charlotte," he said with a smirk, "but an undeniably amusing one. And I'm sure you'll agree I'm infinitely more appealing than, say, Bertie here, although that would be interesting entertainment . . . for me, at least."

The idea of Jason watching and taking pleasure in such an assault revolted her. "You're vile," she said, still struggling between the two men.

Jason leaned his face very close to hers. "You know, I think I will let him have a turn if there's time when I'm through."

Charlotte leaned her head as far away as possible, understanding then that she was not dealing with normal sexual desire. He enjoyed something with pain involved.

"You've got a mother, a sister," she started, while watching him gesture over her head and then feeling Bertie begin to tie her hands. "Would you allow them to be treated this way? I am no different from them," she added.

Jason ignored her words. He sent Bertie from the room before heaving her from the chair and bent her backward over the desk, crushing her arms under her.

"There is a difference," he whispered fiercely into her face, as she struggled and kicked at him to no avail. "You are *not* my mother or my sister, and you are getting in the way of my business, which is to make money."

"And how will assaulting me help?" Charlotte asked, trying to twist and turn and impede his progress. She couldn't fathom how she'd ever thought him pleasant. How did such horridness masquerade in everyday society as normalcy?

It took all her wits not to panic despite her growing fear. She knew her intellect might be all that could save her, as the odds that Reed would find her in time seemed slim.

Jason had shredded the entire top of her dress, as well as her chemisette, but gave up tugging at her tightly laced corset. His eyes, riveted by the curves of her breasts, never met hers as he started to pull up her skirts with one hand while unfastening his trousers with the other.

"It will give me great pleasure to know your body wasn't wasted before you died. Though it will the briefest encounter, I will show you what earthly delights you are leaving behind. I hate to think of any beautiful young woman dying a virgin."

He was grinding his pelvis into her hips, which were pressed painfully against the edge of the desk. She could feel the hardness at his crotch, and a wave of revulsion nearly made her faint.

Yet as Jason's words filtered through her terror, it seemed to Charlotte as though a bell rang in her head. His mouth was now on the swell of her breast, and his hand had clawed its way up under her gown to touch the lace at the bottom of her pantalets.

"But I am not a virgin."

Every part of him, each assault, by mouth, by hand, and by pelvis, halted, frozen by her words. Then he relaxed. "You are lying." And he struck her again, this time, catching her lip on her teeth and immediately, she tasted blood.

"I will be the only man you'll ever know, dear Charlotte. But don't worry, I have taken care of virgins before. Every one of them exceedingly grateful that I—"

"I'm not lying," she insisted, although now it hurt to speak. In a flash she understood the boastful, seemingly over-confident Jason Farnsworth. Here was a man so insecure, he could only be sexually intimate with a woman who had never been with anyone else to whom he could be compared and found inadequate.

A classic example was the term she'd read in one of the psychiatric case studies at the library. *Example*, indeed. Here in the real world, it was terrifying, but she had to press on. After all, wasn't a copy of Christian Wolff's *Psychologia Empirica* sitting on her father's shelf in Spring City? She'd read it and absorbed it, and was fairly certain she could make use of it.

"I've already had extreme pleasure with a man whose prowess you could never match. When he took my virginity, it was the most wondrous day of my life. His manhood was huge. His skill at lovemaking was . . . was beyond magnificent."

She couldn't believe she was saying these things, but the effect was almost immediate. He withdrew his probing hand from under her skirts. He stood up and looked down at her as if she were filth.

"Who is this man?"

"The same man who will rescue me," she told him, struggling again to twist away while he was considering her words.

Jason looked puzzled. "Greene?"

"No." As she said the word, one of the warehouse doors came bursting inward with such force that wood splintered in all directions. Jason grabbed for the pistol on the desk, and Charlotte kicked at him as she dropped to the floor, instinctively curling into a ball to protect herself.

She heard her name called out. *Reed!* Quick footsteps sounded on the warehouse floor and a shot rang out. Then silence. After a moment, Charlotte looked over her shoulder to see Reed clutching Jason's now limp body. He released him instantly, letting him fall like a flour sack to the floor, and rushed over to her, dropping to his knees beside her.

"Charlotte," was all he said as he turned her to get access to the rope that bound her arms. "It's going to be all right."

"I didn't know how long it would take you to get here," she said quietly, mindless of the fact that her whole body was trembling. "I was running out of ways to stall for time." She was unable to continue and tell him how she wanted to adjust her clothing. Instead, she waited almost dispassionately as Reed untied her.

When her hands were free, she tried to pull her tattered chemise and dress closed with shaking hands. Reed stripped off his coat, enveloping her in it before helping her to put her arms through the sleeves and draw it closed.

Crying now, she was feeling almost hysterical with relief. And then he was holding her to him, crushing her against his chest, and she wanted nothing more in this world than the familiar, beloved smell of him against her tear-stained face.

"Charlie," she heard her brother's voice, hesitant as if he wasn't sure what to make of this stranger comforting his sister. Reed squeezed her tightly then released her, and she turned to see her brother escorted by a policeman. Thaddeus opened his arms, and she stepped into his embrace.

"Teddy," was all she could say as a fresh stream of tears started.

"Thank God, you're safe," he said, holding her close. But then he pulled away and looked at her face. "That bastard struck you. I'd like to—"

"Too late for that," Reed said, flatly, gesturing to the corpse, now covered by a dingy canvas sail with two policemen standing by to remove Jason's remains. She could hear other men's voices outside the room, including the man who'd tied her up, along with the familiar one of John Trelaine.

"I think we'd better take your sister home," Reed said, seemingly unable to stop himself from touching her, as he stroked her hair for another moment, before letting his hand drop.

"Home?" Thaddeus questioned, looking down at Charlotte.

"Aunt Alicia's," she explained. "Oh, dear Lord," she added. "The children!" She couldn't wait to hold them.

"Children!" Thaddeus exclaimed.

Charlotte nodded. "There is so much to tell you, Teddy, and so much I want to hear."

CHAPTER TWENTY-NINE

It seemed as if there would be no end to the revelations that night. After a brief interrogation at the police station, Reed, Charlotte, and Thaddeus, along with John Trelaine, sat in Alicia's parlor, drinking brandy. Everyone had a part to play in telling the day's events, including Alicia, who'd been looking out her bedroom window and had seen Jason take Charlotte away.

"Although it didn't look to me as if she was forced into the carriage," Alicia added. "I didn't know what to make of it."

Charlotte explained her stupidity in that matter, drawing frowns from both her brother and Reed. She was glad when John took over, drawing the unwelcome attention off her.

"Before we knew anything of Charlotte's abduction, Reed spoke with a trusted friend on the police force, who agreed to remove the man known as Jeremy Dawson from the Lunatic Hospital and place him in the holding cell at City Hall. Naturally, I decided to accompany the officer."

He paused to take a biscuit from the tray beside him, clearly warming to the task of explaining his part in the proceedings.

"You can imagine my surprise when the hospital room was empty and the superintendent acted as if there never was a

Jeremy Dawson. It was obvious Mason was hiding something, so the officer took him in for questioning," John explained. "And as I understand it, he confessed and pointed the finger at Sergeant Sheffield."

"That's right," offered Thaddeus. "It was Sheffield who came to the cell and said I was being moved. I was starting to feel unsure if I'd seen Charlie or not, and I didn't want to take the chance of moving somewhere she couldn't find me. Unfortunately, I had little choice. My head has been used as a nail by too many hammers lately."

Charlotte moved over to her brother and rubbed the back of his head. Reed's eyes never left her. He'd been watching her like a hawk watches its prey ever since he'd rescued her, as if he feared losing sight of her again. It had been difficult to get him to leave her alone to change clothes when they'd first arrived at Chestnut Street.

"Jason didn't let much slip about his reasons for all this," Charlotte chimed in, as she took a seat next to Thaddeus, "but he did say I was standing in the way of his making money. But I haven't figured out what killing a man, framing Teddy, and kidnapping me has to do with profit."

"Farnsworth was a black marketeer, a common smuggler," Reed began. "John caught up with me after his wasted trip to the hospital. I'd have to say it was mostly instinct that first made me suspicious of Farnsworth—"

"*Instinct* made you suspicious?" Charlotte asked sweetly.

Reed paused, his mouth slightly open, ready to continue. She tilted her head to one side and cocked an eyebrow.

"Instinct," he insisted, although they both knew it was jealousy that had caused Reed to dislike Jason from the first moment he saw her dancing with him.

"I discovered by chance the shay that nearly ran us down the other day belonged to Farnsworth's foreman. After we knew which crime Thaddeus was supposed to have committed, I considered the docks and where Arthur Harvey's body was found. It occurred to me that the Farnsworths owned some of the warehouses on Rowes Wharf."

"But why frame my brother?" Charlotte asked.

"I'm getting to that," Reed said, sounding slightly exasperated, although he fixed her with a crooked grin and warm glance that didn't go unnoticed by Aunt Alicia or Thaddeus.

Charlotte, for her part, lowered her eyes demurely, unable to help the warm tingle racing through her like lightning in a storm cloud.

"I believe you were acquainted with Farnsworth previously," Reed continued, looking at Thaddeus.

"Yes, I met him a few years ago, when I was traveling—"

"Well, at least that was the truth," Charlotte interrupted once more. "He told me about meeting you one day while we were sightseeing . . . ," she trailed off at the look on Reed's face.

"Sightseeing?" Thaddeus exclaimed.

Charlotte shrugged sheepishly, feeling ashamed by her ill-judged choice of companionship.

"Go on," she told her brother.

Thaddeus shook his head before taking a deep breath and another sip of brandy.

"Jason said to look him up if I was ever in Boston, which I did a few months ago. He offered me a job, running his counting house. After a week or so, I realized I didn't care for the way he did business, and I told him so. It's not enough that he has a trust fund from his parents. He wants to own Boston by selling illegal goods and putting in his pocket anyone who can be bought."

"But why didn't you come see me, dear boy?" Alicia spoke up, looking hurt.

Thaddeus was abashed. "To tell you the truth, Aunt, not ever having any contact with Mother's side of the family, I just assumed you were closed to us. I was fairly young when she died, but she'd indicated we shouldn't expect ever to be welcomed by her family. It never occurred to me to come knocking on your door."

It was Alicia's turn to look sheepish. "We should have kept in contact with my sister," she offered. "But I want you to know now that you're always welcome." She sniffed.

After that, Charlotte wished someone would break the morose feeling in the room, but her brother's next words didn't help.

"I confronted Jason about his dirty dealings, and the next thing I knew, I was waking up in a police holding-cell charged with attempted murder. You know the rest. I ended up at the Lunatic Hospital for evaluation. I can't believe no one checked Sheffield's investigation."

"They had no reason to suspect he was being paid off," Reed told him. "The sergeant didn't get too close to anything dirty, making him more useful to Farnsworth."

"Well, he will now," John added. "Sheffield was at the police station when I returned from the hospital with Mason. It was more than convenient, in fact. He went from one side of the prison bars to the other."

Reed leaned over and topped off Thaddeus's brandy glass. "I don't think Farnsworth would have kept you long in the position of overseer even if you hadn't told him how you felt. Anyone handling his affairs learns too much and becomes a threat. No doubt Arthur Harvey had long been aware of Farnsworth's dirty dealings and had even started to use the information to make his own fortune on the black market. Word reached Farnsworth, and he had the man killed."

Charlotte shuddered at the brutality. "As soon as Jason knew I was in town, he looked me up. To think I spent so much time in his company?"

"You what?" Thaddeus exclaimed, looking horrified.

"Partly my fault, I'm afraid," Alicia said, rushing to Charlotte's defense. "The Farnsworths are an upstanding family, or so I always thought."

"It's true," Charlotte added, "I never would have accepted his invitation if Aunt Alicia hadn't vouched for him. Besides, he was persistent. I had no idea why he was so determined to spend time with me." She glanced over at Reed, hoping he didn't think her an utter twit.

"Even if you hadn't acquiesced to his invitations willingly, Farnsworth would have caught up with you," Reed agreed, "as soon as he understood what a threat you were, sticking your pretty neck into both the police department and the Lunatic Hospital."

"Which, by the way, was where Farnsworth stored many of the illicit goods for dispersal, with Mason's approval and complicity, of course," John chimed in. "What better place? It is private, has cells no one ever looks into. Moreover, no one thinks twice about the comings and goings of wagons, and it is close to the train depot."

Reed looked pointedly at Charlotte. "While Farnsworth was showing you around Boston, he could at least keep his eye on you. But he was probably planning how to kidnap you, even before you saw your brother. It was sheer luck you happened upon him."

"And he was about to make certain Teddy and I drew our last breaths before being dumped at sea," she added, thinking of those frightening minutes in Jason's warehouse.

Reed took a swig of brandy as if fortifying himself against the day's happenings. "I guess we had more luck than we knew. After I met up with John again, we came here to inform you Thaddeus was no longer at the hospital, only to find you were gone, too."

Charlotte looked sheepish at her own stupidity, but Reed continued without condemnation.

"When we spoke to Mrs. Randall, she was almost certain it was Farnsworth she'd seen take you away, then it was clinched. We went straight to his house. Empty, of course."

Reed looked over at John, who nodded. "That was a dicey moment. However, it wasn't difficult to figure out that he would never involve his family, who I'm sure know nothing of his dealings. The next logical place to hide people, or bodies, was the warehouse."

"But how did you know which one?" Charlotte asked.

"I didn't really, but Farnsworth didn't seem all that smart to me. He uses his money, not his brains. So, we went to where Arthur Harvey's body was picked up, and you weren't far away."

"I don't mind admitting I wouldn't have felt so brave if we hadn't had the police with us," John Trelaine confessed, "but Reed knocked out that one brute with a single sockdoggler before splintering the door. I was quite impressed."

Reed colored slightly.

"And then there was the gunshot," Charlotte recalled.

"Gunshot?" Alicia repeated. "Oh my." She, too, took a long draught of the amber liquid.

"Farnsworth picked up a gun as I entered, but I was moving forward so quickly I couldn't stop," Reed admitted. "In an instant, we were locked together, and, to tell you the truth, when the gun went off, I wasn't sure who'd been hit, then he crumpled."

"Reed!" Charlotte exclaimed, standing up. "You could have been killed!"

Given the danger everyone had been in—and *her* more than anyone—all the men burst out laughing.

"We've all had enough for one day, have we not?" Reed said after the laughter had died down.

"Hear, hear," said John, getting up from his chair. "I'm going home to sleep."

He kissed Charlotte on the cheek, shook hands with Thaddeus, who professed his gratitude, and took his leave.

Alicia stood next. "I assure you, Thaddeus, you'll find your room under my roof a most comfortable one."

After kissing both her niece and nephew on the cheek, she declared her intention to retire. Just as she reached the door, she turned to give Reed a warm glance.

"Thank you, Mr. Malloy."

"My pleasure, madam." He gave her a small bow of his head.

"Is it truly over?" Charlotte asked, hugging her brother but looking at Reed.

"There are a few legal matters to attend to regarding your brother, but the police don't expect him to sit in a cell while we do it."

"How gracious of them," Thaddeus said, his countenance unsmiling, even as he returned Charlotte's hug in kind.

"It could have been worse," Reed told him. "If the judge hadn't had some suspicions, you could have been sent straight to the gallows or to the state penitentiary, and your indomitably inquisitive sister here would never have happened upon you."

Thaddeus squeezed her shoulders again, and then, to her amazement, he switched topics entirely. "Now, why don't you tell me what's going on between the two of you?"

Reed barely blinked at that, having already seen her brother was an astute individual and knowing he'd caught their glances going back and forth across the room.

It was Charlotte who looked indignant. "I hardly think that's an appropriate topic of conversation."

"It is if Mr. Malloy has intentions toward you. It's my job to make sure nothing untoward goes on. Why, I didn't even know where you were living for the past couple of months."

Charlotte bristled, stepping out of his embrace. "All this time, Teddy, you knew exactly where I was, in Spring City."

"In Spring City?" he repeated, crossing his arms on his chest. "Safely having supper with Doctor and Sarah Cuthins?"

"Well, I was," she insisted. "You took far too long between visits." Feeling herself tear up, she inwardly chided herself for being overly emotional.

"You're right, Charlie," Thaddeus admitted. "I was away having some grand adventures. But I was also hoping to make a decent amount of money and bring it home to you." Then he looked at Reed. "I kept my eye on her from time to time, even had other people check up on her when I couldn't get home."

"What she needed," Reed returned, his voice sounding hard through his weariness, "was companionship. Even brotherly company would have been better than your checking up on her from afar."

Thaddeus frowned, dropping his arms and addressing Reed squarely. "There are plenty of people in Spring. I figured she'd stop writing long enough to be social once in a while with some of them. In any case, I didn't think she'd catch a man with her baby brother hanging around."

The two men looked as if they were going to come to blows—just when Charlotte thought the day couldn't get any stranger.

"I am growing exceedingly tired of you two talking as if I don't exist, so stop it." She looked at each one in turn. "Reed, my life was not as pathetic as you make out. Before you and the children came along, I was used to being alone."

Then turning to Thaddeus, she added, "I never expected you to look after me, but perhaps more than a yearly visit would have been appreciated. And now I have a new life here in Boston," *and a man*, she added silently, "so what do you say to that?"

To her surprise, he smiled. "Amen, Charlie. You deserve it, as long as you don't mind my sticking around Boston for a while." He relaxed and kissed her forehead. Then he smiled at Reed. "Besides, I bet Mr. Malloy can introduce me to a grist of gorgeous women."

"Thaddeus!" Charlotte said appalled, both at the image of her baby brother with a young lady and at his assumption that Reed knew so many females.

Looking innocently at both of them for a moment, Reed said, "Perhaps I do know some."

"Reed!" she exclaimed in the same tone she'd used with her brother.

Both men chuckled again, but Reed wasn't smiling when he added, "I'm afraid you'll be disappointed, Thaddeus, for none are nearly as beautiful as the woman I met in Spring City."

Seeing the expressions on both his sister's face and Reed's as they looked at one another, Thaddeus discreetly retired from the room.

"Nothing untoward," he murmured as he left, determined to make friends with sweet Bridget and obtain a little late-night sustenance before bed.

As soon as the door closed behind Thaddeus, Reed encircled Charlotte in his arms and kissed her on her startled lips.

"Ow," she said.

"Sorry," he murmured, tracing her slightly swollen and injured lip with his thumb. Then he pressed his mouth to the top of her head, her forehead, her nose, her cheeks, and her chin.

"I have never been so terrified as I was today when I discovered you missing from what I thought was a safe haven. I vow, I thought I would go insane."

"My aunt's house *is* safe, Reed. I was an idiot for venturing out of it. What happened with Jason was mostly my fault."

He looked grave at the mention of Farnsworth. She could see he was troubled by something as he took her hand in his, and his voice was extremely gentle when he spoke.

"I didn't want to discuss this in front of your aunt and the others, but I want to ask if you're unharmed. Beside your lip, I mean. When I found you at the warehouse, you were being assaulted."

Charlotte knew what he was asking. She shook her head before Reed could continue. "Jason Farnsworth did no more than tear my clothes and frighten me half to death."

She saw no need to elaborate more on his assault, no point in placing in Reed's head the vile image of Jason touching her. After all, the man was dead and the memory would dim with time. She was not one to dwell on the past, and certainly wouldn't cower because of one horrific incident.

Reed looked hard into her eyes for a long moment but apparently accepted her response. Smiling, she reached up to touch the strong plane of his cheek with her fingertips.

"I knew you would be clever enough to find me, I just had to gain us some time. It nearly got out of hand until I . . ."

"You what?" He had pulled her close against him again, and his tone was becoming less serious as he stroked her hair.

"I used what you might call psychology upon him."

Reed looked down at her in surprise. "You are an amazing woman, Charlotte Sanborn. Most women would have been content to stay locked in the storeroom where your brother was. But you," he held her chin and tilted her head back, "you chose to face the danger head on. And what is your weapon?" He grinned at her. "Psychology! On a mad man, no less."

"Well, it worked and we're all safe." She breathed a happy sigh, to be once more in Reed's embrace and to have her brother safe and sound in Alicia's house. Teddy had briefly met Lily and Thomas, who'd displayed the same degree of shyness as upon first meeting her, but she knew they would warm to him. Yes, everything was right with the world at present.

Except Reed was frowning. "I'll never feel reassured where you're concerned until you are my wife, carrying my name and residing under my roof."

There it was, the marriage proposal again, thrown down like a gauntlet. Her smile died. He ran a hand through his hair, causing some of it to stand on end.

"The way should be clear for us now, but I know it's not. I can see by your face," he said, "that your answer is the same."

Charlotte didn't know what to say. He smiled ruefully. "I ought to be nothing but miserable about that, but all I can feel right now is thankful. I don't think I could have stood it if I'd been too late. If I'd failed you . . . ," he trailed off.

Charlotte knew instinctively that was another key to his closed heart, another reason for his fear.

"It wouldn't have been your fault." Her voice was almost a whisper, as she envisioned how the end would have come if Reed had been too late. "It would have been my own and Jason's fault, of course."

"Sometimes things aren't that simple, Charlotte. The conscience has a way of holding one responsible for lack of action as much as for action itself."

"You're not talking about what happened today, are you?"

He smiled wearily. "No, lady writer, something long ago." He touched her cheek, his thumb barely grazing the small cut at her mouth. "Are you as tired as I am?"

"Yes, I guess I am," She knew he'd closed the subject on purpose, but she had to ask, "Reed, will you tell me soon about whatever happened long ago?"

She saw the doubt and the pain in his eyes, the same flickering shadow over his life that she'd seen before. But he nodded, and with a last, lingering kiss, he was gone.

CHAPTER THIRTY

The story Charlotte turned in to Charles Greene a few days
later was not the one she'd originally intended to write, but
it caught the attention of the city at once. Her article made the
front page, her name was bandied about as if she were the most
popular writer since Jules Verne.

Calling cards and invitations arrived from all walks of society,
and a deeply felt apology from the Farnsworth family, who had
massive black mourning wreaths adorning their residence. Most
importantly, another writing assignment and then another came
her way. Her writing career was assured.

Her relationship with Reed was not.

"Can you believe I'm in the middle of . . . no, I'm actually
causing the hustle and bustle?" she said to Thaddeus over dinner
one day, three weeks after their rescue.

"The Lunatic Hospital is being investigated by the state,
Superintendent Mason is in the Charlestown State Prison, and
I'm busier than I thought possible. I seem to have more
company and more new acquaintances than I would have made
in a lifetime in Spring City, yet—"

"You're lonely as hell," her brother finished for her.

She grimaced. "No, not exactly. I know the way real loneliness feels. Besides I have you." What worried her was that Reed had neither brought up the subject of marriage again, nor done much to pursue her beyond an occasional clandestine kiss in his carriage.

The only real gain Charlotte could see since the night of Jason's death was that Reed and Teddy had become friends. But as for her and Reed, she'd begun to despair of resolving their impasse.

"Welcome to the world of relationships, Charlie." Thaddeus took a sip of his ale. "But I don't see what's wrong. From what I can tell, you have Alicia's unspoken blessing for you and Reed. She's even letting you two go out unchaperoned. And he seems to be playing the dutiful escort whenever your exalted presence is requested at a party or a ball or a cotillion or a dinner. Hell, he'd probably take you to a ladies' tea party, if you asked."

"Teddy," she poked him in the stomach to stop his teasing. "But that's just it. Reed seems as if he is 'playing' or more precisely, acting. He picks me up in his carriage and escorts me out anywhere I want to go, and we dance every dance, and he's sociable to everyone."

She sighed. "It doesn't even bother me anymore when we run into his former flame. Reed has this way of dismissing those collisions with a wave of his hand. But you would have to know how it was between us before."

Thaddeus took a bite of the roast beef in front of him. He chewed slowly. Charlotte could see he was still savoring his return to the real world, eating delicious food and—he burped loudly—drinking local beer. Then he fixed her with his thoughtful green gaze. "More passionate, perhaps?"

She nodded miserably, unable to believe she was having this conversation with her younger brother. "It's as if he's being so careful around me because he's scared I'll break."

"What happened must have shaken Reed to his core," Thaddeus observed. "I know it did me. He loves you so much, he can't stand the notion of anything happening to you."

Charlotte nearly choked on the wine she was sipping. "Loves me!"

"Well, of course." Then Thaddeus looked at her with something akin to horror. "God, Charlie, don't you *love* him? Because I can tell you, I wouldn't want to be standing too close to you if you tell the man otherwise. I mean, look at how he handled Farnsworth. If you're trifling with Reed's affections . . ."

He shrugged as if it were too awful to contemplate.

"Of course I love him," she muttered resentfully. And she wanted to believe Reed felt something similar for her, deep down, although perhaps he didn't know it or recognize the feeling. Or perhaps he simply couldn't express what was in his heart. Or maybe Teddy was just plain wrong.

The lingering doubts weighed heavily on her mind. She sighed. At this point, she would settle for the sparks that used to fly, the way he used to reach for her at any given moment and then kiss her soundly. She had long given up watching for him at her balcony door.

Setting down her glass, Charlotte decided her only option was to tease Reed into some sign of the passion she hoped still simmered below his calm exterior.

"What's that gleam in your eye, sis?"

She merely smiled.

At every opportunity over the next week, she brushed up against Reed, sat close during their carriage rides, and did her best to be both charming and enticing. She thought she could see a reaction in him, in the way he looked at her, the way his pupils dilated when she leaned close, the way he sometimes stepped away from her as if scorched.

However, the very next time he entered Alicia's house, he picked up Lily and checked on her bruised knee, admired Thomas's big-boy haircut, and even talked man-to-man with

Thaddeus about boxing. Yet he did not sweep Charlotte off to his bed or come secretly to hers.

Charlotte thought she'd go out of her mind. It was worse than she feared. Not only didn't he love her, but he didn't seem to *want* her anymore, either.

All she'd done was cause her own level of frustration to peak until she thought she would scream. And Teddy watched it all with a smug and knowing look of amusement. She wanted to wring his neck, not to mention Reed's.

One afternoon, sitting in her aunt's garden, Charlotte made every effort to read over her most recent article in the newspaper. It was giving her little joy. The words were all running together. She put the paper down beside her and closed her eyes.

Her mind was on Reed, on the first time they'd made love after Drake's barn dance It had been magical, the way he'd touched her fevered skin, caressed her breasts, whispered her name.

"Charlotte."

"Mmm," she responded, her eyes still closed. She could almost hear him.

Feeling warm lips brush her own, her lids flew open.

"Reed!" It was exactly the same as when she used to sit in her study, thinking of him, and he would appear in the evenings. He sat down beside her.

"You look so peaceful out here among the flowers, I hate to disturb you, but you also look ravishing."

She breathed a sigh.

"I feel like being ravished," she told him honestly, not caring if he thought her shamelessly bold.

He grinned the most sensual smile she'd ever seen, lowered his head, and kissed her again—deeply, thoroughly, until her nipples had ripened to hard buds, her toes were curling, and all her parts in between were turning to liquid.

At last, he raised his head and groaned. "That's why I need to talk to you. If we don't come to some understanding—"

"Understanding?" Charlotte repeated, thinking of his prior understanding with Helen.

"Arrangement, treaty, agreement, compromise, whatever you want to call it. Otherwise, I'm going to have to break my promise."

"I don't understand." She could remember no promise, unless . . . "Do you mean you won't wait for me anymore?" She had not said yes soon enough to his proposal, and now what? *Was he kissing her goodbye?*

"I can't wait," Reed said, confirming her worst fear. He took her hand. "The vow I made that you would be my fiancée before we made love again was sworn with the best of intentions, but it's as if you're asking a thirsty man to look at a glass of crystal clear, cool water and not touch a drop to his lips. I need you, not only in my life but in my bed."

She was so relieved, she felt giddy. It wasn't that he couldn't wait any longer for her response. It was that he couldn't wait any longer for *her.*

"These past weeks, I've been trying to prove I can be the restrained and respectful suitor you deserve, but damn it, Charlotte, I don't want to be your patient suitor. I want all the privileges and blessings that come with being your husband. I hold you in the highest esteem, but every time you're near me, I want strip off every last article of your clothing, very quickly, and then proceed to make love to you."

She blushed profusely, unable to quell the image he'd conjured.

Reed, however, looked grim. "I thought if I just waited, without Farnsworth muddying the waters and with your career flourishing, you would finally agree to be my wife, but that hasn't happened." He sounded so morose, tears rose to her eyes.

"No," she shook her head miserably. And all her excuses for more time, for the chance to get her career under way were fast running out. He wanted to be her husband, and he held her *in the highest esteem.* But she didn't want simply his esteem, however high. She wanted his love. She wanted . . .

Charlotte looked at Reed's somber face and knew what she wanted most was to remove the shadow from his heart, whatever had caused it.

"Reed, tell me about long ago."

"What do you mean?" He furrowed his brow.

"After you rescued me from the warehouse, you spoke of conscience and holding yourself responsible. Please tell me what you meant. Is it to do with Celia?"

She watched his chest expand as he took a deep breath.

"I've never told anyone this," he said, his voice sounding rough. "It's not Celia exactly, but the baby she carried."

"The baby she pretended was yours. Whose was it?"

"I don't know. I can only assume she knew who the father was." He stood up and walked a few steps from her. "If I had gone along with Celia's plan," he told her, his back still to her, "the child would be older than Lily."

"What happened to the baby?" Charlotte asked, but she didn't think she wanted to hear the answer. Or rather, she already knew.

At his feet was a small weed, sprouting alone in the midst of Alicia's lush green grass. Somehow, it had not yet been noticed by her aunt. Reed bent down and pulled it out with a quick twist of his fingers.

"She never had the baby. She made sure I knew that, too," he said, as he stood up, his thoughts far away. "If I'd known her intentions, I think I would have married her for the child's sake." He let the weed drop from his hand.

Charlotte stood up and closed the space between them in seconds. From behind, she put her slender arms around him and pressed her cheek to his back. She was stunned by the sheer cruelty of the woman Reed had once thought he loved.

There had been no need for Celia to tell him she'd ended her pregnancy, except to make him suffer for having ruined her selfish plans. And Reed, with his love of children, blamed himself for all these years.

"This has nothing to do with us, Charlotte," he said, clasping her arms under his strong hands. Then he turned in her embrace and faced her.

Nothing to do with us. That's what he'd said before when he'd first told her about Celia. However, she knew differently. His guilt over the unborn child and over the possible consequences of loving someone, especially the wrong person, created the fear she had detected in him.

It was clear to her why it had been of utmost importance to Reed that she love Lily and Thomas. And then a thought struck her.

"Reed, why didn't you use any protection the last time we . . . ?" she trailed off.

He rested his chin against the top of her head so she couldn't see him. "I knew it would be all right, either way. I intend to keep you in my life, whatever happens."

Charlotte smiled to herself. It was a good sign. Reed knew if she became pregnant, she would cherish the baby with all her heart. Obviously, he trusted her.

Her expression was wistful, as she thought of all the Celias and Helens in the world who might have won his heart. They'd only needed to look past the powerful, attractive lawyer and see him for the warm, caring man he was.

Yet, she refused to believe any woman, no matter how cruel, had ruined him altogether for love, or that he could close off his heart more securely than she had done. Charlotte had been ready to live alone for the rest of her life, rather than risk losing anyone else. And life had turned out to be wonderful since she opened her heart to loving the children and him. *Could Reed Malloy be as afraid as she had been?*

He lifted his head and looked down at her. To her astonishment, his handsome face split open in a broad smile.

"You look like Thomas," he quipped, "when he has his eyes on the sweet shop."

Oh, yes, dear Reed, my eyes are on the sweets. She pulled his head down and kissed him.

Reed stood by the picture window in his sitting room and looked out to sea. It was nearly the end of summer, the end of another difficult trial, the end of a long day, and very nearly the end of his patience. *What was wrong with the woman, anyway?* It had been so much simpler when he'd been with Helen.

And so much lonelier.

He shuddered to think of their years of endless social gatherings, polished smiles, and loveless sexual encounters. Yes, it was sometimes extremely difficult with Charlotte, but he wouldn't trade what they had, tenuous as it seemed at that moment, for anything or anyone.

Running his hand through his hair, it was all he could do not to pull it out.

True to his word, despite what he'd said to her the day before, he was determined not to bed Charlotte again until she was his fiancée, until he could rightfully make her his own. Yet he was beginning to despair of ever figuring out what she was waiting for. And waiting was definitely what she was doing, looking at him with longing in those emerald eyes each time they were together.

He was nearly ready to haul her down the aisle of the church for her own good.

Rain was falling like sharp needles. With a heavy wind blowing, the ocean waters were pounding relentlessly at the shore, making the pilings underneath India Wharf groan with the strain.

It didn't worry him. These pilings had stood for a century and would continue to do so for many years to come, seemingly invincible and as unchangeable as he had felt himself to be for so long. Until Charlotte.

He couldn't put his finger on exactly what had changed, but something seemed to have opened in him, a weight had been lifted, and he felt eager to start a new life with her, if she would just give in and let him.

"Monsieur Malloy." Reed jumped at the sound of Pierre's voice. His cook had managed to enter the room without him hearing.

"My apology," Pierre said, holding out his employer's warmed brandy glass. "You were drifting, as you have been doing much lately."

Reed smiled crookedly. "I have, haven't I?" He took the drink from Pierre and sat down on the sofa.

Perhaps a good chat with the witty Frenchman, who often bested him in a game of chess or surprised him with his insights into the American political scene, would cheer him. But his hopes for some stimulating conversation were dashed when he noticed Pierre didn't hold a glass of his own.

"I hope you don't mind if I retire early tonight, Monsieur Malloy."

"Not at all," Reed lied, hating to spend another evening with his own brooding thoughts as his sole company. "Is something wrong?"

"It is Jeanine. These storms frighten her so much. And though I tell her we are safe . . . ," he paused and rolled his eyes. "Women, eh? But love makes a man a slave, and luckily, it makes women overlook our faults. Mademoiselle Sanborn has made a slave of you, yes?" He laughed good-naturedly. "Goodnight, Monsieur."

"Goodnight, Pierre," Reed responded, but he didn't notice the man leave. He was thinking of Charlotte, of being a slave to her. A memory of Celia returned unbidden from the last time he'd seen her, the day before she had sailed away.

"I nearly made you my slave, Reed," she'd said, unbowed by her humiliation, unashamed of her own duplicity.

"You nearly did," he had agreed bitterly and with a silent vow that it would never happen again.

No, never again, he'd sworn to himself, *would he let his heart be a slave to a woman.*

Could the answer be as simple as that? It was long ago, but for a moment, it seemed as if it was yesterday, and the feelings were nearly as raw. He'd told Charlotte that Celia had nothing to do with them, but perhaps he was wrong.

Had he been holding Charlotte accountable for another woman's sins? *Impossible!* He loved Charlotte! *Loved her with all his heart.* He jumped off the sofa. Good Lord, he'd been a fool, then and now. An absolute dunce! And he couldn't wait another moment to tell her.

Charlotte heard the door knocker and Gerald's footsteps in the hall, and she put down her book on the parlor table. However, preparing herself for an unexpected late-night visitor and suddenly seeing Reed, without a coat, his hair soaking wet, standing in the doorway was another matter.

There was no preparation for the feeling that started deep inside her, for the quickening pace of her heartbeat.

What on earth was she waiting for? This man wanted to marry her! She stood up and nearly leaped into his arms.

Gerald discreetly bowed out, closing the door behind him.

"Reed, what is it? You look as if . . . ," she trailed off, unable to say what his expression meant for she'd never seen it before, not on Reed's face, nor on any man's. "Has something happened?"

"Charlotte," he cut in, closing the space between them and taking her in his arms, mindless of the damp state of his clothing. He dropped a kiss on her parted lips, "Won't you marry the man who loves you most in this world?"

She was thunderstruck, tears instantly pricking her eyes. "You love me?" Her voice was little more than a whisper.

He looked equally shocked at her words. He'd finally guessed at the problem but couldn't believe that was all there was to it. Still, here was his proof—she hadn't known how he felt.

"Of course I love you."

"You never said it," she told him, sagging with relief and feeling she would disgrace herself any minute by outright weeping. *He loved her.* She could marry him. She sniffed loudly.

Holding her closely against him, he understood finally that the singular impediment had been his own inability to recognize and speak the love he felt. Charlotte had let him into her heart and then waited bravely, even refusing his proposal. And he'd nearly let a shadowy memory stand like a giant in his path.

"I didn't think I needed to say it," he murmured, taking her face in his hands. "In truth, I resisted saying it, thinking I could save a small part of myself from being completely in your power. It hasn't worked. But I honestly didn't realize that was why you were refusing my proposal. I thought I'd stated my case from all angles."

"Like a lawyer!" she exclaimed, pushing away from his chest and searching for a handkerchief in her sleeve.

"But I *am* a lawyer," he said exasperatedly, handing her a linen square from his own soggy pocket. She took it, dabbing at her eyes before scrunching it tightly under white knuckles.

"But *I* am a writer, and I deal in words, and I need to have them spelled out for me. Precisely and with clarity," she added, sniffing again. "I was beginning to think you could never love me because of Celia."

Reed looked surprised. "You're a smarter woman than I deserve." Then he lifted her chin, looking directly at her, his cobalt eyes ablaze with dark emotions. "Let me be precise and clear. Charlotte Sanborn, I love you with all my heart."

She felt a tear slip down her cheek. "I'll need to hear those words a lot, not only once," she told him feeling a lump in her throat.

He smiled at her tears and her sniffles, and he pulled her to him again. "Is this my independent lady writer, brought to crying by mere words?"

"Not just any words, Reed. The words I've waited all my life to hear."

He sobered, gazing down into her glittering green eyes. "The words I've waited all my life to say," he assured her. "And I will tell you often. I love you."

She reached up, drew him down, and kissed him. It was a long moment later when he lifted his head.

"Not that I wouldn't mind hearing them myself," he added, the hint of a smile on his lips.

She beamed at him, feeling the bliss of being encircled in his arms and for the first time knowing she was also surrounded by his love.

"I love you, Reed Malloy, and yes, I will marry you."

Charlotte stepped out of the carriage and walked along the front path of Reed's mother's house. At the top of the steps, on the large open porch, stood her fiancé, taking her breath away and making her heart skip a beat at the sight of him as he talked to someone out of view.

Her brother and aunt were already inside, honored guests of Reed's mother, Evelyn Malloy. Charlotte had stayed a few minutes behind with Bridget to get the children to bed. She loved their bedtime—the stories and warm kisses, and the extra big hugs—and she almost never missed it.

A pretty young woman, a few years younger than Charlotte, rushed out of the open front door and into Reed's arms. He caught her in a warm embrace, laughing as he did.

Charlotte didn't even hesitate, keeping her smile in place and heading up the front steps to her engagement party. Reed caught sight of her and grinned broadly, opening one arm to welcome her while keeping the other firmly around the waist of the other female.

"This must be your youngest sister," Charlotte said, having been taught her lesson the first two times she'd rushed to judgment.

He nodded before taking her hand and bringing it to his lips.

"I hate gloves," the young woman announced. "Who wants to be kissed on the glove?"

Charlotte laughed, and Reed rolled his eyes.

"This is our Rose. Rose, this is my bride-to-be."

"I'm glad to meet you at last," Charlotte said.

"Not as much as I," Rose replied, having recently returned home from a trip to London with her mother.

Hands on hips, she appraised Charlotte from head to toe. "So, you are the woman who has finally tamed my brother."

Charlotte blushed, glancing at Reed whose face had momentarily lost all expression, refusing to give his little sister any satisfaction.

"Rose, quick, come see this stereoscopic thingamajig."

Charlotte recognized the voice of his middle sister, Sophie, having had tea with her the day before.

"See you later, Charlotte." And Rose pushed against her brother's side and was gone.

"We don't normally let her out in polite society," Reed said, giving Charlotte a wry smile before taking her hand again. "But frankly, I hate gloves, too."

He took her by the wrist and proceeded to peel off her dove grey glove, one finger at a time.

Staring at his movements, Charlotte's mouth grew dry. As he took her other hand and did the same, it felt as if he were undressing her in public. A shiver ran down her spine.

When Reed was finished, he kissed her hand again, then entwined her fingers with his.

"Much better," he said, shoving her gloves into his pocket, as they walked into the soiree being held in their honor.

Signaling a passing servant, he snagged two glasses of champagne and handed one to Charlotte.

"I can't wait to strip the rest of you later tonight," he murmured so only she could hear.

Instantly, she choked on the chilled, bubbling liquid she'd just sipped. When she could breathe again, she glanced up at him.

"I'm delighted to know I haven't tamed you at all, Mr. Malloy."

He put his head back and laughed.

EPILOGUE

Although the air was frosty with the winter chill of November, it was a perfect day as far as Charlotte was concerned. She walked steadily down the aisle of the King's Chapel in the heart of the city she had grown to love.

Lily walked ahead of her with a basket of white and pink roses, clad in a cream-colored dress that mimicked Charlotte's own. Thomas had declared her a "princess" in her ivory wedding gown with its trim waist, mother-of-pearl buttons, and leg o' mutton sleeves, tapering to stylishly simple points on the backs of her hands.

The bustle was crowned by a large silk bow over a draped, folded train embedded with smaller bows and trailing out behind her for a carriage-length. Her chestnut hair, swept up in a loose chignon, was decorated with white and purple sweet William, and over this was a gossamer veil.

The dress was entirely Alicia's doing. For her own part, Charlotte didn't care if she wore a sack, or nothing at all, as she made her way between the crowded pews to join Reed at the altar.

Her brother walked beside her, happy to stand in for their father, although he professed himself unhappy at giving her away to any man. Even to Reed Malloy, who was dressed in slate-gray tails, his suit trimmed with black piping. He waited impatiently at the front of the church with John Trelaine at his left. Beside John, little Thomas held a white pillow with their wedding rings.

Charlotte was blissful, seeing Reed's warm gaze upon her. There was that special look, that worshipful expression, and she even had all her clothes on! Scolding herself for improper thoughts in the church, it seemed mere minutes later she and Reed were pronounced man and wife, and Aunt Alicia beamed at them from her honored place in the front row.

Her thoughts couldn't be considered improper anymore, and Charlotte's heart was filled with happiness. Reed lifted her veil, bent down, and kissed her. Opening her eyes, she saw that familiar lock of hair falling over his forehead, and she reached up as any wife would to lovingly brush it aside.

They turned together to face the myriad guests who had filled King's Chapel to see one of Boston's favorite sons marry the lauded writer from out west.

Reed's own family—including his mother, Evelyn, his older sister, Elise, her husband and her children, and his two younger sisters—gave loud cheers, unmistakably pleased he had finally taken a wife, one whom they'd come to love over the past few months.

Middle sister, Sophie, who'd played Mendelssohn's wedding march when Charlotte entered, now began a joyful tune to accompany their first moments as a married couple. Rose jumped up to adjust Charlotte's train before she started the walk back up the aisle as a married woman. And Evelyn Malloy winked at Charlotte as she welcomed a new daughter to the family.

Charlotte sighed deeply when they finally went to bed that night, after hours of celebration with family and friends at the Tremont. There'd been music and dancing, and a wedding feast that would have suited heads of state. And most of all, there were lots of well-wishes.

She had never felt so blessed in all her life. It was like coming out from under a dark cloud that for years had blocked any but the dimmest rays of light, and all at once stepping into the brilliant sunshine. Here were people who cared about each other and about her.

"Now you've had a tour of my entire house," he told her, tracing his finger down the length of her arm, causing goose bumps to raise. She laughed. She had seen his bedroom before, having to pretend she hadn't when his mother accompanied her to advise on changing the décor.

Charlotte had kept silent at that time, not intending to change a thing in Reed's home, except to find places for all her books, her desk, and a few other items she'd had shipped east with Sarah Cuthins' help. The spare rooms would belong to Lily and Thomas, who could not believe their luck in getting Reed for a father. That night, however, they were staying with their grandmother.

"I do enjoy this room the most," Charlotte fairly purred, turning over onto her stomach and pushing aside the thick draperies beside the bed, so she could look out the window.

From this vantage point, she enjoyed a view of the dark sea spread out to the far-off horizon. To her left, in the distance was the Boston lighthouse, shining every seven seconds with comforting regularity.

But Reed wasn't looking at the view. At least, not the one outside. He was eyeing his wife's enchanting backside. In a moment, he kissed it, causing Charlotte to dissolve into giggles.

Releasing the curtain, she turned over to be captured by his strong arms. He stopped her giggling with a tender kiss on her lips, then trailed soft caresses over her breasts and down her slender stomach. Instantly, she was molten at her core.

"Please," she said as she released her breath.

"Please what?" he asked playfully, his voice a whisper as he blew on the curls at her cleft.

"Reed," she insisted.

His tongue touched her, and she bucked, hearing his husky male laugh a moment later.

"Shall I get protection?" he teased.

She simply shook her head, having not yet told him it was too late for that. Grabbing his shoulders, she urged him upward, wanting to feel the tantalizing weight of him on top of her.

"Now, Reed," she demanded in no uncertain terms.

"Yes, Mrs. Malloy. I am yours to command."

They didn't speak again for many minutes. When he finally rested his head on the pillow, she lay hers upon his shoulder

"So, my lady writer wife, will you be happy here?"

"How could I not be? I have an intelligent, handsome, humorous husband," she punctuated each word with a kiss on his bare chest, "who loves me most in all this world, and I have two bright, beautiful children who are so happy with their new home, and I have been published steadily since I came here," she paused, making sure she had all his attention by kissing him on the mouth before whispering against his lips, "and I'm carrying your baby."

She was glad to share the joy of her recently discovered secret. A mere six months earlier, she would have been petrified at the thought. Now, she relished the idea of being a mother to Reed's child. Truly, children were as perplexing and distracting as she'd believed, but they were also the best challenge she'd ever faced.

For his part, Reed was torn between surprise and happiness. "You're—then I'm to be a—but how can this—well, of course I know how, but—"

"Shh," Charlotte silenced her new husband, stopping his babble with another kiss. "You talk too much, Mr. Malloy."

He agreed and proceeded to show his exquisite new wife how very much he loved her, in a manner as timeless as the sea that crashed on the rocks below.

Finis

AN IRRESISTIBLE TEMPTATION
BOOK 2

**and the rest of the Defiant Hearts series
including**

AN INTRIGUING PROPOSITION
PREQUEL

AN IMPROPER SITUATION
BOOK 1

AN INESCAPABLE ATTRACTION
BOOK 3

AN INCONCEIVABLE DECEPTION
BOOK 4

AN IMPASSIONED REDEMPTION
NOVELLA

are available in print and ebook.

ABOUT THE AUTHOR

USA Today bestselling author Sydney Jane Baily writes historical romance set in Victorian England, late 19th-century America, the Middle Ages, the Georgian era, and the Regency period. She believes in happily-ever-after stories with engaging characters and attention to period detail.

Born and raised in California, she has traveled the world, spending a lot of exceedingly happy time in the U.K. where her extended family resides, eating fish and chips, drinking shandies, and snacking on Maltesers and Cadbury bars. Sydney currently lives in New England with her family — human, canine, and feline.

You can learn more about her books, read her blog, and contact her via her website at SydneyJaneBaily.com.